DANGEROUS DARLYNS

TRAILS & TARGETS

KELLY EILEEN HAKE

SHILOH RUN PRESS
An Imprint of Barbour Publishing, Inc.

Cover design by Kirk DouPonce, DogEared Design

Published by Shiloh Run Press, an imprint of Barbour Publishing, Inc., P.O. Box 719, Uhrichsville, Ohio 44683, www.shilohrunpress.com

Our mission is to publish and distribute inspirational products offering exceptional value and biblical encouragement to the masses.

 Member of the
Evangelical Christian
Publishers Association

Printed in the United States of America.

Dedication

For my mother, who taught me to read and encouraged me to write.

For my father, who for many years worked the graveyard shift and enthusiastically supported reading as my favorite (quiet!) pastime.

For my brother, who always tried to snatch away my books and force me to play instead. I didn't appreciate it then— and heaven help you if you try it today—but without your interference, my imagination wouldn't have grown so large.

For Mary Meek, my fourth-grade teacher, who caught my classmates calling me "Bookworm"—then silenced them all by reading one of my short story assignments in class and stopping at the best part. When the worst bully protested and wanted to know the ending, she warned that if I listened to his teasing, I'd never finish it.

For my best friend and first reader— "best" and "first" are fitting descriptions for you!

For my husband, who falls asleep anytime he tries to read my books but insists my writing is wonderful and supports my efforts with enthusiasm (and caffeine!).

For the wonderful folks at Barbour, who've published my stories for more than a dozen years.

And for God, who blessed my life purpose— and plenty of people to help me fulfill it!

The Darlyn Sisters

Beatrix Darlyn: The Leader
>   Age: 20
>   Skill: Sharpshooting with pistols and rifles
>   Physical Description: Mahogany hair falling in waves and curls, hazel eyes, generous smile, tall, strong physique with small waist

Ariel Darlyn: The Wit
>   Age: 18
>   Skill: Archery
>   Physical Description: Straight strawberry-blond hair, seafoam-green eyes, fine features, small, slim, delicate build

Cassia Darlyn: The Beauty
>   Age: 16
>   Skill: Throwing knives
>   Physical Description: Tumbling auburn tresses, emerald eyes, generous curves

Judith Darlyn: The Changeling
>   Age: 13
>   Skill: Trick riding and roping
>   Physical Description: Hair of mixed color, seems to change in various lights—as do her gray-green eyes—coltish, quickly growing frame

Chapter 1

Dakota Territory
Late April 1889

"Go faster!" Pa leaned into a rush of prairie wind, fingers curling around the buckboard seat.

Bea's obedience lost out to common sense. She kept their gait slow, steady, and sure to chafe a man who once raced across these plains in pursuit of buffalo. How could it not, when the sluggish pace vexed her? Unending stretches of grassland begged Bea to gallop past in search of something different—to take a wild, wind-rushed chance for change.

But some chances weren't hers to take, and she'd rather suffer aggravation than see her family injured. Holes made by enterprising ground squirrels and snakes speckled the area, and the Darlyns couldn't afford any catastrophes. Especially with Pa's health even more precarious than their bank balance.

He clung to life like a cocklebur in spite of the doctor's dire predictions, but it took the combined efforts of all four Darlyn daughters to help him hold on. *None of us is ready to let go.*

Bea's hands tightened on the reins. "No reason to rush. Home won't wander off while we're away."

"I got my fill of the Good Book from the preacher, but now I'm hungering for some Sunday supper. You know you're my favorite daughter, but that doesn't mean you can get away with leaving your pa hungry!"

"We started stew before we left and did the baking yesterday." Ariel's matter-of-fact reminder didn't seem to soothe him.

"That's why you're my other favorite," he lauded her. Bea softened at the oft-used endearment, even though she'd been unseated so swiftly. "But I'm thinking we'll need more than one pot of stew and biscuits, to tell you true, m'dears."

"You can't be *that* hungry, Pa!" Thirteen-year-old Judith's chuckle still carried the piping lilt of childhood, a cheery note that never failed to elicit grins.

But Bea noticed Pa's smile slipped away too soon. He cleared his throat with that awful, phlegmy rasp spring hadn't managed to oust. Bea tensed, waiting for the horrible, hacking cough that usually followed. When it didn't come, she felt the tension ease from her shoulders, only to return with a sharp pinch. Cough or a confession, Pa only cleared his throat when he needed to get something off his chest. So whatever came next, Bea knew she wouldn't like the sound of it.

"We might have ourselves a guest or two this afternoon."

"Oooh! Who's coming, Pa?" Though Bea couldn't see her sister from where she rode in the back of the buckboard, she knew Cassia would be smoothing someone's hair.

Bea might work to keep body and soul together, but Cassia—a full-fledged beauty by sixteen—worked to keep them looking as good as possible.

"The Braun brothers..." Pa didn't sound too certain, and Bea hoped the Braun bachelors bellied up to someone else's table. Plagues of locusts left more in their wake than those three.

Apparently Ariel was thinking along the same lines. "We can feed three more, even if they are the Brauns. I'll fill up on biscuits and do more baking tomorrow."

Looks like I'll be making a trip to town sooner than I planned.

"The two Kalb youngsters... Mr. Alderman, too..." Pa's voice broke into her scheming, and Bea realized he'd invited more than just the Brauns.

8

Her stomach soured with suspicion, but she chose to hope he'd finished. "Six is a stretch, but we'll manage."

"And Mr. Huber. . ." The tips of Pa's ears were turning red, a sure sign of guilt. "I'm thinking it's best to let the other guests distract him."

"Do you think that'll work? He stares so."

"You think all the men stare at you, Cass!" Judith teased.

"No! Well. . .yes, he looks too long at me, but he leers at Bea most. Haven't you noticed?"

Pa's voice sounded grim. "Aye, I noticed. But it never pays to anger a banker, girls."

"Let's make the banker pay for angering us," Judith proposed. "Just think. . .if we charged him every time he stared at Bea or Cass—we'd be swimming in nickels before the month was out!"

"Don't say such things, Jodie!" Ariel gasped but broke down and giggled. "Women who make money from their looks aren't ladies."

"You say ladies don't wear britches, throw knives, or stand on horseback either," Jodie pshawed.

"She's got you there, Ariel." Bea snickered. "To hear you tell it, all those poor ladies have no fun and no funds. At least we Darlyns make our own way and know how to enjoy ourselves!"

"My daughters know more than how to have a good time, and today I want you to show off your talents."

Now that she understood why Pa wanted to rush, Bea jogged the reins, speeding the team to as brisk a walk as she thought Pa's aching bones could take. "Pulling together a decent meal takes more time than talent, Pa. You might need to distract them with a game of horseshoes or some such if all seven make haste."

"Eleven. . .I forgot the Fuller youngsters."

"*Eleven?*" Even Cassia sounded more horrified than happy.

"My girls can handle any challenge!" Pa sounded smug. "In fact, that's the entire point of this afternoon. I've invited men from ages fourteen to fifty-five to bear witness."

"Bear witness to the four of us rushing around?" Bea heard her own exasperation and hushed up to hatch a plan. Even if she were willing to sacrifice the six chickens it would take to feed everyone, they wouldn't have the time to pluck and prepare them. *Besides, we need to sell those birds and any mallards I can bring down between now and the trip to town . . . . There's no other choice. We'll have to use the ham I've been hoarding.*

"We'll add sandwiches to the stew," she decided. "It won't impress our guests, but it'll be enough."

"I'm not out to impress anyone with your cooking, fine as it is. Just about any girl can scrape together something to fill the table, but my daughters can do more than that! I've promised the men of TallGrass something they won't soon forget."

Bea tensed, stabbing herself with an ornery splinter. She shifted again, thinking the weather-roughened wagon wasn't the only pain in her backside today. Usually, she and the girls managed to minimize the problems caused by Pa's promises. This time he'd gone too far, too fast for them to intervene. "What, *exactly*, did you promise?"

"A good meal and a display of marksmanship and horsemanship."

"Just shooting and racing?" she pressed, shifting as another splinter stabbed behind her knee.

If she had to put on a show, her sharpshooting wouldn't disgrace the Darlyns. So long as riding in a race was all Judith did, they'd be fine. Anything else—especially if Pa planned for Ariel and Cassia to join in—could ruin them.

"I didn't mention specifics." Pa waved her concerns away.

Bea breathed deep, finding the fresh air tasted of dust and desperation. "Here's what we'll do. Judith can race any challenger, but nothing fancy. Same with my shooting—nothing most of them can't do. We'll send them off with full stomachs and puffed-up egos, and that will be the end of it."

"No! Never give less than your best, and especially not today!" Pa's roar softened as he said, "I won't be around forever, but I'll be hobbled if I see any one of you selling herself short."

"Don't talk that way, Pa." Guilt clawed at her when he sagged against the seat.

"Promise me you'll do yourselves proud today. All of you."

"We will!" Cassia and Judith fell over themselves to reassure him, unable to stand seeing Pa upset.

"Ah, Cassie and Jodie. You go the distance to ease your old pa's heavy mind. It's what makes the pair of you my very special favorites. Now if only your eldest would follow your good example." He stared at Bea.

"Yes, Pa." Though any woman demonstrating her ability to best a man—especially in a "masculine" field like shooting—could expect some animosity. Bea could live with that, so long as she found a way to keep Judith's and Cassia's more unconventional interests a family secret. "But it's not fair to be using that old 'favorite' chestnut against us. You say it to all of us."

"And I mean it, every time," he assured her with a broad grin. Then he turned his expectant gaze on Ariel, who hadn't yet capitulated.

"We enjoy the things you've taught us, and it's done each of us a world of good to conquer a special skill." Ariel's slim hand reached forward to pat his arm. "But our abilities are. . .unorthodox, at best. Scandalous at worst. You don't want us to make a spectacle of ourselves."

"Yes, I do." He sighed. "I'm not the best father in the world, my Darlyns, but I know I've done at least one thing right. I've made sure I won't leave you girls unprotected. And protection works best when people know it exists."

"Perhaps," Ariel conceded. "But we're not men who can intimidate their fellows, Pa. Most often the best protection a woman can carry is her reputation."

"Ach. Reputations don't tell a woman's worth. They're just the sales pitch to tempt a man into making an offer."

"How else does a woman win a husband?" Cassia pointed out. "A good name deserves respect."

"You've got a good name already, and today's showcase isn't to prove that you deserve a man. It's a warning that you don't need one!"

✴

"Needing and wanting are two very different things." Greyson Wilder clapped his arm around his business partner's shoulders and steered him away from the Devil's Lake saloon.

"Not if the wanting is powerful enough." Miles O'Conall shrugged, failed to dislodge Grey's arm, and reluctantly shuffled away from the double doors. Usually the old man walked past problem spots without pausing, but every once in a while, Miles needed a nudge.

No surprise he'd needed one now. Grey hated pulling into a freight station with empty wagons just as much as his partner hated seeing it. Disappointment and failure weighed anyone down. And when a man's spirits ran low, the shot glass beckoned with a fresh supply.

Until the time came when a man woke from his stupor and realized he'd poured the most precious parts of his life away in an amber haze. Grey closed his eyes against the familiar tug of guilt and regret.

"Your want for a drink can't be more powerful than my need for a bath." Now that they'd passed the place, Miles could stand on his own strength. Grey moved away, marveling that after days with nothing but open prairie and oxen for company, a well-established town felt almost as empty.

The bustling outpost fell strangely still on a Sunday. No string of wagons inched toward the weighing platforms. Few trains came through, and those that did were largely passenger or pass-throughs. Laborers didn't swarm around loading docks or construction sites. Even the buildings, huddled in clumps amid lines of track, seemed lonely and divided.

Brick banks and accounting offices squared off against clapboard stables, saloons, and stores. Boardinghouses butted up against fancy houses built by big-headed businessmen who made fortunes on shipping. Railroad tracks snaked through, encircling weighing stations, widening around stockyards, drawing near docks where steamships used to load up for supply runs to Fort Totten.

Miles seemed to be thinking along the same lines. "Feels like the place is holding its breath, don't it? But you can probably get a bath at the hostel. I got us a room at one of the nicer places."

"Of course you did."

"Enjoy the little things in life when they're available," Miles advised. "No need to catch fleas from a boardinghouse bunk when we've the funds for better."

"If you look down on a boardinghouse bunk now, I don't want to hear you griping about a bedroll beneath a wagon tomorrow," Grey warned. "Don't tell me you've gone soft from passenger trains, city visits with old friends, and your fine room here."

Miles scoffed. "Don't you be teasing me 'bout my travels. My connections in the city made the week well worth our while even if the only freight you collected is your travel dirt."

Grey frowned. Joking or not, he needed no reminder that all he had to show for a grueling week were miles left behind and the dust that tagged along. He hadn't expected to come across much over this well-traveled stretch, but a stray skeleton or two would have made welcome additions to rattle in his wagons. Buffalo bones seemed almost as scarce as the living animal these days!

"Maybe you're wishing you went with me?" Miles scrutinized him with a frown of his own. "Been two years since you left Chicago."

Chicago. Grey shook his head. Hard to believe so much time had passed. Two years since he turned in his uniform and turned his back on the town that took everything.

"I know that frown too well, my friend. You're a grand one for grazing on regrets."

"Then I'm in the right place. These plains hold nothing but ghosts and grass."

Miles gave a rueful chuckle. "Used to be buffalo, but between the railroad, the Indians, and us, even the bones have been picked clean!"

Grey groaned at the awfulness of the joke—and the truth behind it. Buffalo ruled the prairie until trains and killers claimed the plains. They came and they conquered, leaving miles of track and millions of rotting carcasses to tell the tale.

It had taken years to produce something useful from the senseless slaughter. But Americans had a knack for creating commerce from chaos, so sun-bleached bones became fodder for the refineries. From hoof and horn to fertilizer and fine china, they transformed testaments of death into life's luxuries.

Though slaughter could never be made right, finding a purpose for the poor creatures lent their deaths some dignity. Grey appreciated that element of redemption amid injustice. But with millions of tons of bones already shipped to the refineries, it looked like redemption was running out for the bone hunters.

"Stop brooding." Miles's sharp elbow prodded him from his musings. "There's a whole world in front of your nose. Why not enjoy some of it?"

"Fine. I'll start by ordering a bath in our room. You can try and knock together something edible from what's left of our supplies."

Miles offered the key with a flourish and a bow. "Would his lordship want his meal delivered to the room, then?"

"Yes." Grey snatched up the key and the offer. As he headed toward the building Miles pointed out, he shouted back, "Make sure whatever you bring is hot, hearty, and there's plenty of it!"

His plan hit a snag when the hotel owner started shaking his head. "We're hit too hard in the dining room on Sunday afternoons to spare anyone for toting bathwater up and down the stairs. You'll have to head around next door and make do unless you're willing to wait another six hours or so."

Unwilling to wait, Grey circled the stables in search of a bath. Some entrepreneur had tacked on a clapboard back room and squeezed in a pair of galvanized tubs, separated by a canvas curtain. The must of mold rose from the hay strewn across the ground, and parts of the curtain rotted away, but Grey wasn't in a position to be persnickety.

"Hot water's eighty cents, cold's forty. Ten if you want soap and ten more for a towel." For a man who put such a premium on bathing, the fellow looked awfully grubby. "Price is double today. Seein' as how cleanliness is next to godliness, folks should pay more for the privilege on His day."

"Most places a hot bath is twenty-five or so," Grey grumbled.

"Not in the third year of a drought."

He'd swallowed enough dust on the way to Devil's Lake to know the man wasn't lying. The town may sit on a lake, but that water impregnated with alkaline salts did little good for drinking, bathing, or farming. This bustling town relied almost exclusively on the railroad for supplies and business—any outlying farmers probably didn't have yield to spare in the dry season.

Money might not buy happiness, but it went a long way toward mitigating misery. Grey handed over his dollar.

To his surprise, the fellow tossed him a dime. "I'm a reasonable man."

Fifteen minutes later and folded into a too-small tub, Grey wondered if they blamed the small baths on the drought, too. Cold drafts rushed through the crooked slats of the makeshift room, making him hurry before the water went frigid.

It also made him realize he hadn't gotten that towel. *If he was out, he could've told me so instead of giving back the dime.* Disgruntled, Grey eyed the grungy curtain and shivered. Cold draft or no, he'd dry in the breeze before he touched that thing.

"Almost forgot! You bought the hot bath and the soap." The proprietor let in a fair amount of frigid air when he lobbed a dingy length of gunnysack toward the tub. "I'm throwing in the towel!"

Chapter 2

P*a means well*, Bea encouraged herself as she sawed her way through the ham. Trying to force thin slices from the dense meat was like trying to reason with her family: far too much effort for such disappointing results.

"Of course he does!" Ariel's agreement took her by surprise.

If I can't contain my own thoughts, how can I corral everyone else this afternoon? She resolved to button her lip better. *Lord, I could use some help. You know I've always been one to speak my mind, but I don't need any fugitive musings going after our guests.*

"Pa always means well." Cassia joined them, resplendent in sprigged green muslin.

"Go change." Bea pointed toward their bedroom. "You aren't prancing around in muslin when it's hardly over fifty degrees outside."

"I'll wear a shawl! This is my most becoming dress, and I want to look my best!"

"Vanity doesn't look good on anyone, and the men already saw you in your checked wool," Ariel advised. "Besides, they'll forget how you look today when you turn up to church next week with your eyes red and your nose streaming."

That sent their sister flouncing back to the bedroom. With dinner ready and guests expected at any moment—in fact, Bea had expected them to show up already—Bea began to wonder where Pa and Judith had gone.

"Where'd Pa and Jodie run off to?"

"He said something about setting up." Ariel rolled her eyes. "Not that it's a comfort. Whatever Pa sets in motion, we have to carry it out. As Antonio tells Sebastian in *The Tempest*—"

"If you didn't quote so much, people would understand you better." Cassia flounced back into the main room, nose in the air and obviously out of joint over wearing her woolen best.

"'What's past is prologue; what to come, in yours and my discharge.'" Ariel finished her thought and the sandwich platter before acknowledging the interruption. "Which means—"

"I know what it means, thank you very much."

"Then there's no problem understanding me."

"Perhaps I should have said that you're more interesting to talk to when you don't sound like compendium." Cassia batted the sofa cushions, stepped back to survey the effect, only to adjust again. She missed her sister's wounded expression, deeply felt but quickly hidden.

"You should pay more attention to people because the ugly things you say make more of an impression than your pretty pillows!"

"Girls!" Bea stepped into the breach before Cassia stopped spluttering. "Ariel enjoys a pithy phrase the way you appreciate a perfectly plumped sofa. Quick wit and a keen eye are gifts to share, not weapons to wield. Heaven knows this house has enough of those already."

"And we're about to show off how well we can use them!" Jodie bounced into the house with a smile on her face and hay in her hair.

Cassia clucked and caught hold of her in a heartbeat, snagging bits of straw and smoothing stray locks back into place. When Jodie ducked around her and headed for the kitchen, Cass followed, busily brushing the rumples from the back of her sister's skirts.

"Stop it!" Jodie batted her off. "The men won't care how I look—go badger Ariel or Bea."

"Whatever were you doing in the hayloft?" Cassia continued to fuss.

"Haystacks. I was helping Pa prop up Ariel's target." At that, the room went still. Taking advantage, Jodie got away from the grooming and grabbed a corn muffin.

"*My* target?" Ariel, already fairest of them all in her coloring, went pale.

"And Cass's," Jodie mumbled around a mouthful of muffin. "Pa's put cans out on Buffalo Boulder for Bea and me, and taken all the men to stick smaller stuff in the hillside. He sent me back to tell you they'll be along in a few minutes."

"All the men? Did they see the haystacks, or did they meet Pa at the boulder?" Bea's heart kicked against her ribs as Jodie, busy with another bite, waved in the direction of the boulder. She grabbed Ariel and Jodie and pushed them toward the door. "Take those targets back to the barn before the men catch sight of them!"

"Now, Jodie!" Ariel yanked her out the door when it looked like she might protest.

They hadn't had time to talk it through, but Ariel knew every bit as well as Bea that Pa's attempt to show the town that they could fend for themselves would set them apart from polite society. Riding, roping, and shooting seemed hoydenish, but unavoidable at this point. If they added archery and knife-throwing to the mix at the same time, they'd be labeled adventuresses.

Or worse.

"Where are the plates?" Cassia came back inside after carrying the sandwiches to the rough trestle table outside. "We've got the stew, corn muffins, with the ham biscuit sandwiches. I saw the coffee and even the mugs and spoons, but no plates."

"We only have ten of the crockery, Cass. This will have to be less formal, like when we feed the threshing crew." She saw her sister's brow knit in disapproval, and her patience slipped. "There's no help for it. When there aren't enough plates, the tins will have to do."

"And when there aren't enough tins?" She pointed to the short stack of only five tins. "You forgot Pa made that fire screen trying to reflect more heat into the parlor and save fuel."

"Plates for the guests, tins for the family then." Bea's stomach turned.

"I'll eat later. . .we'll have to give my tin to one of the men."

"You can't have ten men with plates and one without," Ariel protested as she and Jodie slipped back inside. "It's an insult to whoever gets the tin. Besides, they'll notice if you aren't eating with everyone else, and they'll think you're nervous about shooting for them."

"We can't seem weak! Pa's pride is on the line." Jodie lifted her chin. "Use Ma's plate."

Bea stopped scanning the kitchen cupboards as her youngest sister squeezed through and tenderly took out a single, delicate dish.

Bea recalled that the true test of finest china was holding it up and seeing sunlight through the center. This piece passed the test. A border of blue forget-me-nots encircled a soft glow, set off by the glimmer of gold along the rim.

If only Mama had held up half so well as her china. . .but she'd proven far more fragile.

More than a decade had passed since they were together, but the sight of this plate dragged Bea back through the years.

Jodie hadn't seen her second birthday yet. Newly nine and always anxious to make Mama happy, Bea followed her instructions to pack a picnic lunch. Seven-year-old Ariel baked the cake almost on her own, and Mama held Jodie while they all watched Cassia, a curious five, smudge frosting on top of it.

And around it. And on top of the table, her apron, and anything she touched before Bea cleaned her hands with a damp rag. She'd caught Cass before she grabbed hold of Mama's skirts and giggles turned to grimaces.

During those stretches when Pa left to hunt buffalo, Mama never laughed long, and lately it looked like the effort drained her. Even her smiles faded faster, but not that day. A constant smile belied her pale cheeks and reddened eyes. Bea pretended not to notice the tremor in her hands as Mama unlatched the hope chest she opened so often those last few days.

The soft-sharp scent of aged pine and old memories lingered like a sigh from time itself. Mama unearthed a treasured piece of china, cradling it with both hands so they could all get a good look. She allowed each of them to trace its gilded edges before declaring that their beautiful cake deserved this beautiful plate. High praise, indeed.

Bea would have chosen more time with Mama over any treasure, but didn't get a choice. This delicate plate, and the memories twined into its forget-me-not border, endured long after they lost Mama.

But the recollections didn't have Bea blinking away tears today. Judith's gesture showed that memories weren't what mattered most in this family.

Her sister smiled, sliding her fingertips lightly around the rim before releasing her treasure. "Come on, ladies. Let's do Pa proud and show them what the Darlyns are made of!"

Even as she promised herself not to, Jodie peeked toward the pile of plates. Noticing that Cassia plunked them down on the corner of the trestle table, too near the edge for comfort, Jodie sidled over and scooted them toward safety.

Perhaps it shouldn't make her feel better, but just touching the delicate edge of the plate calmed her. Jodie didn't really believe Mama looked down from heaven to watch over her—that was God's job, anyway—but in a deep, secret spot in her heart, she held a piece of Mama whenever she touched the fragile beauty of what she'd left behind.

They never talked about it, but her sisters felt the same way. No one ever considered putting it in danger by displaying it. They kept it in the cupboard, safe and sacred and saved for special celebrations a mother should share.

Today counts, Jodie told herself as she tried hard to listen to Pa saying grace over the food. *Today's special. The plate can come out of the cupboard because in a way, the Darlyns are coming out of hiding, too.*

When everyone else started to eat, Jodie couldn't choke much down. The corn muffin she'd filched earlier rubbed a sore spot into her stomach, so she stabbed and jabbed at the food on her plate until it looked as though she'd eaten something. The jabbing and the stabbing made her feel better, and it kept her out of any conversation. Not that the men said much. She wasn't the only one focusing on dinner.

By the time the men plunked down their plates—she checked to be sure Mama's dish made it through unscathed—they'd put away enough food to have fed the entire Darlyn family for days.

"Thank you, Jodie." Old Mr. Alderman beamed when Cassia collected his plain plate, and kept right on smiling even when her sister shook her head.

"My name is Cassia," she kindly corrected him.

"I'm sorry, dear. I guess I've gotten the four of you switched around. But you're the youngest, aren't you?"

"Almost, Alderman." Pa snagged Jodie for an introduction. "Judith's my youngest."

She leaned close, loving the feeling of connection more than she hated having all those men stare at her sisters. Too many looked like they longed for more than lunch. Jodie itched to run the lot of them off the farm before they swiped a sister or two for themselves.

Whatever feminine charms the Darlyn blood passed on, it lavished them on the three eldest sisters and ran low by the time Jodie arrived. She hadn't shown any sign of them so far. Too young to marry, too old to dandle on anyone's knee, she endured the awful, awkward area between child and womanhood. Her figure stayed stubbornly straight and lanky, her feet often failing to keep pace with her long legs.

Even her hair seemed uncertain she deserved any sort of crowning glory, changing color at odd intervals as though testing each shade. Golden in summer sun but fiery by candlelight, the changeable strands lost courage under many conditions to leave her mousy brown and utterly unremarkable.

This, of course, was a mousy moment.

Thankfully, it was short-lived, allowing her to scurry off to the side when Pa decided to introduce each of them individually. Next, he brought Bea forward.

"Beatrix is eldest," he informed men who mostly knew that already. They also knew Bea'd broken her engagement to the eldest Fuller brother two years ago and wasn't interested in leaving her family for something so humdrum as a husband. Still, they stared long enough and hard enough to make Jodie see her sister with new eyes.

After all the hullabaloo to get guest-ready, Bea should look bedraggled. Instead, her quiet confidence commanded attention. The too-often washed wool gown Jodie thought of as faded—its gold had given way to watery winter sunlight—suddenly seemed becoming. The color called attention to the amber flecks in her eyes and the glowing mahogany in her dark hair. Worse, those washings wore the fabric to a supple softness that molded to her figure, showing off the strength of her shoulders before skimming in around her small waist.

Jodie hoped none of the men would notice, but knew better. Huber's beady eyes missed nothing, his gaze growing so possessive Jodie wanted to whisk Bea away. None of these men were worth losing a sister to, but Huber made her skin crawl. His had the mean, squinched-up eyes of a snake, the meaty build of an ox, and the puffed-up pride of a rooster. He slapped on a suit and a smile, but Jodie saw straight through it.

"Second eldest is Ariel." When Pa maneuvered Ariel toward the front, Bea came around and snugged Jodie tight against her side.

Jodie nestled in, trying to give as much comfort as she gained because she knew Bea hated this as much as she did. Pa might be oblivious, but both of them bristled at the way the men sized up their sisters like hogs at auction. And they weren't the only ones. Ariel stood straight as a poker, rigid with disapproval and trying to seem taller than she really was.

Small and slight, no one guessed she'd been made of sterner stuff than any other sister. Ariel's name suited her, since she seemed spun from breezes with her milky skin and swirls of hair in that indescribable blend of blond and red. In little girl games, they'd all insisted Ariel play a fairy.

But they'd grown out of those games, and now the men played pretend. Jodie scowled to see them staring at Ariel, imagining her as a farmwife and trying to decide if her delicate build would be a drawback. Deep in their own desires, most of the men made Jodie mad as a hornet.

Only Lionel Fuller looked Ariel in the eye, giving a solemn smile that showed some respect.

If it were up to Jodie, he could stay when she kicked out the others. But it wasn't up to her, and instead Pa turned attention to Cassia, allowing Ariel to slip over and join her and Bea. Ariel stood on Jodie's other side, uniting the three of them in a sister sandwich when she slid her arm around Bea's waist. Together, they tried to keep calm as Cassia came under scrutiny.

The contrast between the two middle sisters never seemed more dramatic than today. While Ariel's soft shades made her a fairy, Cassia's coloring cast her as the princess when they'd played pretend. Nature lavished her with the vibrant tones of precious jewels, framing emerald eyes with ruby red tresses. The men's gazes turned greedy as they drank in her richness. Cassia's curves appealed to men in a way even Jodie understood.

Well, mostly.

But most of all, she understood that Pa's big plan had backfired. Instead of warning the men away, he'd let the whole group get too close for comfort.

Too many men crammed the dining room, but Grey's gut growled at the idea of coming back later. He paid for his plate and plunged into the crowd before Miles protested. After a lot of effort and elbows, Grey claimed a chair and sprawled out. Anyone eyeing a nearby seat could squeeze to the side—Grey wasn't giving up even an inch of his territory until he left the table.

Spoons scraped against bowls, individual voices grew into an overwhelming roar, and Grey didn't think he'd ever seen such a bunch of soup-slurping, table-thumping belchers in all his born days. When it turned out that the soup held more broth than beef and the biscuits could've served as tent stakes, it almost came as a relief.

"No reason to stick around," Grey mentioned as he made short work of the unimpressive meal. "I'll take seconds so as to keep from coming back for supper, but that's all."

Miles nodded and lifted his spoon, turning it so the almost-clear broth streamed back into the bowl. A faint plop punctuated the single scrap of carrot he'd caught in the spoonful. "Not exactly stuff to stick to a man's ribs."

"Ain't so bad." One of the strangers sharing their table crashed into the conversation. "At least it's edible, and you can keep going back for more until you get enough to hold you over."

"Biscuits don't chip yer tooth or crumble from weevily meal," another man pointed out.

"It'll do," Grey grunted. Hopefully the talkers would take a hint and hush up.

"I think these gentlemen have the right idea." Miles encouraged the interrupters. He always liked an audience.

"I'm swallowing what's served." Grey grimaced but steadily emptied his bowl.

"Sounded to me like a lot of complaining for a glad man." The one who'd first addressed them looked as if he'd seen enough years of hard living to warrant respect, so Grey stayed polite.

"Observing the state of things isn't the same thing as complaining about them," he pointed out. "Complaining comes close to whining, and I can't abide a whiner."

"No whining and dining around here!" When the second stranger snorted into his soup and kept eating, Grey set down his spoon for good.

"Unless you head to the saloon, but I'll tell ya what,"—the old-timer grabbed a biscuit and waved it while he spoke—"if you think the soup's watery, you won't recognize what they call wine around here. Best to stick with something in a shot glass—can't cut that stuff too much without the color giving the game away."

Miles pushed his plate away and mumbled, "Don't drink much anymore."

Their newfound friends exchanged a look that warned of questions to come, making Grey bristle. Miles didn't need to explain to strangers why he'd given up drinking. Or why Grey had done it first, then insisted his partner join him. Too many reasons to make the change—and every one of them a reason not to talk about it. Not to think about it.

Grey's substandard soup rose to burn the back of his throat. He tried vainly to swallow back the sensation and the memories that caused it. His boss's betrayal. . .his wife's missed memorial. . .the clawing burn as every shot spread through his chest. No coincidence that they called them shots. Liquor tore through a man's mind and life like buckshot. Every round did a little more damage.

Chapter 3

Liquor leaves a bad taste in a man's mouth, an ache in his head, and a hole in his wallet. Nothing we want to deal with." Grey managed to avoid their good-natured nosiness without giving anything away. "We're heading out first thing tomorrow after we stock up on supplies."

"You oughta come by my place then." The older of the pair straightened up and adopted a more serious expression. "I got the best prices in town to shore up any outfit, and it's set up so a man don't mind spending time inside. No frilly-sillies cluttering up the place."

The description caught his curiosity, and Grey considered continuing the conversation. What would this old-timer categorize as frilly-sillies? What would he deem worthy of stocking to create a place where men didn't mind spending time? And, presumably, money.

"We're headed over there soon as we're done with dinner, if you want to take a gander," the other offered.

"Or join us. We walk the cracker barrel over to the stove and set up the checkerboard on Sundays. Place is named Al's." The owner jabbed a thumb toward his chest. "I'm Al."

"Makes sense to me." Miles grinned. "Don't suppose you sell newspapers or journals at this store of yours, Al?"

Grey wondered whether Miles wanted reading material, or if he was trying to tempt Grey into coming along. Either way, he knew he wouldn't resist the chance to appease his curiosity.

"Sure do. But I don't sell nothing on Sundays."

"What if I picked something out to occupy a few hours today but paid for it with everything else in the morning?" Grey proposed.

"Suppose you don't come by in the morning?"

"You won't have any trouble catching us," Miles promised. "Oxen pull our wagons steady enough, but there's no denying it's slow going. A man could outpace us at a jog."

"Good enough." Al's chair gave a sudden screech as he scooted away from the table and practically plowed into a man passing through. He ignored the glowers shot his way and thumped his pal on the shoulder, making soup dribble down his shirtfront. "Come on, Bill."

"Don't rush me!" Bill scrambled to shove a few biscuits down his dirty shirtfront before following his friend.

"Well." Miles grinned as they headed after Al and Bill. "This should be an experience to remember."

The locals led them around offices, between buildings, and along random rail lengths. They finally came to a stop before a building with a boarded-up window. The peeling paint of a lopsided sign proclaimed they'd arrived at HONEST AL'S SUPPLES.

"You're missing the *i* in 'Supplies,'" Miles mentioned with as much tact as he could muster.

"It ain't missing," Al informed them loftily. "Ain't no *i* because there're not 'lies' at Honest Al's. Get it?"

" 'I' see." Grey bit back a grin at Miles's warning glance.

"And what happened to your window?" Miles rubbed the back of his neck, agitated.

"Trains come close enough to rattle the panes until they break. Pure foolishness to keep replacing the things. If it won't hold up, I won't put it in my shop." Al swung open the door to reveal a dim room divided by shelves, with an uncluttered counter and an open space in front of a potbellied stove. "What you see is what you get."

✳

Watching Jodie race to the barn, Bea wondered whether the Darlyns would make it through the afternoon with their good name intact. Pa's awful "introductions" let the men look them over like hogs for auction, their blatant stares making it clear they'd come to buy. But none of them would walk away with a wife.

In fact, if they didn't start showing her sisters some respect by the time she brought out her rifle, one or two of them might not be walking away at all. A bullet in the boot would stop them in their tracks, and though she prayed it wouldn't be necessary, Bea wouldn't hesitate to hobble the lot if they mistreated Ariel or Cassia. She didn't have to worry about Jodie, who was too young to attract that sort of unwanted advances.

But no longer young enough for her age to excuse a daring display of riding astride.

Worry warred with pride as Bea watched Jodie burst from the barn. Her braid unraveled to stream behind her, the changeable tresses taking up the bronze glow of her mount's sorrel coat. No one watching her ride would imagine Jodie constantly complained about her own clumsiness. Her movements became an extension of her horse's fluid, athletic grace as Jodie put the quarter horse through her paces.

First they galloped around the farmyard, skirting the chicken house, hog pen, and the cleared-off area where everyone gathered near the trestle table. After the first lap, Jodie slowed to a still-smooth run, relaxing into the rhythm and starting to swing her lariat. The loop lengthened as it gained speed, held aloft by the force of its own spinning. The next time she drew near, Jodie snapped her wrist in a sharp motion, sending the swirling rope forward. It arced through the air, settled into a circle around an old bucket, and tightened around its target.

The horse never hesitated or changed its pace, even as they dragged the bucket behind them. Their guests exclaimed at the sight, watching in fascination as Jodie pulled in the slack, loosened the noose, and let the bucket drop back to the ground.

The third time she passed, Jodie leaned back, gripped the cantle, and swung one leg over the horse in a swirl of skirts. Those who'd never seen the maneuver made various sounds of surprise to see her sideways in the saddle. But only for a moment. Jodie turned her torso, gripping the pommel behind her, and with another swirl of skirts suddenly sat backward.

Riding the wrong way, she didn't slacken the pace. Instead, she raised the rope once again. This time she sent it in search of a much smaller target, claiming a can from the ground before looping the length of rope and hooking it to her saddle.

Some of the men cheered, others muttered, but no one could tear their eyes away as Jodie finished the lap and shifted back to the traditional position. She didn't give herself—or anyone else—the chance to get comfortable before she drew up her knees, her feet finding the saddle and supporting Jodie in a crouch.

When she wore a dress instead of britches, this position made her seem like a ball of skirts floating atop her mount. It took several strides for her to center herself and start the heart-stopping process of standing straight. Jodie needed to move swiftly to accomplish the feat, but to Bea the seconds stretched. Jodie unfolded her arms, skirts lengthening by slow degrees until she rose to full height.

Bea's heartbeat borrowed the rhythm of those hooves as Jodie balanced effortlessly. Skirts and hair whipping in the wind behind her, arms aloft in victory, for a breathless moment it seemed as though Jodie had accomplished the impossible, her unbelievable skill overriding any possible propriety problems.

Jodie shifted, knees bending slightly beneath wind-whipped skirts. But she didn't lower herself back into the saddle. Instead, she straightened once more. Then bent and rose again, her smile sliding into a frown of concentration. Bea realized Jodie was struggling to seat herself without getting caught short by her skirts.

The same skirts I insisted on. Guilt gave more weight to her worries as Bea started a fervent string of prayers. *Lord, see my sister through this safely. Please don't let it break her to bow to convention this one time.*

The men began to mutter as the novelty of the trick waned, not realizing the rider hadn't planned to stand so long. Then Jodie seated herself in the saddle and shocked them into silence at the same time.

Unable to maneuver otherwise, Jodie had lowered her arms to her sides, gathered fistfuls of fabric, and hiked her skirts above her knees to sink into a crouch.

Bea began to breathe again when Jodie dropped safely back into the saddle and steered back to the barn. Then and there, she swore she'd sew her sister a pair of split skirts before Judith rode in front of anyone else. Obviously, a woman shouldn't ride astride in fitted britches, but there were other options. Never again would she risk her safety to appease propriety.

Especially since it seemed as though propriety couldn't be appeased. Now that Jodie sat in the saddle without engaging in acrobatics, disbelief turned to disapproval. No one caught so much as a glimpse of skin, but that didn't matter much to these. If anything, it sounded as if some of them were more offended by Jodie daring to wear britches—even beneath her skirts—than they would have been if she'd flashed her legs.

"Bad enough when a woman rides astride," Old Man Alderman fretted, "but to wear men's clothing and attempt athletics?"

"Judith *accomplished* every attempt," Bea spluttered, outraged anew. "It takes time, patience, and discipline to perfect a performance like that!"

"Discipline?" Huber snorted with derision. "I think we've all seen that discipline is something sorely lacking. Put her time toward woman's work, so she'll have some value to a husband."

"Numbers in your ledger won't sum up any woman, much less one of my Darlyns!" Pa thundered. "If you cannot see their worth, the loss is yours—and yours alone."

"The tricks might not be to your taste, but such training takes time and patience." Lionel Fuller stepped into the breach with his own opinion. "Any man well acquainted with hard work can't help but appreciate the same in someone else."

The clever comment shifted the men's focus from denigrating Jodie's character to defending their own. The conversation turned to bluster and boasts as they assured everyone present how well they knew the value of hard work.

Ariel beamed at Lionel, who inclined his head in acknowledgement. Suddenly, Bea wondered whether solemn Lionel wouldn't make a good match for her most serious sister. Now sixteen, Cassia retained too much youthful zeal and flightiness to be ready to settle down. But Ariel had been much more mature at the same age. Enough so that Bea didn't protest when Ben's brother started glancing her sister's way two years ago. But Ariel hadn't encouraged his attentions, and Lionel withdrew when Bea ended her own engagement to his older brother and Ben left for Oregon.

Perhaps time has passed for the Fullers to forgive me. . .and for Ariel to accept a suitor.

"Why encourage women to take up masculine pursuits?" Huber refused to move on. "It's unnatural. Their time is best spent cooking and sewing and seeing to the needs of their menfolk!"

"We'll understand if you feel the need to leave early." Bea slapped on a sickly smile and tried to sound concerned. "Marksmanship is often seen as masculine, and I wouldn't want to offer further offense."

"Everyone knows I'm the best shot in town. Fortunately for you,"— his tongue flicked over his lower lip—"I find myself interested in what else the Darlyns have to offer a man."

"Coffee?" As if on cue, Cassia appeared at Bea's elbow with a set of steaming carafes. The next few moments were filled with good-natured jostling as the men crowded around.

Bea seized the opportunity to escape into the house. She used the pretext of fetching her gun but took a moment to pray for fortitude before going back outside. By now, Pa had been standing for far too long, so Bea waved at him to join her near the table. He raised a brow, so she knew he'd seen her, but he seemed loathe to leave his conversation.

Bea lingered near the table, hoping he'd be able to sit on the bench before the coffee ran out. In the meantime, she set down a box of ammunition, crooked her elbow around the stock of her rifle, and started loading rounds into the chamber until the Winchester reached its capacity of fifteen. Her Colt Peacemaker stayed holstered at her hip.

It took the same .32-20 rounds, but she made a point of keeping the pistol fully loaded at all times. *You never know when you might need to shoot something.*

"Hoyden and a half, that youngest of yours." Huber strutted up to the trestle table, with an empty mug and a mind to match. "When the horse is better behaved than the girl, it's time to rein her in."

"Some need more time than others to master manners." Bea kept her comment neutral, certain he wouldn't catch on that she meant him, not Jodie. "As with any acquired skill."

"Not so much acquired as *instilled*, but the effort can be rewarding. Even, or perhaps *especially*"—he thudded his mug atop the table for emphasis—"when it requires a heavy hand."

Fury froze Bea, leaving her unable to respond for a long moment. Usually her temper ran hot, but Huber's comments made her blood run cold. The man not only advocated violence, he clearly relished the prospect of forcing his will on *her* family.

Bea made a point of moving his mug to an open space, knowing it was no accident he'd struck it against the single piece of china amid the plain plates. She fought to keep her fingers steady when the rest of her shook with rage. Amazingly, the dish escaped his cruelty unscathed—*and so will Judith and the rest of us. I'll make sure of it.*

"Heavy hands can cause harm." Her bland smile might fool the men nearby, because she didn't want to attract attention, but Bea's glare issued an unmistakable challenge to the man before her. "You'll want to take care how you handle what matters to me."

His eyes narrowed to dangerous slits. "You asking me or telling me, Miss Beatrix?"

"Whichever you prefer," she trilled, never letting her social mask slip. Even when he crowded close, she'd give no cause for the others to come over.

"Oh, I like that. Whichever I prefer." Huber leered at her, then made a point of perusing Cassia before meeting her gaze again. "I'll *take care* to let you know which one I choose."

Chapter 4

Miles chose to stay behind at Honest Al's when Grey went back to the room with an armful of news sheets. Who knew how many months he'd be walking the prairie with nothing but oxen and Grey for company? And though he wasn't one to be putting down his partner, sometimes he got on better with the oxen. If he locked horns with them, at least he still stood a fighting chance.

"Not very cheerful sort, is he?" Bill dragged a couple crates over to serve as seats.

"Nah, he just isn't one to joke with strangers," Miles defended. Grey could be better company, to be sure, but he'd be bagged if he let someone else say so.

"Maybe, but I been lotsa places and met many men, and I seen some of his sort. Minds never stop working long enough to start enjoying." Al shook his head. "Think too much."

With that bit of wisdom behind him, Al proceeded to lose spectacularly in the quickest game of checkers Miles ever saw.

"Looks like you need to think things through more," Bill ribbed his friend.

"Guess I got too used to playing you," Al agreed. "Going with my gut usually gets the job done. That, and a little luck!"

"Checkers is more a game of strategy." If this was all the challenge he'd find at Honest Al's, a restless night stretched ahead. Miles barely looked at the board, beating Bill even as he wondered how many other, better games played out around Devil's Lake. He shifted atop the uncomfortable crate, tapping his fingers against his knees to try and ease the itch.

No use. What did a man have to show when he won a game of checkers? Not even a sense of pride when his opponents were such plonkers. Down the way, other games gave better stakes and bigger thrills. *If I step lively, I'll have a go and be back with Grey none the wiser. After Chicago, I could use a pick-me-up.*

Miles rubbed his forehead, feeling the first cold drops of sweat. What good would it do to dodder away the day like a good lad, only to have Grey see him so shook from the effort? His partner didn't ask sticky questions so long as Miles kept off the drink, and Miles didn't correct Grey's idea of why Miles avoided saloons. For that matter, he didn't set Grey straight about the lad's own brush with the bottle. Some things were better left unremembered—otherwise, as Miles knew all too well, they'd never be forgotten.

Much less forgiven.

And he had a lot to repent, but in spite of his Irish blood, liquor left him cold. Always had. What made his blood run hot were high stakes at the card tables. Tables waiting for him tonight, offering a chance to balance the accounts again.

With every trip, Miles gave Grey a summary of what the load earned and what their bank balance was, then counted out a quarter of the take for each of them in cold hard cash. Grey didn't go bothering about checking transaction records, so Miles only needed to keep enough sloshing around the bank vaults to reasonably match their business balance. If he found his pockets light after a hard run at the tables, one good night at a high stakes Chicago game set it straight again.

But this last trip Miles made a right hames of the deal, winning through the night only to be bluffed out of the big pot. A hollow dread spread beneath his ribs, making the itch unbearable. *Wrong or not, I've got to make a play for putting things to rights.*

Odds were Honest Al didn't gamble, but his customers might have given him a feel for the town play. *A man doesn't get a leg up by sitting down*, Miles reminded himself, *and he won't find out nothing to his advantage if he won't ask.*

"How far'd your guts get you in a game of chance, like poker?"

"Better'n checkers." Al stretched his legs, scooting back the barrel he'd perched on. "If you want to go rustle up a game, I'll show you."

"Deal."

Five hands later, Miles decided the night turned out better than he could've hoped, all thanks to Bill and Al. Honest men made bad bluffers, and this pair gave themselves away the second they saw their cards.

The itch left his fingers, and the hollow space behind his heart eased as the pile at his elbow grew. Miles fanned what was sure to be a winning hand and ran through his roster of tricks. How best to swell the bets? When it would be his turn next, Miles shifted in his seat.

A simple shift was a good way to get their thoughts going in the right direction. Now to make them race. . . . Miles eyed cards, started to sigh, and made a point of catching himself halfway to send a panicked glance around the table. Sure enough, Bill and Al caught him out and started smiling.

The other two had the brains to keep straight faces, but Miles saw the sparkle in their eyes and knew he had them right where he wanted them. He gave a slight shake of his head before puffing up his chest and putting on a wide grin that failed to fool anyone. Everything about him screamed to the table that he feared he'd been caught. No sense of surprise from the others when Miles saved face at the expense of his wallet and doubled down. The price of pride might be steep, but every man paid up until he was played out.

Some just had more to gain than the others. . .or less to lose.

"I know you didn't get lost, so why are you hiding?" Ariel slipped up to the stall where Jodie tended to Daredevil.

Granted, Daredevil didn't need the tending, but Jodie needed the time it took, so she brandished his brush and bristled at her sister.

"I won't waltz out of the barn without getting him settled. You know that." A loud snort punctuated her statement, making Jodie peer at the horse in concern before she realized Ariel made the sound.

"We also know it doesn't take this long. Cassia's served up fresh coffee, Bea's loaded her gun, and Huber's gotten obnoxious enough that Bea looks like she might set him in her sights." She patted Daredevil's nose before reaching a hand for Jodie. "The sooner we go out there, the sooner they'll go away."

"You know me too well," Jodie grumbled as she put away the comb. When her sister shoved a candle into her hand, she lifted it in silent question.

"Light it while I signal Bea so she's ready. Once you come out of the barn, hold out the candle and she'll shoot the wick."

"Putting out two fires at once?" Jodie joked, cheered by the plan. While Ariel went back, Jodie poked a finger out the door to get a sense of the wind, then emerged sheltering the fragile flame. The last thing she needed to do after her earlier failure was let the wick blow out before it met Bea's bullet. She shuddered at the thought of anyone doubting her eldest sister's skill—and how Bea might decide to prove them wrong.

She didn't leave the barn too far behind before Bea gestured for her to stop—about thirty paces away from where she waited with her Peacemaker. Jodie stretched out her arm, holding the candle aloft and managing to smile. Usually it seemed ironic to call a gun the Peacemaker, but in this case, her sister's skill with her Colt would end any unrest over how Jodie handled her own horse.

The men watched with mild interest, not hushing as they had for her and Daredevil. Obviously, they doubted Bea would show anything out of the ordinary. And to be fair, the candle trick wasn't one to impress—even at such a distance.

Jodie heard the crack of the pistol at the same time she saw the flame go out. She held it high to show everyone, then brought her arm down and started the applause the others should already be offering.

While the others might be slow off the mark, they eventually began to clap. Only the oily Mr. Huber openly sneered. "Bah! The bullet doesn't have to hit the wick to put out the flame—just pass by close enough to make a breeze. For pity's sake, with prairie winds the shooter doesn't even have to manage that!"

Suppressing the urge to chuck the candle at his foul face—no sense wasting the candle even if she'd been close enough to hit him—Jodie hurried over. Bea ignored the insult, biding her time because she knew that any impressive show started out small, the tricks getting bigger and more difficult until every last observer left shocked.

Ariel and Cassia had already begun passing out targets for the next part of Bea's demonstration. Since the Darlyns weren't about to waste money on glass target balls, they'd long ago perfected the process of forming discs from wet clay and hardening them in the fire. Free, easy, and effective, the clay targets perfected Bea's ability to aim at moving objects. They also perfected every other Darlyn's ability to throw something with accuracy.

"For the next part of my demonstration, I'll tackle moving targets. When Pa yells 'pull,' the first of you in line can throw one of the clay discs. We'll stop when we run out."

"Or when you miss," one of the Brauns added.

"Won't happen," Pa snapped back as Bea raised her rifle.

She shot the first target, then the second, and so on until all dozen men—Pa included—had thrown a disc. She didn't waste a single bullet—not even on Old Man Alderman's low throw. By then, most of the men began to murmur in surprise.

While Bea reloaded, Pa raised the stakes and instructed the men that this round, they'd throw two discs in rapid succession, challenging Bea to hit both before either reached the ground. Some scoffing sounded, but not much, and not loudly.

Jodie figured they'd started to learn their lesson once half of them had thrown their sets and Bea still hadn't missed a shot. She loaded up again, and Pa told the remaining five men to throw three discs instead of two.

"My brother spoke of your skill," Lionel Fuller spoke with obvious approval. "I'm thinking I should be grateful to your pa for inviting us. I've never seen such sharpshooting."

"I've done as well in every competition TallGrass has held," Huber boasted. "Last year I didn't miss a single target."

"No," another one of the Fullers spoke up, "but they were all one-shots. Perhaps this year we'll try throwing three in a single round."

"Maybe we'll see if the little Darlyn can manage what her pa claims before we start changing the way the men make their shots." Huber edged out of line to nudge Pa's shoulder—too hard to be a friendly gesture toward an older man.

Jodie bit her lip as Pa ushered the bully to the back of the line, not bothering to respond. Every Darlyn knew Bea's shooting would prove the point. Even when Huber began making strange noises in an obvious attempt to distract her, Bea hit every target once again. Then repeated the feat when each of their guests flung four discs at a time.

Now openly impressed, none of the men could find a bad word for Bea. They poured out accolades. Even Mr. Alderman, the old-fashioned forgetful excuse for a coot, couldn't bring himself to grumble about her gender. Only one man glowered and sulked like a spoiled toddler.

By now, Jodie considered herself well practiced at leaving Huber alone. But this time the other men noticed his behavior and began to rib him.

"Still think you're the best shot in town?"

Huber grunted. "Better'n you and ready to prove I can best anyone."

"This year we'll have to open it up to the womenfolk! Think you'll keep the title against our new challenger?"

"Sure." His mulish look seemed more stubborn than certain. "Be nice to have a challenge for once. Since none of you could provide any competition, I've been kind enough not to show off too bad about the extent of my abilities."

What a clanker! Jodie never paid much attention to the town games, since Pa and her sisters always maintained that participating would win them more problems than prizes. Even so, she'd seen Huber crowing over his victories, strutting around as though that blue ribbon meant he himself were some sort of gift to the town. Jodie couldn't say for sure, but she figured most folks saw him as a nuisance. If he weren't the banker, more people would probably speak up.

For that matter, if he weren't the banker, the other men might shoot better during those competitions. The only year someone bested Huber, he'd lost his farm to foreclosure in a matter of months. No one commented on the connection, but everybody noticed. Since then, every time it came down to a competition, the other men missed shots they shouldn't. But Bea never missed, and she'd promised Pa to always shoot her best. If the men boxed Bea into competing, she'd beat Huber out of hand.

For the first time, Jodie wondered whether Pa's grand idea might make the Darlyn farm the next target of Huber's ire. Already, his mean eyes went narrow and shifty like he was looking for a way to bring Bea down.

"She's done well enough when she's expecting it, but what about when her pa doesn't yell 'pull' to put her on attention?" He grasped at straws. "What about a surprise shot?"

"I can handle whatever you throw at me," Bea promised. She turned her back on the group and went so far as to rest the butt of her gun against the ground, one palm lightly looped around the barrel.

Something was about to go wrong. That cold, clammy prickle always came when her gut felt something her eyes hadn't found out yet. Jodie stepped forward, worried Huber would throw something and catch the back of Bea's head, or hurt her some other unimaginable way.

With a nasty laugh, he snatched something from the trestle table and flung it high in the air. Bea had her rifle against her shoulder and the trigger pulled before Jodie choked out a scream and stumbled forward.

Too little, too late. Bea never missed. Her sister never even knew what she'd been shooting at until the afternoon sun caught on a glint of gold. Jodie could only watch as bits of blue forget-me-nots became a shower of shattered memories.

Chapter 5

The dim room—a double for those his father once favored—seemed strangely airless. Sour whiskey, cheap cigars, plenty of dust and far too few baths scented the place with a sad desperation Grey remembered all too well. Even the plinked-out piano tunes sounded tinny and far away, trickling around chipped shot glasses, scarred tabletops, and the broken men who claimed them for the night.

He'd been here before, when he couldn't pull his father from drinking, and the stink was the stench of his failure. Later, when he grew stronger, he'd come back and breathed in the same odor hundreds of times in dozens of places, taking them down one by one until it smelled like victory. And then, at his darkest hour, when it smelled like sweet oblivion.

Tonight, the whole thing reeked. Poor choices, it seemed, smelled a lot like poor hygiene. The stale air suffocated him, but escaping the weight of old memories meant leaving Miles to be crushed by their counterpart. He pushed forward and pretended not to be bothered by the place when he reached his partner.

"Evening." Grey gave the table a bland smile. He'd walked into too many dens, clubs, and saloons to saunter up to a game of poker and ignore the other players. He clapped a hand on Miles's shoulder. "Didn't expect to find you here."

"Didn't know you'd be looking." Miles managed not to wince when Grey's grip tightened, a silent message that he didn't appreciate his partner's flippant response. It had to hurt, too, since he'd pinched the soft spot where his partner's neck and shoulder joined.

"Didn't think I'd need to, since usually you steer clear of saloons."

"He ain't touched a drop!" To his right, Honest Al reached around a bunch of bottles and glasses littering the tabletop. His arm fell with a heavy thud as he tried to sweep the evidence of his own excess away from Miles. "These're mine!"

Grey raised a brow in silent question until every man clustered around that sad, scarred tabletop started to nod. Miles stayed rigid—perhaps knowing his protestations of innocence wouldn't carry any weight...perhaps too leery of Grey's grip to risk a nod. Either way, some of his tension eased after the other men vouched for his "good" behavior.

"Gospel truth," Bill avowed. "A man can set roots to anything Honest Al says."

Because he stands his ground, or because he lays it on thick? Grey kept the question, and its inherent insult, to himself. Since Al started giving him the old stink-eye, he still needed to say something. But, unlike Miles, Grey wasn't in any mood for games. He didn't have it in him to play nice.

"Can't say I expected to see Honest Al here either," he griped. "Seems a strange thing when a man who won't open his store on a Sunday sets up shop in a saloon."

"Honor the Sabbath somewhere else if ya need to stick your nose in the air and suck out all the fun for everyone else." One of the men Grey didn't recognize stopped balancing on the back legs of his chair, crashing all four firmly on the ground.

"Jesus turned water into wine." With a nervous glance, Bill tried to smooth things over.

"Seein' as how whiskey's the wine of the West, and I'm a sinner," Al slurred with a self-satisfied smile, "only fittin' that I turn wine back into water!" His joke broke the tension around the table, leaving everyone laughing until Al tried to push his chair away from the table.

"Whoa, now. You can't get up from the table while the game's in play!" Bill waved his friend into staying seated. "You don't wanna forfeit when things was just getting interesting."

Honest Al shrugged and laid his cards on the table. "I call."

As the cards came down, his smile grew. Right up until the last man. Miles fanned his royal flush with a flourish.

Grey glared at the two strangers whose disbelief turned to sour mutterings. He rested a hand on his hip, drawing their attention. The muttering stopped. No one moved as Miles finished stuffing his pockets and said his good-byes, but Grey kept one eye on the table as they left.

Miles started talking as soon as they hit the street. "I swear I didn't drink a drop."

"There's a blessing," Grey acknowledged. "I'm glad you've gotten strong enough to resist—but what if you'd been losing, Miles? Without the rush of victory, you might find a need to fill up on something stronger."

"But I didn't." He brushed his hands over his pockets with a grin. "No harm in a game or two among friends—especially when a man finds one so generous!"

"Don't go trading one vice for another," Grey warned. "And remember that when you mix your money with your friends, you're sure to lose at least one."

"Maybe both," Miles finished. "I can't count how many times your father told me that."

"If he couldn't lead by example, I think he decided to serve as his own cautionary tale." Grey grimaced. The only reason this place didn't dredge up vivid, whiskey-whetted regrets of his own was that when he'd hit his breaking point, he'd almost killed himself with drink. In truth, the days he lost were a blessing. Not only because Grey doubted he'd enjoy the memories, but because he could have lost even more.

But the two-bit saloon still echoed with scenes from his boyhood. How many times had he hunted down his dad in the same sort of place? How many more had Miles himself hauled Dad home following a heavy loss?

At least here the game hadn't been rigged and Miles walked away a winner.

For that matter, at least he'd walked away. Plenty of gamblers weren't so fortunate.

"Ah, I've made mistakes enough of me own to be learning from. And so have you." Miles waved away the warning. "No need to be borrowing bad memories from your pa."

"In that case,"—Grey trudged up the last stair and unlocked their room—"do us both a favor and stop reminding me."

✳

"Member-me's." Jodie filled her pudgy hands with Bea's apron and tugged insistently. "You promithed."

Now missing four of her baby teeth, she lisped some of her s's. And even though Bea knew it really meant her littlest sister was starting to grow up, she sounded so babyish. It caught at her heart the way Jodie caught at her skirts when Bea tried to walk past.

"Mem-or-ies," she patiently corrected, all the while dreading the day Jodie finally listened.

"Member-me's," Jodie stubbornly insisted.

"It fits, Bea, the way she says it." Ariel carefully noted her place in the chapter before she crossed to the kitchen, pulled the forget-me-not plate from its place in the cupboard, and gingerly set it atop the sofa table. "You remember for her now, and later, you'll share the memories of the conversations with her."

Sensing an ally, Jodie abandoned Bea's skirts and rushed over to the low table. She reached for the plate, only to be caught short by Cassia, who pulled her out of reach of her greatest treasure. Instead of struggling, Jodie settled for second best and planted her palms atop the increasingly worn velvet of their album and tried to tug it from the table. Cassia pulled it onto her lap, keeping to the opposite corner and leaving space in the center of the sofa.

Jodie could have wriggled up between the two of them but instead waited for Bea to join them. She always waited for Bea to settle in, then crawled atop her lap to see the photographs. If she'd been very, very good and very, very careful, she might be allowed to stroke the beautiful blue flowers with one fingertip.

Now flanked with reinforcements, Jodie called again. "Member-me, Bea!"

"Of course I will." Bea soaked in the sight of her sisters. *"I* always *will."*

And she had. She'd kept those memories so carefully, for so long, only to destroy them. . . . Bea's heartache thundered in her ears, pounded at her temples, and throbbed in her throat. She couldn't think, couldn't breathe beneath the power of its broken beat.

Only one thing proved more powerful: Judith's pain and Bea's need to lessen it. When her sister raced past, Bea lowered her rifle and followed. Together they sank to their knees and sought out the shards of their shared treasure. Little remained, much of the plate blown into a powdery dust. One precious sliver pierced Bea's knee, a speck of blue rescued from the folds of her skirts and pressed into Jodie's hands.

"Forget-me-not," her sister whispered, slicing her finger along the sharp edge.

"Here." Ariel unearthed another broken blossom and passed it to Jodie, who folded her fist around the pair and kept searching.

Cassia crouched beside them, turning over even the minutest fragments for the gleam of a gold rim. Buried beneath its smaller fellows, she uncovered the largest find—a trio of tiny blooms joined their sisters in Jodie's grasp.

How any of them could see well enough to salvage anything mystified Bea. Tears blurred her vision as first Ariel, then Cassia, then she stopped searching. Jodie looked the longest, at last finding a fragment she folded with the other three in a bedraggled bouquet. Only then did the four of them embrace, a tangle of looped arms, tangled skirts, and tilted foreheads nestled against each other. With their heads bowed and hearts so aching, Bea sought comfort from the only possible source.

"Lord," she breathed, her voice thin, "we ask Your comfort and healing. Love made this piece special in the first place. Help us find solace in knowing the love hasn't left."

She rubbed her palm against Jodie's back in slow circles as they all rose to their feet and stood together. As they walked toward the men, Bea gathered up her trusty Winchester. She caught Jodie glaring at the gun, but Bea knew where to place the blame. *I pulled the trigger, but the fall would have shattered the plate whether I shot it or not.*

Now that she'd seen to her sisters, Bea discovered she wasn't the only Darlyn to see that the dish was doomed as soon as Huber threw it. Red-faced, with that long vein in his forehead standing out in sharp relief against his retreating hair, Pa's wrath put avenging angels to shame.

"How dare you!" Pa's hands clenched into fists. "To destroy something special to my girls."

"Not too special to hold my sandwich."

"It's an honor when your host gives you their best," Alderman admonished. "To destroy any dish is disrespectful, but to take their finest. . .Unacceptable! For this insult, you must answer, Huber."

"It's worth little enough to replace." Somewhat sobered but unrepentant, he shrugged.

"Priceless!" Jodie shoved between Cassia and Ariel, who'd become a barrier. Whether to keep Jodie away from Huber or Huber away from Jodie, it failed. She thrust her fist—now sporting thin red ribbons from clutching the sharp shards too tightly—toward his chest. "You can't replace the last piece of Mama's china!"

"Jodie." Bea used her most commanding, obey-this-instant mothering voice as she put her hands around her sister's shoulders and pulled her away from Huber. "Go wash your hand and put those safely away while we see our guests off."

"Fine!" She wrenched away from Bea's hold and raced toward the house.

"Ariel, Cassia," Bea called, still in a tone that brooked no argument from either the men or her family. "Say good-bye to our guests and see to your sister."

A couple of quick "good days" and they were safely inside the house. Only then did the other guests grasp some of the magnitude of what had happened.

"That's the end, then?" one of the Brauns griped. "What about those targets we tucked into the side of the valley? Or the cans we climbed a boulder to stack up?"

"We've seen enough." Lionel took the lead, but all the Fuller brothers agreed.

"What if we don't want to leave until your girl makes good on your promises?" Huber clamped a thick cigar between his yellowed teeth, drawing a deep breath and blowing the smoke into her father's face.

Enraged more by the treatment of his girls than the smoke, Pa jabbed his forefinger into Huber's shirtfront. "She's already made good. You claimed to be the best, and she bested you so easily you had to hide behind a plate to take revenge."

"You don't know what you're talking about!" Huber splayed one grubby paw against Pa's chest and shoved, but Pa didn't give ground.

"Here, now!" One of the Brauns stepped forward, offering a bracing arm in a show of shocked support. "You don't go pushing around another man."

"He's less of a man than his freakish daughters." Huber drew a deep drag from his cigar and stepped forward to crowd Pa.

"Back away." Bea raised her Winchester. "I warned you to take care how you handled what was important to the Darlyns. You didn't listen. Now I'm giving you one chance to step away from my pa, get off our farm, and never come back."

He froze but didn't give ground. "Murder means you'll swing, so you haven't got the guts. Didn't your pa ever tell you not to point a gun unless you were willing to pull the trigger?"

"As a matter of fact. . .he did." Bea adjusted her line of sight and pulled the trigger, the familiar kick against her shoulder feeling like cheerful encouragement. She moved to stand over Huber, who'd shrieked like a frightened schoolgirl and fallen to the ground. He lay there, puffing like a frog on an unlit cigar, since she'd scared him so badly by blowing the tip away.

"So you should keep out of my sight—and away from my family."

Chapter 6

Too tiny to rustle up any trouble," Miles urged. "Heck, sounds like TallGrass barely counts as a town. Not so much as a saloon."

While it took the oxen a day to cover fifteen miles and three to travel between Devil's Lake and TallGrass, a horse-drawn buckboard could make the trip in a few hours. Grey wondered whether the distance deterred TallGrass men from making many trips. It all depended on the town women.

Females had a funny way of changing how men spent their days. Some drove their husbands to the saloons, some pulled them back and straightened them out. Seeing as how they'd built a church before a saloon, Grey guessed they got the good kind.

"They must go to Devil's Lake to raise hell."

"Clever." Miles didn't say anything more for a while, but Grey knew his partner planned to. Miles liked people. Grey liked making good time on their way to the next bone field. The only reason to give in to his partner's social tendencies involved plentiful food cooked by someone else—unlikely that they'd find a café in such a tiny town.

"No food, no stop."

"Now, now, I know there won't be a hot meal handed to us, but I'm thinking a little farm-town store should be stocked with some supplies worth stopping for!"

In spite of himself, Grey considered the point. The morning after his big poker loss, Honest Al hadn't been happy to see him and Miles.

They'd left town with the bare necessities: dry goods, jerky, salt pork, beans, some canned goods, and coffee—but none of the perishables or specialties that turned grub into a real meal.

Still, Grey held out until Miles mentioned the mother lode. "Bet they've got fresh-pressed butter. . . ."

Of all the things they'd done without, he missed butter the most. Butter and bacon. . .not a dish in the world that couldn't be improved by one or the other. Or better yet, both.

"A quick stop, then."

It seemed as though they'd hardly made the decision to swing by TallGrass than they rolled into town. Grey made short work of watering the oxen, figuring he'd catch up to his partner in the store. But Miles found something more interesting along the way, and Grey spotted him too late to intervene as Miles headed toward a newly arrived buckboard. A buckboard that happened to carry two young women. Grey couldn't make out their faces beneath those sun bonnets, but their lithe figures told him to steer clear.

Too bad Miles didn't look beyond the ladies to see problems on the horizon. He met the buckboard with a cheerful bow and a big smile, reaching up to lift the first gal from her perch and place her safely on the ground.

Grey groaned. Miles might not resist the urge to talk with the girls, but he knew better than to touch them. Married or not, it didn't matter. Wives were watched over by protective husbands. Unmarried maidens made potential husbands overly possessive. Either way, it came down to a simple truth: the better looking the girl, the more trouble she attracted.

Grey hoped to head off any problems by ending the conversation quickly and getting his partner into the store, but knew he faced failure. When it came to women, Miles moved faster than a man of his age had any right to. As Grey reached the trio, Miles outmaneuvered him with a generous offer: "Lovely ladies like yourselves shouldn't be toting so heavy crates. What say you let my partner and me unload this wagon o' wonders?"

Bowing to the inevitable, Grey peered into the buckboard and discovered Miles hadn't exaggerated. Fresh-from-the-farm goodness filled the buckboard—and his visions of future meals. Naked greed must have been evident in his expression, because an oh-so-feminine and slightly amused voice called him to the conversation.

"Something catch your eye?"

"Yes'm. I've never laid eyes on a more beautiful—" Grey reluctantly dragged his gaze from the feast to the woman and promptly forgot how to form words.

He'd gotten used to seeing attractive women in one of two ways: fragile, frail, and finicky or bold, brassy, and blunt. But here stood the most compelling woman he'd ever seen, defying such description.

Mahogany curls escaped her bonnet, framing her face with cheerful waves. Fine-boned features fit to carve on a cameo, with a delicate tip-turned nose to keep her from looking snooty. The hazel of her eyes warmed with good humor. Her complexion, tinged with a touch of tawny color, told of time spent in the sun. Strong shoulders and straight posture tattled that she'd spent it working. She stood tall for a woman— Grey imagined she wouldn't need to tilt back her head to meet his gaze if she weren't wearing a bonnet.

Then he imagined her with no bonnet, luxurious curls tumbling over her shoulders. . . .

Behind him, the second woman's question prodded him to finish his thought. "A more beautiful what, now?"

Woman. "Wagon. Load." Grey cleared his throat and scowled at his own awkwardness. "Wagonload. Such a bounty near enough takes a hungry man's breath away."

"He's hungrier than most." Miles chuckled, and Grey knew his friend hadn't missed his lapse—or its cause. "Too many weeks with nothing but his own cooking and company makes a man forget his manners. I'm Miles O'Conall, and this is my business partner, Greyson Wilder."

"Don't mean to offend, but do you mind me asking if these goods are already bought and paid for?" Grey's own lips curved at her generous smile.

"You caught us before we got into the store to strike our bargains." Those full lips didn't frame the response, and Grey belatedly recalled the second woman. No sooner had he convinced his eyes to act polite and at least look at her, he had to blink.

Deep red hair marked the youngster as kin to the first and too gorgeous for her own good. And well she knew it, coyly playing with her bonnet strings. "I'm Cassia Darlyn, and this is Beatrix, my older sister."

Miles, old enough to be her father and then some, smiled indulgently at her preening and asked whether she ever tired of having every man call her Darlyn.

Grey gave her a quick nod of acknowledgment, then ignored their foolish flirting to look back at Beatrix. Mystery always held more appeal than the blatantly obvious. While her beauty might not be as classic, it held a warmth and depth that drew him in. He sensed that she could surprise him, and that intrigued him too much to turn away.

Bea tried not to sigh as the handsome stranger fixed his intense gaze on Cassia and exchanged names. She usually shrugged it off when she met a man, the man met Cassia, and the man forgot she existed. Even Ariel, with her dainty elegance, suffered the same scenario. Now that Cassia had turned sixteen, men didn't pretend to see the girl beneath the curves. They saw her as a grown woman—and stopped looking anywhere else.

Not that it mattered who caught Mr. Wilder's eye—he'd be passing through town and out of their lives. At least she wouldn't add him to Cassia's list of conquests—or her own list of concerns. If Bea liked what she'd seen when he met her gaze, she liked keeping him off her lists even more. And that was telling, because this man could catch any woman's eye.

God sketched Greyson Wilder with the unrelenting lines of a lawman. Straight brows and a strong nose angled over a square, stubble-roughened jaw. His black hair, long enough to tickle his collar, carried no hint of curl. No bending. No yielding. Every inch bespoke a man who would not compromise. . .but could be counted on.

Perhaps. Those wide shoulders and strong hands might never carry burdens for anyone else. Appearances deceive.

And surprised, too, because the object of her inspection was now looking right back at her!

Disbelief dulled her wits, rendering her incapable of looking away in time to preserve decorum. After Ben, she'd never thought to find another man who turned his interest toward her instead of her sisters— *and found me ogling like an old maid!*

Beneath the cover of Cassia's tinkling laugh, low enough so only she could hear, Mr. Wilder leaned in to ask, "Something catch your eye?"

Mouth dry and face aflame, Bea needed a moment to recognize her own question. She'd teased him over his preoccupation with her goods—now that he caught her looking him over, Mr. Wilder returned the jibe. If she weren't so mortified, Bea might have laughed at the joke.

"Yessir." She kept a straight—albeit reddened—face and elaborated, "I like to see that a man offering to carry my cargo can be trusted not to drop the eggs. You seem solid enough."

He raised a brow but didn't pursue the matter, and Bea decided she didn't care about the crates. She could forgive a few broken eggs from a man who knew when to drop a subject!

"Your sister said that no deal's been struck." The other one—Mr. O'Conall—waved at the wagon. "Are you open to selling some of your selection to us directly?"

How many times had Bea considered making the five-hour trip to Devil's Lake to turn more profit than the TallGrass shopkeeper would offer? But five hours there meant ten altogether, and an entire day wasted. It also meant exposing at least one of her sisters to unsavory characters and corrupt business practices, which Bea wouldn't countenance. She could, however, countenance a slightly unconventional offer here in town.

"Let's be quick about it." Bea lowered the back of the wagon along with her voice. "Tell us what you want, and how much of it, then you can carry everything else into the store with no one the wiser."

✳

If fools and their money were soon parted, the hungry ones didn't stand a chance. Facing a pair of pretty women with a wagonload of good food, Grey practically felt his wallet shriveling. *If we're doomed before we begin, at least I can make sure our last meals make it worth the expense.*

He joined Beatrix—Bea, as her sister called her, though neither one did her justice—at the back of the wagon and reached for some crates. As he leaned in and slid the stack across the rough bed of the buckboard, he caught a whiff of something wonderful.

Breathing deep, he immediately recognized two things: First, nothing in the back of the wagon smelled that good—in fact, the caged chickens and freshly shot mallards overpowered the scent as soon as Grey moved away from its source. Second, Bea was the source. She smelled fresh and clean and sweet, a bright blend of sunshine and lemons.

Just one more reason to be glad I took that bath. Better to wash up in the back of the stables than to smell like them. Especially when I'm standing next to a woman like her.

Grey didn't bother asking what she wanted to charge. His foolish side would pay high prices, all the while hoping she'd tucked a few bars of soap alongside the rest. "What have you got and how much of it can you spare before the shortage makes your shopkeeper suspicious?"

"The crates hold five dozen eggs each. I imagine you wouldn't want more than one of those in a wagon." Bea shot him a sideways glance and waited for his nod before tallying more.

"Half a dozen ten-pound wheels of hard cheddar, twenty two-pound bricks of butter—"

Grey cut in to ask a crucial question before it slipped his mind. "Salted?"

"Salted," the younger sister assured him. "It keeps for weeks if stored out of the sun."

"And the butter and cheese vary for any number of reasons, so take what you need." Bea motioned toward the jars. "Mr. Muensch doesn't expect the pickled cucumbers or eggs, though we brought five of the pickles and half a dozen of the dilled and brined eggs."

"We'll take a crate of eggs, five bricks of the butter, two cheeses, and however many of the pickle jars you're willing to part with." As he spoke, Grey started stacking his purchases off to one side of the wagon, then paused over the pickle jars for her decision.

"Why don't you take three of the pickles and four of the dilled eggs from us, and keep Mr. Muensch happy by buying the others from him?"

"Wise lass." Miles craned his neck for a better look at the wagon. "Are the birds spoken for?"

"There's four frying roosters—anyone with hens will already have one and won't want another—and the three ducks I brought down during the drive into town. I thought to roast a brace of those for supper, but I suppose I can spare one if you'd like."

"Brought down during the drive?" Grey stared at the mallards with new respect.

"Well, a flock of them flew overhead when I had my rifle handy," she explained. "It's only prudent for unescorted women to arm themselves when heading into town."

"No denying the truth of that. Well then, we'll take the duck for dinner today and a rooster for tomorrow." Miles poked at the rooster cages.

Visions of the four of them chasing after escaped chickens made Grey intervene. "Leave the rooster. I'll have my fill of feathers when we're done with the duck."

"So we wait awhile." Miles cheerfully schemed to give him the dirty work. "Fatten him up between now and the pan."

By the time he and Miles finished ferrying their prizes, Bea Darlyn tallied things up.

"That's fifty cents for the rooster, twenty-five for the duck, a penny apiece for the eggs, twenty per pound of butter." As she ran through the prices, a smile growing on her face, Grey felt himself frown. "The cheese is fifteen cents per pound. . .and I'd say a quarter a jar for the pickles."

"That comes to eight dollars, ten cents." Grey felt his brow furrow and tried not to glower while she checked his calculations and gave a hesitant nod. "What are you playing at, with numbers like those?"

She stiffened, a beguiling fire lighting her eyes. "Those numbers are more than fair! You'd pay at least a third again as much in the store, and most likely more."

"More," the younger girl judged.

"Of course, more!" Grey grabbed two five-dollar silver certificates from his wallet, folded them over, and held them out.

She refused to accept the money. "We'd have counted ourselves fortunate if Mr. Muensch offered us four dollars in trade for the same goods."

"Then turn around and charge these men fourteen," her sister pointed out.

"Ten dollars is a bargain, and we won't let you take a penny less." He nudged her hand with the bills. "Those eggs alone would set us back a buck and a half."

"Bea,"—her sister's tone took on a note of urgency—"men are making their way over here. From the bank."

Without another word, she snatched the money from his hand, tucked it into her own pocket, and loudly thanked him for his help before following her sister into the shop.

Grey's eyes narrowed. He knew a tactical retreat when he saw one, but their abrupt departure held an anxious note he couldn't account for. Whatever their reason, it went deeper than worrying whether a greedy shopkeeper caught wind of their dealings. Since the Darlyns didn't strike him as the sort of women who let fear rule them, Grey wanted to know what—or whom—they wanted to avoid.

Chapter 7

Huber?" Bea murmured as she followed Cassia into the shop.

"I can't say for certain," Cassia whispered back. "I didn't want to be caught staring."

"No." She sighed. "You definitely don't want a man to catch you staring."

"If it isn't two of my favorite Darlyns!" Mr. Muensch gave Bea a smile, which widened as it lingered on Cassia. Every time they came to the store, he made them just a little bit more thankful he'd found a Mrs. Muensch so many years before.

And, really, that was saying something, since Mrs. Muensch made herself a master of the fine art of insult. She could slide a pointed comment between another woman's ribs and be gone before her victim felt the wound.

"Darlyns, did you say?" Mrs. Muensch stuck her head through the curtains cordoning off the back room, spotted them, and whipped out of sight.

When Mr. O'Conall and Mr. Wilder came through the door, arms filled with goods, it offered a welcome distraction. They set the first load atop the counter with respectful nods all around before heading back outside for more.

Mrs. Muensch, now emerged from her cocoon of a back room, followed their progress with avid interest. "Who were those strange men, Beatrix?"

"Yeah, who are they?" The eldest Braun brother, followed by a few other men, crowded toward the counter. "I don't like the looks of them."

Cassia calmed the men. "They're just passing through. Kind of them to offer to unload the wagon, since they don't even know us."

"I bet they'd like to get to know you." The jeer died a swift death at Braun's scowl.

"We would've unloaded your wagon for you."

"There's plenty left," Bea pointed out, though none of them moved toward the door.

Mr. Wilder stacked the four wheels of cheese alongside the eggs and butter. His efforts earned him nothing but glares from the good gentlemen of TallGrass.

"Best look over everything real careful and make sure nothing went missing between the buckboard and the store, Beatrix." Mrs. Muensch's mean mind held true to form, though for once she waited until the object of her disparaging remarks moved out of earshot.

"I'm not worried. But why don't you and Mr. Muensch look things over while Cass and I pick out our purchases?" Neither of them waited for her agreement. Bea skirted her way through the men and began pulling items from the shelves.

Cassia, of course, stayed at the counter. It kept the men from trying to brush against her when she walked past, it offered the best chance to bargain with Mr. Muensch, and it gave her an enjoyable opportunity to order his wife around.

"Oh, no, I'm afraid I don't like that pattern nearly as much as I thought I would from over here. Would you mind taking it back and bringing over that one—no, one more over. . .to the left. . ." While polite, Cassia's voice held a note of glee as she made the unpleasant woman heft and shuffle twenty-pound sacks of flour, keen to find the prettiest pattern on the cotton sacks.

Cassia really did have an eye for that sort of thing, always coming away with a color or pattern sure to suit the sister she had in mind. Watching Mrs. Muensch huff and puff just made it more fun. In fact, that was the best part of coming to the store, and Bea resented the crowd of men who blocked her enjoyment of the scene.

While Mrs. Muensch struggled to stack rejected flour sacks into neat piles, Cassia haggled with her husband, tutting loudly. "Surely you can do better than that."

"I could have used these goods when I went to Devil's Lake yesterday," he protested. "Now, there's not so much demand or profit to be found."

"I understand about timing things right," Cassia cajoled then kindly threatened the man. "If you can't manage at least eight for the cheese and ten for the butter, we'll take it back and tuck it in our springhouse until our next visit. The timing should be perfect then. With the spring planting and butchering, we won't be back for weeks and weeks!"

"All right, all right. Eight and ten, then." He made some changes to his figures and totaled up the goods. "That comes to seven dollars, eighty-five cents."

Bea said nothing as she slid her selections next to Cassia's flour and moved to the corner to keep shopping. *Lord, thank You for Your timing this morning. If we'd sold everything to Muensch, we wouldn't have earned twelve dollars. Instead, You've blessed us so we'll walk away with almost eighteen!*

"I don't see the jars here. Two of pickles and two of pickled eggs." Cassia frowned at the ledger, looked at the counter, then back toward the door. "Oh, Mr. O'Conall is bringing them!"

"Pickles!" One of the milling men spotted the jars in Mr. O'Conall's hands and just about started a stampede to open the door for him.

"Now, fellas, keep your hands to yourselves!" Mr. Muensch looked up from his scales, where he weighed every brick of butter and every wheel of cheese even though they'd been coming to him for years. "Don't go grabbing at my customers, and stop trying to call dibs on those jars."

While he shouted, the jars circled around the store as one man after another swiped them from his neighbor. Poor Mr. O'Conall looked rumpled by the time Bea reached him.

Nevertheless, he gave her the cherry-cheeked smile that so reminded her of Pa. Between those cheeks and the thinning red hair, the two men could have been related. He leaned close, eyes twinkling, and confided, "We told you ten bucks was a bargain! Looks like you could've named your price for those pickles."

By now, Mr. and Mrs. Muensch abandoned their posts to wade into the fracas, scolding the assorted culprits but unable to gather the jars.

"A town too tiny to rustle up trouble." Mr. Wilder sounded amused as he edged over. "TallGrass defies your description, Miles."

"I'll say." Bea didn't know whether to be embarrassed on behalf of the men or plain angry. A flash of yellow near the counter had her shoving her way to the back of the store in an instant. She couldn't see more, but her hackles told Bea she needed to be by her sister.

"I'm fine," Cassia was insisting as she slipped around the side of the counter—and away from the biggest of the Braun brothers.

"Don't worry, Cassia. Get out of there and keep close to me." He reached out and closed one hand around Cassia's wrist, trying to pull her to him. "I'll protect you."

"Protect yourself," Bea snarled, seizing the nearest glass container and smashing it over his crown. Cassia jerked her arm out of his grip, and they watched with satisfaction as he stumbled, tripped over a loose floorboard, and crashed to the ground in a heap.

The squabbling stopped, and the store went silent. None of the men moved to help their fallen friend. Mr. Wilder, who didn't know any of them, pushed through and crouched down, reaching out to find Braun's pulse. After a few minutes, he rose to his feet with a shrug.

"He'll wake up with an aching head, but he deserved a lot worse."

"It'd take more than one bottle to kill a Braun," someone shouted. "I remember last summer, when we went up to Devil's Lake and—"

"Hush, Clyde. That story's not fitting for ladies to hear." The word *ladies* brought Mrs. Muensch from her stupor.

"Every last one of you, get out! Be sure to take this one"—she nudged the bottom of Braun's boot with her toe—"with you."

"And you can tell him we've charged his account for whatever Miss Darlyn used to knock some sense back into him," Mr. Muensch added, giving Bea a grim smile. "No one lays a hand on any woman in my shop."

She managed a smile in return, relieved at the support and pleased by the notion Braun would pay even more for his bad behavior.

"I'll note it on his record." Mrs. Muensch gave her a conspiratorial nod. "Just tell me what you broke over his thick head."

"Oh." Bea still gripped the metal lid and sticky remains of some sort of ointment. A glance at the raised lettering sent her into a fit of giggles. "Dalley's Magical Pain Extractor!"

Well, I wasn't wrong about her ability to surprise me. Grey wondered whether she'd surprised herself, or if the irony of her chosen weapon startled the laughter from her.

"They say the best cure is hair of the dog that bit you!" Miles guffawed.

Of course Miles immediately thought of advice for a man who'd over-imbibed and suffered an ale headache the next morning. Many of Miles's references could be traced to seedy beginnings. Grey kept the observation to himself and moved away from where the women hastily completed their transactions. He made a show of examining the store's shelves, though he didn't expect to find much to pique his interest. *We already got more than we bargained for.*

When he spotted a few remaining jars of the pain extractor, Grey began to grin again. He hadn't immediately understood why Bea tensed up and sprang into motion, shoving her way across the shop. If he'd noticed her sister's situation, he would've beat her to it. But some woman's intuition sent her flying to protect her family before anyone else saw a problem.

Though the circumstances were unusual this afternoon, Grey got the idea she always kept fierce watch over her loved ones. For one thing, though the blow shocked the men into silence, they'd recovered with surprising speed. It seemed as though they'd been astonished by Beatrix Darlyn before, and expected to be again.

The whole thing made him powerfully curious about what other exploits she'd entertained the town with—and what she'd do next. Grey actually regretted that he wouldn't be on hand to bear witness—or bring help.

We've stayed long enough. Leaving Miles to settle up with the shopkeeper, Grey walked out the door before that small domestic voice convinced him to spend another moment around Beatrix Darlyn.

The woman was a menace that no amount of pain extractor could cover.

He planned to go straight to his own wagon, but the sight of men clustered around the ladies' buckboard brought him up short. As he watched, trying to determine whether he needed to shoo them away, a puffed-up prig in a too-tight suit planted one boot on a wheel spoke and pulled a rifle from beneath the seat.

The two men flanking him darted nervous glances toward the store. Glances that hitched on Grey for a second too long before sliding toward their friend. The man in the center showed no concern about being caught holding someone else's firearm. He did, however, seem very intent on inspecting what looked like a fairly ordinary Winchester '73.

Grey's hackles prickled. Instincts he'd once relied on every shift, almost every day, rose to the fore as though Grey never stopped using them. Little enough proof presented itself in this scenario—after all, the man hadn't attempted to walk away with the gun. Nor did he seem at all inclined to use it on someone.

But here stood the man the Darlyns wanted to avoid. Grey knew it in his bones, but he didn't have time to warn the women. They'd face the situation as soon as they stepped onto the street. Worse, they'd face him with their defenses down, their arms full, and their weapon held by their adversary.

Unacceptable.

"Put it back." Grey barked the order loud enough to startle them. While they jumped, he pounced. Swift, long strides carried him to the buckboard before they so much as turned the rifle his way.

"I don't know you." The troublemaker looked him over and tilted the rifle more purposefully. "That means you don't belong in TallGrass, and you sure as hell aren't going to tell me what to do."

Grey flicked back the side of his coat, unsnapped his holster's safety strap, and looped his thumb through his belt so his hand hung over the butt of his pistol.

"Bet you push plenty of people around, waltzing into town with your hand on your holster and no one who knows your name. But you've got no roots here, nothing at stake. No reason to risk getting hurt over a stranger's rifle that hasn't even been stolen."

Grey hoped the bully never knew how close he was to being right. But in this case, he knew all too well whose gun and whose safety were at stake.

"Put back *Miss Darlyn's* rifle."

The bully's buddies backed away, and even their leader turned green around the gills.

"You weren't going to keep it anyway," one of the others urged. But he'd taken a stand and his pride was at stake, so he kept his hands clamped around the rifle as he tried to find a way out of his own foolishness.

Time ran out as the shop door opened and Miles escorted the Darlyn sisters outside. Arms filled with sacks, crates, and packages, all three froze at the tableau before them. Not surprisingly, Bea corralled her composure the quickest. Barely a pause before she descended the steps and walked past Grey to put her packages in the back of her buckboard.

Everything in him demanded that he pull her out of harm's way and shield her behind his larger frame. But Grey understood who belonged to this fight and who would handle the next encounter. He was only visiting.

"If you want a Winchester, Mr. Huber,"—her voice carried down the street, clear and calm—"surely you can afford to buy your own?"

Huber. Grey filed away the name.

"I can afford any gun and got my eye on a Sharps carbine. Shoots better than some beat-up old Winchester." He demonstrated his disdain for the piece by half-tossing, half-shoving the rifle back where he'd found it.

"The gun's only as good as the person pulling the trigger." Bea edged around her wagon, drawing level with the seat to slide her rifle into her arms—and back into the conversation.

"Every ribbon and award this small-time town offers, and most of the ones in Devil's Lake, prove I'm the best marksman in these parts," Huber sneered. "And the ones I don't have from Devil's Lake are only because I didn't enter the competitions."

If Grey had to guess, he'd say those competitions Huber hadn't entered were ones he knew he couldn't win. But the really intriguing thing about the entire exchange revolved around the implication that Bea Darlyn's skill with a firearm threatened his masculine pride.

"Marks*man*," Mr. Muensch emphasized, emerging from his store to join the conversation. "From what I've heard about Miss Bea's shooting demonstration last Sunday, I missed out on quite a show. Not every day a woman shoots a cigar out of a man's mouth."

Huber turned the swollen purple of an old blood sausage. "She didn't. The shot came so close to my face I moved back, and the ash dropped from the jostling."

"She put the cigar *out*," one of his friends burst out, unable to contain his enthusiasm. "Maybe you didn't notice, on account of how hard you landed when you fell."

Grey snickered.

"Yep. Sounds to me like she could best you." Muensch hooked his thumbs over his apron and nodded as though imagining the scene. "Something I wouldn't mind seeing."

Bea stepped back a few paces, but only a fool would see it as retreat. With her rifle looped in the crook of her elbow and the barrel facing Huber, the maneuver sent a distinct message: she could shoot any time she chose.

Chapter 8

I'm not interested." Bea didn't like being cornered into anything, and a shooting competition would put her in an impossible position.

If she lost, she'd disappoint Pa and lose the element of caution he'd tried to instill in the townsmen. Failure left her family vulnerable, so losing wasn't an option. Yet if she won, any respect would swiftly turn to resentment. Poking the pride of every man within a fifty-mile radius might leave the Darlyns excluded from the cooperative aspects of a farming culture, with no help during threshing or half a dozen other necessary activities.

Either way Bea looked at it, a shooting competition was something she couldn't win.

"Bet I can *make* you interested." In spite of the fact that she held the gun he'd tried to take, Huber managed to roll a threat into his innuendo.

"Get yourself another girl," she advised. "It'd take more time and effort than I'm worth."

"I don't make a habit of wasting my time or effort when something can so easily be bought." Huber's insinuation that she was no better than a prostitute left Bea reeling.

"We told you when you destroyed Mama's china that there are things worth more than money," Cassia shouted, trying to storm forward, only to be stopped as Mr. O'Conall and Mr. Muensch became a human blockade before the stairs.

"Just because you're willing to sell your honor doesn't mean everyone else will sink to the same level. Bea can't be bought. Treasured mementos can't be replaced. And greed can't compensate when a man abandons his values."

Cassia's outraged defense gave Bea the strength to remain calm. Both irate and erudite, their sister's outburst would have done Ariel proud.

"I offered to pay for the plate—your own pride cost you that much."

"It's not pride we stand on, Mr. Huber." Bea drew herself up to put down the problem once and for all. "It's principle. If you had a few of your own, you might be better able to recognize them."

She didn't realize Mrs. Muensch had joined her husband to bear witness until Bea heard her shocked gasp.

So did Huber, who puffed up like a gassy hog and started snarling. "I've more principles than your father has overdue mortgage payments, missy. So get off your high horse and pay attention. You oblige me in a shooting competition Sunday after next, and if you win, I'll forgive the amount you're in arrears."

✳

"We pick bones, not fights." Grey wondered whether anything he said would deter Miles from his line of conversation. He didn't like the questions, and Miles wouldn't like his real answers.

"I didn't ask you to pick a fight," Miles defended. "Though you seemed to be doing a fine job all on your own, from what I saw. No man stands with his coat flipped back, hand over his holster to say howdy. Stop acting like you don't want to teach that hooligan a lesson for disrespecting those Darlyn girls."

Yeah, the banker made Grey's blood boil. Of course he wanted to see the man pay for the way he'd mistreated Bea and her family. Problem came when seeing justice served didn't seem half so satisfying as dishing it out.

Grey cracked his knuckles and kept walking. He planned to keep walking until he'd put so many steps between them and TallGrass that Miles stopped talking about it.

"Not our business to get involved, Miles." He didn't wield that sort of authority. *Not anymore.*

"Like I said, you don't have to pick a fight. But don't you want to watch that shooting match? A woman sharpshooter's not something most men get a chance to see unless Buffalo Bill brings his Wild West show to town."

What man wouldn't want to watch Bea? And sharpshooting! How many afternoons had Grey enjoyed at Bogardus's Shooting Gallery, back in better days? If he stayed, Grey didn't want to watch the competition— he wanted to participate. That way, when Huber lost to both him and Bea, he couldn't claim she'd been given any unfair advantage.

The thought of them beating the banker together made him far too content. It landed him right back where he knew he couldn't stay: involved.

"Bill brings his troupe to Chicago regular enough." The warm feeling from thinking of shooting with Bea went away at the mention of his old town, lending a cranky strength to his statement. "If you want to see a woman sharpshooter, go for the world champion."

"More fun to cheer on a woman I've met. Besides, there I'd have to pay for a ticket. Here, she'll make the banker pay. Now that's what I call something worth watching, and a beautiful irony, besides."

Beautiful, indeed. And he'd always appreciated a healthy dose of irony.

Grey scowled. Too much more of this conversation and Miles might talk him around. But the long-dormant instincts that kicked in this morning were still kicking, and he knew better. If Grey turned around now, there'd be no going back.

"There has to be a way to undo it. We can't owe that much!" For once, looking at Cassia could have been looking in a mirror, so clearly did her sister mirror Bea's own disbelief.

Bea forced herself to stop grinding her teeth. The last thing she needed was a headache to rival Braun's. Her temples already ached from the pressure of their unexpected problem.

"We can't. And we do." Abandoning her own stringent rules about driving at a decorous pace, Bea urged the horses to a jog. What use was trying to coddle an old wagon through another few years when financial ruin already found them?

"When did Pa do this?" Cassia tugged off a glove to start picking at her nails—her own version of teeth grinding.

"The first year of the drought, when he caught the fever."

"When you and Ben broke up?" Cassia counted time by social events rather than harvest or even illness.

"It had nothing to do with that," Bea gritted, but before the words finished, she wondered whether they were true. She and Pa always made large decisions together, whether for the farm or the family. Could it be coincidence that he'd set his own course once she'd done the same?

It has to be. Ben was supposed to build us a home nearby and add on to the barn. Pa knew I wasn't leaving the farm or the family—the marriage should have been a blessing for both! In spite of one year's bad harvest, we would have been able to keep going.

"Then why else? Pa owned the land free and clear, and I remember the harvest before that first dry year." Cassia's nervous hands stilled, soothed by the memory.

"We put all our profit back into expanding the farm." They'd expected a return on all of their improvements and all the hard work they'd put into the fields before the drought took hold.

Hogs joined the chickens in their yard, adding to a ready supply of fertilizer. They'd ordered a manure spreader and a disc harrow to ready the ground for oats. Best of all, they'd replaced the well and bucket with a shiny red hand pump. *We'd come so far. . .and now we're so close to losing it all.*

Bea tried to remind herself that as head of the household and landowner, Pa didn't need her approval for any decisions. But betrayal gnawed at her, breaking through to a swell of bitter resentment. Pa might not need her approval, but he'd certainly needed everything else she had to give for the past dozen years. *And I gave it. Right up to my chance to leave TallGrass with Ben and strike out in a new corner of the world. I gave everything. Why couldn't Pa give me more consideration in return?*

Instead, he dishonored all their efforts with this loan, falling behind without speaking a single word on the matter. Even were they to catch up, next year's final bulk payment, equal to the entire amount borrowed, loomed large.

One thousand dollars. The sum kept ringing in her temples. They'd have to come up with it in time, but Bea couldn't see how.

"Oh, look. I think that's Mr. O'Conall and his friend." Cassia shaded her eyes to peer toward the distant left, where two slow-moving shapes shadowed the grass. "I wish you'd accepted their offer to escort us from town, so we could see more of them. Perhaps invite them for supper."

"I needed to see Huber's paperwork." Bea decided not to mention her opinion that none of her sisters needed to spend extra time in the company of the handsome and quick-witted Mr. Wilder. Especially since he'd be on his way directly after the meal. "We did not need an escort. Nor did we need to give Huber or the other townsmen the impression that we need one. That defeats the entire purpose of Pa's demonstration."

"And your handling of Braun." Cassia's giggle faded to a sigh. "But Mr. O'Conall and his partner were so helpful. . .first with the wagon and the store, then standing up to Huber when he tried to take your gun. I hate to think that he might've snatched it and secreted it away before we left the shop."

"I doubt he wanted the Winchester to keep." Bea figured the man had a surfeit of faults without letting Cassia's imagination add to them. "But Mr. Wilder watched out for us, and I'm sorry I didn't think to thank him before I went to look over those accounts."

"Wouldn't it be lovely if the men around here were as gentlemanly and considerate?"

"However lacking you find our local men, comfort yourself that you'll have your pick of them. They'll be fighting tooth and nail to beat out the competition."

"Stop looking so grim. After Mrs. Muensch yammers to everyone and their oxen about Braun's 'pain extractor,' they'll all be on their best behavior. Especially since word of your shooting will spread—whether or not you agree to Huber's challenge." Cassia stopped looking back at the wagons to scrutinize her sister. "Would he really credit us the overdue amount?"

"If so, do you think I should take him up on it?" Not that either of them had any choice in the matter. They couldn't pay up, and they needed time to pull together a way to pay off the rest.

"I know Ariel's right about the importance of a ladylike reputation . . .but to tell the truth I desperately want to see Huber's face when you make him eat his insults."

"And pay for the privilege?" Bea smirked at the picture her sister painted. Cassia's unbridled enthusiasm had a way of lightening her darkest moods.

"So all you have to do is outshoot him, and we're caught up for a while. So long as we can keep Pa from getting too worked up over the whole thing, we'll come up with the rest."

"We'll find a way." Bea's thoughts jumped from one prospect to another, considering and rejecting half-hatched ideas. The drought dried up any chance of finding a farmer who could afford the machinery and equipment that might have brought ready cash a couple of years ago.

Bones were the last thing left to consider. Almost every homesteader trying to cultivate his fields first had to clear them. Though the plains didn't provide many obstacles when it came to tree stumps, skeletons of the slaughtered buffalo scattered the land like so many spilled marbles. They moved them out of the way, but what once seemed an annoyance suddenly became an asset when the railroad came through and bought bones by the boxcar. Over the past dozen years, every bone pile from cleared fields and every massacre site had been harvested, the last traces of the buffalo shipped off to refineries.

Except for the concealed cache on Darlyn land. Pa refused to consider taking their grim crop to market. They'd tried once—Ben, with his reassuring grins and grand promises convinced Pa when she couldn't—but abandoned the idea when their engagement ended. Without Ben, Pa adamantly refused to do anything with any of the bones. *He doesn't have the luxury to refuse anymore.*

Bea knew Pa wasn't the only Darlyn repulsed by the thought, so she tried to make light of the idea. "Looks like the Darlyns are down to bare bones."

Cassia shuddered. "You came up with a pun almost as bad as the idea itself. You know I side with Pa on this. It's against the natural order to go digging up old bones."

"You side with Pa because you're squeamish, not because you believe the blarney."

"Deliver bones or plant crops—we don't have time for both. And that's not blarney."

"I know." Bea rubbed her forehead. "Some of the men might help in exchange for a share of the profits, but anyone we know would put it off until they saw to their own crops."

"Bea?" Cassia clamped a hand around her wrist. "You know how you're always telling us that God's plans might surprise us, but to trust in His timing?"

Bea learned long ago to be wary when her own good advice came back as a question from Cassia. The only time any of her sisters sounded happy to tell her she'd been right about something was when it made her wish she'd been wrong. "Yeees..."

"Today's surprises couldn't have been better timed." Cassia's grip tightened, and she started to tug. "Turn the wagon around, Bea. Mr. O'Conall and Mr. Wilder won't have gone far. Their oxen go at such a slow pace, we can invite them over for supper, and still have time to get home and talk it over with the others!"

"Talk what over, exactly?" Bea pulled her wrist away before Cassia's excitement left a bruise. "They're already cutting things close by setting out so late in the year, if they have any hope of crops. Those men don't have time to stop and help us."

"Bea, what on earth made you think those two are farmers?"

"I overheard Mr. O'Conall saying something about heading toward Canada and trying to find a good area that hadn't been picked clean. They must be well prepared, with two huge wagons full of equipment and supplies." She tried not to wince as Cassia clamped on again.

"No! Those wagons are *empty*, Bea. Mr. O'Conall told me—he and Mr. Wilder aren't farmers. They're *bone pickers*!"

✳

"Buffalo bones and business, no other distractions. You swore up and down that we'd never stay in a town or make a return trip for any woman after that last gal in that Kansas backwater." Grey looked back at Miles, who dragged his feet as though it would make a difference. "What was her name again?"

An impish smile flitted over Miles's face at the memory. "Mary."

"I should have known. They're all Mary."

Miles laughed. "It's a good Christian name. And an Irish favorite, to boot. Can't say as how I've ever known an upstanding Irish family without a Mary or two mixed in for good measure."

"True enough."

For a while it looked as though he'd won. But Grey should have known better.

"Funny thing about names. How they usually fit folks, I mean. Take Mary, for example. It's an honest, straightforward, feminine sort of name. Strong hearts and soft smiles, those are my Marys." Miles started slow, but Grey saw where he headed. After all, it never took Miles long to move on from his Marys.

"Then there are your more exotic names, like Cassia. Says her name comes from some sort of cinnamon tree, and that suits her just as well. Fire and spice to make men lose their heads. Good thing that older sister of hers keeps a sharp eye out."

"Bea looked to have things well enough in hand." Not that a woman like her should have to dirty her hands dealing with her sister's soft-skulled suitors.

"Had her hands full, more like." Miles cleared his throat. "And 'Bea,' was it? Can't remember the last time I heard you call a woman by her Christian name, much less a pet name."

"When it's proper to call a woman 'darlin',' Bea seems more appropriate." Grey could've kicked himself. He should've known Miles would jump on his slip like a tick on a hound.

"But not 'Beatrix'?"

"Unless she's a beagle or an old biddy, no woman should be called Beatrix." *Particularly not one so full of fire and life.*

"Could be she'll grow into it then." Miles's observation almost goaded Grey into stopping.

Almost—but not when the comment boxed him into a corner. If Grey protested that he'd never seen a woman look and act less like a broody old biddy than Bea Darlyn, the conversation continued. If he didn't protest at all, he basically conceded that he shouldn't have called the woman Bea. Either way, Miles would keep on pestering him.

"I deal with the days as they come, Miles." Grey slipped the noose. "Why waste my time wondering about a woman I'll never see again?"

Chapter 9

Miles spotted them first, nothing more than a speck in the distance. Grey shrugged off his partner's attempt to slow their progress, but a strange awareness stirred. Steadily, his own over-the-shoulder glances grew more frequent, and all too soon he knew he'd been outmaneuvered. Leaving town didn't do a lick of good when the town tracked them down.

"Stop walkin' away," Miles ordered, halting his own team. "Those women don't need to chase after any man, but they're comin' after us. I aim to be an easy catch."

When they get close enough to be more than blurs in bonnets, they won't be as striking as they looked in town, Grey tried to tell himself as he halted and kept vigil, the girls closing in the last few hundred feet. *After too long alone, a man finds any female attractive enough. But since I saw her before, I'll be better prepared. This time she won't seem so special. She won't look as good as my memory made her.*

The next minute made a mockery of his memory. Now close enough to see clearly, Bea looked even better than before. Handling the reins with capable grace, she seemed utterly at home in the untamed plains. The contrary prairie wind tugged more mahogany locks free from her bonnet to wave around cheeks now tinged with pale pink. She reined in the horses and slowed the wagon to a stop.

"Definitely *not* going to be a biddy," he muttered toward Miles, then moved forward to greet the girls.

"Miss Darlyn, and Miss Darlyn." He nodded to Bea, who'd flattened those full lips of hers into a straight line. Whatever prompted her to trail them, it didn't look good.

"Always a treat to see such lovely ladies." His compliment caught him a smile from the younger Darlyn, but not her sister, though that straight line softened somewhat.

"Thank you for your assistance earlier." Bea broke her silence. "I should have given you both my gratitude before I went to look over the accounts."

"You didn't need to drive out of your way just for that," Grey chided, surprised by a surge of disappointment that the Darlyns didn't want . . .well, he didn't know what he wanted them to want from him, but whatever it was, he'd hoped it would be more than this!

"Oh, we didn't!" The sister's exclamation made him an eager audience once again. "You deserve more than a simple thank-you for your trouble. We wondered if you'd trust us with that duck you bought while you make your way to our farm and join us for supper."

"It's not too much out of your way," Bea added, brows raised as Miles turned his back on all of them, rushed to his wagon, pulled the duck from the back, and returned in the space of a few seconds.

Hand fisted around the bird's neck, he thrust it toward the women before Grey got a chance to think things over. "We'd take you up on the offer no matter how far your farm sits."

"Stop dangling that dead duck at the ladies, Miles." Grey grabbed Miles's elbow and forced his arm down, amused in spite of himself by his partner's enthusiasm. "They're not going to hold a bloody bird all the way home."

"Sorry." Miles gave a sheepish grin before going to put his prize in the back of the buckboard.

Bea's smile kicked back into place. "That took less convincing than I thought."

"Not hard to sell a man on good food," Grey told her. "Especially when it's served alongside good company."

"And especially when that company's made up of two beautiful women." Having seen to the supper arrangements, Miles rejoined the conversation with his customary charm.

"And Pa, of course," Bea hastened to clarify. "Though there are four of us sisters."

"Four!" Miles beamed at the thought of that many women, not noticing the eldest Darlyn daughter's frown.

Grey swiftly stepped in before she started to worry she'd invited a pair of lechers for supper. "Any man able to raise four daughters is a force to be reckoned with. I look forward to meeting him."

She gave him a measuring look. Then, apparently satisfied with his sincerity, began issuing instructions on how to reach the Darlyn farm.

"Head due northwest for two miles or so. When you first see the flatland give ground to rolling hills up ahead, turn straight west. After another mile, more or less, you'll come to what looks like the world's edge—the grass ends in a sheer drop. The coulee creates a valley stretching all the way to Turtle Mountain.

"Follow the ruts worn by our wagons, and you'll find the decline into the valley—it's the only entrance for at least twelve miles. The angle's fairly constant and not too steep, though it carries a bit of a curve. Before you reach the bottom, you'll see our place to the right."

"Should take us three hours or thereabouts," Grey calculated.

"I guessed about the same." She lifted the reins. When he and Miles stepped back, she set the horses into motion. "Until then!"

Grey watched until they were once more a smudge of shadow against the grassland. "We aren't getting involved."

"Not involved," Miles agreed a little too readily. "Just sitting down to some supper."

"That's right." Though something about the entire situation felt wrong to Grey, he couldn't resist the invitation any more than Miles. "Just supper."

✳ ⁄

"Just supper!" Pa's roar made Jodie jump as she returned from the springhouse. While Pa often raised his voice over all four of them, he almost never shouted at any of them. Especially since that terrible fever and its following pneumonia left him weak in the chest.

Pa thundering at her sisters set off every one of Jodie's alarms. If he'd started yelling even a few seconds sooner, Jodie wouldn't have opened the door. If she'd listened in, Jodie knew she would've gotten a much more complete idea of what had Bea looking grim and Pa sounding so riled. Instead, the sight of Jodie stopped the conversation in its tracks.

"What about supper?" She tried to poke them back into talking but got scowls for her trouble. Jodie scowled back. After all, *she'd* spent the past half hour seeing to the horses and carting Bea and Cassia's purchases to the springhouse. Pa hadn't been thundering at *her*.

Jodie watched as Bea poked one of the birds with a wooden spoon, wedging it against the side of the pot so she could grab a feather. It slid free with ease. "We'll be having guests for supper."

"Who'd you invite?" Jodie stiffened at a terrible thought. "Not Huber!"

"A pair of bone pickers we met in town today. They helped us unload and load up the wagon. . .among other things." Cassia went quiet at a quelling look from Bea, but it was too late.

"Bone pickers?" Jodie sank into a seat, hand reaching out to cover Pa's. Cold. These days, he always felt cold. It didn't matter if it was the middle of the day or he sat right in front of the fire. Same as his cough, his coldness got worse whenever something upset him. They all knew that. And they all knew he'd been upset since Sunday. So what were her sisters thinking, inviting strangers over and stirring up the old argument about the bones?

"Stop glowering, Jodie." Ariel looked up from the columns of numbers marching across the family ledger, where she accounted for today's transactions. "There are worse professions."

"Besides, Bea thought they were farmers." Cassia plumped dough into her mixing bowl and carefully covered it with a towel to rise. "We only invited them for supper as a thank-you."

"For unloading the wagon?" Jodie didn't buy it for half a second.

They never lacked volunteers to help unload the wagon—especially if Cassia came along.

Bea'd begun peeling sweet potatoes into the sink, so Jodie couldn't read her expression. "One of them also caught Mr. Huber taking my rifle from beneath the wagon seat while we were in the store and confronted him."

"He tried to take Chester?" Aghast, Ariel abandoned her accounts. The way Bea babied the rifle, down to its affectionate nickname, the Winchester was as much Bea's pet as her protection. She cared for it almost as carefully as she watched over them and Pa.

"I don't *think* so." Judging by the speed and strength with which those peelings struck the sink sides, the idea alone aggravated Bea enough. "At any rate, he said he wanted to look the gun over before challenging me to a shooting match, and gave Chester back."

"Good thing!" That gun was more than a weapon, and Jodie couldn't stand the idea of Huber taking one more memory out of their hands. Chester gave them peace of mind, called back the fun they'd had helping Bea practice her aim, and brought them many a fine meal. Like tonight's ducks.

Jodie gave them a guilty look but stayed put. She managed to make an almighty mess of plucking, but her sisters seemed to control which way the feathers flew. They could pluck birds on the kitchen doorstep and not miss a thing. But Jodie? To do the same job, Jodie would have to leave the kitchen—and the conversation—so she didn't volunteer.

Luckily, Ariel prodded the birds with a cautious fingertip, finding them cool enough to touch. She open-rolled the plucking pillowcase and spread it on the stoop to catch all the down and feathers. Then, she fished the ducks from the pot, plopped herself down in the doorway, and began divesting them of their downy coats.

Seeing supper progress and talking about rifles had Pa perking up. "Shooting match? My favorite daughter could whip the stuffing out of that nodcock!"

"Careful, Bea. It's some kind of trick." The memory of the last time Huber made a challenge crashed through Jodie's thoughts. "Since everyone knows that he can't beat you, he'll have something up his sleeve or he wouldn't want to try."

"It's something to think about later, when we don't have guests coming." Cassia carefully rubbed butter all along a pan in preparation for the dinner rolls.

"Only for supper," Pa repeated. "No bones. I let you talk me 'round once, and it cost Bea's fiancé his uncle and Bea her fiancé—proof that the old warning holds true. Whoever removes remains forfeits a life, be it their own or that of close kin."

"Superstition!" Ariel dismissed from the doorway.

"There's things on earth we can't fathom, and what you call super-stition I call having sense enough not to tempt fate!" Pa's hand fisted beneath hers, obstinate and unhappy.

Jodie rubbed her palm across his knuckles, hoping to soothe him a little. At least Ariel didn't argue, able to vent her irritation with every handful of feathers she wrenched free.

"We didn't say a word about any bones." Bea gentled her tone, trying to coax Pa into a more comfortable state. "Though I wouldn't mind seeing the matter settled. We can't keep those bones hunched under straw forever, and they've already been moved from the boneyard—"

"After you've met these men,"—Cassia clamped onto Bea's comment before she finished it—"you can decide whether or not you'd be willing to work out an arrangement with them."

Bea abandoned her heap of grated sweet potatoes, drying her hands on her apron and approaching Pa. "Huber raised some. . .considerations . . .about finances."

"Like what?" Jodie didn't like anything to do with Huber, and she absolutely hated the way Pa's shoulders slumped at the mention of finances. "What's there to consider?"

Should've kept quiet. Jodie bit her lip as Bea and Cassia shared the sort of sidelong look Bea and Ariel used to share before they asked Cass to go "teach" Jodie something. Now Cassia turned traitor, standing with the others if Jodie earned herself an eviction. Any minute now, they'd come up with some pressing chore demanding her immediate attention.

Milking, she hazarded, *because first I have to go to the pasture and fetch the cows.*

"Why don't you see to the milking a bit early today?" Bea made it sound like a question, but Jodie knew better.

"Plenty of time for milking before supper even after we finish our discussion." Jodie stood firm. "Whatever concerns the farm and the family equally concerns me, so my opinions should matter as much!"

"Why? You wouldn't seek Bea's thoughts on horse training, nor my archery advice. It is the weight of experience that gives words their worth." Ariel pointed a befeathered finger at her. "You're not entitled to an opinion until you master your mathematics work."

"Problems you put on paper aren't the same as problems in life."

"No, they aren't." Pa's sigh gave Jodie hope, only to dash it. "Life is more complicated, without such clear solutions, sweeting. With this, you cannot help. Now tell me: Are you going to leave an old man thinking that his favorite daughter is the sort to waste her time regretting what she *can't* do? Or are you going to buck up and work at the things you *can*?"

"I'll tend to the cows." Jodie never could refuse Pa when he called her his favorite. Sure, he said it to them all—that's what made it wonderful—but just the same she couldn't forfeit the moments when she'd won his highest honor.

She slid her chair back to see a still-duck-plucking Ariel blocking the kitchen door—along with Jodie's last slim chance of circling back to listen in.

Her mood stayed sour while she fetched the cows and waited for them to drink their fill from the stock tank. But the barn, filled with friendly horses, fresh hay, and a thousand memories. . .the barn never failed to soothe her. There, Jodie settled the cows and allowed the familiar pattern to settle her, too.

Jodie gathered her one-legged milking stool, hooked a foot through the handle of the milking pail, and flipped it into the air. As always, she caught it on the upturned leg of her stool and carried both to the cows. Silly trick, but it took so long to learn that it still made her smile.

The scratchy warmth of the cow's side, rising and falling with each breath, tickled her cheek as Jodie started the first verse of "Down the Old Mill Road." Pa insisted songs made the cows give more milk, so long as they selected a simple tune that suited the splashing rhythm.

Ariel and Cassia didn't like the cows and never found the music that made milking such a soothing task. Then again, they'd never mastered the trick of tucking the cow's tail between their leg and the bucket. Nothing enjoyable about getting slapped in the face with a bovine's back end.

Chapter 10

Jodie smiled at the memories and kept singing, stopping only when she half-wrestled the heavy tin milk can out to the springhouse. Backing her way in, she almost bumped into Ariel.

"Sorry! Didn't see you there! Someday we'll get ones with handles..." Jodie angled her ten-gallon container toward the milk-can corner, hands slipping on the slick galvanized tin. She still smarted from her sister's math comments but hated to see Ariel looking so lost.

"Need help finding something?" she finally burst out, startling Ariel into motion.

"Someday, but for now we need cream for the creamed onions." Ariel pulled a pail of heavy cream, stepped toward the door, then stopped to look back around. "Hard to believe we lived here when we first came."

"Hard to believe, after half a dozen years," Jodie agreed. How many times had she brought milk, eggs, and more out here without stopping to remember?

Partly carved into the valley wall and finished with sod pulled straight from the prairie, the squat room served as their first Dakota home. For those miserable months, they'd all squeezed in and tried not to complain about visiting insects. Sod made good insulation against the weather but issued an open invitation to nature's other elements. Thankfully, once Pa wagoned in enough wood, the Fullers and Whites came to help put up a real house.

A real house with a duck supper sitting in the kitchen. Jodie poked her unmoving sister to get her out of the springhouse. "If you're planning on moving back in for the evening, I call dibs on your share of duck."

"Oh no you don't." Even though she couldn't see Ariel's smile as she led the way into the kitchen, Jodie sensed a pun in the offing. "If my duck goes missing, your goose is cooked!"

Jodie followed her into the house, snorting with laughter. She was still snorting when Ariel moved out of the way and she caught sight of their visitors.

The laughter died an abrupt death as her breath hitched. Vaguely she noticed the older gentleman next to Pa, but the other man commanded attention. Not too tall or too short. Not too unkempt nor too fussy. Like some handsome, much more interesting version of the old Goldilocks story, everything about the stranger struck Jodie as just right.

Granted, his hair hung dark and straight instead of in blond ringlets, but it suited him. Besides, when he turned to smile at her—really smile at her, not just throw her a nod before staring at another sister—his brown eyes held a golden glow any fairy-tale character would envy.

Jodie had only seen eyes that color in cats and, once, a proud eagle. Little wonder her sisters came home in such a flutter! No doubt he'd inspired Cassia's latest round of primping and Bea's busy afternoon! Now Jodie understood the reasoning behind those focused preparations, but she couldn't blame her sisters for being preoccupied.

Belatedly, she realized her mouth hung agape, as though still waiting for the rest of her strangled snickers. She shut it and closed her eyes, wishing she hadn't let Ariel come in first. *Then I would've seen him and smiled softly like a lady. . .instead of snorting like a village idiot!*

She didn't know how, but Jodie resolved to erase her undignified first impression.

Before he leaves, the eagle-eyed stranger will remember me as something more than a slack-jawed snorter!

How's a man to keep them all straight? Miles entered the house, pleased to spot Bea in the kitchen as Cassia introduced them to their father.

Simple, straightforward, and smelling better than he'd dared hope, the arrangement made a man feel at ease.

Then another two girls came bustling through a back door. The first, with hair the golden-pink of a soft spring sunrise, had a waifish way about her. Between her green dress and the pail of cream she carried, the girl looked like a sprite dressed up as an Irish milkmaid.

The second—or should he say the fourth?—sister all but stomped in, head thrown back in the sort of boisterous guffaw that can be brought on by a bawdy tavern tale. Obviously, that wasn't the case here. Nevertheless the youngest girl, with her untamed laugh, smattering of freckles, and coltish air struck him as the least civilized Darlyn.

I like her more for it. Miles gave her a broad grin, expecting her to share his good cheer. When she didn't so much as acknowledge him, he followed her gaze straight to Grey and suddenly had to stifle his own chuckle. Judging by the gal's wide eyes, as he'd be kind enough to overlook her wide-open mouth, his partner had an admirer.

And judging by the way his partner kept stealing glances at the eldest Darlyn daughter, he was too busy doing his own admiring to have noticed.

With so many skirts and smiles swirling around the place, Miles almost missed the names of their father and his other two daughters. But either Cassia caught on to his plight or she'd learned early on that too many names and faces confused a man at first. Either way, she smoothed things over.

"Mr. Miles O'Conall, meet Seamus Darlyn, our pa."

"A pleasure!" Miles snagged the other man's hand for a hearty shake, but gentled his grip. The chilled palm, cane kept close to hand, and a pallor unconcealed even in the kindest candlelight. . .it all tattled that the man's health had gone a-wandering.

"Mr. O'Conall." Cold it might be, but Seamus Darlyn's hand clenched his with surprising strength. He searched Miles's face as though looking for something.

Miles pulled his hand away quickly but covered by grabbing Grey's shoulder and steering him into the introductions. It always gave him the collywobbles when people stared too long. A man never knew who might be looking for him—or whether he wanted to be found.

"Mr. Darlyn!" Grey, too, handled their host with care. He also withstood his silent scrutiny with more equanimity than Miles managed, though he relaxed to see Darlyn's intense inspection hadn't been personal.

Had I a passel of daughters half so pretty as his, I'd be giving the old stink-eye to every man who walked through the door myself. Despite Darlyn's dour expression, the scent of supper and the sight of those sisters promised a pleasant night.

Even better, it held potential. His partner let the past haunt him—both of them—for too long. He'd resisted every invitation for over a year, but Grey gave no argument against dining with the Darlyns. He blustered about being on their way as soon as supper ended, but the Darlyns might have a surprise or two in store for them.

Bone collecting had run its course, and the pair of them couldn't chase after broken bits forever. But Grey had grown comfortable with ghosts for company. He'd need some powerful convincing before he'd put the past to rest. . .but Miss Bea struck Miles as a mighty powerful woman. She might be just the ticket to return Grey to the land of the living.

And absolve Miles for his part in making his friend so lost.

Whatever these women brought to the table, Miles meant to make sure Grey took them up on it.

"I'll take that." Bea gestured toward the largest platter. Moments ago heaped high with roast meat, it lay bare but for a thin film of fatty juice. Delicious though that juice might make the duck, it made an unappetizing, slimy smear across the crockery.

Two extra guests squeezed around their table left no room for empty dishes—much less one so unappealing. Mr. Wilder hesitated, his expression more exasperated than appreciative.

But that made no sense whatsoever, considering the excellent meal awaiting him. Bea felt her brow furrow at the sight of that untouched meal. The inroads on everyone else's plate bore mute testament to the excellence of her food. What kept Wilder waiting?

"Is something wrong?" She tried to not to sound irritated. Why his opinion mattered so much, she couldn't fathom—but snapping at the man wouldn't improve his digestion.

"Everything looks perfect to me." He raised a brow, but since he didn't follow suit with his fork, Bea remained unappeased.

"Would you like anything else, Mr. Wilder?" Ariel produced a frown of her own at the sight of his too-full plate.

"Yes." He leaned forward slightly so he could see past his partner. Still looking toward Ariel, he tilted his head back toward Bea. "I'm desperate to try this fantastic food, but I need your sister to stay seated for more than two seconds so I can start."

Bea blinked, too taken aback to reply. Ariel's shoulders rose in the smallest of shrugs. Cassia pressed her napkin against her lips as though pushing back giggles. Jodie glanced from her own partially cleaned plate to Bea's full one, then to Mr. Wilder's before she deliberately set down her fork.

Pa chortled like a madman, tapping the end of his cane against the side of the table before pointing the top of it toward her. "Man makes a good point, Bea."

Disgruntled that the duck—not to mention the rest of dinner—sat cooling, Bea snatched up the offending platter, placed it on the kitchen counter, and regally regained her chair. "I don't know what you mean."

"A woman knows when she hasn't had a hot meal in a decade," Pa pointed out.

"He's right—and we should've stopped it long ago." Cassia looked shamefaced.

"Stopped what?" Bea stabbed at the side of a creamed onion. Smooth, savory, and slightly sweet, the onions made the perfect accompaniment to offset any gamey flavor from the duck. They also made satisfying targets for a frustrated fork.

"You see to the table, you check the fire, you clear used dishes and serve up seconds," Jodie chimed in with a conspiratorial glance toward Mr. Wilder. When it came to the delicacies of dinner conversation, her sisters needed a lesson in loyalty. "By the time you try a bite, your food's gone stone cold and the rest of us are near enough finished."

"Your bone picker here's a canny one to have caught on so quickly. Even better, he's got a mouth smart enough to say something on the subject!" This time, Pa's chuckle hitched into a hacking cough.

Belatedly, Bea realized he'd emptied his mug without telling her. She snatched her own cup of water, splashed a bit into the bottom of his mug, then swiftly fetched the teapot to fill the rest. Normally she wouldn't dilute Ariel's concoction of soothing herbs, but better to weaken the brew than serve it scalding.

He downed half the tea in two swallows, paused for another bout of spasms, then finished. She poured another cup, breathing easier now that he could, and set the teapot on the table. Exactly in the empty space from the platter. Triumphant, she slid her napkin onto her lap, picked up her fork, and scooped a bite from one of her sweet potato cakes.

Bea sampled some duck, finding it succulent and scrumptious. And warm—proof that her family fretted needlessly. Savoring vindication along with her food, Bea lifted her chin and looked around the table. Mr. Wilder's gaze snagged hers before she completed her victory lap, but Bea couldn't bring herself to look away.

She imagined his eyes lightened with amusement—then realized she wasn't imagining it. Warm molasses brightened to gold around his pupils. It always had, but before there'd been more of the brown and less of the brilliant gleam. *I wonder if it only happens when he's amused? Or if it works in reverse, and annoyance will darken them? Or perhaps some other emotion? How long would it take to learn how to read his mood?*

The prospect tantalized her. And as she watched him, his gaze grew brighter still.

Which made her realize how long she'd been staring. Bea blinked and set her fork across the top of her plate, searching for a way to cover the awkwardness.

"Would you like me to warm your plate?" she asked pertly, knowing full well the food was as warm as her cheeks.

"Even if it did need warming, you'd be hard pressed to pry this plate away from me now that I've sampled the fare." His compliment at least gave her cause to blush, if the others hadn't already noticed. "Truly, it was more than worth the wait."

"Not many home-cooked meals come our way," Mr. O'Conall told Pa. "Much less a feast the likes of this. Mind you, we'd already been looking forward to much-improved meals courtesy of your daughters."

"My girls make the best butter and cheese money can buy, though I hear you paid a fair price." Pa pulled his attention away from his plate and squinted at their older guest.

"*Insisted* on paying a fair price." Cassia pounced on the opportunity to talk up their guests. "Even when Bea tried to charge them less, they wouldn't hear of it!"

"I can't remember the last time someone outside the family got Bea to give way once she'd made up her mind." Jodie gave their younger guest an admiring glance.

"Not a thing wrong with knowing your own mind," Mr. O'Conall defended her. "Most of the world's trouble comes from plonkers who can't put two thoughts together for themselves."

Pa nodded vigorously. "Well said. Been ages since I heard anyone say 'plonker.' Puts me in mind of Grandda."

"I've heard it said Irish blood shares the same soul. That's not something I hold to—met too many men I wouldn't care to claim!" Mr. O'Conall drank a long swig of coffee. "But those with roots on the Emerald Isle aren't hard pressed to find their fellows."

"When Bea and I first met you, we were both struck by your resemblance to Pa." Cassia encouraged the growing sense of connection. She knew as well as Bea how hard pressed Pa would be to find fault in a fellow Irishman. Most homesteaders hereabouts came from German stock. Inevitably, they created a community built on that shared heritage, and equally as inevitably, it rankled Pa's pride. Both as an Irishman and as one of the first to settle the area.

Mr. O'Conall shifted uncomfortably and waved away their interest. "Come now, don't you all begin comparing our noses and chins. So many stares might put me off my eating!"

"No need to dissect the resemblance," Bea soothed. "It's easy enough to imagine Ireland as full of rolling green hills and cherry-cheeked men out making mischief."

"Mischief and whiskey!" Pa guffawed. "The type of trouble Irishmen make best!"

"And should best keep clear of," Mr. Wilder reminded. "Though without a pub or saloon, TallGrass won't have whiskey troubles."

"We've troubles enough without adding to them." Pa swallowed his last potato cake, clearing his plate for the first time all week. Leaning back and folding his hands over his full belly, he looked more at ease with their guests than Bea had dared hope.

Mr. O'Conall relaxed against his own chair back, unconsciously adopting the same position. "One troublemaker, in particular, from what I saw."

Pa's face darkened. "Sometimes one is all it takes to change everything."

Chapter 11

McGarigle." Grey's soft dinner roll turned into a clump of clay.

"Who's McGarigle?" The youngest sister cocked her head in interest. An interest her family seemed to share, as everyone looked his way.

With effort, he swallowed. The bread went down, but resentment surged stronger than ever, burning the back of his throat.

"William McGarigle," Miles supplied. "Chicago police chief-turned-warden of the Cook County Hospital. Two years back, they indicted him for graft and fraud, only to have him slip loose of the sheriff and escape to Canada. Quite the tale." A glance at Grey made Miles falter. "Though a story for another day. Grey don't like being reminded how far his station house fell."

"Used to be part of the police force, did you?" Mr. Darlyn eyed him with a new respect.

Returning that respect, Grey gave more of an answer than he had in years. "Served with pride, until black-market politics put people in power I couldn't be proud of."

"Grey took it personal, having to arrest the first chief he'd served under." Miles's misguided attempt to end the conversation only pro-longed it.

"Who wouldn't take that personal?" The youngest sister's immediate indignation was so endearing it helped him regain his good temper.

Grey waved dismissively, hoping to rid himself of the bothersome memories along with any further questions. "Let's just say I understand how much havoc one man can wreak."

"Or try to." Determination strengthened Bea's beauty. "I dislike bullies and don't intend to bow to ours."

"More bluster than bite to most of'em, in any case." Miles straightened in his seat. "We left town wondering whether you'd grant him that shooting match."

"Something we're considering." Mr. Darlyn spoke for his daughter without answering the question. A certain set to his jaw told Grey the older man knew Huber announced his mortgage difficulties to the world at large. "Letting Bea beat the stuffing out of him is tempting."

Tempting. If one word could sum up a woman, Grey would choose *tempting* to describe Bea.

In town, she'd been confident and capable of looking after her own. Grey recognized a fellow protector when he saw one, and she'd taken on the role as surely as any man bearing a badge. Even when she relaxed, responsibility remained her watchword. After all, you can't guard against what you don't see coming.

Like a Darlyn who turns out to be a temptress. Grey stole another glance at Bea. The more time he spent in her company, the more he wanted to add to those hours. The indulgence would cost him—this evening, alone, took a toll.

A man can't have what he can't hold on to, Grey reminded himself, only to have his good intentions trampled by a herd of thoughts about how nice it might be to hold Bea Darlyn. When the confusion cleared, he tried again. *Let her go now, or let her down later.*

A straggler from the idea herd moseyed along to offer a helpful observation. *Gotta grab something to let go of first!*

Grey relegated the stray to join its fellows—squashed far away and deep down. Miles trying to convince him to stay made things challenging enough without his own thoughts trying to sabotage his attempt at self-preservation. *When I said "just supper," I meant "just supper."*

And supper's over. He carefully laid his napkin alongside his plate. *Time to leave.*

"We wish you the best, but we won't be here to witness any competition. A week and a half's worth of waiting won't fill the wagons. Our thanks for a superb supper to send us on our way."

He ended with the sort of good-natured grin Miles used when he wanted to get out of something. In return, Miles shot him the sort of disgruntled, broody stare Grey usually gave him, while the women abandoned the table ahead of them. With a rustle of skirts and the clatter of dishes, the women cleared the table. They talked the entire time, but four feminine voices speaking over and under each other garbled everything.

He caught the word *stay* more than once, which made his stomach sink. But it perked right back up again when he heard someone mention *dessert*. Technically, Grey only agreed to stay for supper. . .but he wasn't about to turn down dessert. He picked up his napkin and put it back in his lap, trying not to look overeager.

Miles smirked, but Grey let it pass. *Just dessert*, he swore to himself. *Then we'll leave.*

"Stay put!" The startled squeak stopped him from scooting his chair farther back. Good thing, else he would've run into the youngest sister, who'd popped up behind him with a carafe of hot coffee.

"Thanks, Miss"—he groped for her name but came up empty—"Darlyn."

"Judith," she supplied as she snagged his mug, filled it, and set it down to steam enticingly. "Too many Miss Darlyns to stand on ceremony unless there's good reason."

"Must not happen much." Miles wrapped his hands around his own freshly filled mug.

"More than you'd think. Pa insists that the men use the formal address when they want to come calling." The girl shared a wide smile with her father.

"Puts their noses out of joint." Mr. Darlyn chuckled. But when his youngest turned away, his eyes narrowed. He might be older and in poor health, but he was every inch the formidable father. "No man comes sniffing around my daughters without showing proper respect. Even then, most aren't worth the time it takes to be rid of them."

Grey inclined his head slightly, the silent gesture acknowledging the difficulties of discouraging eager suitors—and a father's warning against becoming one of them. He felt no need to cobble together any greater response than that. After all, they'd be leaving directly after dessert.

The warning didn't worry him, but the idea of ill-mannered men overrunning the Darlyn farm left Grey unsettled. Although Mr. Darlyn's presence probably deterred some problems, he wouldn't bet on the man making it through another winter.

With no male to maintain the boundaries, the sisters might not be able to hold the lines. Where one barrier blurred, others weakened, and the women were grossly outnumbered. Greedy landowners would encroach upon the property. Lonely bachelors would push the bounds of propriety. Without a father, the girls might well need the force of the law to keep their neighbors in check. Otherwise, they'd be overrun. No matter how well they shot.

"I don't recall seeing a sheriff's office in town." *Maybe I missed it.*

"There isn't one." Bea's expression as she slid a plate in front of him told Grey all he needed to know. A woman with her hands full of chocolate cake should never look grim.

"The town is big enough to warrant a keeper of the peace," Grey ventured as the women took their seats once more.

"Probably time and past for TallGrass to take that measure," Miles encouraged. "Good thing to bring up at the next town meeting."

"Don't think I haven't." Mr. Darlyn jabbed at his slice of cake as though it had done him a great personal wrong. "Did no good."

"Try again." The demand slipped out before Grey could soften it.

"Any time the subject is broached, Huber volunteers to take on the job." Frustration tightened Bea's features, compressing her lips, wrinkling her nose, and furrowing her brow. Scrunched up and steaming, she still looked better than the cake.

And despite the fact that no one touched their piece—except to poke at it—the cake looked mighty good. Grey plunged his fork into the cake, delighted to find it soft and moist, with a thick texture to keep it from crumbling. "Put it to a vote."

"No one votes against the man holding their mortgage," the second sister pointed out, looking resigned. "We're better off with no sheriff than one who'd abuse the authority."

"Agreed. But you're isolated out here, too far away from Devil's Lake to rely on help in times of trouble." Grey refused to let it slide. "Wait until Huber leaves town, then move fast to get it done. Whatever it takes, get someone to keep order around here."

"I will." Mr. Darlyn's shoulders straightened with resolve. His vigor renewed, he finally sampled some of his dessert.

This served as a signal for everyone else to dig in. For a few moments, no one spoke. Hums of pleasure and *mmmm*s of appreciation paid homage to the deliciousness of what had to be the best cake Grey ever ate.

No light-as-air, melts-the-second-you-taste-it sort of dessert here. Rich, thick, and sweet, this was something to sink your teeth into. A cake with a bite of its own, an elusive underlying hint of tang Grey couldn't place. But he wouldn't mind going through another slice to try and figure it out.

"Speaking of letting things go until it's too late. . ." Mr. Darlyn polished off his piece and picked up the conversation right where he left off. "I wouldn't recommend you boys try to navigate your way out of the valley at night."

Mouth crammed with cake, Miles couldn't try to wrangle an invitation to stay the night. He glared in a wordless demand Grey refused to follow. "Just supper" already became "just supper and dessert." He had no intention of tacking on "and an overnight stay," or the next thing he knew, a week would pass without them leaving. Small steps made big differences, and Grey planned to put them between himself and temptation.

"I wouldn't try that for the first time at night." Remembering the none-to-wide but not-too-steep wagon trail down into the valley, Grey couldn't imagine coaxing the oxen back up it in the dark. "We'll head north until we find the next route back up to the plains."

"Or you can bunk down in the barn tonight. The hayloft might not be fancy, but it keeps warm even through a cold spring, and—"

"Thank you!" Miles broke in before Darlyn could finish—before Grey refused. "My bones aren't so young as they once were, and the damp chill of morning fashes me more than it used to."

Amid womanly exclamations of sympathy and offers of various ointments, Grey fumed.

"Just one night," he gritted. "We'll head out first thing in the morning."

✳

Jodie eased out of bed, quiet and careful not to bounce around or flip back the covers. Last year they'd replaced the lumpy, rustling cornhusks with the soft, silent down they'd collected for so long. Good thing. The feathers kept their peace, but shifting cornhusks always woke the other person in the bed. Getting past Bea presented enough of a challenge without a tattling mattress!

Bea slept lightly, jolting awake at unfamiliar or imagined sounds, and waking Jodie in the process. Back when they first moved into the new house, with its separate rooms, she'd scramble after her sister, unwilling to let either of them face the night alone. Eventually, she grew out of it.

But Bea never did. Every night she traced the same pattern still etched in Jodie's memory: check the door latch, peek out the windows, tend to the stoves. Then she'd look in on Pa and return to their bedroom, pausing beside the bed where Ariel and Cassia slept. Only then would she climb back between the covers.

Jodie used to find it reassuring. Now, even with the feather bed to soften things, it chafed. They'd all grown up, more or less. So why did Bea still shoulder the same worries? Those short snatches of sleep shouldn't be enough to keep anybody going, especially one as busy as Bea. *Maybe if she weren't such a busybody, she'd be able to rest.*

And I'd be able to sneak out easier! She balanced on the balls of her feet for the final few steps to the kitchen door, pulling her cloak from its peg and slipping into the misty morning.

When she reached the barn, Jodie cracked open the door and slipped inside as swiftly as possible, trying to block out the cold and the noise—anything that might awaken their guests and waste all her efforts.

Jodie grabbed an oil lamp, felt the wick, and turned the knob to lower it. Lighting it, she replaced the glass chimney and levered the handle upright to seal the lantern shut. Shadows stretched and shivered around the faint flickering glow as she hung it on the highest peg, as close to the hayloft as possible. No matter how well made the lantern, no flame could be taken up the ladder and allowed close to the straw. Hopefully she'd have enough light this early.

She certainly couldn't wait for it to get any brighter. Bea always rose at the rooster's call, and she'd be after her in an instant for coming out here alone with strange men in the loft. But if Bea came after her and found that she'd climbed the ladder. . .no excuse would save her.

Is it worth the risk? Jodie wavered. Such a simple thing she wanted. A short moment or two when she could look her fill at Greyson Wilder with no one noticing. No sisters' teasing. No golden gaze pinning her and making her heart flutter like a caught moth. Just a short private stare so she could commit him to her memory before he left.

It went deeper than the way he looked, though that alone gave a girl good reason to stare. She'd grown alongside the males TallGrass had to offer and found them an unappealing lot. Greedy, selfish, small-minded, and cruel, most of them. Often lazy, always acting superior to girls, giving orders and not taking baths. . .none of them were worth considering.

But Greyson Wilder put them all to shame. He looked around and really noticed people—even an awkward girl too young and plain for most men to bother with. He knew how to be forceful without becoming unkind—you could tell he cared about keeping people safe. Best of all, he didn't reek of sweat, manure, or sour milk. Jodie even checked to make sure.

Last night, when she poured his coffee, she'd given him a quick sniff. That clinched it. There, right under her nose, sat a man worth having. Since she couldn't keep this one, someday she'd like to find another one like him. Was it so wrong to want to carve Greyson Wilder's example into her mind?

If he leaves this morning, I'll have wasted my only chance.

Jodie put her hand on the ladder frame, listening for the sounds of shifting straw or male voices amid the background noises of the barn. Hooves on hay, the soft whicker of horses, swishing tails, the loud rumbling breaths of sleeping cattle. . . What she usually heard as a welcoming chorus became a deafening distraction. She stepped carefully on the first rung, pulling herself that much closer before reaching for the next rung.

The scratchy shriek of a young rooster pierced the air, startling her so badly she jumped from the ladder—mere seconds before Bea shoved the barn door open.

Chapter 12

The patchy crow of a late-sleeping cockerel announced Bea's arrival as she reached the barn. Loud, shrieking, and warbling, Bea always thought young roosters sounded like someone snuck up while they were gargling and goosed them. At least, Cassia produced a credible imitation under those same circumstances.

Even in the dim light of the barn, a wide-eyed Jodie looked scared spitless. It made Bea wonder what frightened her hard-to-startle sister so badly—the tardy squawking or her own appearance? She wouldn't bet on the bird—Jumpy Jodie sprang from a guilty conscience.

Jodie knew better than to be in the barn alone when strange men were staying in the hayloft. Occasionally they extended the courtesy to other homesteaders passing through or hired hands. It didn't happen often, but it happened often enough for Jodie to know better.

"Aren't you going to close the door?" Jodie hissed, recovering rapidly. "You'll wake the bone pickers after I tried to keep so quiet!"

"Quiet or not, you don't belong in the barn this morning and you know it!" Bea hissed back. "Get out of there this instant!"

Jodie extinguished her lantern and sulked her way out the door. Bea shut it behind them.

"What were you doing in there in the first place?"

A brief hesitation, then: "Wanted to get my chores out of the way before breakfast."

"Before breakfast?" None of them could manage to complete

their chores—or even most of them—before the first meal of the day. Especially Jodie, who took care of most of the livestock.

"As much as possible." Her jaw worked side to side, the swift sign of agitation. "Give the rest of you less reasons to send me off when you deal with the bone pickers."

Beneath the youthful petulance, Bea heard the echo of last night's accusation and recognized a genuine grievance. Nor could she deny strategically assigning chores to her siblings. The gambit served Bea well for as far back as her memory reached.

In younger days, her sisters didn't notice the ploy. Gradually, they became good-naturedly aware of the system. When it rankled enough to provoke arguments, Bea started giving the sister more responsibility—and authority—over the younger ones. Ariel and Cassia made the same transition; Ariel had been two years younger than Jodie was now. But Ariel had the old soul, and Jodie was the baby of the family, so a few extra years didn't seem unreasonable. Until now.

That needs to change, Bea admitted to herself. *After the bone pickers are on their way.*

Until then, Bea planned to severely curtail any interactions between her sisters and the strangers. For however long the men remained, the Darlyns would take a page from Noah's Ark. Two at a time, or they didn't go at all.

Since Pa hadn't promised to do business with the bone pickers, Bea saw no sense in ruffling feathers—especially with Jodie already complaining about her clipped wings. Bea hated to see her plucky sister slumping toward the house, shoulders hunched as though trying to hold herself together against attack.

Bea stooped a little, stretching out one arm and scooping her sister close before Jodie protested. With some wiggling, she worked her arm around Bea's waist in return, and the two of them fell into step together.

"Stop growing so fast. You make me feel old!" She turned her head and planted a kiss against Jodie's temple, earning a reassuring squeeze.

"I can't stay a kid forever." But no whine sharpened the words.

"Growing up doesn't give you more freedom, Jodie. Just a different kind." Bea wondered whether the warning would make any difference.

"What do you mean?"

"It's a trade. You're allowed to make your own decisions, but as an adult, you don't just answer to family. All of society keeps track of your actions and holds you accountable." Bea groped for a simpler explanation. "Fewer rules mean more responsibilities."

Don't be so eager to leave childhood behind, Bea wanted to tell her sister. *Once you shoulder the obligations of an adult, no one will lift the load. There's no choice but to carry on.*

For Bea, part of carrying on meant never letting her sisters suspect that she harbored regret over the past. Or feared for their future.

Lord, we've come so far. I can't say I understand why it's been so hard—or why You've seen fit to add more challenges. Help me rest in Your provision. However hard I try, it feels as though my worries are winning.

"I don't think any farm girl fears responsibility." Jodie's joke poked through Bea's prayer, bringing her crashing back into the conversation.

"Good. You can start pumping water and help Cassia set up for wash day." Bea arched her brow a fraction higher—what Ariel called The Final Fraction. More than a warning, it essentially dared Jodie to protest the added chore.

She didn't. In return, Bea didn't smirk. Pumping and lugging water to fill the boiler and the washtub would keep Jodie busy, and out of trouble, for a good while. By the time she finished, she'd have worked off a good deal of this morning's extra energy. Not a bad outcome considering the hog butchering and trip to town skewed this week's schedule.

"Should have known better than to think finishing my chores early would do any good," Jodie surrendered. "There's always something more to be done."

"We work hard, but there are certain rewards." Bea waited for Jodie's questioning look before she took pity and gave her sister something to smile about. "Ariel's baking cinnamon rolls this morning."

"What?" Jodie tensed, pulling away from the close embrace. "That would've gotten me out of the barn lickety-split!"

"I know." Bea waved her onward.

Nothing smelled—or tasted—half so good as a hot cinnamon roll fresh out of the oven. Especially first thing in the morning, still sticky with a slathering of Ariel's honey glaze. Since Jodie grew tall enough to reach things in the kitchen, she'd eagerly "helped" by separating the still-steaming rolls—and pinching a few bits along the way to stick in her mouth.

But this morning Bea didn't mind if Jodie helped herself to an extra taste or two, so long as it distracted her sister so she could steal something equally irresistible; a few moments to herself!

Leave her alone, Grey's common sense warned.

He'd heard someone below and looked down to see Bea enter the barn. So for the second time that morning, he ordered himself to sit tight and stay quiet. He could have kicked himself. *Of all the days to turn slugabed.*

Grey rarely slept past daybreak. Be it a clattering racket or a burst of bright morning light, at dawn something always summoned him. But here in the loft, neither noise nor nature held sway. No big-city bustle badgered him from his bed. No newly spun sunshine glared Grey into getting up. He overslept, jolting awake at the garbled alarm of a confused rooster. Trust Miles to choose the chicken with a cockeyed schedule.

Birdbrains. Grey glowered at the pair of them, who remained united in their defiance of the new day. Miles slept on, utterly undisturbed. The rooster, regally satisfied that his screeching discharged his daily duty, settled in for another snooze.

No matter. Lazy ways and tardy timing made no difference to a frying pan. Grey earmarked it as a victory feast, to be enjoyed after he evaded his own version of flames—the bright-eyed and fiery Bea Darlyn. She heated his blood and fueled his imagination, keeping him up half the night with unanswered questions.

Another reason he'd overslept. . .and more than enough reason to leave. Immediately.

Grey wanted those answers, but he also knew better than to dismiss the urge as idle curiosity. His interest in Bea was anything but idle, and answers wouldn't be enough to satisfy him. He wanted to know *her*. Then, judging by the time he'd already spent in her company, Grey would want even more.

Shoot, Grey *already* wanted more. Once he'd fallen asleep, his more respectful wonderings were replaced with fevered, half-remembered dreams—the sort of things that belonged between a man and his wife alone. No matter how long ago Alice passed away, no matter that he'd been asleep, his mind's meanderings betrayed them both. A man who couldn't control his own thoughts wouldn't be able to withstand temptation.

But he could avoid it.

The sooner the girl left, the sooner he and Miles could do the same. The first step was getting out of the hayloft without finding himself alone with Bea. So long as Grey kept his head—which meant keeping it well away from the edge of the hayloft—Bea would never know he hadn't slept through her presence. He shifted back, fighting the urge to look down into the barn.

Even so, Grey itched to know where Bea was. . .what she was doing. . . whether she'd slipped off her bonnet while she tended to her chores, allowing the soft lantern light to play along the rich length of her hair.

He could shore up his resolve later, once he'd left the Darlyn farm far behind. Today, he'd satisfy his curiosity. Grey lowered himself onto his belly, thankful for the restless shifting of animals awaiting their breakfast. Their rustling obscured the rasping sweep of straw as he inched forward.

There! He halted at the very edge of the loft, not even letting his nose past the border. By rolling his neck and angling his head just right, he caught sight of her.

Or, more accurately, her shadow. She'd closed the barn door behind her, most likely out of consideration for him and Miles, so she navigated by the flickering light of a lantern. A light that illuminated precious little for a man in Grey's undignified position.

Disappointingly, she hadn't doffed her bonnet. Not only did the blasted fabric hide her glorious hair, it further obscured her features. Add on the insulating folds of her cloak, and Grey felt further cheated. Hair, face, form. . .the woman couldn't have withheld more of herself if she'd tried!

Still, she captivated him. Grey followed her movements with a greedy eye, grabbing any detail he could impress upon his memory. He admired the graceful economy of her motions, even when they took her beyond the narrow scope of his vision. When she returned to view, she stopped near an enormous tin pail filled with what looked like wet sand and drew a deep breath. He stared at the stuff, trying to identify it. Then he saw her fingers snag the nearest handle and curl around it.

Grey tensed, pressing his face farther over the edge. Surely she couldn't mean to pick up such a heavy load? But before his very eye, she reached around the pail, her free hand groping for the other handle.

He pushed himself from the floor and hastened down the ladder. "Hold on a minute!"

Startled by his sudden interruption, she released her grip and straightened up.

Grey took advantage of the shift to wedge himself between her and the bucket, only belatedly recognizing his folly. He'd been so anxious to keep her from harm that he'd pushed his way in to the most perilous position imaginable—improper proximity with Bea.

Now they stood indecently close. In spite of the pungent aroma emanating from the sludge, Grey caught a whiff of lemon freshness he couldn't evade even if he wanted to. Her skirts brushed against his knees, though the back of his boots pressed against the bucket. He'd heard of getting caught between a rock and a hard place—but what sort of fool stuck himself between glop and a hard-to-resist face?

Grey would have closed his eyes against the temptation to take her in his arms, but he feared freeing himself from one of his senses would incite a mass exodus. His good sense, in particular, felt far too flighty to take that risk. Right now, Bea's wide-eyed surprise was the only thing stopping him from making more—and more enjoyable—mistakes.

Then those wide eyes narrowed in annoyance. "What do you think you're doing?"

Trying not to kiss you. He took a deep breath, determinedly ignoring any hint of citrus. "You shouldn't try to haul something this heavy without help."

Grey pivoted and picked up the goop before she could stop him. No more scent of lemons, but under the circumstances, he counted that as a blessing. Especially since the swill didn't smell nearly as unappetizing as it looked.

"I do it every day," she informed him, stepping back to give the bucket wide berth.

"Not today. It's the least I can do before we head out." He thought he played the part of the gallant knight fairly well, but the damsel looked more distressed than before he offered assistance.

Grey wondered how she would have looked if she guessed his less chivalrous thoughts. At the very least, he'd be cast in the role of villain—just before she cast him out. The thought tickled him. Maybe the easiest way to shore up his defenses was to provoke hers.

It would have borne serious consideration if she were anything less than the noble woman she'd proven herself. Bea might not be royalty, but she deserved to be treated like it.

Grey shifted a bit to get a better hold on the pail, which managed to be even heavier than it looked. Incredible to hear that she hauled this every morning.

Then he reconsidered. Her father surely couldn't lift it. Of all the Darlyns, Bea stood strongest. Her feminine charms and tiny tapered waist belied that strength. Grey doubted he was the first man to underestimate her abilities. Or her temper.

"You should put that down." Her arms crossed, a mute message that she didn't plan to lead him wherever the pail needed to go.

"Do me a kindness," he appealed to her soft heart. "A man likes to feel useful every now and again. Let me help."

"Helping is a mistake when you don't fully understand the task you've volunteered for." But the bite had left her tone. A spark of humor quirked her lips. "All right then. On your own head be it."

He grunted his assent as he followed her from the barn, knowing his voice would give away the strain of carrying the pail—which was swiftly starting to feel like penance for his presumption. Since when did rescuing a lady reveal a man as a fool?

"Any experience with animals other than horses and oxen?" She paused. He gave a harsher, negative-sounding grumble. "Well then, Mr. Wilder, this will be an experience you'll never forget."

His heart nearly stopped right along with her when she halted in front of the hog pen. Grey might be new to farms, but even he had heard horror stories about being mobbed by hogs overeager for their morning meal. No backing out now; not when he'd been too proud to heed her warning. Grey eyed the pigs, disconcerted to find their beady gazes fixed upon his pail. Slowly, the biggest of the pink-bristled brutes started toward the gate, swiftly followed by his fellows.

Grey guessed the smallest of them to be just under four feet long and probably matched him pound for pound. The other four grew progressively larger, with the most formidable standing hip-high, over five feet long, and probably double his weight. As he took the measure of his opponents, they grew impatient, nodding their sloped heads and making strange woofing huffs that sounded strangely like. . .

"Are they *barking*?" As though in answer, they grew louder. Some of them tilting their heads back and showing their teeth. Grey wondered why no one ever mentioned that hogs had so many teeth.

"They do that when they're hungry. Along with crowding and trying to get to the slop before you can dump it in the trough." She slid the latch on the gate and gave a few final words of advice before flinging it open. "Move fast, and whatever you do, don't stop."

Chapter 13

Grey rushed ahead and kept going, shoving his way forward through the crowding, hopping hogs. But they were big pigs, well versed in strategies he'd never seen. Some of them would jump so they half-straddled one of their fellows in a literal piggyback ride. They crowded around his knees, pressed against his arms, nudged the pail so he couldn't hold it straight, and some of the mixture slopped over the sides.

And over his coat, but the oh-so-helpful hogs were happy to clean up the mess, slicking globs off his jacket with eager grunts. Grey managed to make it to the trough without falling face-first to his doom. He gratefully dumped the stuff out, but most never made it to the trough. As soon as the pail tilted, the beasts shoved their heads and entire front ends into the stream, sending slop splashing everywhere.

By the time he exited the pen, drying blobs of grainy slop spotted his coat, pants, boots, and hands. It almost made him miss the drafty, mold-smudged stable bathhouse back in Devil's Lake. But he bit his tongue against any complaints. Bea had warned him repeatedly and would have every right to remind him that he'd asked for it.

Grey couldn't deny that he'd earned this comeuppance—many times over. Now he'd finished with such foolishness. As soon as he got himself mopped up and Miles out of bed, they'd leave this farm—and all his foibles—far behind.

For some reason, the thought didn't do much to lift Grey's spirits. He followed Bea to the water pump, where she filled a few buckets waiting nearby, then back to the barn. She didn't laugh at his sorry state or issue any tart I-told-you-so lectures. Without a word, she fetched a few rough towels and a chunk of slightly yellowish soap from the tack room, passing them to him along with one of the water buckets.

He nodded his thanks, wetted a towel, and started scrubbing. As the stuff dried, it crusted over and became almost impossible to remove.

Bea picked up the filthy pail and carried it over to the stall where a third horse stood. "Here, Daredevil." She slung it over the partition and let it drop to the ground with a muffled clang.

He heard the vaguely metallic rasp of tongue against tin as the horse slicked up every last trace of the mess. And while she looked away, he took the opportunity to smell the soap she'd given him, hoping to find traces of her sweet lemon freshness. Sand, soda, and lye. No lemons.

"When you're finished cleaning up and your partner is awake and ready, come on down to the house. After feeding the pigs, you've more than earned your own breakfast!"

His fist clenched around the towel, sending small streams of water sluicing over the edge of his coat. Breakfast? Of course he wanted breakfast. What man wouldn't want to enjoy as much of this family's fine cooking as possible? But he'd have to come to the table half soaked. If he changed into his other set of clothes, he'd have to roll up the wet ones and stick them in the pack. His pride wasn't worth wearing damp, musty clothes later.

Besides, he had better reasons to avoid the table. Meals with the Darlyns seemed to stretch. Just supper. . .just dessert. . .just a night's hospitality. . .what would "just breakfast" rope him into? Part of him was afraid to find out. The bigger part was afraid that he *wanted* to find out.

"Thanks for the offer, but we should already be on our way. We'll eat some soda biscuits and salt pork to tide us over until midday." Grey cast an uneasy glance toward the hayloft. *As long as I can get Miles out of here before you or one of your sisters issues him another invitation.*

Surprise widened her eyes. "Soda biscuits? For breakfast?"

Miles popped his head over the edge of the hayloft like an eager puppy. Or, more closely, another hungry hog ready and willing to walk over Grey to get to a good meal.

"Did I hear someone say 'breakfast'?"

Cinnamon rolls fresh from the oven weren't just a better breakfast— they were weapons of war. Bea was convinced that if politicians ever stumbled upon the power of stealth baking, the secret could change the course of history.

Luckily, her goals remained on a much smaller scale. She'd put the pieces in place as best she could. Allowing Mr. Wilder to slop the hogs might have been a mistake—for a moment, when he'd pressed between her and the bucket, she'd been certain of it—but he'd proven himself more gallant than grumpy. If he remained to collect buffalo bones from the property, Bea suspected the man wouldn't be so swift to disregard her warnings.

Then again, she wouldn't be so quick to turn down a helping hand. Honest, hardworking, chivalrous. . . Greyson Wilder started looking like a pattern card for a white knight. Trade in the oxen for a steed, and he'd play the part to perfection. Sticklers might insist on swapping dragons for the hogs, but Bea knew better. Hogs were harder, and still not one complaint crossed his lips. No griping, no attempts to blame someone else for the poor outcome of his efforts.

She'd done her part by managing not to laugh.

As things continued, she was more inclined to admire the man than be amused by his predicament. He hadn't backed away. Instead, he straightened his shoulders and struggled through. He might have emerged stained and sorry he'd taken on the task, but now Bea knew she'd been right in her first impression of the man; he possessed the courage of his convictions and the commitment to see them through.

As soon as Bea got back from the barn, she'd pulled Pa aside and related the episode. His own failed attempts to feed the hogs made him sympathetic toward Mr. Wilder. Between that telling incident, the circumstances of their original introduction in town, and the stock Pa placed in police guards, Bea would be surprised if he didn't broach the bone business.

On the other side of the equation—and the table—sat the visiting bone pickers. Bea boasted more experience trying to make men leave than luring them to stay, but she and her sisters addressed the essential elements of good food and enjoyable company—hogs excepted, of course. She couldn't imagine a reason why they'd turn down a profitable business opportunity.

The trap was set, the table laid, and the secret weapon deployed. Any minute now, when he stopped chewing the cinnamony deliciousness long enough to breathe again, Pa would ask them to stay.

Any minute.

She tried not to fidget or huff with displeasure as her father reached for his third roll, then helped himself to a few more sausage patties.

Lord, grant me wisdom rather than this anxiousness. I don't want to disrespect my father, but I don't believe we have the ability to overlook this opportunity. Thank You for this chance, and thank You for restoring Papa's appetite. I hope and pray he regains more of his strength.

The prayer soothed her stretched nerves enough to let her nibble at her own breakfast. Good thing, too. The way everyone tucked in, there wouldn't be a crumb left for later!

"Sourdough!" Mr. Wilder's triumphant exclamation caught everyone's attention. "The cinnamon rolls and the cake last night, too."

"I like using a bit of our sourdough starter for some of my baking," Ariel confirmed. "A little tartness mixed in makes a more interesting sweet."

"Little bit of tart adds interest to something sweet," Mr. Wilder murmured thoughtfully, as though applying the idea to something beyond baking. His eyes found Bea's, his gaze gold with good humor once again. "Interesting way to spice things up."

"Works for me! Don't know when I've eaten better than I have these past two meals." Mr. O'Conall clapped a hand over his stomach, managing to look both replete and regretful. "Don't know when I'll next see such a fine meal either."

Bea caught Pa's eye and raised a brow, urging him to bring up the bones—and asking why he hadn't done so already. Not that it mattered, so long as he took care of the matter now!

"So you two are planning on heading off to Canada?" Pa's conversation compared to the way Bea drove the buckboard—safe and slow, but at least progressing in the right direction.

"That's right." Mr. Wilder straightened in his seat. While he answered Pa's question, he looked at his partner as he added, "Time and past to move on northward. South's picked over, and there's next to nothing to find here. No bones, no business. . .and no business staying."

Bones and business, we can give him. But would it be enough? Mr. Wilder seemed oddly intent in his determination to leave TallGrass.

"What if you found business here?" Pa must have picked up on Mr. Wilder's emphasis on leaving. "Would you stay? Or does Canada hold some added allure?"

Novelty. Adventure. The challenge of the unknown. Bea knew next to nothing about Canada, but that was the entire point of going to another country—exploring! It almost didn't matter what a traveler found along the way, so long as it stayed a departure from the familiar.

"I can't imagine anything in Canada that can compare to the treasures we've found in TallGrass." Mr. O'Conall all but oozed charm, saying exactly the right thing to please Pa.

But not Mr. Wilder. His jaw clenched, and his lips thinned as though pressing back a protest. Apparently, Mr. Wilder didn't place as much value on "the treasures" of TallGrass.

"Hard to say, since we haven't given Canada a chance."

"A good businessman takes more chances than he gives out. That's where you find the biggest return for your efforts."

Wilder shrugged. "Never know what you'll find if you're willing to look close enough."

"Are you willing?" Bea blurted out, then blushed for the second time in two days—which she thought might be the only two instances in the past year. She frowned, more at herself than everyone else, and clarified, "To look closer, I mean."

"Closer?" He returned her frown, with interest.

"Closer to home, so to speak." Ariel intervened. We've gathered up a quantity of bones, but the time and effort needed to transport them to Devil's Lake outweighed their worth."

"Would you gentlemen have any interest in a business arrangement?" Pa gripped the head of his cane but did not stand.

The bone pickers shared a dumbfounded glance before Mr. Wilder answered.

"While we appreciate the offer, we deal in large loads. Tons at a time, at times enough bones to fill a boxcar." He paused, obviously searching for a way put it politely. "If what you've collected wasn't even worth your own time, there's not enough to go around."

"What if we said that there's too much?" Cassia challenged.

"There's no such thing as too much profit," Mr. O'Conall chortled.

"Explaining would be a waste of time. Come." Pa surged to his feet, signaling everyone else to do the same. "Judge for yourselves."

Judging by the family's confidence as they headed through the yard and around the barn, they truly believed they'd collected enough buffalo bones to warrant some sort of business arrangement. If Grey hadn't already noted every building and bump surrounding the place, he would have worried.

Nothing but the barn and silo were big enough to hold much, and he'd already been inside the barn. Whatever skeletons they'd set aside while clearing their fields wouldn't be enough to worry over. At best, he'd be able to give them a few dollars for their finds, then be on his way. At worst, they'd put too high a value on the things, and he'd still be on his way.

"Mind your mouth," Miles muttered so the others would have a hard time hearing. All but the youngest daughter were several steps ahead of them, obviously itching to display their prize. "Don't be so eager to go that we leave on bad terms."

Grey's mood improved to hear Miles talk about leaving without any wheedling. Once Grey got past this hiccup, he wouldn't accommodate any other delays—no matter how "Darlyn" they might be.

Bea...

She walked alongside her father. The more weight he placed on the cane, the closer Bea kept. Her siblings followed a little farther behind, their motions blending with and blocking Bea's. Impossible not to notice the differences between the sisters.

Judith loped along, each too-swift step kicking into the next. Her skirts bounced, bunched, and swung with unpredictable enthusiasm.

Ahead of her in sharp contrast, Ariel all but glided. Only the brush of her hem against the grass attested that her feet touched the ground.

To the side, Cassia's rolling gait set her hips and skirts swaying in the classic "come hither" call most men would fall over themselves to answer. But coquettes left Grey cold.

He far preferred the efficient elegance of Bea's stride. Long and fluid, each movement flowed into the next with unexpected ease. Her skirts mimicked the motion of waves, softly surging forward and sweeping back in a sinuous ripple.

Grey couldn't bring himself to look away until Bea came to a stop. Even then, it took him a beat too long before he realized they hadn't reached any unexpected building. They'd halted in front of a haystack behind the barn.

Dumbstruck, he watched as the girls fanned out around the sizable stack, standing eight feet tall and about six feet around. Without warning but in perfect unison, they launched some sort of attack. All manner of yanking, jerking, pulling, and tugging ensued as the girls gathered armfuls of straw and ruthlessly pushed it aside. Within minutes, small piles of the stuff clumped around the heap they seemed so determined to disassemble.

No. That can't be right. Grey rubbed his eyes when he caught sight of the first patches of white peeking through the brown and yellow straw. He looked again to find more white, now uncovered enough to take on shadow and shape. The girls weren't disassembling a structure—they were dismantling a disguise!

Chapter 14

The Darlyns had employed a strange—and strangely effective—way to conceal a cache of buffalo bones. Torn between amazement and aggravation, Grey began to circle the stack. He eyed the dimensions and began calculating a rough estimate of what the pile contained. It depended on how much straw they'd layered over the top of the stack. The higher they'd piled the bones beneath, the higher the value.

But unless he badly missed his guess, a ton of bones sat before him, still sprinkled with straw. Not enough to fill even a third of one of his and Miles's wagons but more than worth taking to market! How much time and effort had it taken to gather dozens of eggs, churn and press bricks of butter, and turn curds into ten-pound wheels of cheese?

More investment, surely, than the time it would take to get these bones to the weighing station—and given the ludicrously low rates they accepted from the greedy shopkeeper, this load of bones would have brought better profit in a shorter span of time.

The process of loading, freighting, and selling the bones before returning home would eat up a week or so. . . . Suddenly, Grey spotted the problem. A week away from crops and livestock was a long time to lose for a farmer—and the Darlyn women were too smart to make such a trip alone. So they'd lose two of their workers for a week. . .for every trip it took to bring in all the bones, because their buckboard wouldn't hold half this much. "I'm starting to see what you meant by too many," he conceded.

Mr. Darlyn lifted his cane and jabbed it at the top of the stack, raining straw atop himself and his daughters. Cassia made a sound halfway between a squeal and a squawk as she scurried out of the way, picking bits from her hair all the while. Bea looped her arm beneath her father's elbow, enabling him to lower his cane without toppling over. Once he steadied, she brushed some scattered straw from the top of his head and shoulders, smiling as he returned the favor with a few clumsy swipes.

"They'd be more than worth your while, I'm thinking," Miles judged. "Seeing as how the stations in Devil's Lake will pay nine dollars a ton."

"We know." Bea moved to her father's side to face them. "The problem lies in how much time it would take to transport them."

"Time, the one tool no man can replace," Mr. Darlyn mused, then sharpened his focus on Grey and Miles. "Yours is just as valuable. Would you consider assisting us for a division of profit?"

"Of course!" Miles all but shouted, adding his agreement to Grey's nod.

"What would you say to a two to one split?" Bea negotiated. "Two to us for owning and gathering them, one to you for transporting."

"Done." Grey would gladly offer to pay them the entire nine dollars they would have received in Devil's Lake. Only he knew the Darlyns would protest, then Miles would manage to make things more complicated, and before he knew it, they'd have wasted half the morning bickering over how much he'd be allowed to pay.

If he avoided the time trap, he and Miles could get this load into one of the wagons and be done before lunch. Not that he expected to leave before the midday meal. Miles wouldn't allow it even if the Darlyns did. *Load the bones, then lunch*, Grey vowed. *Just lunch—then we leave.*

This time, the increasingly familiar refrain made him smile. He liked the idea of helping the family, even in such a small way, to find the funds to silence their big-mouthed banker. Grey even admitted lunch with the Darlyns gave him something to look forward to while he worked.

"After we load them into one of the wagons, we'll have a clearer idea of the worth," he told them. Miles wouldn't mind fiddling a bit with the numbers to leave the Darlyns with a little more than they expected, but he might make it impossible by blurting something about the value in front of the family.

"We can't weigh them to say for certain, but according to my calculations, this stack represents a ton of bones," Ariel announced, neatly dashing his scheme to bits with her all-too-accurate evaluation before tacking on a prim, "Approximately."

"I thought the same." Amazement colored Miles's voice. "After hauling boxcars' worth of bones, my eyeballs do the estimating. How were you figuring?"

"By placing the bones—"

"What were you onto, Ariel Darlyn, 'placing' bones? You weren't to be touching a one of them!" Her father's roar effectively ended her explanation. Face reddening, he waved his cane in a shaky arc. "None of you!"

His agitation came on so sudden and so strong, Grey had a hard time making sense of what the man said. *Don't ask. Don't get involved,* he reminded himself. *Anything that doesn't affect our business arrangement is no business of mine.*

"Now, Pa." Bea laid a comforting hand on his shoulder. "None of us took any of the bones from their. . .er, place of rest. We kept our agreement."

"Wait. . .what?" Curiosity got the better of him. Grey could've kicked himself, but as long as he'd started firing off questions, he figured he might as well make them more specific. "If you didn't bring the bones here, who did? And why would you promise not to help?"

"Whoever removes bones will lose life or a loved one," Mr. Darlyn insisted, face still flushed. "As every Irishman well knows!"

"My forebears were British." Grey shrugged off the indictment and looked to Miles.

"Well-known wisdom, though I always understood it to be a warning about churchyards and cemeteries—hallowed ground where human souls were laid to rest." Mile spoke slowly, careful with the convictions of a fellow Irishman. "And we've been collecting buffalo bones going on two years now, without provoking anything of that sort."

By the time we began bone collecting, neither one of us had any loved ones left to lose. Grey grimaced at the unwelcome memory—and its morbid conclusion. *If the saying held true, Miles and I would have gone six feet under long ago.*

"There are consequences we can't fathom for our actions." Mr. Darlyn ran a weary hand across his face. "Easy thing for a man's errors to outlive him."

Grey swallowed. He knew all too well how a string of simple decisions could cut through a man's life and scar his soul. But the only curse he could blame was his own stupidity.

"Pa, we know you're good at everything, and buffalo hunting was no exception. But you've got to stop claiming credit for killing them off single-handedly," Ariel chided, her wry humor easing a few lines from her father's forehead.

"There's death enough to be laid at my door without bringing bones to it," Seamus Darlyn insisted, revealing the true source of his aversion. Good, old-fashioned guilt gave an ancient superstition new strength. He waved a hand toward the pile of bones. "I relented, and you saw what happened. You know the price was paid."

"Who moved them, if not the girls?" Miles repeated Grey's earlier question.

Jodie looked at her eldest sister and shrugged. "Bea's fiancé."

Fiancé. A single word, but Grey had to take a step back to absorb the force of it. Of course she had a fiancé. The men he'd encountered in TallGrass weren't blind. *Just lucky. Unless. . .*

"Did he die?"

"No." Cassia snuffed out the shameful hope. "His uncle, in Oregon."

"A coincidence," Bea scoffed. "Ben's uncle had been sickly for two seasons."

"Ben?" Grey never met a Ben who'd been worth the time it took to say his name. Of course, he'd never known any Bens, but minor details didn't diminish his deepening dislike of the name.

"Bea's fiancé," Jodie repeated. "Well, until she threw him over."

He straightened at that last bit, ears perked.

"Jodie!" Cassia demanded. "Do you mean to make Bea sound like a jilt? Or a heartbreaker?"

"She *did* jilt him." Jodie seemed unconcerned about the state of the man's heart.

Broken. Poor Ben. In spite of his name, he didn't sound like such a bad sort after all. So long as he hadn't done something to hurt her. Grey glanced at Bea and tried not to smile.

No lovelorn sighs from this lady. She looked mad enough to spit. "We called off the engagement when he chose to move to Oregon," she gritted out. "None of which has anything to do with the business at hand."

"Unless—"

Grey dug an avenging elbow into his partner's side, stopping Miles from whatever disastrous comment he'd hoped to unleash. "Now who needs to mind his mouth?"

"Stop using my ribs to sharpen your arm!" He jerked out of reach and rubbed the sore spot. "I'll fix it."

He waved and called everyone to attention. "No use speculating over superstitions! Point is, none of us were first to move these bones. The girls kept their promise, and we can all move forward."

"Ariel's experiments came after Ben moved the bones," Judith affirmed.

Mr. Darlyn's ruddy cheeks went white. "Experiments?"

"A simple test to weigh the bones. Nothing ungodly, Papa," Ariel assured him. "I filled an empty twenty-pound flour sack with the bones of a single skeleton, then compared it to a still-full flour sack. Repeating the comparison with a few different skeletons verified that twenty pounds was a surprisingly accurate average, so from there—"

"Ariel?" Judith spoke over her sister. "No need to detail the exact equations!"

In spite of himself, their resourcefulness impressed Grey. Without the looming threats of superstitions, fiancés, or unending delays to weigh on his mind, he could focus again.

"Clever. Clever, too, the way you concealed them. No one would suspect that you stuffed one of your haystacks with something more than straw." Grey gave Bea an appreciative smile, perplexed to see her brow knit.

"We didn't."

"Clever of Ben, then." Grey figured he could afford to be generous to a jilted man several states away.

"Oh, it was our idea, but we didn't stop at one." The sweep of her arm encompassed the haystacks around them as Jodie finished the explanation.

"We filled *all* of them!"

"All of them?" Miles gave a low whistle as he counted a dozen haystacks. At a ton apiece, they'd come within kissing distance of completely filling both wagons. Twice. "Now there's a rapid change."

Grey's expression turned from astonished to stony. Sure as he knew his own tells, Miles mapped the train of Grey's thoughts. When he'd accepted Darlyn's deal, he'd planned to pay the family and keep heading toward Canada. Less than one-third of a single wagonload didn't demand any detours.

Then, in a blink, everything changed. Everything but Grey's commitment, of course. He'd already struck the bargain.

No way to duck out now that the bargain struck back. And it hit Grey hard, knocking out his hopes of heading out that afternoon. Why the man wanted to abandon an oasis of beautiful women with better cooking stumped Miles, who deeply appreciated those little luxuries. Even a hayloft trumped a cold, frost-soaked bedroll.

He had little tolerance for deprivation these days. While he'd been busy looking for buffalo bones, old age crept up to claim his. No longer a spring chicken, Miles O'Conall was ready to find himself a new roost.

As soon as he saw Grey settled someplace safe enough to give Miles some peace of mind. Deadly dull, though, most peaceful places. Even a settled-down sort of fellow needed something stimulating to while away the years.

And what stimulated a man more than a fiery female? A safe place and a sassy lass, that's what Grey needed. Someone to brighten his days, spark his smiles, and warm his heart, among other places. The right woman would make Grey want more from life than he allowed himself now. More, Miles even dared hope, than he'd once lost.

Otherwise, Grey would remain lost. And alone. Miles couldn't settle for that.

Especially when the solution stared him straight in the face! Something about this family—the eldest daughter, in particular—disconcerted his partner. *Good. Maybe if I keep dangling the Darlyn gal in front of his nose, Grey will take the bait.*

"Looks like we'll be going back to Devil's Lake," he pushed.

"No other choice." Grey's growl of agreement sounded anything but agreeable. "We'll be loaded up and on our way by Saturday. From then it won't take more than a week to get out there and come back, then it would be another week for the second trip. But. . ."

Miles saw that pause as a signpost, the sticking place between two possibilities.

The easy way sold the bones in Devil's Lake for a measly nine dollars per ton but got them back on their way to Canada the quickest.

The other road altered their course completely, bringing in a sight more profit but also doubling their delay.

Miles didn't expect his friend to make the right choice. Grey had been heading in the wrong direction for a long while. But men and maps often changed course. Grey wasn't so far gone he couldn't find his way back—especially if he rediscovered some of the priorities he'd let fall by the wayside.

Miles struggled against the inclination to step in. So simple, to offer the Darlyns both options and make things easy for everyone. Easy for him to get his way, easy for the family to get their funds...

And all too easy for Grey to keep his distance from a woman who brought back the best of his character.

Miles balked at the thought. Stepping in was one thing. Stepping in between? Unthinkable! Grey needed to deal with the Darlyns on his own terms.

Despite appearances, Grey's sense of chivalry wasn't dead—just dormant. The warrior within craved a call to arms to stir his blood...or a fair lady to do the same. He'd found both in Beatrix. What else to arouse Grey's better nature than this most potent of lures? And, it had to be said, the most predictable.

After all, even the most errant of knights couldn't resist a Darlyn in distress!

Chapter 15

Victory! Bea savored its sweetness. Today, triumph tasted like spring itself. The bright note of new beginnings cleansed her palate and sharpened her senses. No longer did these haystacks reek of sullen censure. The straw smelled simply of trapped dust and stale sunshine, the scent of summers gone by. Old arguments and broken hopes didn't haunt the haystacks. For the first time, Bea saw more than a long-standing reprimand. Today, these piles stood for redemption.

Thank You, Lord, for transforming an old injury into such a blessing. Even through our sorrows, You provide. I need to trust in Your timing.

"From then it won't take more than a week to get out there and come back, then it would be another week for the second trip. But. . ." Mr. Wilder paused, thinking something through.

Even as her fields and family stood idle and waiting, Bea couldn't begrudge Mr. Wilder a few moments to adjust his plans. The value of this man's time couldn't be measured in money or minutes. Some gifts were priceless. Like the fighting chance he'd just offered her family.

Seed money started the farm, but the bone money will keep it. Bea hadn't realized how heavily Huber's threats had weighed until the pressure eased. No longer crushed with concern, her lungs luxuriated in a rush of cool morning air. How freeing to know that the extra funds, along with Huber's forfeit when she trounced him in that shooting match, would buy them enough time to turn the farm around.

"There can be some flexibility." Mr. Wilder seemed to have finished considering his options. "If your banker is too impatient, we can advance your expected earnings before we take the load to Devil's Lake. Save some time."

Startled by his generosity, Bea didn't respond quickly enough. Where she might have considered that proposition, Pa emphatically refused it.

"Absolutely not!" He raised his cane and thumped it back against the ground. "You might reach the freight station to find the price fell. Never pay out what you haven't earned. Someone's bound to come out poorer for the practice. Bad business."

No worse than taking out a loan with Huber. Bea closed her eyes, lest she roll them. From a practical perspective, it made more sense to take payment before the goods left the property. The entire agreement, as insisted on by Pa, relied on the honor of Mr. Wilder and Mr. O'Conall.

Strangers. With no ties to TallGrass, no acquaintances in common, and no way to find them after they left. Once they had cash in hand, there was no incentive to give any back and no consequences if they cheated.

Too late to change things now. Bea wouldn't undermine Pa's decisions. Already he struggled with his increasingly limited physical abilities and the need to surrender the reins this season. Add in Huber's disrespect, and his pride needed no further blows.

When she'd collected herself enough to open her eyes, Bea found Mr. Wilder watching her. Intently. As though he understood that she disagreed but forbore to contradict her father. Bea narrowed her eyes. If he could deduce her thoughts, the man could very well figure out that he should mind his own. . .well, mind. *Oh, never mind.*

Struck by the silliness of her own thoughts, and uneasy with the idea Mr. Wilder might somehow infer them, Bea shrugged off her earlier doubts. Mr. Wilder seemed too shrewd not to know she'd be looking for him if he didn't pull through.

✳

For all the world it looked as though he were trying to puzzle his way through something, and she had no earthly idea whether she should feel flattered or offended by such scrutiny. Vaguely, she realized it couldn't be all that remarkable or have gone on overlong, else one of her sisters would have taken note—and taken action. It only felt like something significant to her.

He ended her growing unease by turning to her father. "If your timetable is flexible enough, there is a way to increase your earnings."

"Oh?" Bea made sure they'd hear the man out before Pa dismissed anything out of hand.

"Miles, that is to say, Mr. O'Conall—"

"No, no. Miles is fine! In fact, I insist on it." The man seemed absurdly pleased to be included in the conversation, now absolutely beaming at his partner. "We both do."

"We do?" Mr. Wilder sounded more dubious than enthusiastic, but only Bea seemed to share his reservations.

Bea caught herself noting the connection and resolved not to seek out any more similarities between them. Dangerous to start believing they shared any sort of sensibility. Dangerous, too, the use of his given name. Giving them that privilege took away the barrier of formality—a barrier Bea felt her family needed.

In this area, she'd always set an uncompromising example for her sisters, relaxing the rule only for Ben and his brothers. But an easygoing fiancé was a far cry from this self-contained stranger. Mr. Wilder might be helpful and handsome and even honest, but hard edges roughened those fine qualities. The set of his shoulders and the jut of his jaw telegraphed a clear desire for distance. Bea recognized that stance; she respected that message. She sent the same one when a man came too close to her or her sisters. *Keep away.* It actually reassured her. If he'd seemed eager for any increased sense of intimacy, Bea might have resisted. Instead, she found something comforting in his discomfort. It gave so little to guard against.

By now, Mr. O'—Miles—was deep into explaining his rationale for the name exchange.

"Since we don't call all the women 'Miss Darlyn,' it's awkward for them to call us 'Mister' all the time." He paused. "Lopsided, for them to address us with more respect than we return—particularly under the circumstances. Don't you agree, Mr. Darlyn?"

"I don't mind you calling me 'Mister.'" Pa's mischievous twinkle made an all-too-rare appearance, and Bea couldn't help but smile. If the loan weighed heavily on her, its burden must have been crushing him. Not so surprising, then, that spring hadn't improved his health. Guilty secrets sapped strength.

"But seein' as how you use my daughters' given names, it's only polite to extend the same privilege to them."

"It's uncanny, the way you wear the same roguish gleam." Cassia looked between the two older Irishmen. "If you and Pa met as young men, there would have been high jinks aplenty and just enough charm to get away with most of them."

"High jinks!" Miles scoffed. "Sounds like some sort of mincing fop kicking up a fuss."

"When Irishmen get ornery, they stir up shenanigans!" Pa guffawed right along with their guest.

Bea let loose a rueful smile. She understood Pa's need for laughter and what he called the "little things to make life worth living," but his timing was deplorable. Even now, with the possibility of increased income hinging on this conversation, Pa cared more for shenanigans than security. Horseplay pulled no plow, and funny phrases finished no business deals.

But I can. Galvanized, Bea fixed her focus on Mr. Wild—*Greyson*—and redirected the conversation back to the matter at hand.

"You were saying?" she prompted. "About increasing our earnings?"

Bless the man, he didn't miss a beat. "Would tack on more time—over a week, bringing it up to at least three. If you can't wait that long, no use discussing the details so you're dissatisfied with what we can manage."

Figures of overdue payments, loan amounts, and timetables jumbled around her brain, but Bea reasoned that after the shooting match, time wouldn't be such a pressing issue. She slanted a glance toward Pa, who gave the go-ahead motion.

"We can swing it if there's enough of a difference to make the time worthwhile." No commitment either way, but she kept their options open.

"I've got a connection at the Chicago Refinery," Miles jumped in. "Grey and I ship the freight ourselves and I deliver it in person for the going market rate."

"There must be a considerable margin of increase to support the added effort, time, freight, and passenger fees," Ariel remarked with great interest.

"Never you mind the passenger fare," Miles ordered. "The freight comes to just under five dollars per ton to get it from here to Chicago, loaded, and unloaded."

Bea drew in a sharp breath, managing not to gasp. "That's more than half the value of the bones themselves!"

"The market value at a refinery is considerably higher," Mr. Wild—*Greyson*, Bea reminded herself—corrected her. "Remember, the outfit in Devil's Lake makes a profit even after paying freight and giving collectors nine dollars per ton. More, even—some people don't know to portion out the hooves and horns separate, but those bring fourteen."

"What's the ratio of the hooves and horns to the other bones?" Bea broke in, wondering whether they'd come short of a ton.

"Five to one." He inclined his head toward the haystacks, answering the unasked portion of her question. "You'll have two premium tons."

"So in Devil's Lake this load would be worth one hundred, eighteen dollars," Ariel deduced. "Possibly one hundred twenty?"

"Let's say one-twenty," Miles obliged Ariel's craving for concrete numbers. "But nine dollars turns to twenty in Chicago, and the fourteen brings in thirty-two."

Dazzled by the "twenty," Bea gasped at his offhand mention of "thirty-two." She saw Ariel's fingers curl as though clasping a pencil, obviously desperate to be doing the sums. Her sister worked this sort of thing through much more quickly than the rest of them, but Bea narrowed in on one key truth.

"That's more than double!" she marveled.

"Less freight costs," Pa muttered, still sorting through the figures.

"Still comes awful close to double," Jodie pointed out, "when you add in the extra hoof-and-horn money."

"Approximately two hundred and five dollars, after shipping fees," Ariel announced. She paused while everyone else absorbed that, then added, "If we'd dropped everything off at Devil's Lake ourselves, all mixed together, it would have been one hundred and eight, give or take."

If the men hadn't said anything, we would gladly have accepted seventy-two dollars as our share. Bea calculated. Enough for the next nine interest payments.

But their share of the grand total would be one hundred thirty-six! Enough for a year and a half's worth of payments! Along with the four months Huber would be "forgiving" after the shooting match, they could earn enough to pay off two years' worth of interest on the loan— when they had only one year remaining!

It left them with enough to start saving toward the looming one-thousand-dollar balloon payment coming due at the end of the mortgage. But most importantly, it gave them time to earn the rest.

"We can front the freight costs, if that's a concern." Greyson seemed to think there was more to their silence than stunned disbelief.

"No. We'll pay our share from the start," Pa insisted, puncturing Bea's giddy joy. As it seeped away, practicality stepped in; he'd just committed to giving these men sixty dollars—on top of trusting them with the entire supply of bones!

"We're putting up the goods," Bea reminded him. "It's a sign of goodwill that they're willing to invest in the venture, Pa."

"They're paying the passenger fare, and they're investing their time, contacts, and knowledge," he persisted. "We've just heard how valuable that is to us."

"Yes, Pa." Chastened, Bea looked at the bone pickers. For the first time, it occurred to her that they could easily have taken the load to Chicago for a fantastic sum without admitting to it, then paid only the seventy dollars the family expected.

"Let's compromise. We'll take two-thirds of the freight costs and pay our share, so we won't need to factor it when we divvy up the profits." Grey's hasty intervention, and his increasingly obvious integrity, staggered Bea.

"Thank you both for your honesty, and your assistance. I can only believe God brought you both here to help us make the most of things."

✳

"Make the most of it," Miles repeated beneath his breath.

Grey ignored him, instead addressing himself to the Darlyns. "Since we parked the wagons right here, beside yours, they won't need to be moved. I'll grab our gloves and hammers, and we'll get straight to work."

A glance at the sky told him a surprising amount of morning slipped past while he'd been busy slopping hogs, breaking his fast, and blithely agreeing to things he shouldn't. Obviously he'd gone as gooey as one of those sinful cinnamon rolls, unable to hold himself together once the Darlyns poured on their honeyed charm.

"A hammer?" Judith cocked her head to the side, eyes bright with interest. "What do you use the hammer for?"

"Breaking up the hip bones."

"Are they worth more that way?" she persisted.

"I'd imagine he means the pelvic cradle, Jodie." Ariel looked consideringly at the straw-strewn stack of bones before her. "As one piece, it's awkwardly shaped and most likely takes up too much room."

"Yep." Grey nodded to soften his short responses and took another step back. Come to think of it, he should probably keep all of his responses short from here on out. Otherwise, who knew what else he'd get himself into?

"Do you think I can watch and see how it's done?" The youngster sounded oddly eager to bear witness as they broke down the bones.

He stopped, unable to say why it seemed like such a bad idea but unable to agree to her request either. It might take a little while before they unearthed a pelvis. Then, too, once she saw the procedure, would she trot off—or would they be working through the day with a ragamuffin girl watching their every move?

Then they'd be watching their every word. . .and Grey had a few choice ones to share with Miles, once he got the chance.

"The day's already gone ahead without us, Jodie. We've plenty to keep us busy and no time to waste watching other folks get their work done. You take care of the horses." Bea paused, her gaze flicking toward Grey. She drew a breath as though fortifying herself to finish. "And leave the bones to Miles and Greyson."

Greyson. The sound of her voice, wrapping around his name for the first time, stopped him cold. Then hot, as warmth spread from his chest through his limbs. She said it softly. Hesitantly. Lingering over those two syllables as though exploring new territory. For a moment, he forgot his irritation. Forgot the fact that his name now served as an indictment—a constant reminder of how he'd blurred his once black-and-white principles.

On her lips, he became a benediction. Grey wanted to drink it in. Straight from the source.

Chapter 16

He walked away. Without another word, Grey turned on his heel and headed for the barn. Behind him, he heard Miles smoothing over his abrupt departure, mentioning again the gloves and hammers, before his quick steps followed Grey's.

"You call that making the best of things?" Miles demanded as soon as they were out of earshot.

"Yes." He didn't bother to explain himself. Right now the best move he could make put distance between him, Beatrix Darlyn, and all the things she'd unwittingly saddled him with.

Every moment he made the most of would make it that much harder to leave. If, indeed, he ever managed to leave. Each encounter with Bea and her family spilled into the next. Another meal, another night. . .one surprise after the next brought him here, before a haystack holding a secret. That secret seemed worth half a day's delay.

Until one haystack turned out to be twelve, and half a day stretched into a fortnight. His old superiors back in Chicago would have been ashamed at the way he'd been hoodwinked. A guardsman never closed a case or deal without a thorough investigation. But Grey couldn't seem to keep his head straight when it came to the Darlyns. Wanting what's best for them meant muddling through what was worst for him, while the project mushroomed once again. *Three weeks, maybe a little more— so close it might as well be a month.*

No. Grey sucked in a breath. *If I start thinking along those lines, it'll grow to a month for sure.*

If the girls were lash-fluttering flirts, he'd leave them to the local swains. If they were dishrag damsels, weak-willed and washed-out, Grey would've walked past. If they were bold as brass, careless and crass, he wouldn't give them a second thought.

With such a wide variety of acceptable options, Grey figured one of the women would oblige him with a redeeming flaw. But no suitable shortcomings came to light, nothing to slow his growing fascination with this fierce little family. Nearly everything about them, from their loyal affection to their dogged self-reliance, got him in the gut. Still, his good sense might have prevailed if it weren't for the added appeal of Bea. *She* was the test Grey feared he'd fail. She was the lure who left him no choice.

To escape temptation, he'd go to the devil.

And Devil's Lake offered precious little to look forward to, aside from driving out his demons. Or letting him drive away from them. Grey never did enjoy cooling his heels while Miles traveled back and forth from Chicago.

Grey grunted his way up the ladder, venting some of his frustration until a rusty cackle reminded him that even the livestock were guilty of conspiracy. As if the women and their father and Grey's own partner weren't enough, he'd had to fend off a phalanx of pigs and put up with an unreliable rooster. In the scheme of things, the bird ranked last—but if he'd crowed on time, Grey might have gotten on the road before breakfast—and before anyone brought up the bone business. It galled him to realize how much the fowl's sloth had cost him.

"You're too young to be grunting your way up ladders and glaring at chickens." Miles reached the top of the ladder and smacked Grey's boot in silent command that he move over. When Grey obliged, he hoisted himself into the hayloft—with a grunt.

Grey cleared his throat. Pointedly.

"Don't you start. I'm about twenty years older than you. Two decades give me the right to whuffle like a geezer if I want to." He paused, losing some of his bluster. "And sometimes even if I don't."

"Fair enough." In spite of himself, Grey couldn't resist asking, "What is an appropriate age to start one's chicken-glaring career?"

Miles snagged the rooster cage and turned to face him. "You're fishing for an argument and I'm not taking the bait. Cut that grumpy line of thinking, before you catch hell."

"Better catch than that bird of yours," Grey snapped back, all traces of amusement gone. "Glad to see you claiming the useless thing. I don't plan to play nursemaid to a chicken—especially one that's good for nothing but a frying pan."

"Nobody asked you to play nursemaid over anything." Miles clutched the cage against his chest for all the world as though cradling a baby. "If you're looking out for someone other than yourself, it's because you made that choice. Most folks would say that's a good thing."

"You're not most folks, and you know better. If you'd been the one to pledge us to a project without knowing its full extent, I'd be angry as all get-out with you." Instead, Grey got to be angry as all get-out at himself, which made him twice as touchy about the whole thing.

"You need to stop being so angry all the time." Miles shuffled over for his bag. "Gotten to be a grouchy git, but there's hope yet, if you can see this is the best deal we ever made."

"How's that?"

"A couple weeks is a small price to pay for putting your priorities in order. Or to regain a friend who's been gone too long." Miles settled the cage into the crook of his arm.

"Gone?" Grey got the message but didn't want to hear it. "Two years as partners, and I've been at your side the whole time."

"The whole time. But not the whole man." In spite of the rooster in his arm and the straw sticking out from his hair, Miles managed to project some solemn dignity. "It's good to see you comin' back into your own."

My own what? Grey didn't want to ask, aware that the answer wouldn't be flattering. Withdrawing might have kept him together for the past couple years, but Miles was right—"together" didn't mean the same thing as "whole."

"Hello?" Bea's hands closed around the doorpost and her head leaned into the barn, as though checking to make sure the rest of her could follow.

She's respecting that these are our quarters as much as the livestock's. At least, for the next couple of days. Her reticence struck Grey as adorable. He remembered she'd done much the same thing earlier that morning when she shooed her youngest sister out of the barn at sunup.

His smile lightened his response as he snagged his gloves and called back, "Just a minute—coming back down."

Her head whipped out of sight. "I don't want to embarrass anyone or sound as overly forward, but we're doing wash today, if either of you would like to add anything in. . ."

"Absolutely!" Grey didn't hesitate to take her up on the offer.

"On a Thursday?" Miles's surprise dredged up a snippet of old memory.

Butterflies stitched onto dishcloths, each one emblazoned with a day of the week and a chore. *Wash on Mondays, Iron on Tuesday. . .Bake on Saturday.* Days became weeks, weeks became a life he and his wife shared right up until he lost her. Fire on Thursday stole her, their unborn babe, and every shred of that life—right down to those towels.

What did it matter if the Darlyns didn't hold to the typical schedule? Dishcloth didn't order anyone's days. The fabric of life could be torn apart in the blink of an eye.

"Normally Monday's wash day, but this week we pushed things back to butcher and process a spring hog." Bea's explanation didn't offer any fodder for happier thoughts.

Grey edged farther back into the hayloft and started stripping as quickly as possible, eager to feel clean again. At least he could launder his slop-splotched clothing. No man could throw his memories in the boiler and be done with them.

Regrets never washed away.

※

Miles scratched the pesky itch between his shoulder blades, then flicked the culprit—a sticklike bit of straw—to join its fellows beside a newly unearthed bone pile. Yesterday they'd managed to get through two of the things, but keeping that slow pace would be harder today, since they hadn't wasted half the morning before starting out. *Couldn't have worked out better if I planned it myself.*

Not that he'd stopped planning. When God saw fit to give a man a fine start, the man still needed to build on it. The Darlyn family, along with their farm and their fine stands of bones, presented the sort of foundation Miles couldn't stand to see lie fallow.

A sidelong look told Miles that Grey wasn't bothering to ponder their place on the farm. He was too busy trying to work his way off the property. The boy set a punishing pace that told Miles he meant to be finished in record time.

The worse Grey wanted to leave, the more Miles meant to prolong their stay. He shoved aside armfuls of prickly straw then shoved them slightly farther, making a lot of grand motions with very little movement to show for them. Grey and the girl needed time to get to know each other. To talk without being knackered. Maybe to show off their shooting skills or something of that sort. But with summer fast approaching, the Darlyns wouldn't rest more than a minute until Sunday.

On Sunday, there'd be no work beyond basic chores. Only church and plenty of time spent with the family—the sort of relaxing time to make a man reconsider living alone. If he convinced Grey to alter his path, Sunday would be a big step in the right direction. Especially if that foul little banker misbehaved some more.

The true catalyst for Grey's grudging changes came not from merely meeting the Darlyns—but from seeing the eldest sister stand against a pack of savages to look after her brood. Her courage stirred a man's convictions, and Grey needed to stay on the farm long enough to see that the Darlyns waged a losing war.

Fine women and hardworking lasses though the girls may be, they didn't have the numbers, the strength, or the time to make the most of their acres before planting season ended. Though they'd done much of their morning chores before breakfast and the bone discussion yesterday, the family spent the rest of yesterday racing around as though they'd wasted weeks instead of lost an hour. If they could hire laborers, they might do better and have more time to relax.

Then again, if they could afford laborers, they wouldn't need him and Grey to help with the bones. Miles frowned at the thought, and frowned still harder at the notion of strange men swarming all over the farm, leering at the ladies while lending a helping hand. Most men couldn't be trusted to keep those helping hands to themselves around such appealing lasses.

Maybe their da's empty pockets held a silver lining after all.

Chapter 17

Don't mind me." Their host's voice grabbed Miles's attention as he passed behind. "Going to take advantage of this fine weather to oil some equipment. Give me a chance to keep an eye on your progress."

Miles turned and touched the brim of his hat in silent, good-natured acknowledgment. Darlyn didn't intend to watch his and Grey's progress picking bones—he planned to keep an eye on where they worked and make sure they stayed as far away from his daughters as possible. Smart father.

Miles got back to work. In no time, he'd denuded two stacks and edged his way toward the wagons, where Seamus mixed turpentine and linseed oil. Strong, sour, and earthy, the concoction protected wood, wheels, and gears alike from the worst that bad weather could offer. Rain and drying, rot and cracking, the linseed oil seeped in and strengthened.

Miles figured the Darlyns acted like linseed oil, restoring Grey's stronger qualities. He acted more like the turpentine. Without the turpentine, wagons and tools resisted the linseed for weeks on end, making precious little progress. He and the turpentine just sped things along.

Though in this case, the best way to make that progress was to slow down Grey's pace. What better way to waste daylight than in conversation with the girls' father?

"Not much to see here, Seamus," he joked, daring to use the man's first name even though they hadn't been given explicit permission. For middle ground, men usually dropped the "Mr.," but Miles couldn't take that step. No chance he'd be calling another man "Darlyn" without the "Mr." attached—even then it made for a bit of awkwardness. So Seamus it would be, unless the farmer protested. First names set them up as friendly—like they needed to be.

"Seamus, am I now, Miles?" He popped his head up from the back of the buckboard, where'd he'd been crouching.

"Seamus you are, if you're looking for friendly conversation while you're watching over us." He decided to draw the boundary, secure enough that the other man would fall in line. "Otherwise we'll work without words."

"Job gets done just as well." The observation made Miles doubt himself for a moment. "Doesn't get questions answered though."

A quick glance toward Grey, who'd halted long enough to hear that last bit, made Miles suck in a breath. Grey hated questions. Come to think of it, Miles didn't hold much fondness for them either. Unless he was the one doing the asking, of course.

"What's on your mind?" Miles addressed Seamus first. That way he had a better chance of directing the course of the conversation. This first talk would be the most important—if it didn't go well, there wouldn't be a second chance.

"Wilder worked with the police." Seamus jutted his chin toward Greyson and rubbed linseed oil into the back of the buckboard seat with steady, measured swipes. Then he looked at Miles. "What about you? You don't strike me as one for the guards. How did you spend your days before you took up bone picking?"

Gambling. Trying to keep ahead of the McDonald crew until I had the money to repay the latest loan. Watching my business partner—Grey's father—drink himself into oblivion without being able to stop him. Answers clotted in Miles's mouth, thick with guilt and bitter to taste. He licked his lips and looked for something more suitable to say.

"Contractor," he spat out. "Grey's pa and I ran a contracting business. Construction, brickwork, foundations, sidewalks, repair, you name it.

Anything and everything a building might need, we had a man or two on the lists who specialized in it."

"Sounds like a good setup." Seamus's hand stilled then started wiping back the other way, as though he'd reversed his thoughts. "Takes a lot to get everything in line for a business like that."

"True." He saw where this headed, but wasn't overly worried. He'd managed to talk his way around the same questions with Grey, and no one interrogated like Grey.

"Amazing thing, to build a business from the ground up. Then watch that business build structures all over a major city. Seems the sort of thing a man would sit back and eye with pride in his middling years." Seamus's rag moved in short, tight circles, narrowing in. "What makes a man abandon a business at that stage?"

"Bad time to be a contractor in Chicago." Miles settled on the most basic summation possible, hoping the man would take a hint and drop that line of questioning. "After the Great Boodle Trial, city and county contracts froze. Laborers found other work. . . . I moved on."

"Rough times, when a few bad apples spoil the barrel for everyone." Seamus worked his mixture into the nooks and crannies around and beneath the buckboard seat. "Maybe after you're through picking bones, you can go back and pick things up again. Couple years ought to have changed plenty of things out there."

"Chicago never stops changing. I'll keep an eye out." Miles had gotten to be very good at keeping an eye out, in fact. But until Michael Cassius McDonald passed away and a new mob kingpin rose to power, he knew better than to go back for more than a swift visit. Every time he got back from Chicago, Grey expected him to be rested up, but constantly checking over his shoulder wore Miles out.

"Good. Look to your city. Look to your bones and business. Plenty of things in this world to catch the attention of a smart man." Seamus scooted out toward the back of the wagon and eased himself down. He picked up a pile of rags and walked to where Miles and Grey stood. "And a wise one won't waste time casting glances at my favorite daughter."

Miles gawked. What sort of father outright admitted he had a favorite?

"Which one would that be?" his partner asked, almost smiling. "Your favorite?"

"All of them, o' course." Seamus's expression darkened into a menacing frown as he defended his daughters. "For different reasons."

By now Miles couldn't help but wonder which girl the man meant to scare them away from. Seemed to him that a father would pass out the most warnings over Cassia, but maybe Seamus noticed Grey's interest in Beatrix? That might make things tricky.

"Then which one did you mean in your warning?"

"Don't be a bunch of dopey dossers!" Seamus grabbed his cane from where he'd rested it against the wagon wheel spokes. He raised it and jabbed Miles square in the center of the chest before repeating the maneuver with Grey. "Whichever one's caught your eye, that's the one you stay away from. No pass-through men are going to go chasing after my girls, you hear?"

"Yes, sir," they chorused.

But that wasn't all they heard. From across the yard and out in the fields, a shot rang out.

Grey never broke a promise, much less one that still hung on the wind—but off he went after Bea without a second thought. And not even the gal's father could object to that sort of chasing!

Bea chased down the rabbit she'd shot from half a field away, debating whether to wait for Jodie to come fetch it or walk it back to the house herself. Any time the family heard her shoot from the field, they figured she'd bagged something for supper and sent Jodie to pick up the spoils.

Best way to keep the kill pest-free. Hawks, in particular, had no qualms about carrying off a rabbit or other bird once it'd been shot. They preferred to do their own hunting, but just because something wasn't moving didn't mean they ignored a fresh meal.

Bea shaded her eyes. No hawks circled overhead, but a figure raced across the fields toward her. Too big and too quick to be Jodie—it looked like one of their guests thought something had gone wrong. For a fleeting moment, Bea felt bad. *Maybe I should have warned them not to worry about gunshots?*

Greyson burst through some scraggly shrubs they'd planted as a windbreak. Hopefully the man didn't scratch himself half to death in his haste. "Are you all right?"

"Fine." She held the rabbit aloft, glad to note he wore his freshly cleaned coat. That should have protected him fairly well from the dry, snagging branches. "I'm rarely without my rifle, so it's not infrequent that we rustle up some supper."

He stared at her then the rabbit. "We?"

Bea lifted the rifle at her side and back down again in a sort of half shrug, battling the rising heat of yet another blush. *Useless things, blushes.*

Useless, but surprisingly resilient, since they defied her best efforts to end them. Perhaps bad habits gained late in life were made of sterner stuff than vices acquired early on?

Less than a fortnight had passed since she and Ariel laughed over Elizabeth Barrett Browning's thoughts on the subject. Something along the lines of drawing too close to the fire of life and, like a gnat, flaring up as the heat consumed them. The poet had little pity for any such gnat of a girl.

Neither had Bea. . .until she joined their ranks. Inwardly, she struck up a chant of "not-a-gnat, not-a-gnat, not-a-gnat," hoping to shame the pesky affliction away.

It worked more as a trade than a triumph, since giggles threatened to take its place.

Luckily, Greyson broke into a grin of his own. "Should have guessed. I've said the same sort of thing about my pistol back when I still served on the force."

"Few things in life stay at your side or cover your back better than a trusted firearm." She realized too late that most women would have spoken about their family or old friendships in such a fashion. *He probably thinks I'm some sort of trigger-happy recluse.*

Anything she tried to add would make things worse, so Bea shrugged and started back toward the plow, where her team had begun to shift restlessly. Even-tempered and strong-backed, by now the horses were familiar with the feel of her fetching the gun from the harness she'd rigged between the plow handles. They no longer flinched. Her livestock were better equipped to handle her hunting than their guests.

She reached the plow and placed her rifle back in its sling, wondering whether it would be rude to ask him to carry the rabbit with him back to the house. Then wondered where she'd left her mind.

Send a man up to the house? Insanity! She kept strange men as far away from her sisters as possible! No matter how well mannered they might be, or how kind they were to race into the fields to check on her, or how brilliantly the brown of their eyes flashed to gold when they were amused or interested. Like now.

"Never heard a woman describe it that way, but you're right on target. A well-cared-for, properly handled gun serves as more than a weapon. It's an ally." He tugged off his hat, a stray breeze toying with some of those long, straight strands.

Bea hefted the rabbit a bit higher, determined to bring the conversation back to more practical ground. "Even if you're only putting supper in a pot?"

"I'm glad it wasn't anything more serious. I figured if you were bringing down dinner it'd come from a passing flock. So that single shot set me running. My mistake, but I didn't imagine rabbits invaded the fields while you worked."

"Rabbits take a keen interest in the planting process. When we cast grains and oats it's the easiest meal they can find, since we've fenced in the gardens."

"So he's not an unfortunate passerby. He was a scout for enemy scavengers."

Bea smiled at the way he depicted her ongoing battle against foragers but swiftly sobered. "Around here, we have to look after our own. No use wasting time or ammunition on warning shots."

"So you were aiming for the cigar then?" His swift change in topic didn't faze her—a benefit of living with three sisters.

Bea nodded, not sure whether to be amused or indignant at the idea she might have been aiming for the man's head—and missed.

"Should've known. The man's head is too big to miss."

She couldn't help but laugh at that, but the silence afterward stretched too long. With precious little experience in encouraging men to share their thoughts, Bea let the silence spread between them. If he chose to bridge the distance, she'd gladly listen. If not, she'd churn up any disappointment along with the soil beneath her plow.

"Impressive feat, stubbing that cigar. And a bigger risk." His tone gave no hint of admiration or approbation, leaving her with nothing but the words themselves.

She resisted the urge to respond defensively. "Sounds like a question's prowling around those observations, but I don't know how to respond to it."

"Hard not to wonder how big a risk you took."

It went without saying that if she'd missed her target and hit the hothead instead, Bea would have committed an unthinkable crime. Nor would the deadly consequences have been confined to Huber, once the law handed down the only possible judgment.

A shiver pebbled her skin as Bea considered the possibility for the first time. In the heat of the moment, fueled with rage and regret, she hadn't thought at all. Only acted. Foolishly.

I never would have forgiven myself if I flubbed that shot.

Not only would she be guilty of murder, she'd be every bit as guilty as her mother—throwing away the life and family she'd built to chase after some fleeting temptation.

How did I not consider it fully before? Forgive me, Lord. She closed her eyes and confessed it not only to Greyson but to God. "I risked everything."

Chapter 18

Whoa, *there*.

Whatever Bea meant, it meant an awful lot to her. There she stood, a bit apart from her plow, wearing the same dull dress Grey remembered from that morning. Nothing special about the outfit, save the woman inside it. At breakfast, with its faded skirts masked with a clean white apron and the rest of it brightened by her smile and platters she carried, it looked fine. Ordinary.

Now, she wore it differently. It still looked plain, but no one could accuse Beatrix Darlyn of looking ordinary anymore. With no pristine apron to interfere, the muddy brown of her skirts sank straight into the dirt, rooting her to the land. It fit her better this way.

At least, it had until she'd gone white as paper and started looking like she wanted to fold in on herself. With a start, Grey realized she looked like a woman who might start crying.

"Don't." He slapped his hat back on his head. Worn felt wasn't a man's first choice for a helmet, but in a pinch. . .*at least it's waterproof.*

Her chin came back up, shoulders straightened and eyes blessedly dry. "Don't what?"

"Cry." He tapped the barrel of her Winchester. "I'd rather borrow a cigar and play practice dummy for you."

"I'm not the blubbering type." Her rolled eyes raised his spirits. "What is it about tears, that the very idea makes a man panic?"

"It's not panic." Bad description but a point worth considering.

"Assuming he's not the reason she's crying. Then all bets are off."

"Then what—" Bea broke off, looking like she was doing some considering of her own. "Never mind."

"I never do."

"You never mind." The blue in her hazel eyes sparked bright. "Unless you're the reason for something. Then all bets are off, right?"

Grey chuckled at her quick wit. "So ask."

"You didn't answer the first question!" Her brows pinched together, as if she wore her hat brim too tight. "About why tears make men panic?"

"Yes I did. I said we don't panic."

"Quibbling over the description isn't the same as offering an explanation," Bea huffed. That tiny puff of air seemed to vent her frustration, since her brow smoothed. "Whether at fault or not, men seem eager to escape a weeping woman. Why?"

"Escape? That makes us sound a cowardly bunch." Though no worse than "panicked."

"Semantics aside, why would they want to flee the scene?"

"You make it sound like the location of a crime." Grey realized the more interested and animated she became, the more he liked listening to her, even if he didn't like what he heard. "Crying is no crime."

Though the comparison held merit. Whether the scene of a crime or a cry, no man wanted to loiter—especially if he committed the offense!

"You're evading the question. Again." She peered up at him. "Questions and tears. . .why would a man want to avoid these?"

"Some call it self-preservation." Yep. Somewhere along the line, he'd lost the upper hand in this conversation.

"Self-preservation?" Eyes bright, corners of those full lips twitching, she put him in mind of a kitten batting at a dust mote. "What can be imperiled by tears or conversation?"

My peace of mind, for one thing. It had been too long since Grey matched wits with anyone but Miles. His rusty skills needed more practice before he sharpened them against the keen edge of Beatrix Darlyn's intelligence.

Not that he'd be staying long enough to invite another encounter. Grey frowned.

"I wasn't trying to fluster you." If a woman could sound intrigued and apologetic, Bea managed it. "At least, not much."

"Flustered" made him sound like some fussbudget in need of smelling salts! He all but growled. "You don't blubber. I don't get flustered."

"Unsettled?" At his continued scowl, she dredged up other options, each worse than the last. "Discomfitted? Unnerved?"

"Nothing wrong with my nerves."

"Rattled?" Obviously, the woman enjoyed baiting him. "Perturbed?"

"No."

"*Discombobulated?*" She dissolved into laughter. Not delicate chimes, silvery peals, or sly titters, but a genuine invitation to share her amusement.

An invitation Grey found almost irresistible. If he gave in, the moment would turn into a memory that belonged to both of them.

Not mine. The truth pinched him. Bea wasn't his diversion to enjoy, nor his responsibility to protect. He couldn't allow gunfire to draw him into guffaws. He should have walked away as soon as he knew she wasn't in danger.

"Disgruntled." The word dropped between them like a rock; its heft weighed down her levity. Maybe too much. Grey fought to strike a better balance so he could leave. "You should've taken me up on my offer to play cigar stand the next time you wanted to take a risk."

She sobered in degrees—lips thinning, light leaving her eyes, color leeching from the apples of her cheeks. Each alteration stabbed at him, a silent accusation. "And if I'm not willing to risk it again?"

"Even easier." A nice change for a complicated encounter. "Never take the shot if you can't be confident in your aim."

Advice he should've applied to his dealings with the Darlyns, but hindsight always gave the most accurate scope. Useless, of course.

"I've no reservations about my ability to make the shot, Mr. Wilder."

"Greyson." The correction slipped out before he could stop it. No matter how profound the need to establish distance, something deep-seated rebelled at Bea's formality. After hearing the sound of his name on her lips, there was no going back.

The look she shot him should've withered the scrub brushes bristling against his boots. Distance was one thing. Earning her animosity. . .well, that went a step too low.

He gave talking another try. "If you're convinced you can make the shot, why did you say you risked everything when you made it before?"

"No matter how practiced, no shooter should make assumptions. One misfire or a sudden distraction, and skill doesn't count for much." Her lips twisted in a grimace. "I aimed at Huber's cigar out of anger—never an acceptable reason to point a gun at another human being. Definitely not a good reason to put lives at risk."

"Ah." Lives. Plural. "You mean you risked your own, had the shot failed." *And made you guilty of murder* seemed too cruel and intimate an accusation to speak aloud.

"My family's way of life would have been irrevocably changed." Sorrow clouded her expression at what was obviously, to her, the worst possible consequence. "Not simply because of my absence, though I'm sure they'd miss me, but because it would ruin the Darlyn name."

"Though I'm sure they'd miss me." Even sandwiched by self-reproach, the guileless acknowledgment of her family's love shone bright as a beacon, calling to Grey. What a dismal contrast to his own days. Other than Miles, Grey couldn't dredge up the name of a single person who would miss him.

Because I'm always the one left behind to do the missing.

"You didn't miss. Not the cigar, and not in the impulse to shoot it." He looked off in the distance, back toward the house. "Every police officer knows there's more than one motive for any action. There was more to it than anger."

His conviction stabbed through Bea. "Vengeance isn't any better."

"Maybe it is." Grey rubbed his chin, an absentminded gesture that emphasized both the hard edge of his jaw and the size of his hands. "Bet it's closer to the core. Vengeance is retaliation for something taken. He took something of yours; you responded without even thinking."

"Hardly a comforting fact." If he kept trying to cheer her up, she'd need an extra handkerchief.

"Yes it is. You didn't plan out your revenge and make the shot in cold blood. You reacted instinctively." He caught her consternation and shook his head. "Don't berate yourself. It's a good thing. Huber threw the plate as an act of aggression. If he thought he'd bested you, he would have grown more aggressive."

"You're right." Bea stood a little straighter. "I recognized the same thing. It's why I made the shot then told him to get off our land and not come back."

"Bullies don't back down until someone stands up to them."

"Believe it or not, you made me feel better." Bea ignored the fact that he didn't look overly excited about that. "Though Huber's as hostile as ever, challenging me to that shooting match."

He shrugged. "Haven't seen you shoot, but I've seen enough of the results to think you'd beat the tar out of him."

"Thanks." Anything else would sound disingenuous or boastful, so Bea didn't trust herself to say more. Greyson seemed to approve of her skill, but Bea had precious little experience talking about her shooting with anyone outside the family. And Ben, who'd seemed surprised and then seemed to forget the matter entirely. She'd shrugged off any disappointment that her husband-to-be hadn't lauded her efforts, content to know Ben didn't mind her shooting. Of course, Ben never minded much of anything.

"Have to admit, it makes me wonder if you can outshoot me." Almost as though he'd known what she was thinking, Grey grabbed her attention.

She didn't try to quell her eagerness. "Do you fancy yourself a marksman?"

"No."

Disappointment flooded Bea. She'd never met anyone who'd trained and practiced and prevailed in honing their ability with firearms the way she had.

"I don't 'fancy' myself anything—though I bet your Mr. Huber does."

"He's not mine!" Revolted, Bea all but snarled. "I don't want him."

"Can't imagine anyone would." If he'd said it in a lighthearted way, she might have shrugged it off. Instead Greyson looked so earnest, he made the subject too sober to ignore—and, suddenly, too funny.

Bea chuckled. "Can't imagine he calls himself a marksman either. When you denied being one, were you saying your shooting skills aren't up to par, or were you taking exception to the term 'fancy'?"

"Fancy ways aren't for me. As for shooting, I'm a devotee of the sport, and I put a good deal of time and effort into making my aim accurate."

"You *are* a marksman!"

"Not professional grade but a step or two above amateur," he conceded, his confidence keeping him from sounding too modest. "Would you call yourself a markswoman?"

Bea blinked. "No one's ever asked me that before. Partly because no one but my family—and my fiancé—knew about my affinity with firearms until this past week."

"Why's that?"

"It's not considered very ladylike," she mumbled. The idea that Greyson Wilder might see her as less than a lady bothered her more than she cared to admit. Although he seemed to approve of her unconventional interests, Bea wondered whether he'd be so supportive if he planned to settle in TallGrass.

Passing curiosities were one thing; ever-present oddities quite another.

"Idiocy, the idea women should pretend to be less capable than they are. But I wanted to know what made you bring your talents into the open."

"Pa decided the men of this town needed to be set straight on a few things."

He raised a brow, his mouth pressing into a thin line Bea didn't like nearly so well as his natural expression. "That mess in the store was an example of improved behavior after they'd been set straight?"

"No," she hastened to reassure him, then realized the truth wasn't very reassuring. "The incident at the store surprised everyone. Jodie says the whole demonstration idea backfired."

"Your family has a way with the phrase." Greyson didn't smile though. "Between showing off sharpshooting skills and breaking jars over their heads, you'd expect the men to get the message not to mess with the Darlyns."

"To be fair, the Brauns boast thicker heads than most—I like to think that seeing him laid low will keep the others in line until the shooting contest. The more people who bear witness, the greater the impact."

Her hopes didn't run overly high, but Bea felt oddly reluctant to reveal her doubts. Not because she doubted her shooting, but she held little faith that the people of TallGrass would receive the demonstration well—much less take heed.

"Fools follow a leader." His estimation of the townsmen matched hers so closely that Bea gaped. "The strongest or the richest idiot usually holds sway over the pack—in this case, it looks like Huber calls the shots."

"Even mine, this time around."

"You had a choice." Instead of offering empty assurance, he looked back at her, steady and sure. She noticed that his eyes returned to brown—no longer amused but somehow warmer than before.

"With him holding the future of our farm over my head, there wasn't a choice. Not really." She paused, realizing how petulant that sounded. "So I'm not thinking of it as giving in to his demands. Instead, I see it as an unexpected gift—the opportunity to bring down our payments and his pride."

"Sounds like the right choices to me." He gestured toward the rabbit. "Do you want me to take that back for you?"

Bea realized she'd been standing motionless for far too long. No matter how interesting the conversation, nothing excused such laxness during planting season!

Pa remained at the homestead. Her sisters knew better than to spend time alone with their guests. Greyson proved, perhaps, too interesting for Bea's peace of mind, but he'd also demonstrated an unshakable integrity. She thrust the rabbit toward Grey before she could think her way around it.

"I hope you like rabbit stew for supper."

"Sure, but I wouldn't turn down a serving of anything that came out of your kitchen, and neither would Miles."

"I can't take much of the credit for that. Ariel and Cass have been doing most of the cooking these days."

He looked down at the rabbit then back at her. "I'd say you contribute your fair share."

"We all turn our hand to whatever needs doing." Bea didn't mind agreeing with him. Greyson wasn't a man to flatter. She had a hunch that they shared the same philosophy—the truth could stand on its own. If people didn't like it, they were free to walk away.

"Speaking of what needs doing, I'd best get back to those bones before your pa comes after me."

"If he did, I'm the one who'd be in trouble," Bea assured him as she headed back to her plow. "I'll need to move fast to keep on schedule. Thanks for taking the rabbit!"

"No problem." He crunched his way back through the dry shrubs and a fair ways beyond, when the breeze played tricks with Bea's mind.

It had to be the breeze because she wouldn't have imagined Greyson Wilder would mutter anything on his way back. Hints of good humor were one thing, but she doubted he'd indulge in outright silliness.

Even so, she couldn't stop smiling at the very thought as she followed the phantom advice.

Hop to it.

Chapter 19

The next morning dawned dark and dismal. Bea tried to shrug it off, assuming she'd risen earlier than usual, pestered from her bed by half-formed thoughts of what her family would face after church tomorrow. Normally, she tried not to worry over what the other women said, but this time the Darlyns deserved at least some of the censure aimed their way.

The TallGrass sticklers were sure to have plenty to say about last Sunday's demonstration—not to mention the display at the mercantile. Bea knew better than to think a smile would soothe the ruffled feathers of the other townswomen. Sadly, a frown might make more headway because it showed that she took the situation as seriously as they did.

The matrons would leave no opportunity to escape or defer the coming judgment. Trials weren't staged for the sake of the accused, and Bea knew better than to expect an opportunity to explain or defend last week's impromptu invitations. She and her sisters had been found guilty long ago—possibly even before Pa informed them they'd be having guests.

That turned into a trial of another sort—no less infuriating, and equally avoidable.

Suddenly, Bea couldn't help but smile at the idea of being bracketed by womenfolk—it meant Pa's plan worked. Not in the way he'd wanted, but at this point Bea would claim any victories she could find for her family.

The Darlyns might finally succeed in driving back the men, but not because Bea's skills frightened them. No, if the TallGrass bachelors kept their distance this Sunday, it would be because they couldn't get through the throng of scandal-sniffing women!

Her smile fell when she heard loud sniffing of an entirely different sort coming from behind Pa's door, followed by the rumbles of a suppressed cough.

He shouldn't have oiled the wagons. When worrying did no good, Bea resorted to tracing problems back to their cause. Partly so she could avoid future pitfalls, but partly because it felt good to find something to blame. In this case, she found fault with the turpentine in the oiling mixture. Linseed oil smelled strong and sour, but turpentine never failed to aggravate Pa's condition. Had she known his plans, she would have put a stop to them.

Which he knew all too well, otherwise he wouldn't have waited for me to be plowing the fields before he brought out the rags and set his plan in motion. Vexed, Bea added some honey to the mug before pouring hot liquid over. The honey sweetened a somewhat bitter brew, making it more palatable for Pa but also, Ariel told her, helping soothe some of the sting from his throat.

Just like Bea's understanding of why Pa went out to the wagons helped soothe some of the sting from the results. He'd gone to keep an eye on their new business partners, doing his level best to protect his daughters from possible threat. Bea would have done the same thing. A series of coughs—no longer muffled and quite clearly worse than they had been earlier that week—sped her steps back to Pa.

She cracked the door and nudged it open with her hip, just enough to slide through with the tea tray. Bea didn't need to move far to reach the bedside—once Pa started feeling poorly, they'd shifted his furniture to keep his bed along the wall that his room shared with the kitchen. Farthest inside and closest to the stove, it kept him as warm as possible. Bea set down the tray while he straightened against his pillows.

Unless he remained still, she knew better than to pass him his mug. Only when he felt his poorest did she dare wrap his hands around the vessel and help nudge it toward his mouth. Nor would she fluff his pillows or offer to fetch him another. In return for suppressing her instinct to fuss and fret, Pa wouldn't quibble while she tended to other, smaller matters.

While he swirled a spoon in the liquid, clinking around the edges of the mug, Bea picked up the second cup from the tray, enjoying its warmth as she made her way around the room's perimeter. She casually broke the layer of ice atop his washstand bowl, wordlessly dumping most of the heated water from her mug into the basin.

His slurping sip brought a smile to her face, which she hid by crossing the room to open the curtains. Normally, she frowned on such poor manners, but Bea didn't begrudge her father his small rebellion when it came time to take his tea. So long as he drank it and allowed the concoction to ease his coughs, he could do as he liked.

Especially if it kept him distracted long enough for her to slip down to the barn and make a few arrangements of her own!

"We aren't changing the plan." Grey kept the leather shade aloft, letting the heat waft away and bone-chilling cold seep in to replace it. The view beyond the haymow opening matched his mood.

"Man makes plans, God laughs." Miles eyed the charcoal sky, limned blue and lavender whenever lightning spiked, and did his best to hide his grin. "In this case, maybe the rumble you hear is as much laughter as thunder."

Grey dropped the panel back into place, plunging them into deeper darkness. "No matter what new schemes you're hatching, we roll out today."

"If you want to tell an old man to go to the devil, come out and say so." Miles shrugged into his overcoat, grateful for its weight but shivering to find it colder than he'd been.

"Devil's Lake—though I've thought much the same thing."

"Most any place would seem hellish after the haven we found here." With so little light, Miles couldn't see his partner's expression well enough to attempt more subtle conversation. Besides, they were running out of time. If he'd gotten up and dressed already, certainly the Darlyn sisters would be bustling into the barn any minute.

Grey's pause—a shade too long—told Miles more than the man's answer.

Ah! Miles rubbed his hands together as much in glee as to generate some extra warmth before sliding into gloves. Now they were getting somewhere. His friend wouldn't sound so disapproving unless he, too, were tempted to see the Darlyns as more angelic than earthly.

Though I don't want him to think of them too angelically. Miles's plans for his partner definitely required that Grey's interest in at least one of the sisters sprang from a more earthy awareness.

"It's a mistake, making this place out to be heaven on earth." Grey's delayed response broke through his musings with another intriguing question.

"Mistake?" Miles echoed. He could think of reasons why it would be dangerous to become too contented on the Darlyn farm, but they ranged too far and too wide to narrow down the conversation. But the *why* of it didn't matter nearly as much as the *who.* "For which one of us?"

"Greyson?" A cold blast of charged air accompanied the call as Bea opened the barn door. "Miles?"

She said Grey's name first.

"We're up!" Grey called down as the warm glow of an oil lantern spread through the barn. Shadows licked along the rafters, shrinking back as she lit another lantern and carried it toward the ladder.

"Rainstorm headed this way." She hesitated, as though debating whether to keep shouting up to the loft or to wait for the pair of them to come down to meet her.

Grey made things easier on her. "Coming down."

Miles waited until he heard his friend's feet hit the floor, then swung himself onto the ladder and followed. No sense moving too fast and causing an accident. If the situation warranted, Miles could manage some way to incapacitate Grey and keep him on the Darlyn farm, but he wouldn't try that unless he had absolutely no other option.

"There's a lot of lightning," Bea started slowly, searching both their faces for some sign of understanding—though Miles noticed she spent a lot longer looking at Grey.

"We noticed." Grey folded his arms across his chest as though bracing himself. "Miles and I still plan to load the last of those bones and move out today, but we completely understand if the weather keeps you indoors."

"It wouldn't." Her chin lifted. "There's too much to be done and too little time to finish the planting to let a little rain chase me from the work. Especially when we need the water so badly, I can't see the storm as anything but good for the farm."

Grey's expression darkened swifter than the storm-soaked sky. "You've too much to do, in too little time, if you'd put yourself in harm's way to see it finished."

Miles seized the chance to make a last-ditch maneuver. "You know, I've been thinking the same thing. Seems to me the Darlyns could use an extra hand over the next week or so."

When his partner turned that shadowed, grim gaze on him, Miles's mouth went dry. But now wasn't the moment to lose his courage. "It's not ideal, but if the Darlyns would be willing to teach you how to help with planting, I can hitch the wagons together and take the load to Devil's Lake on my lonesome, then turn right around and come back for the next round."

Hope brightened Bea's face, but Grey missed the encouraging sight. *Look at her!* Miles willed his friend to turn his gaze in the right direction so he'd be inspired enough to change course, but to no avail. Grey wouldn't turn, so he got things backward.

"Works well enough with the wagons empty, but nearly full they'll make a much bigger burden on the oxen and the riggings. You shouldn't go it alone this time." In spite of the practical concerns he laid out, Grey's gaze bored into Miles with the precision and pressure of a drill bit. "Especially with storms blowing about, there's too much of a chance something will go wrong."

"Oh." Disappointment rang through the single syllable, catching Grey's attention a moment too late to make any difference. "We wouldn't want to endanger either of you or make more difficulties when you've delayed your own business to help ours. Much as we'd love to have help planting, it sounds best that the two of you keep together. Storms can cause all sorts of problems."

"So tell me you won't go out plowing fields in the rain." Grey demanded the promise as though he had a right to it.

"Only liars make promises they can't keep, and I told you the lightning won't keep me from work. But today. . ." Worry knit her brow. "It offers a good pretext to keep away from the cold and the damp. If my sisters and I go outside, Pa would insist on working alongside. He's still coughing from the turpentine yesterday."

Miles and Grey exchanged a layered look, full of doubts about how long Seamus had been coughing, as well as the cause behind it, but also brimming with a shared determination to keep the man close to home and out of the storm.

"Aye, the sear of turpentine does lungs no good," Miles vouchsafed. "And if you don't mind my nerve in saying so, it seems your pa got a bad dose some time ago and hasn't yet made his way fully back from it. Would be downright diabolical to put him in the perishing cold of a lashing storm."

"I don't mind your nerve, Miles." She favored him with the sort of smile she usually bestowed on his partner, and suddenly he understood a bit more why Grey'd gotten so smitten with the lass. "No more than I begrudge Greyson's determination to see the job done. But I'll admit, I'd hoped to persuade you both to wait out the storm with us. Pa won't rest on his laurels while we work, and I fear he'll be even more intractable if the other men go on."

She didn't press the issue or plead with them to change their minds. If she had, Grey might have discarded her request as overly dramatic. Clever lass, to leave the decision entirely up to them. Holding back hysterics gave guilt the chance to grow.

"No good comes from being so stubborn," Grey muttered.

"You've never spoken truer words." Miles fixed his partner with a penetrating stare. "I, for one, would just as soon spend another morning here. That narrow incline out of your valley isn't something I'd fancy facing in the rain."

"Oh, no. You mustn't try to take such heavy wagons through mud." She looked properly horrified. "If you insist on leaving today, you'll need to take the long way. Go north for six miles or so. There's a broader, more established path to the left. That means you'll have to go around the ravine, but at least you'll be safe."

He could've done a jig, but Miles made a point of keeping his expression serious. "Sounds like a miserable day to circle around and end up in almost the same place."

"All right, all right, we'll stay." Not even Grey could withstand guilt *and* logic, no matter how stony-faced he looked. "But just through the storm."

Miles prayed the storm let loose enough water to keep the roads muddy through the afternoon. Then, "just through the storm" would turn into another night.

And tomorrow was Sunday!

Chapter 20

He might not deserve it, but Grey gave himself full license to enjoy the cozy circle around the table. The company gave a man something to relish that ranked right up there with strong coffee, the tantalizing smell coming from the oven, and the welcome heat that had almost finished drying his clothes.

"When obstacles arise, it's good to come up with a creative way to correct course." Seamus lauded Miles's ingenuity in becoming a bone picker. "We do the same sort of thing around here, though on a smaller scale. Nothing to turn our world on its ear, just ways to make the most out of the small surprises God sees fit to give us."

"Yes!" Jodie hopped up from the table and returned toting a large Bible bound with cracking leather. She cautiously nudged her mug aside before plunking the Word atop the surface.

Grey might be giving the thing more weight than it truly displayed, but he fancied he could practically hear the thud of it hitting the tabletop. To him, bringing the Gospel to the table doused the morning's enjoyment just as thoroughly as the deluge he'd braved outdoors to get from the barn to the house.

"On rainy days, we make extra time to worship," Jodie graciously explained as she reclaimed her seat and scooched closer to the table. She bracketed the Good Book with thumb and forefinger, gently sliding it toward Bea. "We choose a passage to ponder over and discuss together."

"Together?" Grey choked out.

"Absolutely." Bea flattened her palm and slipped it beneath the Bible, supporting its back even as she opened its pages and flipped forward. "Last time we ended a cycle of turns. This week, we start again. I choose which book of the Bible, Jodie will select the chapter we read for this time and the next, and all of us will discuss which verses spoke to us most deeply from the first half."

The neck of his coat, still buttoned to his chin, constricted enough to cut off Grey's air. He realized he was starting to sound like an echo but couldn't seem to stop himself. "All of us?"

Even me? seemed well enough implied, even if he couldn't squeeze it out after the first part of his question.

"Does it make you uncomfortable to share which passages resonate with you?" Bea stopped riffling through the pages to fix him with a concerned stare. "We've only ever done this as a family, but this might be too personal for some people. Do you all want to proceed?"

Her voice trailed off as she looked at her sisters, waiting for each of them to nod in turn. But it took Miles's nod before her tension visibly eased.

Grey couldn't know for sure, but he imagined his tension visibly increased with each nod. Each one pounded another nail into his hope that someone—anyone—would object to putting this plan into practice today. How could it be that none of these sisters seemed shy about sharing such deeply personal thoughts with men they'd just met? More to the point, how could he protest that it made him uncomfortable when the women were more than willing to undergo the experience?

Share which passages speak to me? Grey couldn't even swallow his sip of coffee. It sat on the back of his tongue, becoming increasingly bitter. It didn't matter what book Bea chose or what passage Judith picked, Grey could already predict precisely what any one of them would "say" to him. Everything in the Good Book brought back memories of how he'd failed its precepts, reminding him how incredibly unworthy he was to so much as sit at the same table as this fine family. He could no more share thoughts on Bible verses than he could give birth to babes.

"We won't ask you to divulge anything you don't offer to share." The entire time he'd been trying to find a way out of the situation, since her sisters hadn't obliged him, Bea's eyes hadn't left him. She tilted her head, half in question, half in signal that she was ceding to his needs—the very portrait of compromise.

At the lack of judgment, and this offer of acceptance, Grey found himself able to swallow again. Once he'd gotten the coffee down—without making himself cough, no less!—he scraped up a smile. "Thanks. It's new to me, so if it's all the same to you, I'll probably do more listening than sharing."

"You've already shared a lot with us." Judith's attempt to make him feel better made him feel even worse.

Mornings. . .meals. . .memories. She was right. He'd shared a lot with this family.

And every bit of it would make it that much harder to leave tomorrow. Grey already knew he'd be reliving those memories time and time again—during slow walks alongside oxen, to drown out one of Miles's monologues, and, most of all, when he couldn't sleep. Men with memories didn't count sheep, and Grey already knew he'd be tallying up things about Bea.

How many times he'd seen her smile, and which ones were for him alone. How many different sorts of smiles there were—a lot more than he'd seen anyone else wear, he felt certain. The number of times they'd touched—even accidentally or because they were helping each other. Then he'd hunt out the rarest ones, when her bare skin touched his, or his touched hers, or best of all, they'd brushed against each other. So far, only twice. They both wore long sleeves and almost always one of the other of them had on work gloves, too.

The list stretched so long, Grey figured he could always resort to counting the categories themselves. Maybe, by the time he'd tallied up all the different pieces of her he'd saved inside his mind, it wouldn't add up to a woman quite so amazing as he thought, and he'd be better equipped to face her when he and Miles came back. He needed to be better equipped—that's why he'd wriggled out of the trap his partner laid earlier, trying to convince him to stay behind and plow fields for an extra week or more. It took Grey aback how difficult it had been to nip that suggestion in the bud.

Staying sounded so appealing.

Which gave him all the more reason to hit the road, just as soon as the rain passed and the roads dried. Grey needed that time to gain perspective on the things he could never have. Hopefully, he'd reaffirm his conclusion that taking a chance on another family couldn't be worth it. That Bea herself wasn't worth his peace of mind.

The many small details that made her so gorgeous could comprise an entire list in itself—a dangerous list. Grey could pretty much guarantee it would keep him up instead of helping him sleep.

It'll probably be my favorite.

"One of my favorites." Bea tapped a tapered forefinger against the flowing script proclaiming *Philippians*, then passed the Bible back to Judith.

Why? Grey stopped himself from asking. He'd decided not to join them, loathe to attempt to explain any personal meaning gleaned from scripture. How could he turn around and ask anyone else to do what he would not?

No one else evinced much curiosity at her comment, so he figured her family already knew the answer. Judith certainly seemed familiar with the material, thumbing through and looking over pages with astonishing speed. After she'd gone all the way through, she flipped back to her selection, then passed the Bible on to Ariel.

"Chapter four," she announced. Her sisters each seconded her smile, giving Grey the impression this particular passage was much loved by the Darlyns.

"Ah, now that is one of *my* very favorites!" Seamus approved, earning grins from all his girls.

"You know you say that every time?" Cassia's question seemed asked more for Grey and Miles's sake than to get an answer from her father, explaining everyone's amusement.

"When it comes to the most wonderful things in life, there's always room for another favorite." Seamus wagged his finger at each of his daughters. "You ought to appreciate that your old pa ranks scripture chapters and his children as the best parts of his days."

Grey couldn't agree about the scripture, but he couldn't help but grin right along with the girls. He didn't think he'd ever met a man more unabashedly adoring of his family—nor a family who deserved it more.

"Pa can never decide on a favorite." Ariel stretched across the table to pat his hand, the fond gesture keeping the statement from sounding stern.

Down the table, Miles chortled. "We found that out the other day. He mentioned his favorite daughter, so Grey and I had to ask which one of you he meant."

"And I told you the same truth I've been telling everyone for years." Seamus paused for a spate of coughs, but this one seemed shorter than some of the episodes from earlier in the morning. He drank more tea, then looked around at his girls. "You're all my favorites, for different reasons. And the same goes for many, many chapters from the Word. So I'll ask a blessing over our studies, Ariel will read aloud Philippians four, up to verse. . .nine is a good breaking point."

While Seamus asked guidance and blessing over their study of the scripture—and gave thanks for the much-needed rain—Grey racked his memory. Philippians, chapter four. . . Something about the reference tickled a recollection, but he couldn't quite call it forth. It'd been too long since he'd picked up a Bible or listened to a lesson. For the first time, that bothered him. Not because he hadn't added to his knowledge or attended those missed Sundays, but because he'd lost so much of what he'd already learned.

Compared to the other things he'd lost, old lessons weren't all that important. But it bothered Grey. This feeling of being less than he once was. . .it left him restless. He shoved the feeling down and devoted his attention to Ariel's reading, searching for distraction. Things that couldn't be changed weren't worth wasting time or thought.

"Finally, brethren, whatsoever things are true, whatsoever things are honest, whatsoever things are just, whatsoever things are pure, whatsoever things are lovely, whatsoever things are of good report..."

That's why Philippians chapter four sounded so familiar! Grey tilted back his head and rolled his shoulders, as relieved as though he'd taken off the weight of a heavy pack. As soon as Ariel started the verse, the rest rolled through his memory, and he almost mouthed the rest of the exhortation right along with her.

"If there be any virtue, and if there be any praise, think on these things." Ariel didn't stop reading, but at that point, Grey stopped paying attention.

True, honest, just... He ticked off the qualifications, matching them against the woman who'd taken over so many of his thoughts. *Pure, lovely, of good report... Yep. Every single one applies to her.*

Grey looked to where Bea sat across from him, one hand folded around her father's, the other cupped around the warmth of her mug. It seemed to him as though the list fell short of the mark when it came to her good points, but he figured that's what the phrase "any virtue" was intended to cover.

How about that? He raised his own mug for a long sip, finding the coffee sweeter at the bottom of the cup. No dregs here. Only confirmation that the most powerful source of sweetness sometimes took a little longer to be enjoyed.

But he'd have more than enough time to enjoy the sweet memories on his way to and from Devil's Lake. Grey hadn't realized he'd be doing so with the Bible's blessing—well, on most counts. Some of his thoughts certainly stepped over the "pure" line, but for the most part, musing on Bea would give him plenty of good things to occupy his mind.

Too many people occupied the house. Jodie fought not to fidget, but knew she failed. All too often she caught her fingers drumming, her toes tapping, or her heels shuffling. Whenever that happened, she covered the movement by crossing the room and peeking past the curtains, hoping to catch a glint of sunlight through shifting clouds.

Shameful, for a farmer's daughter to wish for good rain to go somewhere else—especially in a time of drought!—but she itched to get out of the house.

Except it wasn't really the house. She'd weathered much longer stretches inside with her family, but somehow this single morning seemed more constraining than months of snow. Two more people shouldn't crowd the place so badly, but it felt as though she all but tripped over Greyson no matter which way she turned or what she tried to turn her hand to.

Literally tripped. And with such close quarters, no one could miss her flailing and fidgeting and all-around foolishness. She did better outside, where the space soothed her soul and offered enough room to absorb a few of her mistakes. Jodie might never be graceful, but going outside offered a tomboy like her a little extra grace.

Grace she obviously needed if Grey were to see her as anything but a klutz. . .

Wistful wishes drummed a tattoo inside her skull, keeping time with the sound of rain striking the roof. Jodie's temples thrummed in time with the beat, distracting her so much that she missed the first signs when the rain started slowing.

Cassia noticed first, her head rising from the miniscule stitches of her embroidery. Then, almost like a colony of prairie dogs popping their heads from their holes, the others followed suit. One by one, until everyone stopped what they were doing and sat perfectly still, heads tilted and ears cocked to catch even the slightest sound.

When the insistent thrumming dropped down to intermittent splashes, Jodie rocked forward to her feet. Slowly, almost as if she were superstitious and feared that sudden movement might call the rain rushing back, she made her way to the nearest window.

She carefully peeled back the curtain. Fog from the warmth inside filmed the window, and she leaned close to rub her cuff along the cool, slightly bumpy surface of the glass. Jodie held her breath, both in hope and to avoid fogging the glass again as she peered through it.

Things didn't look nearly as gloomy as they had even a quarter hour before. Snatches and scatters of small drops struck the water pump and garden, but not even enough to match the steady dripping from the eaves of the roof. Even as she watched, the clouds shifted and roiled, pushed away by an impatient wind. White patches showed amid the pale gray and charcoal, with pure light seaming the edges where the different fabrics joined together.

Everything shifted again, and a brilliant beam of sunlight struck forth, hitting what few haystacks remained standing behind the barn. Jodie's breath rushed forward in an exultant exhalation, and she hurried to push back the curtain so everyone could share the sight.

"Rain's passing!" She didn't bother trying to hide her excitement any more than anyone else tried to hide theirs.

Amid a rush of bodies toward windows, only Pa sounded a note to dampen their joy. Ariel hurried to fetch him a fresh pot of hot tea as a spate of coughs nearly shook him from the sofa. A sideways motion of her head kept the rest of them from flocking to him. Such attention could only embarrass him before their guests.

"Water's so scarce, seems almost a waste to keep making tea," Pa grumbled, repeatedly clearing his throat. "We need that rain, and 'tis sorry indeed I'd be to hear that any of my girls were wishing it away!"

"Don't blame your daughters." Greyson stepped into the conversation—and the line of fire. "I've never yet managed to make so much as a dent in a drought or a storm in all the times I've tried, I doubt TallGrass weather responds to wishes."

"True enough." Pa relaxed and folded his fingers around the mug as though trying to draw every scrap of warmth into his bones. "As soon as I'm done with this, I'll go see how badly the wagons fared. They'll need another coat of linseed and turpentine. Maybe if I wipe them down, I can start it today."

"You can't!" Jodie protested right along with her sisters—a well-worn chorus, if not a welcome one.

"What are you four goin' on about?" Pa gulped the last of his tea and surged to his feet. "You all act as though—"

Grey stepped in, smooth and sweet as fresh-turned ice cream. Only difference was that Jodie felt like the one melting as he appeased Pa. "As though I mentioned that I hoped to enlist your advice for a small project while the mud dries."

"What project?" This time, Jodie spoke along with Pa. *At this rate, Grey will think I don't have a thought in my head that isn't an echo. . . .*

"A surprise is spoiled by the telling," Miles admonished.

"You ladies go about your day, but leave the barn to us menfolk for a short while." Grey shrugged into his overcoat and passed Pa and Miles theirs.

Jodie couldn't help but notice that Miles didn't look very thrilled to be ushered out into the chilled damp. The set of Grey's jaw—boasting a manly shadow that sent a little shiver through her shoulders—spoke of determination. Only Pa, ambling with a slight swagger, seemed enthusiastic at the prospect of an afternoon's extra work.

Her eyes narrowed when she spotted Grey peering around the farmyard with unwarranted interest. Was it possible Grey didn't have a project in mind, and only stepped in to keep Pa from pushing himself too hard?

Jodie felt melty all over again. She gave it a little time before she edged away from her sisters and crept toward the barn.

All around came the sound of water dripping and dribbling from eaves and fences, and the strengthening songs of birds as they emerged from cozy nests. She breathed deep, loving the way the crisp air chilled its way down her throat and tickled her lungs, but wishing it warmed swiftly so Pa wouldn't be bothered by the sensation.

From the sounds of things, he wouldn't be. Grey kept them in the barn, where the hay insulated and the livestock generated enough heat to keep the air warm and cozy. Mutters rumbled through the walls, too low to distinguish words. The rasp of a saw competed with the metaling kiss of hammer and nail.

What are they building? Jodie tried to nudge the door open a smidge—just enough to glimpse what was going on without capturing any attention—when a hand smacked against the wood and pushed the other way.

"Do you want to ruin the surprise?" Cassia hissed.

"Not for anyone else," Jodie grumbled. "I just wanted to know."

"We all do—and we all will." She grabbed Jodie's elbow and steered her back toward the house. "Later."

For the rest of the afternoon, all three of her older sisters watched her like a hawk, dispelling any hope of wandering back toward the barn. At least she had the run of the yard again. Jodie didn't mind watering, feeding, mucking under the chicken coop, or helping spread her gatherings over the vegetable garden. Doused by the rain, the fertilizer didn't reek nearly as badly as usual, and she knew it would help seal moisture into the soil.

She did mind being sealed inside the house when Miles bustled outside and asked them to stay indoors until Pa came to fetch them. It felt as though they waited for ages. This time, Jodie didn't try to stop her fidgeting. If she didn't move around, she'd burst through the door just to keep from going mad. Finally, Pa threw open the door and led them to the hog pen.

Where Grey and Miles stood, side by side, obscuring the corner nearest to the barn. They waited until everyone hushed and stilled, then moved to the side, flinging their arms forward in a dramatic dual flourish to highlight. . .

The corner of the hog pen.

Jodie squinted, spotting some extra wood running along the top of the fence, toward the trough. If it hadn't been a lighter, less weathered color than the rest, she would have missed it entirely.

"Oh!" Bea rushed forward to peer over the fence, reaching out to trace some of the new wood. "You didn't need to do this! But thank you!"

She positively beamed at what looked like a narrow, shallow trough leading down to the main one. Bea even patted the thing!

"It's like a flume." Ariel tilted her head to the side the way she did when evaluating something.

Cassia tilted her head to the side the way she did when trying to figure out what Ariel meant. "What's a flume?"

"They build flumes to help with logging. Much larger ones, of course, and pipe water down them, so the water runs down the mountain and will carry the logs with it." At Ariel's explanation, Jodie finally understood the purpose of the addition.

"Is this so we can feed the hogs, too?" She shouldered her way forward for a closer inspection. "We can pour the slop in here, and it'll flow down into the trough without us needing to enter the pen!"

She didn't even care that she'd answered her own question. "It's brilliant!"

"Simple enough to knock together." Grey shrugged off their accolades but couldn't hide his grin. "Much simpler than trying to get in and out of the pen in one piece!"

They all chuckled at that. "Good idea. Should have thought of it ages ago, when the pigs started outnumbering my daughters."

"Ah, pigs will always outnumber beautiful lasses." Miles waggled his brows. "Beware those on two hooves more than these portly fellows!"

Jodie sobered at the truth of that. The TallGrass bachelors needed several lessons in how to behave. Too bad Pa's idea of demonstrating their skills hadn't done any good. "Hamlet, Brutus, Volumnia, and Porktia are better behaved than most men around here when it's time to tuck in."

"What were their names?" Grey turned the full force of that golden gaze on her, making her breath hitch.

"They're all named after Shakespearean characters," Bea explained when Jodie didn't get her breath back in time. "Ariel dredged them up from her excellent memory."

"We started with Hamlet—which seemed obvious," Ariel admitted. "Then it became a challenge."

"Other than Hamlet, I can never remember what plays they're

from." Cassia tapped her chin. "What were they?"

"Brutus and Volumnia are from *Coriolanus*—a play that takes place in ancient Rome."

"Brute. . ." Miles grinned. "And voluminous, or something like it. You chose names that fit hogs."

"I could've sworn Jodie said 'Porktia.'" The fact that Grey listened closely enough to pick up on the syllable swap helped Jodie breathe again.

"Yes. I chose that one. It's actually Portia, so it needed a little changing." The words poured out of her in a rush. "From *The Merchant of Venice*. She's one of my favorite characters."

"Why's that?" He actually sounded interested.

"Because she's smart enough to choose her own husband and even outwits all the lawyers and creditors to save a man's life." Jodie paused. "And I liked her even before I knew we had our own creditor to outwit."

"Sounds like a strong woman." Miles gestured toward Jodie and all her sisters. "Cut from the same cloth as the Darlyns."

I hope so. Jodie trailed along as everyone moved toward the house for a special treat of hot cocoa. *I think I'm clever enough and stubborn enough, but if I'm going to be like Portia, I'll need to get a lot wiser!*

Portia knew better than to moon about over a man she couldn't have. Instead, she devoted her efforts into catching and keeping the one she wanted.

A wise woman, indeed.

Chapter 21

Wisdom was promised to those who turned in early and rose with the sun, but Grey thought his partner's tactics might change people's minds. Miles made sleeping late into a strategic art form, banking on a good night's sleep to soften Grey's irritation. Failing that, Miles still avoided unpleasant conversations by the simple expediency of sleeping through them. Grey couldn't be entirely sure, but he put the odds at ninety to ten in favor of Miles pretending to fall asleep last night. The ten percent leeway came only because those snores of his sounded awfully convincing.

Grey didn't doubt for a minute that Miles manipulated things to prolong their stay at the Darlyn farm and that he'd been avoiding the discussion every time they had a moment in private. Granted, yesterday's storm stole a significant bit of time, but not so much they couldn't have left in the afternoon if Miles hadn't been lollygagging. It drove Grey half mad, deprived of his chance to put this place behind them, then denied any opportunity to vent his spleen about it.

But though he'd gone to bed angry and expected to awaken the same way, a good night's sleep softened Grey's ire. His cushion of straw kept him surprisingly cozy through the night and even now, after the barn doors had been opened and closed multiple times. It was a far cry from trying to slide out of a dew-slick or frosted-over bedroll, maneuvering to keep his behind dry while forcing half-frozen feet back into his boots. Bunking under the wagon cut back on the cold and damp but kept a man too cramped for comfort.

Grey gave a mighty stretch, allowing himself to fully appreciate his spacious accommodations. He might as well relish these comforts for as long as they lasted because he had the feeling he'd find more to miss than he expected. *Just one more morning.*

For now, there seemed little use getting steaming mad over Miles's tactics, no matter how underhandedly effective they'd proven. Grey'd bitten his tongue and gritted his teeth through the past couple days, watching his partner deliberately waste daylight. He'd dawdled and chatted, slept in and slow-chewed his way into a day's worth of delays until Saturday evening—when the sun set on Grey's dwindling hopes that they'd leave before having to navigate another Lord's Day. Before he'd have to explain to Bea and her family why he never went to church.

Church! Grey bolted upright, his slumber-soaked brain awakening along with his wrath. How could he have allowed himself to be lured into such complacency? Miles's machinations didn't just mean an extra night in the warm hayloft or another day with the Darlyns. It meant stepping into a church for the first time since his wife's death.

After he'd missed Alice's memorial, he'd determined that attending any other, lesser, church service further insulted her memory. No mere sermon merited more attention than his wife's passing, thus no services were worth attending.

He'd held firm to that logic for two years, but today would end his stubborn streak. No matter how serious his shortcomings, they wouldn't shadow the Darlyns' good name.

Light spread through the barn as the door opened, prompting Grey to abandon his cozy nest and scramble into his clothes. He moved as silently as possible, loathe to awaken Miles or startle Bea. He didn't need to glimpse the woman's face to know who moved about below, quietly and competently caring for the livestock. Grey descended the ladder only to be rewarded with the proof. And what pretty proof it was.

The soft morning sun sought out Bea Darlyn, kissing her upturned face with enough light for Grey to appreciate her beauty anew. No matter that she stood in a barn and conversed with horses. Nothing detracted from her allure.

Grey drank in the sight of her with greedy gulps. When she spotted him, her eyes widened with surprise, and Grey couldn't resist peering even more closely to see their color. The shade eluded him, the barn too dim for that final detail. When he saw her surprise ebbing away, Grey regained enough sense to greet her.

"Good morning."

"Good morning. Did Marco, Polo, and I awaken you?"

"No, I was awake." He reached up to pat one of the horses. "Marco and Polo? You named your team after the explorer?"

She visibly brightened. "Have you read his travelogue?"

"Years ago." He racked his brain to recall the particulars but was distracted by the way her lips tilted in amusement. "Fantastical stuff."

"Absolutely! So many wonders that most of the world never knew, now long gone. But he preserved it for us on the page. I read, and it's real again."

"I seem to recall something about birds big enough to hunt elephants by picking them up and dropping them from great heights."

Gruesome passage, now that he said it aloud. Of all things, why did he remember the elephant-eating birds? No wonder she was frowning at him!

"Marco didn't claim to actually see the giant white eagles, and it's an ancient legend. *One Thousand and One Nights* calls them *rokh* birds in the tale of 'Sinbad.'"

"Sounds like I should read it again." He shrugged. "He described plenty of customs, beliefs, and legends from the places he visited."

"That's why people of his own time didn't believe it. They thought his account was fiction. Later, when more merchants traveled, they confirmed his writings." She made an expansive gesture, eager once again. "All true, and almost none of it appreciated!"

"To me, that's the most believable part of his story," he pointed out. "Something ordinary folks and epic adventurers have in common."

The bright gleam of Bea's excitement dimmed. "Grand adventures aren't for everyone."

"No?" He tried to tease her smile back. "Why give your horses such exotic names if you weren't planning a few exploits?"

"That's exactly why I gave them the name." She stepped past him and propped the shovel against the stall.

Unable to think of a response, Grey watched as Bea stroked the noses of both horses at once, crooning for them to come closer. For one mad moment, he envied the horses. The lucky beasts sidled over until they stood shoulder to shoulder. Close enough for Bea to slip her arms under their chins and lean forward, embracing the team.

"We won't circle the globe, Marco, Polo, and I. But together, we cover a lot of ground. Especially during spring planting!"

When she withdrew from the hug, her wistful smile wrenched him. How many women pushed a plow without complaining? How many of those looked past the horse's backsides blocking their way and found something to smile about?

Grey stared after her as she crossed the barn. Beatrix Darlyn might never explore the far-flung reaches of the earth in search of adventure. But if she wanted to discover a one-of-a-kind wonder, she need look no farther than her mirror.

Bea peered at her reflection, fighting an unfamiliar—and all too feminine—surge of despair.

Brown as a berry. The saying never made much sense, since Bea never saw a brown berry before, but not even the flickering flame of her lamp softened her sun-browned skin. She smoothed her fingertips across her cheekbone, suddenly aware that all the hours spent out-of-doors were writ plainly upon her face. Sadly, that "plain" might be the best term for the results.

Oh well. At least her freckles hadn't cropped up—though she owed Cassia's lemon face cream for that minor mercy. Bea turned her head to the side, wondering whether her sun-bronzed skin made her lips too pale, then noticing for the first time that her lashes had lightened. They'd always been long, and she'd never been vain over them, but this morning they didn't seem so long as before. The tips weren't dark and dramatic anymore—perhaps they'd been bleached by the sun?

Bea's lips tightened. The reverse should hold true. The harder a woman worked, the better she should look for all her efforts. If there were any fairness in the world, sunshine would fade spots and darken a lady's lashes so she sported a dramatic, eye-enhancing fringe.

Not that her eyes offered much to enhance. Not Jodie's changeable gray-green jade. Not Ariel's delicate shade of silvery seafoam. Not Cassia's bold, flashing emerald. Bea hadn't been blessed with any of those beautiful colors. She'd inherited Pa's steady and ordinary hazel.

It suited Pa, but Pa's eyes held a habitual twinkle that spoke of merriment and mischief. On him, hazel was always alight with a warmth that welcomed conversation and confidences. But for Bea? Especially when seen beside her sisters' more exotic examples, hazel seemed plain. Maybe. . .frumpy.

She looked closer, searching for anything to refute her frumpiness but finding precious little. Even her hair, pulled back into its customary bun, no longer seemed simple or elegant. This morning it looked old-fashioned and unlovely, as though her hair deserved nothing better than to be hidden beneath a sagging bonnet.

In spite of herself, Bea drew closer to the washstand mirror. She forced herself to stand straight and look ahead until she saw something positive.

After an absolutely disgracefully long stretch of time, the only good point she uncovered was gratitude that she couldn't see any lower than her neck. The longer mirror attached to the wardrobe would present a more complete—and completely disheartening—reflection of her lackluster charms. She knew without needing to look down that her Sunday best, once a vibrant marigold that seemed almost too ostentatious for church, dimmed to the dull, hollow shade of old straw.

The elbows were worn too smooth, so in certain lights they seemed to shine. Once heavy and well weighted, the fabric held up against heavy wear, stiff enough to offer some construction and concealment. Now, well worn and wrung out with too much use and too many washes, the fabric fairly wilted, following the lines of her undergarments instead of holding its own shape. No longer marigold, no longer standing proud, Bea's best dress drooped.

She didn't need the mirror to confront her with the fact. No more than she needed a mirror to confirm that her sisters inherited whatever beauty the Darlyn line had to offer. Facts weren't worth wailing over, but somehow old truths held fresh horror after hearing Grey so easily decide against staying.

Golden eyes, their color more compelling than any cloth on earth, flashed through her mind before she pushed back thoughts of Greyson Wilder. No sense wanting to impress a man who'd be leaving. Only a fool would waste time wishing he'd stay longer.

I'm already a spinster. I won't play the fool, too. Bea lifted her chin and turned away from the glass.

Only to find herself under even more intense scrutiny.

Chapter 22

All three of her sisters clustered behind her, gaping. Even Cassia abandoned her own ablutions to gawk.

"Are you all ready?" Bea pressed her smile into service, trying to stave off any questions. "Early, even! That's a first."

"That's not the only first," Jodie marveled. "I don't think I've ever seen you spend that long in front of a looking glass."

"What were you looking for?" Cassia wanted to know.

Change. Bea didn't share the first answer that came to mind—or the second. *Assurance that my best years aren't all behind me.*

Instead, she turned the question back on her sister. "You've more experience with looking glasses than I do. What are you looking for?"

"Things to improve, of course." Cassia didn't think twice.

"Well then, I found them."

"There's always room for improvement," Ariel soothed, hearing the chagrin behind Bea's half-hearted joke. "Fortunately, your appearance offers far more to celebrate than to shore up."

Bea fought the urge to glance back at the glass. Its message wouldn't have changed in the past few moments. Love didn't always reflect reality.

"It would depend on what you're trying to celebrate." If even Cassia couldn't find anything redeeming about her appearance, it counted as a lost cause.

"That Bea is beautiful, just the way she is!" Jodie rushed to her defense, moving to loop an arm around her waist.

176

"Who said she wasn't? Bea's been blessed with a fine figure, clear complexion, and a host of other assets she keeps hidden." Cassia began to circle her older sister—a swift, sleek cat with its sights set on a rather slow mouse. "It wouldn't take much to fix that though."

Jodie glowered. "She doesn't need any fixing up, Cassia. If the other men around here haven't noticed her, don't bring Bea to their attention. They don't need any extra reasons to try and separate us!"

I'm not the sister they'll see as marriage material. But Jodie wouldn't be reassured by the prospect of losing Ariel and Cassia. Bea reached down and pried Jodie back, then stooped down a smidge to look her in the eye. Bea sought for the right tone, a blend of reprimand and reassurance. "You know better than that, Jodie."

"Not with all those men ogling the three of you during their visit! Not with Bea standing up in front of the entire town for the shooting match, so all those men get another good, long look!" she burst out. "You're all old enough to marry and move on—I'm the only one who isn't ready for a husband. I'll be the one left behind!"

"Jodie!" Ariel looked upset, as did Cassia. "Nothing will change the fact that we're sisters. We'll always be close to each other."

"Besides, who says we're all ready for husbands?" Cassia demanded. "I say none of us is ready until we meet the right man. I don't know about you, but I'm not sure any of us has managed that."

Jodie gulped back a big breath and pulled herself together. "Really?"

The rest of them variously shrugged, shook their head, or looked puzzled. To Bea's eyes, Ariel's shrug seemed a smidge halfhearted, and Lionel Fuller floated to mind again. For now, Bea pushed the notion aside. "I don't know what the future holds, but I think it's safe to say none of us is jumping ship just yet. Stop your fussing."

A few more big breaths, and Jodie summoned a sly smile. "I'll stop fussing if you stop making me think you want to change things!"

I do. Bea shook her head, banishing old wishes along with new desires. "What would I change into, even if I did?" She tried to keep the mood light.

Ariel's frown warned she'd failed. "True. None of your work dresses are suitable, and your summer best isn't warm enough unless you'd wear your cloak all through church. Then no one would see it anyway, so there's really no use."

Not that my summer best is much better. Bea refused to encourage that line of conversation.

"Don't be so literal, Ariel! I meant that I'm not a fairy-tale character. I'm not going to change into a pumpkin or a toad." *Much less a princess.*

"Too late to hide behind tall tales now," Cassia crowed. "And that's what it would be if you said you don't need—and deserve!—something beautiful to wear. Next dress has your name on it, and no arguing about the color, pattern, or style I choose!"

"What makes you think I'd argue?" Bea knew full well her yellow dress wobbled on its last legs because she always debated her way out of a new one. The other girls grew so quickly that they needed new clothing to accommodate the changes. One of her sisters always deserved something special to celebrate the wonderful women they were growing into.

I must've gotten that impulse from Pa, along with his hazel eyes. This time, the comparison warranted a grin. Pa insisted on surprising the four of them with little luxuries, always saying that his girls were the best and they deserved the same in their day-to-day lives.

"You always argue." Ariel rolled her eyes and reached out to snag Jodie. "This time, we're standing together to see you dressed up in something pretty."

"You two give us a moment." Cassia seized Bea's arm and tugged her back toward the bedroom, closing the door behind them.

"No lectures. No explaining anything I do to Ariel or Jodie—it takes too much effort already to keep their noses out of my beauty practices. If you squabble, I'll start asking who you want to impress." Her sister's threat was underhanded, but effective.

Nevertheless, she couldn't allow her younger sister to start issuing orders without at least a token protest.

"Every woman in town is itching to denounce us after last week. Who says I want to impress any one person in particular?"

"Not a person—a *man*." Cassia plunked her down atop the mattress and burst into a flurry of motion. Her sister seemed to have sprouted extra hands as she teased tendrils free from Bea's bun and spun them around her forefingers, coaxing curls from the loose waves. "You've never been vain, but at least you used to do a quick once-over when you expected to see Ben. Then he left for Oregon, and you've scarcely glanced in a mirror since."

"Horse feathers!" Offended, Bea pulled back, wincing at the sharp yank at her hairline, as one of her locks still curled around Cassia's finger. "I use a mirror daily, every time I wash my face and scrub my teeth. Why do you make it sound as though I've turned into some sour-smelling spinster?"

"Is that what you're worried about?" She produced a suspiciously dark, rose-scented lip balm. "Spinsterhood?"

"For pity's sake. Don't start taking things as literally as Ariel does." She would have said more but couldn't speak while Cassia dabbed the balm on her lips.

"Press together," came the short order. Once obeyed, Cassia squinted, then dabbed on some more. The stuff smelled wonderful and felt even better, so Bea decided not to launch into a lecture over any suspected tinting.

Besides, both sisters couldn't lecture each other at once, and Cassia beat her to it.

"Don't tell Ariel I said so, but sometimes it's smart to pay attention to how someone says something. Words are like colors. Cherry and brick are both red, but the shade makes all the difference. Brighter, darker...cheerful, dour. Woman...spinster." She arched a brow at Bea. "You haven't mentioned marriage since Ben. Today you referred to yourself as a spinster. Why?"

Because I've become one? Bea bit her lip and swiftly released it when her sister tutted and reached for more balm.

"I thought I was the bossy one," Bea muttered, fighting against the urge to fidget.

"Ariel may be the wordsmith, and you might be the leader, but I can be clever and give guidance in my own way." Cassia planted her hands on her hips. "Don't limit any of us to just one thing."

"You're right. I'm sorry."

"Two things you rarely say!" In spite of the reprimand, Cassia softened, stooping down to clasp Bea's hand for a moment. "In spite of this morning and what I'm doing, remember that we're all more than the mirror sees—because we're all more than we show everyone else."

Bea squeezed her hand, then let go and watched her sister pluck a candle from the nightstand. "If we're so much more, then why do you bother so much with what other people see?"

"Because seeing yourself at your best helps you be your best to those other people. I should have done this for you long ago." Cassia pinched the burnt tip of the wick and told Bea to shut her eyes.

"Why?"

"No more questions—or I'll go back to the ones you didn't answer, about why spinsterhood is on your mind these days and who you might be trying to impress."

Bea snapped her eyes shut. She felt a soft tug on the tips of her lashes and suddenly understood Cassia was coating them with a fine dusting of soot to darken them. Which meant someone else had noticed the lightening, too.

"Where do you come up with these ideas?" She tried to gloss over her discomfort but pulled back when she felt her sister's cool fingertips briskly rub something along her cheekbones. Bea's eyes flew open and reached out to snag Cassia's wrist. "Is that rouge?"

"I don't know what you're talking about."

Her sister pulled away and tucked a small pot into the private, locked box she kept inside her hope chest. Cassia narrowed her eyes and tilted her head first to one side then the other, as though trying to decide something. Her brisk nod made Bea's heart sink.

"Close your eyes again."

"I don't want to."

Cassia flourished a set of pincers and advanced relentlessly. "Suit yourself."

At the sting of the first plucked hair, Bea's eyes screwed shut and stayed that way until her sister finished attacking her eyebrows and stepped back. "What happens now that my eyes are watering?" she wanted to know, imagining sooty streaks striping her face.

"Keep them shut for another moment." Something soft pressed beneath her eyes then gently flicked upward to remove any excess moisture.

"Open." Cassia scrutinized her once more but this time produced a small smile and a nod of approval. "Much better. By the time we get into our cloaks and meet Pa by the wagon, any redness will have gone."

"Why did you pull out parts of my eyebrows?"

"So they looked more delicate and framed your eyes better." Cassia swirled one hand in a nonchalant gesture. "I do mine and Ariel's, but until now, I thought you'd squawk over it."

"I would've, if I'd been allowed to protest." Bea gave in and fidgeted as Cass opened the door, delaying the moment when she'd have to get up from the bed and see her altered reflection. She couldn't say what she feared more—that her sister's attentions would turn her into someone she scarcely recognized. . .or that they wouldn't.

Ariel and Jodie swarmed in, but stopped and stared when they caught sight of her. This time her sisters' astonishment seemed less insulting and more approving.

"You look different." Jodie's brows drew together, a sure sign of an impending storm. She cast a fulminating glower at Cassia, then reconsidered Bea. Her tone softened in a sort of wonder. "What did you do to her?"

"A few extra curls, some rose lip balm. Nothing much."

Along with sooting my lashes, rouging my cheeks, and plucking my brows like you're preparing a chicken. But by accepting Cassia's assistance, she'd agreed not to give Jodie any explanations. Which, considering the speculative light in her youngest sister's eyes, was probably the wisest course. They didn't need Jodie experimenting.

Bea turned to Ariel. "Is it too drastic?"

Cassia harrumphed from the back of the room, but Ariel considered. "People are bound to notice the difference."

"You look wonderful," Cassia defended.

"Too wonderful," Jodie griped.

"Jealous?" Cassia's guess must have hit home because Jodie's face flamed brilliant red in a matter of seconds.

"Calm down, everyone! Each one of you is beautiful; there's no cause for jealousy." Bea ignored the fact that she often had to suppress a pang of her own when she surveyed her sisters. Instead, she reached up and began tucking some of the loosened curls back into her coiffure.

She couldn't lessen the changes to her newly shaped brows, but she pressed and rubbed her lips to wear away the balm. Bea noticed her lips felt softer and smoother than usual, but the color seemed believable. As Jodie threw a triumphant glance over her shoulder, Bea took advantage of her distraction and swiftly swiped the backs of her hands along her cheeks, then rubbed away the resulting tinge of faint pink.

"I don't want the change to be conspicuous," she soothed the room at large, casting a questioning glance toward Ariel—the only sister who held no stake in the proceedings.

"That'll do. You look very nice, but not so different as to invite comment."

Or laughter.

"Still different, but more yourself. You look nice, Bea, and you deserve it." Her youngest sister scrounged up a sincere smile. "No matter who notices."

Chapter 23

They'll notice if I don't show up. Grey braced himself against the urge to hunker down in the hayloft and avoid Sunday service, same as he had for almost one hundred weeks now.

But Alice would never have approved of him avoiding church, and she would've broken into one of her rare, gentle reproofs if she saw him turning down the Darlyns' invitation. The realization wrenched him, strengthening Grey's urge to avoid the entire ordeal—until Bea emerged from the house and dealt his resistance the final blow.

She walked out and Grey just about smacked into the back of the wagon.

He caught himself in the nick of time, avoiding the painful humiliation of stabbing himself in the gut with the back of the buckboard. At least, he thought he had. It was kind of hard to tell because his stomach clenched and his lungs stopped working the second he clapped eyes on Bea. Strangely right, and altogether wrong, how seeing her in her Sunday best made him feel his Sunday worst.

Which was saying something, all things considered.

She barely glanced his way, busying herself with shepherding her father and sisters toward the wagon. In return, Grey barely glanced away. Heaven and hell, to watch her and know other men would, too. A just reward for his many sins, to know such as she would always be beyond his reach.

But not beyond his gaze. While everyone else kept too busy to notice, Bea filled his vision. Not for the future—Grey wouldn't allow himself so much—but for a few precious moments.

More than enough to see she looked more radiant than ever. The morning air didn't hold enough nip to flush her cheeks. Even her lush lips looked fuller and more tantalizing than before. Her eyes looked wider and brighter as her gaze flicked toward him then shifted away just as swiftly. She urged her sisters to hurry as though eager to be on her way—but why?

What would make anyone excited to spend a few hours perched on a hard pew, hearing harder truths? Unless it wasn't the service Bea anticipated so highly. After the service, church presented an opportunity to socialize. Maybe she looked forward to speaking with some friends?

Or a man. Grey blew out an aggravated breath as a clawing, clenching creature shredded its way around his ribs. *What if Bea has a beau?*

The idea that some local swain put that sparkle in her eyes banished any lingering thoughts of allowing the Darlyns to navigate town without him. Grey steeled himself for an unpleasant morning, vowing to keep a close eye on all the women.

Easier said than done. Once they reached town, eager bachelors besieged the buckboard before Grey had a chance to hitch Daredevil to a handy post. Some of them Grey recognized from the melee at the store a few days ago. His fists clenched, first in remembrance of the past offenses, then in all-too-present irritation as one of the men cinched his hands around Bea's waist and lifted her down.

Grey's own hands tightened when the stranger's hands lingered around her tiny waist for a moment more than necessary, and he added to the crime by carrying her too close to his own body. By the time Bea's boots touched the ground, her skirts had slid along the upstart's knees. Too close for comfort—his or Bea's, to judge by her disapproving expression.

That disgruntled look restored some of Grey's equanimity. The instant Bea gained ground, she stepped back and forced the swain to release his grasp.

Good thing. Grey moved toward the pair. He took care not to crowd Bea overmuch but deliberately angled his stance so his boot became a barrier between her and the grab-happy gentleman who had yet to stop gaping at her.

How many men turn lackwit when they catch sight of her? If Grey looked like a love-struck ox, her father would've knocked him upside the head with that cane of his. Since his skull wasn't sporting any soft spots, Grey figured he could rest easy on that score.

On every other level, he tensed tighter than a miser's fist. It looked like they'd cut the timing close—once the women were out of the wagon, the last few clusters of townsfolk disappeared into the church. The tide carried him and the Darlyns inside, and before he half realized it had happened, Grey crossed the threshold of his first church in years.

He scarcely had time to register the fact before he spotted the over-interested townsman trying to sidle into the pew after Bea. Any hesitation evaporated on the spot. Grey curled his hand around the interloper's elbow and tugged in one abrupt motion, setting the man off balance enough to step backward. By the time he righted himself, Grey shoved his way around and claimed the last space in the pew.

Bea dipped her head the smallest fraction in an unmistakable message of approval—and, Grey hoped, appreciation. He removed his hat and plunked it on his lap, tickled to discover that the pew tucked him close enough to Bea that he caught her scent. Every other time he'd passed near a church, his past closed in and carried away all the air in the area. Today Grey breathed deep, filling his lungs with the faint freshness of lemon.

It seemed fitting, sitting in a highly polished wooden pew, sniffing after an elusive hint of lemon. Back when he was a boy, his mother mixed lemon and beeswax to polish the furniture. Fresh. Clean. The smell spoke to Grey of the care that went into comfort, of the often unappreciated effort behind keeping one's world in order.

Before Bea, he hadn't breathed in the rejuvenating scent in ages. Even before the fire—that unkind beast so merciless as to take his wife and unborn son but leave him to live without them—Alice's stomach churned at any strong smell.

Since her death, Grey's stomach churned at anything that reminded him of the loved ones he'd lost and the life he left behind. And almost everything reminded him. Memories haunted every Chicago corner. The sight of a child in a pram sent him to the nearest bench before he fell to his knees.

If Miles hadn't dragged him into his buffalo skeleton scheme, Grey might well have gone mad. Strange, to find escape in such a sad endeavor, but bone picking issued both purpose and penance. The grim work and rough conditions suited him. A man who'd failed to protect his family, then failed to honor their memory, didn't deserve creature comforts or company. He owed no obligations to anyone but Miles, and that was good enough for Grey.

Or it had been, until a buckboard filled with butter slipped him up. Everyone lamented slippery slopes. Why did no one warn against wayward wagons, waiting in front of general stores to bowl over unsuspecting men? Those were the true dangers of the world.

One look at Bea, one hint of her lemon scent, and suddenly his simple life seemed insufficient. He began craving the comfort of a warm home and, even more damning, the warm welcome of a good woman. Such thoughts betrayed Alice's memory in a new and powerful way, giving Grey solid proof that he'd been right to resist Miles's gambit yesterday. If he stayed to help with the spring planting, who knew what he might let himself be lured into? Already he'd crossed the threshold of a church!

At a rickety-looking podium, an aging man with a slight stoop and not-so-slight set of wrinkles led them in a short opening prayer before urging everyone to their feet for worship.

Grey hadn't noticed the piano when he came into the building, and now he searched in vain for a hymnal. He didn't intend to pay lip service to the words, much less sing them with any sort of conviction, but he wanted to be able to follow along. Besides, bowing his head over a book would help mask the fact that he wasn't participating.

" 'Awake, My Soul,' " directed a younger man as he walked up the aisle to join the throat-clearing preacher.

Grey didn't recognize the title or the words, but the melody stirred memories. Grey puzzled over it, trying to remember why it sounded so familiar...but different. At the leader's instruction, they skipped the next verse, and Grey found himself wishing they hadn't leapfrogged. Maybe he might have recognized the second stanza, but the third didn't match his memory any better than the first:

> *In conversation be sincere;*
> *Keep conscience as the noontide clear;*
> *Think how all seeing God thy ways*
> *And all thy secret thoughts surveys!*

It got him thinking how that sort of "welcome" back to church made a sinner want to clap his hat back on his head and hope to go overlooked! Every line made Grey more and more aware of his position as the fraud among the faithful.

He tried to shrug off his discomfort as the piano plinked out a new tune. Grey's ears perked for the song title, hoping he'd know the words to this next one. Then he caught himself. Even if he knew the words, he wouldn't be raising his voice in praise; even mouthing the syllables said he shared the sentiments they sang about. Worship without joy became the worst sort of hypocrisy.

So he kept his mouth clamped shut as the leader mumbled something he couldn't catch and everyone started to sing words that made no sense.

No. Not everyone. While most of the town sang something that still made no sense, the Darlyns' voices didn't contribute to the harsh but happy cacophony. Seamus and Jodie stood stiff and silent while Cassia and Ariel folded their hands, the very picture of patience. Only Bea showed any sort of enjoyment of the music, swaying slightly and mouthing along even though the movements of her lips didn't match the shapes of the syllables sung all around.

Grey stared, trying to trace the softly shaped, silent words. He failed, but he wouldn't have minded whiling away the rest of the service trying to cultivate the skill. Her lips transfixed him, but her eyes fluttered open at a sudden swell of music, ending his fun.

And bringing him back to his senses. No longer distracted by Bea's lips, his brain resumed its duties and realized that the man hadn't mumbled and the hymn wasn't incoherent—it was German! Grey remembered some of the surnames from the melee at the mercantile— Muensch, Braun, and Kalb. Even today, they'd identified the old-timer behind the podium as Alderman. In a place settled so thoroughly by Germans, the Irish Darlyns would always be odd men—and women— out.

The Darlyns would stand out in any setting, but Grey couldn't help thinking they'd find more acceptance and appreciation in a larger, more diverse town. Not that they showed any inclination to leave. Drought and debt inspired redoubled efforts, not despair. Their crops might fail, but Darlyn roots ran too deep for them to seek out greener pastures elsewhere.

Impractical, but understandable. When they'd cut a road into a ravine and coaxed crops from a dry streambed, they'd built more than a farm. They carved a place for themselves amid the unforgiving plains, a home so cozy that even Grey fought a reluctance to leave.

All the more reason to go as soon as possible, before the pull became too powerful to easily escape.

"You can't escape the Lord's will for your life," Mr. Alderman thundered from the front of the church, an eerie parallel to Grey's thoughts as he launched into the tale of Jonah.

Jonah, the reluctant prophet who earned what Grey considered the most inventive punishment ever meted out. Fleeing God's order to witness to a sinning nation, craven Jonah boarded a ship headed the opposite direction. But he didn't make it far before a mighty storm threatened to tear the ship asunder. Jonah begged the crew to save themselves by tossing him overboard and appeasing God's wrath.

A dramatic series of events, but what came next trounced even the most fantastical passages of Marco Polo's travelogue.

Jonah didn't drown.

Instead, God sent an enormous fish to swallow him. The wayward believer survived for three days in the belly of the beast before his prayers turned to promises that he'd make good on the mission he'd abandoned. Only then did God command the fish to spit Jonah on dry land.

As a child, Grey judged Jonah as unforgivably idiotic to think he could outrun the Almighty.

As a police officer, he'd appreciated Jonah's sense of justice. His attempt to spare the sailors by willingly sacrificing himself showed integrity, making him more than a fool.

Later, as a father-to-be watching his wife swell with new life, Grey marveled at the sheer size of a fish that could carry a grown man.

Though Alderman focused on the futility of going against God, he raised a point Grey hadn't considered before. For all the verses of prayer, lament, and praise detailed in the scripture, it wasn't until the final verse that Jonah relented and gave himself to God's will. Immediately afterward, the fish spat him onto land. Three days trapped in the stomach of a fish. Three days of what had to have been an unbearable, sickening stench. Three days of unrelieved, pitch-black darkness pressing around him before Jonah repented.

It bespoke a man of astonishing—albeit misplaced—conviction. Grey started to see Jonah in a new light; not as an idiot who'd fled, but as a man who'd protested his unfair fate and dared to try shaping his own. Grey couldn't help but admire the man's mettle.

Jonah failed—but at least he'd found the courage to fight first!

Chapter 24

*C*oward! Of all the Old Testament tales where God's chosen people chose to follow their own desires, Bea most loathed Jonah's.

The man didn't care if he condemned an *entire city*, so long as he escaped any personal inconvenience. Bea didn't pity hard-hearted Jonah for his three-day stint in the stomach of a whale. The *whale* was more deserving of sympathy! *Poor thing probably suffered indigestion after swallowing something so vile.*

Fleeing their obligations wasn't an option for any man—or woman—of integrity. No matter how unpleasant the prospect, they pushed forward. God granted strength enough for the struggle ahead.

Bea sought that strength for even minor skirmishes, such as the one awaiting her family after service. When the preaching stopped, the ladies' lecturing would begin. Their vexation over last Sunday's impromptu demonstration had festered for an entire week, bolstered by the ruckus at the general store. By now, their ire bubbled over like a long-overlooked batch of sourdough starter—sure to end in a sticky mess that stank to high heaven.

When it came to home-brewed poisons, fermented indignation ranked right alongside moonshine.

Fermented Indignation: Every Bigmouth's Favorite Fodder! The irreverent thought helped Bea smile at the crowd as she led her family down the church steps.

Into battle.

To her astonishment, none of them returned her gaze. Mrs. Muensch and Mrs. Fuller, the two most formidable biddies in the territory, abandoned their long-standing partnership to glower at each other. Considering how close Mrs. Fuller stood to Mrs. Braun—who kept darting pointed glares from her oldest son's head to the shopkeeper's wife—it didn't take much sleuthing to deduce the cause of the rift between them.

Without their stalwart leaders, the younger women shifted restlessly, lacking enough standing to initiate a scene. The unmarried ones—and even a few wives—pretended to mill around aimlessly, all the while craning their necks to get a gander at the new arrivals. Suddenly, their silence made more sense.

Sharpening their tongues on the Darlyns could cut their chances with the handsome new arrival their opponents brought to church. Their dilemma widened her small smile. Between the dissension among the ranks and the greedy gazes aimed toward Greyson, it looked like the ladies were too caught up in their own interests to stir up trouble!

As though summoned by the very thought of trouble, Huber shouldered his way through the crowd until he stood nose to nose with Bea. Since they stood at roughly the same height and he shoved his way ludicrously close, it wouldn't take much for his nose to impinge on hers. His breath certainly did.

Bea grimaced but gave no ground and offered no greeting. He'd twist anything she said, either accepting a nonexistent compliment or accusing her of inappropriate conduct. Instead of speaking, she looked over her shoulder. The motion let her give her sisters—as well as Pa and their new friends—a reassuring wink. It also provided a pretext to alter her stance, gaining precious inches of space before she returned her attention to Huber.

Only to find his attention, while still fixed upon her, had wandered about a foot too low for him to meet her gaze. Quicker than thought, she crossed her arms as a barrier, nearly knocking into him because he crowded so close.

"Your eyes must be failing, Mr. Huber." She used her sternest voice. "I'd imagine they're unable to tolerate light if you have to keep your gaze so low."

His head snapped up, but he didn't take the not-so-subtle hint to step back. Nor did he show any signs of embarrassment at her reprimand. Only anger.

"Nothing wrong with my eyes. You're looking for a reason to wriggle out of competing in that shooting match, and I'm not going to oblige by giving you one." His chest puffed up, stealing that much more of the space between them. "We'll see whose sight proves sharpest."

Bea dipped one shoulder as though the matter didn't merit a full shrug—the better to show she wasn't attempting to "wriggle" out of anything. Besides, she didn't feel comfortable shrugging both arms while she kept them folded around her chest. It might draw his gaze back where it didn't belong, and she couldn't guarantee that she wouldn't knock him over next time.

"Mine." Greyson's deep voice came from so close behind her, Bea almost jumped. When he'd gotten so close—or how she'd failed to notice—she had no earthly idea. "Even from a distance, I can see you're crowding Miss Darlyn."

"And who might you be?" Had the demand come from one of the groups of men clumped around the yard, it would've sounded surly and rude.

Bea would have welcomed surly and rude if it replaced the coquettish lilt of an impertinent miss. Bea scanned the crowd, unable to identify the speaker since she found every eligible female preening, giggling, or blushing for no discernable reason. It didn't matter which of them called out the question when every single one of them anxiously awaited the answer.

Thankfully, they'd hatched a plan to handle introductions. Omitting any mention of their business arrangement with the bone pickers, Ariel's carefully crafted explanations stopped shy of any outright lies. Cloaked with Cassia's easy charm, they shouldn't raise any suspicions, and Cassia needed no further prompting to take center stage.

"Mr. O'Conall is an older friend of Pa's."

"Older" really referred to his age, but no harm done if people assumed that the two Irishmen enjoyed a long-standing friendship. Standing side by side, they seemed so alike.

Pa built on Cassia's introduction, preempting any questions about occupation. "I'm happy to welcome him, along with his partner, as they look into a prospective business venture along the Canadian border."

Huber's squinty eyes swiveled from Miles to Grey, but Cassia steered the topic away from occupational concerns before anyone had a chance to follow up. "You can only imagine how dearly Pa esteems Mr. O'Conall's company."

No one need know that "dearly" referred more to monetary value than fond feelings.

"Though Mr. O'Conall has known him for years," Ariel chimed in to introduce Greyson, "we've only just met Mr. Wilder this past week."

Never mind that they'd only just met Mr. O'Conall, too.

"Mr. O'Conall. Mr. Wilder." Huber offered no welcome. "How long do you think you'll be staying in my town?"

"Last I checked, no one owned TallGrass." Pa thumped his cane as though claiming the ground. "My guests are no concern of yours."

"One of them has no townsman to vouch for him." Huber jabbed a stubby forefinger toward Grey, who fought the immediate impulse to smack it away. "Strangers in the area should concern everyone, and we've every right to ask how long you plan to play host."

"I've some old business that needs finishing back in Chicago." To anyone who didn't know Miles, he sounded perfectly amiable, but Grey could practically hear his partner's molars grinding. "Early morning I'll be setting out."

"Taking him with you?" Huber crooked a thumb in Grey's direction without sparing him a glance.

"I go where I want, when I want." Grey waited for the banker to meet his gaze before adding, "Not a minute sooner."

"You want to go to Chicago with your partner."

"Don't think so." No one needed to know that he and Miles planned a couple trips to Devil's Lake before his partner headed for Chicago. That was their business with the Darlyns, and no one else's.

"Don't think you've got any reason to stay." Huber looked pointedly from him to Bea then back again. "Everything of value around here is already spoken for."

The idea of Bea belonging to anyone was laughable, but Huber's implication that he owned any right to her made Grey see red. His sense of self-preservation buckled beneath an even more overpowering urge. In that instant, he reversed his earlier decision to accompany Miles the next morning. No sense of self-preservation could compete with the visceral imperative to stand guard over Bea—most specifically to stand between her and Huber.

"I'll be sticking around to lend a hand with spring planting. Miss Darlyn extended the invitation yesterday." He lifted a brow at Bea, enlisting her cooperation. "Clear as day that only a fool would give up the chance to stay."

Huber's eyes slitted. "For how long?"

"However long we choose." Bea shifted slightly, closing some of the distance between them to present a united front.

Grey's heart gave a gallop at the sound of that *we*, no matter that she could have been referring to her entire family. Combined with her movement, it made it sound as though she'd paired the two of them. As a team—a force to be reckoned with.

Or to provide a reckoning. While he played the part of farmhand this week, Grey figured he could sow some seeds here in town about how to hire a sheriff. He needed to ensure that the Darlyns were provided for before he hit the road. Funds from the buffalo bones were a good start toward keeping their farm, but money made for one sort of security. The shooting competition offered a more primal platform, a chance for the Darlyns to prove once and for all they had the guts, gumption, and guns to protect themselves.

"Sounds like you'll choose to still be here for the shooting competition next week."

"I never agreed to the shooting match." Bea wasted no time correcting him.

"We had an understanding. Don't try to back out of it."

"It sounds like we have a *mis*understanding."

Huber started riffling through his jacket pockets. When he didn't immediately find whatever he sought, he searched the hidden pockets secreted into the lining of his coat and produced a folded sheaf of papers.

"This ought to clarify things. I wrote up the contract the day we discussed holding a match. Now we'll make it official." Although he'd challenged Bea to the match and she'd be the one required to fulfill any agreement, Huber didn't hand her the contract. He extended the papers toward her pa instead, all but slapping them against Seamus's chest.

"I don't conduct business on the Lord's Day." Seamus flattened his palm like a blade, using his forearm to force Huber's hand away.

"So agree that the match takes place a week from today, and sign at your leisure."

"We'll let you know if Bea accepts your terms." Seamus emphasized his daughter's name, leaving no doubt as to who would make the final decision.

Smart man, to trust Bea's instincts. And a good father, to show such support in front of the entire town.

"If she agrees, we hold the match next Sunday." Stupid man, to keep pushing.

"If Bea agrees and no sudden lightning storms bar our way," Seamus grudgingly conceded. "I won't endanger my daughters."

"Agreed. I'll allow no excuses for missed targets or accusations that the judges didn't have a clear view. If next Sunday dawns stormy, we'll wait for a clear day so everyone can see me trounce anyone who dares challenge my skill."

"Anyone?" Grey couldn't pass up the opportunity to help Bea teach a much-needed lesson in humility.

Huber shook himself like an old bull trying to dislodge flies, but grudgingly agreed. "Yeah. Anyone. You think you got a shot, you compete. Ten-dollar prize for the victor."

"I won't be shooting for the money." Stepping forward, deliberately crowding the thug in much the same way he'd tried to crowd Bea, Grey gave him the steely-eyed glower he'd once worn with his uniform. "Putting you in your place will be satisfaction enough."

Shifting away from Grey, Huber bellowed at the ladies. "Speaking of satisfaction, it's midday and I've a powerful hunger."

"Then I suggest you make haste heading home." When Bea didn't bow to his bullying, Huber pushed harder.

"You won't refuse a hungry man a place at your table on the Lord's Day."

Seamus shouldered his way forward. "We offered you our hospitality last week, and you returned it with disrespect and destruction."

"A mistake." Far from retreating, Huber sent Bea a look so possessive it turned Grey's stomach. "One which won't be repeated."

"Of course it won't! How could you think otherwise?" The honeyed sweetness of Cassia's question could have hidden enough poison to fell a few moose.

Or one overeager idiot, as Huber gave a pompous nod. "Good!"

"We don't repeat our mistakes because we learn from them." In sharp contrast to Cassia's sugary tones, Ariel's strict schoolmarm manner left Huber stunned.

And vulnerable as the youngest Darlyn moved forward.

"I'm sure Mr. Huber will be gratified that we've taken last week's lesson to heart and won't disappoint him with another invitation." Triumph blazing in her eyes, Jodie dealt the final blow. "While we can offer food to *share*, we just don't have a dish to *spare*."

Chapter 25

Ill help with the dishes. Anything still needs scrubbing, I've got the elbow grease." After lunch, Miles seized an apron, knotted the strings into a hopeless mess, and joined Cassia at the basin. Ariel, arms filled with towels for drying, dragged a reluctant Judith forward.

"Bea, why don't you and Greyson go haul out the targets?" Seamus sounded particularly smug from his station in an overstuffed armchair. "May be a week late and a few townsmen short, but no matter. Where your old pa's plans failed, the Heavenly Father brought unexpected opportunities."

Meaningful looks flew among the sisters. Intense expressions and abbreviated gestures comprised a silent language Grey couldn't completely decipher. But he enjoyed watching it play out, particularly amused at how Seamus pretended not to notice any of it. The unspoken conference apparently reached a consensus, as Bea slipped back into conversation with her father.

"We've had enough of the unexpected to keep us busy for a while, don't you think?"

"I think I asked my favorite daughter to set up the targets." Steel reinforced the order. "*All* of the targets."

Ariel edged closer, but Bea waved off any further attempts to evade their father's edict. "Yes, Pa."

"I'd be happy to help." Grey waited until they'd left the house far enough behind to be out of earshot, then couldn't resist asking, "What 'unexpected' situation were you and your sisters hoping to avoid?"

She blinked but recovered quickly. "Who says we wanted to avoid anything?"

"No one. None of you said a word, but I sure wouldn't go against your sisters in a game of charades."

"Wise decision." She chuckled. "As you'll find out soon, we're a competitive bunch."

"They're markswomen, too?" How had he missed that?

"Of sorts. You and Miles will be the first outside the family to see Cassia and Ariel demonstrate their talents." She took a deep breath. "Ariel practices archery, and Cassia throws knives."

Grey didn't try to hide his surprise. "Unexpected" seemed too weak a word. "Markswomen, one and all."

"Not all of us." More relaxed now, she began gesturing while she spoke. "Jodie does more than lassoing and rope dancing. It's hard to explain to someone who's never seen her, and after last week's debacle I doubt anyone outside the family will see it again. She and Daredevil have their own sort of routine, filled with tricks."

"A trick rider?" Grey slowed down at that. "You mean, like the ones with the Wild West Show, who ride standing up and backward and flip and drop in and out of the saddle like it's some sort of wingchair?"

Her laughter burst free with an undignified whoop as they rounded the barn and she opened the door to a narrow storage shed. "We've never been able to describe what she and Daredevil do, then you all but paint the picture without having seen it. She'd be tickled to hear your colorful description."

"Must've taken her years of training." Grey groped for a polite way to ask the obvious question, came up empty, and tried anyway. "Hard to fathom how she talked you and your pa into letting her take up such a dangerous pastime."

Her back stiffened into a line as rigid as her response. "I keep as close an eye as possible on my sisters, and always have."

"Always?"

"As far back as I remember, and more so after mother moved on." She shrugged as though hoping to escape old memories.

Or avoid further questions. His old *dig-deeper* impulse, once so crucial during his days as a cop, resurged with a vengeance. Grey recalled something about them losing their mother before the Darlyns moved out to the Dakota Territory, about seven years before, and he'd assumed the two events were related. It gave a young girl time to grow into the woman of the home, but Bea hadn't mentioned years.

In a world overfond of exaggeration, Grey had yet to hear Bea offer anything but absolute facts unless she made an obvious joke. If Bea said *always*, she meant it.

"When did you lose your mother?"

She edged her way into the storage area, eluding his observation. "When I turned nine."

Grateful she couldn't see his expression, Grey leaned against the wood frame. *Nine? Ten was too young for me to lose Ma, even without any siblings to look after. Bea's eldest—how old were the others when she stepped in to help raise them?*

Her head popped into the doorway. "I can practically hear the wheels in your head, so I'm going to save you the trouble of trying to figure it all out. When I was turning nine, Ariel was seven, Cassia five, and Judith hadn't reached her second year. Now she's thirteen."

Never married, never bore her own children, but a mother for most of her life. The burdens she shouldered so early on would have staggered almost anyone, but not Bea. Far from being stunted by such heavy responsibilities, carrying that weight strengthened her. It explained both her uncommon composure and her constant motion. Little wonder the woman never sat still—she'd been running ragged since before she'd celebrated her first decade!

She's spent more than half her life parenting her sisters.

"That's not 'keeping an eye' on your sisters," he burst out. "You *raised* them!"

Those luscious lips thinned, her irritation compressed to a terse reply. "More or less."

"Undeniably more." Grey refused to play polite and let her casually dismiss the past eleven years. "Discounting the extent of your efforts diminishes the enormity of your success." *And your sacrifice.*

"I don't discount myself, my family, or our accomplishments. My sisters give me plenty to be proud of, as we'll happily demonstrate if you'll kindly carry this"—she shoved a painted wooden target through the doorway, forcing Grey and the conversation back to more comfortable footing—"out toward the haystacks."

"Got it." Amused, he wondered whether Bea employed such tactics as routinely as she made use of the obviously much-loved target clamped in his hands. More than weather marked the wood. Age and exposure accounted for the splinters sticking up around the edges, but that didn't tell the true tale. A wealth of wounds scarred the surface, its impressive array of scrapes, gouges, and pockmarked holes a transcript of various talents. Still more markings lay beneath flaking layers of a paint job that made Grey fight back a guffaw.

Standard concentric circles of white, weathered wood, blue, and yellow narrowed in to a bull's-eye that was anything but typical. There, in the middle of perfectly circular rings, someone had painted a red heart in the place of the bull's-eye.

"Who's idea—"

"Cassia." Bea traced the outline with her forefinger, lips quirking at the whimsy of the shape even as she categorically denied responsibility for it.

"To give herself a bigger bull's-eye?" Grey asked lightly but listened closely. If the sister who threw knives expanded the bull's-eye to give herself a wider margin of error, it behooved everyone to keep well out of the way while she practiced.

"She thought it needed a feminine touch." Bea kept a straight face, but he heard the smile in her voice. It made him smile in return.

"None of the Darlyn women need worry that anyone will mistake them for men. You may be independent, intelligent, and even intimidating with weapons in your hands, but that doesn't lessen your femininity."

"I'd appreciate it if you mentioned that to Cassia." Bea huffed as she shoved against her target, driving some sort of stake attached to the back deep into the muddy ground. "Ariel, too. She worries what would happen to our reputations if word got out."

"Considering the upcoming shooting match, it seems word is already out." Grey straightened the target so it sat perfectly center. No crooked hearts allowed among the Darlyns.

"About my shooting and Jodie's riding, which are plenty scandalous enough."

"I'm not sure what's scandalous about handling a rifle. Everyone should be proficient with firearms."

"In truth, Jodie's riding ruffled more feathers. She wore skirts over her britches for last Sunday's performance, for the sake of decorum. But the skirts made it almost impossible for her to reseat after standing in the saddle, and the britches made it too improper for the persnickety people to accept."

"Fools, the whole lot." Grey eyed the target he'd set up and decided it sat much too low to be of any real use. Plunging his arms into the haystack, he began shoving straw aside so he could prop the wood higher. "Folks who stick their noses too high in the air will step on something special long before they bend enough to see things clearly. No one needs those sorts of people."

"We do. In a farming community, no one can stand alone." Grey couldn't identify which sister spoke, aside from excluding Bea. Her tones held a richer warmth than the speaker. "We come together for harvesting and threshing, working bees and so on. Any one outfit tries to go it alone, they're certain to fail sooner rather than later."

Whichever girl made the admonishment, Grey couldn't deny its truth. As soon as she started detailing the ways a farming community depended on each other, he understood her concern.

Understood, but didn't like it.

He pulled himself from the haystack, yanked the bandanna from his back pocket, and succumbed to a series of sneezes. The straw in the hayloft didn't bother him whatsoever, but straw set outside, soaked and dried in cycles of rain and sunshine, set him sneezing like a bellows. After the spasms subsided, he identified Ariel as the speaker. She radiated a sort of stern disapproval Grey remembered receiving back in his primer days.

"Ever consider taking a position as schoolmarm?"

"I did." Her fine features contracted with remembered rage. "Then Huber demanded I sign a contract saying I would stay unmarried and wouldn't miss a single day of the school year, no matter the weather or the needs of the farm."

"No man should be allowed to make so much trouble—particularly when he's not Irish!" Miles struck the perfect balance between lament and levity, diffusing the tension before it took over the afternoon.

"Small minds make trouble. The Darlyns devise more interesting creations. Like this impressive. . .contraption." Grey made a sweeping gesture to encompass all its parts. "What do you call it?"

"Spinster's Doom." Bea patted one of the wooden support posts, pride in her sisters' achievement warring with embarrassment at its name. Time turned whimsy to irony, its point never sharper than now. Saying it in front of Greyson Wilder, the name felt ominous, like a self-fulfilling prophecy.

He's staying. Like a single wish borne by a blown dandelion, the knowledge kept floating across her mind. During the ride home. All through lunch. While talking over the targets. *He's staying an extra week. Maybe it will grow into something more.*

No matter what busied her hands, soft seeds of hope kept gliding through Bea's thoughts.

Desires every spinster's heart harbored in secret, destined to go unfulfilled. Forever.

It will never grow into something more. Bea ruthlessly crushed those fragile, floating hopes before they could crush her. Between the man and the machine, only one of the marvels standing in front of the barn could spell doom for this spinster.

"Spinster?" Grey and Miles half-asked, half-exclaimed in unison.

"Part of it spins!" Jodie darted forward, her enthusiasm redeeming the name. She lightly rested her fingers against one of the spokes of the old wheel Pa repurposed as a turning target. Twelve spokes sliced the circle into segments, each of which they'd filled with a flat wooden wedge, creating a dozen potential target areas. Plain white—or, at least, white when it started out—peeked from eleven of those wedges, but the twelfth boasted one of Cassia's red hearts—a spinning bull's-eye that whirled into a scarlet blur when the target twirled.

"Surprising." Grey looked first at the wheel then past it to the other components of their odd invention. "But clever."

"Why surprising?"

Grey hooked his thumb through a belt loop and shrugged, the inherently male stance distancing him from any hint of sentimentality. "I figured you'd call it 'Heart's Something-or-Other' to match the bulls-eye, but you took the opposite track."

"I'm not surprised." Miles chortled. "From what I've seen, it makes more sense to expect the unexpected from the Darlyns."

"Imagination over expectation," Pa bragged. "Never a dull moment with my girls!"

Greyson circled their invention, obviously trying to pick it apart and find the function for each part. "How does it work?"

Bea waited for Ariel to launch into an explanation. After all, Ariel understood the mechanics and mathematics of the machine better than anyone. But her sister gave a faint shake of her head.

"Bea, why don't you explain?" There was something significant in the way Ariel enlisted her, but now wasn't the time to dwell on it.

"You'll notice the red heart in one of the twelve sections of the wheel." She started with the most striking feature. "Once Judith sets it in motion and gets clear of the area, Cassia has until the wheel slows to hit the red heart with enough force and accuracy to push the panel back and release the spring."

"What spring?" Miles craned his neck as though trying to see behind the target.

"The spring-loaded hinge holding that panel in place. Once struck with enough force, it snaps back and releases the lock on the pulley." Bea pointed toward the post, standing tall and featuring a pulley system attached to a crossbeam. "The weight drops, the sandbag rushes up, and Ariel has seconds to shoot the rope before the sandbag strikes the top of the beam."

"With an arrow?" Greyson shot a dubious look at Ariel's longbow. "How many shots do you have time to take?"

"One." For all those endless hours spent honing the skill, her sister had no practice fielding questions or compliments. Ariel offered a tight smile and rushed to change the topic.

"The sandbag becomes the counterweight for the trebuchet, swinging the arm to launch Bea's targets into the air."

"Targets?" Greyson stressed the final *s* so strongly, no one could possibly miss the point of his question.

"Yes." Bea figured he could count them when the time came. Offering a number struck too close to making a pledge. Better to let the shooting speak for itself. If the unthinkable happened and she failed to bring down every disc, at least she wouldn't fail to deliver on a promise.

"It took us the longest to work out the catapult portion." Ariel glided over to point out the swinging arm mechanism.

Cassia laughed. "You can't imagine how many discs went flying too far or too low. We baked more clay targets than bread for a good while, until we worked out the length of the catapult arm, the depth of the sling, and so on."

"Every time we altered the weight, it changed the speed of the bag and the dynamic of the entire challenge." Seamus brandished his walking stick in short arcs, then long ones, circling back to the apparatus. "Yet we needed to experiment with the weight until we found a range that consistently triggered the catapult without overloading it."

Jodie joined in. "Especially once Bea caught the hang of it and started asking if we could add more targets! Every time she gets ambitious, everything else needs adjusting."

The Darlyns all talked over one another once they got excited, and for people outside the family, the babble got overwhelming. Greyson's brows hiked toward his hairline, a clear indicator that he'd about hit his limit.

Bea tucked her middle finger and thumb between her lips and blew out a screeching whistle, stopping the ruckus instantaneously. Sometimes the only way to stop a racket was to make a bigger one. Bea rarely used her ear-splitting skill since the girls grew old enough to stop wandering out of sight, but when she did, it worked like a charm.

"What?" Cassia's head spun as far around as it could without popping from her neck as she searched the area for trouble. "What's wrong?"

"Even I'm getting a headache, hearing the group of you talking our guests half to death." Bea softened the reproach with a smile, since the whistle proved punishment enough. "We can chatter after our friends see it in action!"

"From what I gathered, it seems like we'll be seeing the *Darlyns* in action." Miles took care to step back as he spoke. "The target just bears the brunt of it!"

"Better the target than any of us!" Jodie flashed a grin. "So far, we haven't come up with a way to use my roping in Spinster's Doom, but maybe some fresh eyes will see an opportunity we've missed."

What if I miss? Bea gave a mighty swallow and forced her feet to move so she joined Ariel and Cassia. *After all that talk about shooting competitions and marksmanship, if I make a mistake, Greyson will think I'm an absolute goose!*

"Enough yapping." Pa thumped his cane into the dirt. "Ready?"

Jodie rested her hand on the pull lever, prepared to set things in motion. Directly across from the target, her knees slightly bent, Cassia held her knives at the ready. Ariel tightened her grip on the notched arrow, pulled it back, and held her stance with rigid precision.

The tip of Bea's rifle barrel rested against the ground, her grip light and supple against the butt of the gun. Because Bea trained her line of sight in Ariel's direction—and more specifically the pulley system beyond her—she waited until the last possible moment to raise her rifle. Even then, Bea didn't aim it anywhere near her sisters.

Thankfully, she didn't need to. Bea refined her method in slow degrees, aiming first and foremost to safeguard her family. Trial and error, her most effective instructors, proved that she could swing Chester up and around without sacrificing any speed. If anything, combining the upward motion with an arc to the left gave her a broader scope and better ability to track her targets' descent.

At the best of times, she could shatter more than one disc with a single bullet, but she held no illusions that she'd manage it today. Her nerves stretched as tight as Ariel's bowstring.

Pa's yell snapped her attention back to the target.

"Pull!"

Chapter 26

Judith yanked the wagon-wheel-turned-target into a spinning illusion, sending the red from the heart spilling and streaking into a blurred ring. How Cassia kept her eye on the correct section stumped him, but the thunks of two solid sticks proved it possible.

Trying to track the target when he should have watched the woman, Grey missed the moment when she let her knives fly. Now he could only wonder whether she threw the blades overhand or underhand, and if she threw with both her left and right hands. Cassia could have lobbed the first blade then transferred the second from her left to her right for the second strike. Only the slight delay between the surprisingly loud thuds as they hit their mark told him she hadn't thrown the pair simultaneously.

The panel snapped back, springing the post and pulley system's lock. The rope zipped through the wheel channel with a thin hiss, sending the weight plummeting and yanking the sandbag heavenward with astonishing speed. Ariel's arrow streaked by in a blur. It severed the rope with an audible snap, closely followed by the thump of the sandbag striking its target.

Years of trap shooting and target practice in shooting galleries gave him a slight advantage when it came to watching Bea's portion of the performance. He knew better than to watch the release mechanism or try to follow the flight path of the projectiles. If he'd been behind the gun, he would've ordered a "look-see" round to better judge where the arc of the targets would peak and map the pattern of their descent. Then, when called upon to bring them down, he would've transferred his attention to that area, primed and ready before they began to fall.

But he wasn't the one shooting, so as soon as the sandbag dropped, Grey focused all his attention on Bea. With an ease born of practice, she pivoted to the left, raising her rifle in the same swinging movement.

Fluid, graceful, powerful, and sure, Bea's movements snared his interest too thoroughly for him to spare any attention for the target discs sailing through the air. If he hadn't counted the number of shots, he wouldn't have any idea how many of the things she brought down. Three shots, and by the time he looked toward the heavens, he saw nothing more than dust and several broken bits of clay tumbling toward the earth.

Three shots, and the amount of refuse seemed far too high for two targets. He could safely assume three targets, but Grey suspected her skill extended far enough to bring down four discs with those three shots. Had she used a shotgun, he would've given the idea more credence— shot scattered in a wider arc, so bringing down four targets with three rounds became much simpler.

But Bea used a rifle, with solid bullets. No scattered buckshot to widen the radius of impact, no hedging her bets and helping her bring down more marks. Everything she did—and everything her sisters did—relied entirely upon mastery of their respective weapons.

"Amazing!" Beside him, Miles brought his hands together in loud, enthusiastic claps. "You're all markswomen—and more than that, inventors!"

"Ariel used the project to help me learn about math and science." Judith looked pleased to have been included by the "inventor" aspect. "It took a lot of trial and error."

"Gave good times, too," Seamus added. "Not to mention hours of entertainment for me!"

"And a sense of accomplishment whenever we got things to work properly or if we conquer the course." Bea looked fondly over her family. "Together."

An intense longing to be part of that "together" surged over Grey with enough force to make him lock his knees. He pictured days with the Darlyns, tinkering on targets and constantly challenging what seemed impossible. They had a way of making the most unlikely scenarios seem reasonable—like his increasing interest in staying. Grey steeled his resolve to withstand the week ahead. If he eased his vigilance, who knew what alchemy the Darlyns would work against him?

The next morning, Bea woke earlier than everyone, as usual. But when she cracked open her eyelids and spied the familiar halo of pale lavender light around the curtains, she jerked upright as though shocked by a cattle prod.

She never slept well unless she knew her family did. Getting up a few times each night assured her that everyone was safe and sound, so she could snatch some more rest herself.

I slept through most of the night! Heart thudding at the discovery, grateful to find her abrupt movements hadn't awakened Jodie, Bea carefully slid from beneath the covers. A quick look reassured her that her sisters slept on, comfy and cozy as could be. But what about Pa? Bea sent up fervent prayers that her laxness last night hadn't left Pa to battle through a difficult episode on his own.

Cold crept through the woven rug carpeting the wood floor, making Bea's toes tingle. They'd gone numb long before she reached the door to Pa's room and pressed her ear against it.

When she heard a rumbling snort and the rustle of covers as he turned over, she sagged against the frame. So powerful was her relief, she almost let herself slide right down to sit on the floor—but without worry to ward off the cold, Bea became much more aware of it. Luckily, Cassia designed their dresses to be practical above all else, so it took next to no time for Bea to slip into her clothes.

Why did I sleep so soundly last night? And for so long?

Bea frowned and felt her own forehead, glad for the confirmation that she didn't seem to be running a fever. On the rare occasions she fell ill, she managed to sleep through the night to awaken guilty and groggy the next morning. Working herself into utter exhaustion sometimes provided long stretches of sleep, but that wasn't the case this time either. Sundays meant precious little work to tucker her out. Aside from necessary chores, her only activity had been shooting with Greyson and the girls.

Her frown flipped at the memory of how quickly he'd gotten the hang of shooting targets launched by catapult. He claimed he'd come to the field with an advantage from shooting trap in a fancy Chicago gallery that used machines to launch glass balls into the air, but his facility impressed Bea nevertheless.

It also made her itch to visit Mr. Bogardus's business, but she knew better than to hope for such outlandish adventures.

Our new business partners were the appreciative audience Pa hoped for when he invited the contingent of TallGrass bachelors last week. Bea felt her smile slip a notch at the thought of how dreadfully wrong that went— and the gamut her family would be facing next Sunday. With Grey.

He's staying! Bea didn't even mind knowing she had Huber to thank for it—Grey hadn't changed his mind so much as risen to Huber's challenge. Bea didn't imagine there were many challenges Grey couldn't conquer.

From what Bea had seen, he'd easily outstrip any of the TallGrass contestants, which offered the tantalizing chance that Huber would be beaten not once, but twice at his own game. Greyson's high score would make her own a little less conspicuous. But Grey gave them more than good company and an unexpected ally.

His readiness to tackle farm chores would help make the most of spring planting, offering a surprising source of hope—and some much-needed hard work!

The thought made her eager to tackle her own chores. She hurried to the springhouse, letting her nose lead her to the strongest-smelling milk can.

The thinner fluid left after they skimmed away the cream could be used in plenty of ways, but some batches languished too long for anything but hog fodder. A firm shove of her boot pushed the barn door open enough to squeeze through. Jodie might have a point about getting cans with handles, but Bea chose inconvenience over insolvency—even before Huber's unwelcome revelation!

She shoved the big tin pail beneath the chute to the oat bin and pulled up the block, letting a healthy measure of ground oats stream into the pail. She stood back from the dusty, chalky cloud. No matter how hard she tried to breathe through her nose, the scratchy stuff stuck to the roof of her mouth.

The earthy aroma from several scoops of linseed oil meal blended with the sour milk in a pungent scent Bea found strong, but pleasant. She breathed deep as she stirred the thick mixture, then carried the shovel over to let her plow team enjoy a taste and lick it clean.

"Good boy, Marco," she crooned softly once they finished, rubbing their noses and necks as they nudged against her. "Hello, Polo. We've a long day ahead, but I'll be sure to sneak you some extra carrots and maybe an apple or two tonight. This week will bring better days. . .I promise."

For a moment, she closed her eyes and pretended away the worst parts of the past week or so, refusing to let her doubts spoil the day ahead. No dwelling on demonstrations gone wrong, madness at the mercantile, or sudden declarations of debt. . . No sense letting difficulties overshadow the bright spots of the week.

Especially when that intriguing golden-eyed bright spot would be staying!

Grey didn't think he'd ever awoken to a better sight than Beatrix Darlyn, clutching a shovel and crooning to her draft horses. Hardworking, kind, with a streak of whimsy nearly as strong as her stubbornness, she made the smallest things seem precious. She heard him coming down the ladder and favored him with a smile

"Good morning. Is Miles awake?"

He took advantage of the assumed need for quiet and leaned close to answer conspiratorially. "If he is, he's pretending not to be."

Startled, her grasp loosened on the shaft of the shovel just enough to send it sliding downward to thump against the ground. Bea tightened her hold, darting a glance up toward the too-still loft. "Does he do that often?"

"Hard to tell." He relished the tiny laugh that bubbled up before she remembered to stay silent. Grey appreciated the way her sense of humor balanced with her more serious side.

He suspected she took what people said at face value because her own deeply ingrained sense of honesty permeated her view of others. In a good way—but if she trusted the wrong people, perhaps the inclination could prove dangerous. Before the possibility could cause too much concern, Grey recalled the way she'd tried to steer her father toward the more prudent course when striking their agreement over the bones.

Though she'd bowed to her father's wishes and respected his decisions, the fact that she'd spoken up regarding the freight costs eased Grey's mind. Horse sense, business sense, and feminine sensibility wrapped together in one appealing package. Bea boasted more facets than a well-cut gem, but rock-hard strength formed every angle.

As she lost ground to the giggles, her shoulders shook, and Grey swiftly amended his observation. Angles? Blessed with such a feminine figure, some of Bea's finest features came from her *curves*.

"Sometimes I can't decide either." For a moment, her words seemed to fit his inappropriate thoughts too well.

Cursing himself for losing track of the conversation, Grey stooped to pretending he hadn't been able to hear her. "What?"

"My sisters." She raised her voice ever so slightly, lifting one hand to cup around her lips as though to funnel her words to him. "When they were younger, I could sniff out a false snore from half the house away, but now that they've grown, sometimes I can't decide if they're sleeping or stealing a few more minutes to snuggle under the covers."

"Can't blame them," Grey croaked. Hopefully, she attributed the strained quality of his voice as an attempt to keep quiet.

His initial relief that she hadn't somehow discerned the direction of his thoughts rapidly gave ground to a new round of improper imaginings centered around snuggling under the covers. . .beside Bea.

"Why not?"

She really needs to stop encouraging me to explore these ideas. Grey blew out a breath, knowing Bea wasn't issuing any invitations but unable to ignore the way her responses could have been tailor-made to suit his meandering imagination.

"Because we all give in to moments of weakness." As Grey'd been doing more and more often since he'd met the woman in front of him.

"What some call weakness, others call strength." She slowly started toward the other side of the barn.

He couldn't follow her logic, but darned if he didn't follow the soft sway of her skirts—even as she led him toward the massive pail of hog slop. "How so?"

"Overcoming flaws makes people stronger."

"If they're strong enough in the first place to admit any weakness."

"It's a conundrum," she admitted with an impish grin. "Probably why unclaimed opportunities abound."

Grey couldn't hold back a laugh.

Bea raised one forefinger to her lips and raised the shovel upward, reminding him that they'd drawn closer to the loft where Miles may or may not still be sleeping. At his shrug, she replaced the spade where it hung against the wall, bracketed by two wooden pegs.

Grey's hand shot out and captured hers before she reached the handles of the heavy pail. He'd only meant to keep her from lifting the thing, but the unexpected speed of his movements nudged her off balance just enough to make her curl her hand around his.

The clasp kept her on her feet, but judging by the way she went stock-still, the contact knocked them both off balance. Grey couldn't resist the chance to prolong his contact with the soft warmth of her skin. He stroked his thumb across her wrist, relishing the telltale flutter of her pulse before she pulled away.

It took everything in him to keep his gaze fixed on the bucket of slop. Grey knew if he saw her face, her eyes, those lips. . .he'd kiss her.

And he couldn't. Giving in to temptation would leave him no choice but to back out of his commitment to stay behind while Miles went on with the bones. He wouldn't leave Bea in the lurch. She deserved better than that.

She deserved better than him. If he lost sight of that, this arrangement wasn't going to work.

My plan worked! Miles tolerated false modesty in others but eschewed the practice when it came to his own accomplishments.

And getting Grey to stay on the Darlyn farm counted as an impressive accomplishment, even if he had to say so himself. As soon as his head hit the pillow last night, Miles sank into the deep sleep enjoyed by all successful schemers.

Sleep cut short by the toe of his partner's boot digging into his spine.

"Up 'n' at 'em." The boot followed Miles's motions when he wriggled away, jabbing that much harder. "Keep going and you'll hit the ground groaning."

Miles stopped mid-scooch, before he inched himself clean out of the hayloft. He poked his head out of the top of his bedroll to glower at the ungrateful wretch. "Keep your boots to yourself and let an old man enjoy his last morning waking up dry and warm. You won't be the one sleeping under a wagon this week."

"Would've been under my own wagon if you hadn't volunteered me to hang back," Grey grumbled, but the boot stopped bothering him.

"You turned the invitation down so fast you left its seams showing." Miles knew better than to admit he'd planted the seed, but on the inside he couldn't help gloating that they'd borne fruit so fast. Looked like he had a knack for farm life.

Grey scoffed. "Keep your mind on the seams you're about to scramble into so you can grab the last flapjacks before you lose the chance."

Miles bolted upright, arms pinned to his sides by the bedroll. "I'm up!" He scrambled into his clothes, down the ladder, and skidded to a stop before the kitchen door. Miles rubbed a palm over his chin, loathe to let the ladies see his graying whiskers. On the trail, necessity trumped niceties. But whenever he bunked somewhere civilized, he made a point of keeping clean-shaven.

If he went back to shave, every swipe of his razor meant Grey could swipe another flapjack. Looked like necessity won again. Shaving was out. Miles reached up and felt his hair, chagrined to discover competing cowlicks. He hurried to the water pump and slapped a few handfuls on his head, then did his best to slick it all down.

"Quit primping." Grey beat him to the kitchen.

Miles barreled after him, only to find all five Darlyns standing together, waiting for him. Cassia and Ariel offered fragrant platefuls of flapjacks and sausage. Judith toted a steaming carafe of coffee, and Bea handed off a bulging rucksack to Grey, who hefted it up and down to emphasize how much they'd stuffed into the thing.

"Stop your gawking," Seamus chided. "My girls wanted to give you a proper send-off."

"It's the least we could do!" The heartfelt chorus rose.

Cassia added an extra verse. "We were fortunate to find you two the day you stopped in TallGrass."

Looking at all their smiling faces, Miles could only shake his head. "You got that back-ways, Cassia. We're the lucky ones."

Even later, after he'd finished his breakfast and finally set the wagons in motion, Miles almost didn't mind the prospect of spending the next week with the oxen while Grey got to stay. Because he believed what he'd told Cassia and the others; his luck had changed for the better.

Miles only hoped it lasted long enough to squeeze in a good night's worth of cards once he reached Devil's Lake!

Chapter 27

Grey wouldn't go to Devil's Lake with Miles, but some practical considerations kept him from plunging into field- and farmwork straightaway. Hitching all eight oxen together and keeping them moving on pace would challenge Miles during this trip, but the biggest trouble came from sheer weight. The oxen and the first load inevitably created deep grooves and ruts in the ground, a complication usually avoided by leading the second wagon several feet to the side.

Handling both wagons on his own, Miles wouldn't have that luxury. But Grey refused to take any chances when it came to the somewhat narrow, certainly steep incline out of the coulee. The drought worked in their favor, leaving the land hard-packed and dust-dry, but the slow pace of the oxen steadily wore away Grey's patience. He tried not to look too gleeful as he waved Miles on his way and went back to the farm.

Grey's guilt didn't even kick in, easily outweighed by all the times he'd handled the wagons while Miles made the business deals back in Chicago. But even after he'd gotten back to the barn, bones remained the order of the day. He headed for the water pump for a quick drink, then poked his head into the house to let the Darlyns know he'd returned.

"I'll be at the haystacks, if anyone needs me," he called. At breakfast he'd mentioned his plans to finish pulling, sorting, and breaking down the remaining bones.

"Sure you don't want to leave that until your partner gets back?"

Seamus responded with surprising swiftness and vigor, before Grey could so much as close the door.

Why's he questioning the plan now? Did something change while I worked with Miles this morning? This time, Grey pulled his head clear of the door before hollering—the better to snap it shut and be on his way after.

"Yep."

"Ready." Seamus shoved through the other door, the one close to the kitchen, brandishing a ball-peen hammer in one hand and his cane in the other.

Obviously, at some point between breakfast and now, Seamus decided to take a swing at busting buffalo bones. Considering how much he'd protested anyone in his family so much as touching the skeletons when Grey and Miles first arrived, his current enthusiasm was disconcerting.

At least he hadn't brought out the turpentine, like he had in his last bid to keep a fatherly eye on the newcomers. The hammer made for a more direct warning for Grey to stay on his good side, but it wouldn't damage Seamus's ability to breathe the next day.

Neither of them wasted many words for the first half hour or so, which Grey counted as a mixed blessing. The silence suited him, but he couldn't shake the feeling that the longer it lasted, the more thoroughly Seamus intended to break it.

"Why'd you come back?"

"Said I would."

"Hmpf. Never did like a man who dodged questions." The older man swung his ball-peen with more force than needed, splitting the pelvis into several pieces instead of two. "Why'd you say you'd stay on instead of go to Devil's Lake with Miles?"

Two questions, and Seamus honed in on the sort of specifics Grey didn't plan on examining himself, much less sharing. Better to be a question dodger than the dope who handed over answers.

"Why wouldn't I?"

"Not interested in why you wouldn't. I'm interested in why you did."

He thumped the steel head of the hammer against his open palm. "Let's see if a doting father can agree with your logic."

"If you thought I'd harm one of your girls, we wouldn't be having this conversation. You'd have sent me off with Miles before the breakfast bell rang."

"I trained my girls to handle themselves well enough, with the four of them looking after each other as a safeguard. No need to worry about you trying to harm one of them—but I need to know if you've got any intentions toward my favorite girl."

"No." Grey stopped working to meet Seamus's gaze. "And the answer holds no matter which one happens to be your favorite at the moment."

"And why not?" Eyes narrowed, he tapped the hammer against his hand in a slower, heavier rhythm. "Are you addled?"

Since Seamus was so earnest in his attempts to warn Grey away from his girls—and so affronted by the idea he might not need to—Grey managed not to laugh. "Your daughters are incredible women, and any man would be blessed to claim any one of them as his bride."

"Aye." The hammer moved more rapidly as Seamus shuffled a step closer. "But don't be thinking you can sweep one away so easy."

"I don't." The memory of Bea's laughing eyes flashed through his memory, but Grey shook it away. "I won't. Truth be told, I don't plan to marry again." *Ever.*

"You're no lackwit, but whatever you say, grief leaves its mark on every man. That—and not planning to take a second wife—I can understand."

"I figured as much, since you chose not to marry again."

Seamus's laugh held a rueful edge. "Even after I lost my wife, I could never look to another woman. Gwen made sure she could never be replaced."

Seamus stopped handling the hammer like a man ready to work through aggravation, so Grey got back to work. Better that then leaving the opportunity to delve into the reasons why each of them chose not to seek second wives.

Grey knew better than to take on a responsibility he couldn't fulfill, accepting his position as widower for the ending it was. He got a strong impression this wasn't the case for Seamus, who seemed to stay single as a way of keeping the memory of his marriage alive.

"So if you're not angling for a wife, why sign on for farmwork?"

"No sense in a man walking away and doing nothing when he can help good people." Grey ignored the fact he'd kept walking for years before he'd hit TallGrass. "Especially if he's helping hand out some comeuppance. Seems past time for someone to stop Huber in his tracks."

"That's a reason I can't argue against," the older man mused, tackling the task of separating horns from skulls. "Some things need more than time to make changes."

"True." Grey turned the topic to something that interested him. "When Miles and I first arrived, you seemed dead set against anyone touching these skeletons. Today you're swinging a hammer without a second thought. Good to see you let go of superstition."

"Easier to part with superstition than one of my daughters. I'd dig up every buffalo from here to the Mississippi if it meant safeguarding them." The sharp crack of a shattered skull punctuated the statement.

Grey closed in. "Besides, what's-his-name already took on the worst of the job, right?"

"Ben." The look Seamus sent him said he knew Grey hadn't forgotten the name—or the man's identity as Bea's former betrothed. "One I thought worthy, but proved to be stupider than the beasts whose bones he moved."

Grey snorted but didn't press. Showing too much interest now would destroy the fragile balance they'd struck.

"Back in the days I hunted buffalo—before anyone realized we were hunting them to extinction—every man felt justified in thinning the herds. Even when we didn't put the kills to any use besides collecting their hides." Seamus winced, and Grey winced right along with him.

But Seamus already suffered belated conviction over his role in the slaughter of a species. Haranguing him wouldn't help. "Why?"

"Easy pickin's, you see. We figured God made them for killing, since it took so little effort. Buffalo travel in groups—sometimes several herds will come together. Social sorts, so not much surprise to figure out the women led things. All we had to do was find the oldest, biggest female. Bring her down, the rest of the herd milled around like lost lambs until the next biddy took the lead. All a hunting party had to do was keep picking off the new queens until they'd blasted through the whole herd."

"Not exactly a fair fight." Grey bit his tongue to keep from saying more. It hadn't been fair to go after the animals for the sake of railroads, and shotguns and rifles gave man an advantage that "unfair" didn't cover.

"Not at all. And the whole time, we kept thinking how dumb the creatures were, that they'd die before trying to fend for themselves without their queen mother."

"Loyal." Even Grey had to admit that such poor survival instincts meant the buffalo contributed to its own demise.

"Smart. Buffalo worked out something we men still struggle against." Seamus sent a pair of horns crashing into the nearby horn 'n' hoof pile. "Without a woman to hold everyone together, things fall apart."

"I see your point, but you might be taking it too far. Plenty of men go through life as bachelors." He and Miles scraped by.

"They've got mothers. Sisters. Aunts. You can always tell a man who's gone without the influence of a good woman for too long. Loners, if not worse. Though there ain't much in this life that's worse than loneliness."

The words sank in through Grey's ears and sank down to twist his gut. There'd been times in his life when he'd more than scraped by. . . before his mother died, and again while he had Alice. . . .

"Women make the heartbeat of a life well lived. Look at us. After we lost Gwen, Bea became the glue keeping the Darlyns together. Even at such a young age, she managed in a way I never could."

"In a way few other women could, I'd imagine." Easy to see Bea was exceptional.

"Exactly so—and exactly why I say Ben didn't have the brains of a buffalo. He got Bea; she should've been the center of the life he wanted to build."

"Makes sense." And temptation, too.

"Instead, the fool changed the deal. Expected her to trot after him to Oregon and leave everything she loved behind." Seamus hooked his hammer in his belt and uncapped his canteen for a long drink, then stared out at the horizon. "If he'd known what he had—if he'd known her at all—he'd have known better."

"Bea would never leave." Grey knew it within hours of meeting her.

"Never." Seamus pulled his hammer back out of his belt loop and jabbed it in the direction of the fields where Bea worked.

"She's our center."

Three clay discs exploded midair, dancing to the rhythm of Grey's rifle.

"Well done!" Bea finished loading Chester and closed the chamber, ready to take her turn.

"Not so well as you. Clay makes for an easier target than those marbles Ariel tossed for you." He lowered his own smoking rifle to grin at her. "After practicing with you, I'll never see marbles the same way."

This time Bea didn't bother to fight the blush. Heaven knew she'd already been flushed from exertion. And, even if she only admitted it to herself, enjoyment. Grey made a good marksman—and even better company.

"You'd hit them, if you wanted to try." Of that, she had no doubt. "Watch for them to catch the light."

"With practice, perhaps. But your sisters are right about the range—they have to be far enough away that there's no chance the glass or a ricochet will hit someone. Until we've put Huber in his place, I'll practice with targets I can reliably bring down."

"Maybe we'll break out a fresh batch after the competition," she proposed. "In celebration."

"I'd like that."

I like this. Bea raised her rifle and readied for the next volley. *Maybe too much, but I'm going to let myself enjoy it for as long as it lasts.*

And when they trounced Huber, she'd have something more to enjoy. Hopefully the satisfaction of victory would fill the gap when Grey moved on.

"Three questions." He sounded smug, but Bea didn't blame him. She felt smug every time she successfully completed a round and earned the chance to ask her own questions. Their little game turned practice into another sort of competition—with the reward of getting to learn more about her unexpected ally.

"Shoot." She saw him roll his eyes at the pun, but his chuckle meant more.

"Who taught you? To shoot, I mean. You said it wasn't your father." Curiosity sharpened the gold in his gaze to a point almost as dangerous as this line of questioning.

Bea felt her smile fade. "My mother."

"Why?"

Thankfully, Ariel lobbed a set of marbles through the air. Blasting them to smithereens helped Bea regain enough composure to carry on the conversation.

"Hunting buffalo kept Pa away for long stretches over the years. Ma knew how to use a gun, and after she taught me, she felt better about leaving us girls behind when she went to town." *Or to the neighboring ranch, to sneak time with her lover.* Sometimes Bea wondered whether Ma would've gone so often if she'd refused to learn how to handle the rifle. If her surprising knack for shooting had been the final blow to knock her family apart.

Another scatter of marbles hit the air. Reflexively, Bea followed the arc and pulled the trigger, taking aim as if she could shatter old memories right along with the marbles.

"I see." Maybe he did. Bea couldn't shake the feeling Grey saw more than anyone else she'd ever met. This time, he saw that she didn't want another question about her mother and thankfully changed course.

"Keeping in mind that I don't entirely remember the story, if you could choose one wonder from Marco Polo's accounts, what would it be?"

"The Golden Tablet." A way out every bit as enticing as the change in conversation.

"Didn't even have to think about that one." He moved forward as she moved back, preparing to take another turn as soon as Jodie brought more makeshift targets. "And I remember that. The emperor's gift to Marco's uncles—the ticket granting safe passage and provisions."

"A ticket to travel anywhere in the empire." Bea sighed. "Even though the kingdom no longer exists, I wouldn't mind something similar."

"There's an idea. Maybe the railroads should make a universal pass that can be used on any line for a certain length of time."

"Instead of the Gateway to the East, they could sell it as the Gateway to the West." The idea captured her imagination. "An opportunity for adventure."

"Seems to me you and your family make your own adventures just fine."

"Maybe."

"If you really wanted to travel, you would've gone to Oregon." He looked at her intently enough to make Bea uncomfortable. Time to turn the tables.

"Uh-uhn." She wagged a finger at him. "You're trying to sneak in questions without actually having to ask. And it's my turn. Since you're the one with experience traveling, and you're so good at shooting targets and questioning people, I'll have to ask. . . What made you leave the police? It seems the perfect job for you."

Maybe, if she could convince him to think of it that way, he might consider taking on the position of sheriff.

"I liked the work itself. At first, Chicago was pioneering advancements in enforcement. From the first record of homicide cases to John Banfield's signal sources, the force dedicated itself to bettering the community."

"Signal sources?"

"Devices placed on every telegraph pole. Officers held keys, along with upstanding citizens nearby. It took one citizen and one officer key to open a signal box. It gave the police a way to check in to the station house, and citizens the means to summon patrol wagons or ambulances. A badly needed advancement to make the most of too few officers."

"Fascinating." He didn't look very happy with the conversation though. Bea tried another track. "We don't have a single officer here in TallGrass, so I can only think Chicagoans fared better."

"One officer per twenty thousand citizens." His jaw worked. "Counting all of them—even the ones off duty. At any given day, unless there were riots or a major bust, we could expect the numbers to be one of us to forty or fifty thousand."

The magnitude of that responsibility staggered her. "That can't be effective."

"So long as the citizens respected the force, we kept things under control." His brows slammed together, eyes narrowing with old anger. "When the former police chief was indicted for fraud and graft and several other officials came under scrutiny, all officials became suspect. When even respectable citizens don't respect the police, it's almost impossible to maintain any kind of peace."

"So you left?" It didn't make sense. From what Bea saw, Greyson wasn't the sort of man to give up. To the contrary, the greater the need, the more he'd give.

"It got bad enough, officers were almost never allowed off duty. Even when we weren't on active patrol, we slept at the station house to stay on call six days a week—seven if anything major happened." He shook his head in an angry, abrupt jerk. "My wife was expecting our first child, but she might as well have been a widow for how often I came home to help. She'd. . .lost one before, early on. With this one, the doctor finally ordered bed rest for most of the time."

"You left for her." Bea saw the way his throat worked at the memory. *How much he must have loved her. . .*

Chapter 28

Y ou're out of questions." He turned away, gesturing for her sisters to launch his targets. The report of his rifle sounded louder than before, the thundering crack angry where before it had been companionable.

"My turn again." His brow still furrowed, his expression fierce, he started his own interrogation. "Why didn't you follow your fiancé to Oregon?"

She sucked in a sharp breath. Bea realized she had no one to blame but herself. Her curiosity turned the questions from a lighthearted game to a deeply personal interrogation. Grey had every right to fire queries right back at her and expect the same level of honesty he'd given.

"I couldn't leave. Maybe, if Pa hadn't fallen ill, Ariel could have seen to things. But Cassia was just starting to. . .erm. . .grow into a woman, and already attracting a troublesome amount of attention." Difficult things to handle under any circumstances, but not her deepest reason. "But more than that, I couldn't leave Jodie. She was still so young. Out of all of us, she has no memories of our real mother. Just me. I owed Jodie more than to abandon her before the most difficult transitions every woman grows through."

The hard line of his jaw relaxed. Grey kept quiet for so long, Bea started to wonder whether her talk about womanly transitions disconcerted him into silence. But she doubted it. Most likely he was sorting through options and deciding which question he wanted to ask.

"Ever regret not going with him?"

Why would he want to know that? Bea wasn't sure she could put the answer into words—and she told him so.

"Try." An order. . .and an invitation.

"Not the way you think. I thought Ben and I made a good pair. Jodie called him a smile on legs, and I tend to be too serious."

Grey snorted at that but didn't comment. Even so, the indication that he didn't think she was too serious helped Bea find her answer.

"But enough time's gone by for me to know that I'm serious when I have to be. My family needs me to look after them, and of course I don't take that lightly. Ben took almost everything lightly. . .and now I see that if I'd married him, he would need someone to do the serious work when it came to running a household. I don't mind work, but that's not what I want." She avoided his interested gaze as she finished. "A husband should be a partner. Marriage should bring change—for the better."

"You're right. It should." He seemed lost in his own thoughts, but he couldn't have gone very far because he lobbed his last question quickly enough. "Why did you agree to marry him in the first place?"

"He asked." Spoken aloud, it might have sounded flippant if the truth weren't so sad. Ben had been the only one interested. The only one who saw Bea as a woman in her own right, not just a tether chaining him to her aging father and three younger sisters. Bea wanted to be wanted, so she chose to accept the only man who'd chosen her.

"A smart move from a foolish man."

Bea found herself grinning as she signaled her sisters and took her own practice round. This time, the marbles caught more of the waning light, looking like small sunbursts.

But what to ask, now that she'd earned more questions? They'd reached a new level, and she hesitated to press any further. So after due consideration, she decided not to ask him about himself at first. Instead, she'd ask for his opinion.

"Do you think I made a mistake?"

"When you agreed to marry him, or when you decided not to?"

"Either one."

"Yes. Then no. Walking through life with a man like that meant squeezing into shoes too small. You're more, and you deserve more." He saw her squinting up at him and reached out to tweak her hat brim a little lower. It meant she couldn't see his expression as well, but Bea didn't mind. The gesture—along with his answer—more than made up for it. "Every woman deserves to be taken care of."

"That's why you left the police. For her." A powerful, roiling mix of regret, envy, compassion, and longing churned through her words. What sort of woman inspired that sort of dedication from a man like this? And suddenly, her next question came blurting out. "Why did you marry Alice?"

"She said yes." His answer countered hers about why she'd agreed to marry Ben, and Grey's tight travesty of a smile told her he'd done it intentionally.

"Fair enough." But not enough. Bea couldn't stand not knowing... "But why did you ask her, specifically? What was she like, your Alice, that she caught your attention?"

No chance he could wiggle around such a clear question.

"Her family lived in the same building as mine. I knew her for ages, even if I didn't know her well. She grew into a pretty thing, with a certain way about her. Sweet...quiet...shy..."

Bea couldn't help but realize exactly the sort of woman Alice had been. *Everything I'm not.*

✳

She didn't have half your fire or your strength. Grey bit back the observation. Comparing Bea to Alice wasn't fair to either one. It wasn't Alice's fault that he'd misinterpreted her shyness and silence for serenity. If he'd looked closer, he would've found the fear behind it.

"Alice struck me as peaceful, an example of what we police fought to protect but rarely experienced for ourselves." For good reason. If he hadn't been so busy looking after his corner of the city, he would've done a better job protecting the most precious part of it. But the realization came too late. The day he resigned was the day he'd lost everything.

Grey pushed back the mounting regrets and focused on finding a way to answer Bea's question. He'd pushed her about Ben; she had every right to ask about Alice.

"Work filled my days, and I wasn't looking for a wife. . .but other men were. Her mother remarried. Badly." His hands flexed at the memory. Grey always wanted to get his hands on that brute. "I knew the signs. First, I saw Alice's mother less and less. Before, she'd never let her daughter step foot on the streets unguarded. Now, I saw Alice alone. Then one day I saw her blackened eye—I married her that same day."

"Always protecting someone." He read admiration and regret on Bea's expressive face. "You rescued her, gave her a better life."

"I gave her a death sentence," Grey snapped back. "I took her from her home; I took responsibility for her. But I failed to protect her and our child when they needed me most. They both died in a building fire the day I left the force. I left. . .and I still wasn't there in time to make a difference."

She reached a hand toward him, but he jerked away before her touch could sear him. He was already too raw.

"You can't blame yourself for the fire, Grey."

"I blame myself for not being there." Negligence, that's what he was guilty of.

"No. We can't control everything that happens to the people we love—especially when we're not there." Her voice lowered but didn't soften. "You aren't God."

"Nope." Grey jammed his hat harder on his head and grabbed what was left of his box of bullets as the sun sank below the grass line. "That's why I was a heck of a lot closer to her when she died. I should've gotten there before heaven edged me out."

Church didn't bring much in the way of celestial peace that Sunday.

After Jonah last week, Alderman tackled Mary and Martha this time—another one of those biblical examples Bea felt less than fond of. Not because of the sisters themselves, or the lesson Christ gave them— but because of the way men chose to hold up a single incidence as a model for all that a godly woman should be.

Bea held that a godly woman could keep busy with more than serving and that many times she had more to offer to a conversation than an extra set of ears. Why was it that Christian men missed the crucial point that Mary had been listening so fixedly to *Jesus*—the average male shouldn't count himself worthy of the same regard as Christ Himself!

She'd left the pews certain she and her sisters would be subjected to an abundance of comments about women minding their place—particularly in light of the looming competition. She dreaded having to grit her teeth through self-satisfied proclamations from the men and pointed comments from the ladies.

Encounters with what Jodie called the Biddy Brigade won first prize for Things-To-Be-Avoided, but at least they were infrequent. Last week they'd gotten off easily, with the town too preoccupied with the new arrivals and even newer dissent between two of the biggest biddies.

This week worked another wonder: the women didn't pick up their dropped opportunity. Instead of the disapproving glowers Bea expected, she spotted several small smiles and the sort of measuring glance that meant she was suddenly someone of stature. Nor could she attribute all of that silent goodwill to the womenfolk's natural infatuation with Grey, because the younger girls should have gone right on glowering at their rivals!

Of course, everyone wanted to see her shoot holes in Huber's pride, which explained a lot of the change. But Bea still suspected the other members of her gender were pulling for her much more than their men.

The men, who gave her sisters wide berth for the first time in ages. Some might be put off by Grey, who doubled the number of men in the Darlyn camp and more than doubled their ability to intimidate. Others might be cowed by the prospect of Huber interpreting their attention to the Darlyns as a show of support. Whatever the reason, Bea decided to be grateful. Things would return to normal all too soon...and, of course, some things never changed.

When everyone drifted toward the trestle tables lined against the shady side of the church, manners flew to the wayside. Men jostled to get to their favorite dishes first, heaping huge helpings onto their tins and ensuring there'd be little left when the women reached the remains.

The men did exhibit the basic consideration of allowing their elders enough space to make their selections without being pushed aside. Good thing, too. Bea hated to think what she would've done if she'd spotted any of the younger men elbowing Pa.

Whatever is good. . . Bea smiled at the positive side of the setup, then found herself finding a second, even better realization. At least the established social convention of "men first" served Grey well. It allowed him to escape the all-too-eager interest of the women, who'd be hard pressed later to sidle back up to the stranger. They'd already been introduced, so the girls would have a hard time dredging up a pretext to approach him again.

I don't need to manufacture a reason to talk to Grey. She tried not to feel smug but failed when she saw him walking alongside Pa, heading straight toward her. Cassia's brows rose in a mute expression of triumph and surprise, so Bea knew she wasn't the only Darlyn relishing this moment. The dour denizens of TallGrass, who'd so often scorned her sisters since Bea's failed engagement, deserved some comeuppance.

No. Bitterness serves no good. While the feeling might be true, honest, and even just, it certainly couldn't be called virtuous, pure, or lovely. Why let past wrongs ruin an afternoon that shaped up to be so much more than she expected? Bea willed away any unpleasantness and moved forward to help Pa. The blanket spread across the ground wouldn't cushion the impact if he sat too heavily. He needed the use of both hands and his cane as he settled into a comfortable position.

"Isn't that thoughtful?" Cassia's murmur directed Bea's attention back to Grey, who held two heaping tins.

At first, she assumed he'd taken Pa's plate, but that wasn't the case. Ariel and Jodie relieved Pa of the two tins he'd brought to the blanket, allowing Bea to offer him her arm to steady himself while he hunkered down. Once she'd seen him settled, Bea looked back to find Grey offering one of his dishes to Cassia. The other, he proffered to her.

"Oh, no." Bea refused to even consider allowing him to go hungry for her sake. "We know how these gatherings go—it's why we ate so much at breakfast this morning!"

He nudged the tin into her hands, leaving her no choice but to accept it or let him smear the front of her dress with food. "I put away twice as much as any of you gals, and you need to eat enough to keep your strength up so you shoot your best."

"You're shooting, too."

"That's right, and since I'm as much of a competitor as you are, you should be ashamed for hiding crucial information from me."

"What do you mean?" Cassia cradled the tin Grey had given her, looking as uncertain as Bea felt.

"I knew you faced drought, but you didn't mention the worst of the blight." He jerked a thumb toward the tables, which had been all but picked clean. "I would've been better prepared to bring back more if you'd warned me you were also afflicted by locusts!"

His joke startled a laugh right out of her, and Grey seized the opportunity. His hands closed over Bea's when she attempted to give the plate back, coaxing her to loosen her grip without letting go.

It shouldn't have been possible, but he sensed the warmth of her hands through the worn fabric of her gloves. The way her breath caught in her throat, he figured the sensation snagged at her, too. He recovered from the distraction first, nudging a second tin from where it nestled up against the first.

Grey pushed aside any regret over breaking contact and waggled his prize toward Cassia and Ariel. No fools, the girls swiftly mimicked his motions and pulled the extra tins from beneath their own overflowing dishes. Smiles blossomed across all their faces, but Bea's thunderstruck appreciation made him feel about ten feet tall.

Together, the girls made short work of portioning out the food. He noticed they conspired to give him the lion's share, but didn't quibble.

The Darlyn family shared his sense of fairness; this was their way of returning a measure of his own thoughtfulness. They also went out of their way to pile their pa's plate with his favorite foodstuffs. No matter what the circumstances, they were consistently considerate—a glaring contrast to the remainder of the town.

They all enjoyed their food and did a fair job of ignoring the people who stared their way. While people from other families easily visited among each other, the Darlyns received no well-wishers. Only stares reached their blanket, though stares didn't describe the astonishing range of looks cast their way. Grey spotted glances, glares, glowers, and stares—pretty much every kind of notice ranging from avaricious to admiring.

Grey thought it an odd and unpleasant state of affairs until their first visitor made him miss the seclusion. Their intruder ended the isolation but replaced it with aggravation.

Huber grunted, "Came for Bea."

Chapter 29

You can't have her. His good manners owed more to a mouth full of dry cornbread than social grace, but Grey managed not to growl.

"Oh?" Bea tensed but didn't rise, her lack of reaction more effective than any insult. She wouldn't jump at his bidding or dance to his tune but gave the man no cause to complain.

"Show you the traps and targets, go over the rules and such so you can't claim you weren't familiar. Don't want to leave any handy excuses for you to use after I beat you."

"Or you want to avoid the extra embarrassment when she beats you." Grey got to his feet. No sense letting Huber look down his nose at him when Grey could tower over the man. "Or, I should say, when more than one of us beats you."

He didn't even need to raise his voice to make the statement carry— by now, the rest of the town crept close. Sharpshooters weren't the only people who didn't want to miss anything that afternoon.

"As though I'd be bested by some pass-through weakling." A collective gasp punctuated Huber's taunt. "You abase yourself by dancing attendance on a group of girls. A real man doesn't need to curry favor with females. He makes his way with his wits and his weapons."

"You'll see my way with a weapon during the competition. As for the other. . ." Grey shrugged. "A man with even half a wit knows to honor women."

Huber reared back, at least smart enough to catch the insult.

"Weren't you paying attention to this morning's sermon on Mary and Martha? It's the women's place to obey and serve the man's strength!"

Grey waited for a few fools in the audience to stop murmuring their agreement, certain they'd pay for their misplaced allegiance ten times over in burned meals and badly starched shirts. The women in TallGrass might be small in number, but a wise man recognized that only made each one a greater force to be reckoned with.

"And men are to use that strength to protect and provide for their women." No surprise to see the men stand straighter, puffed with pride.

"Seems to me the women did their part by serving up a fine meal." Most of the men nodded along, happy to encourage good cooking, blithely oblivious to the snare closing in around them. The ladies caught on quicker, a fervor of bobbing bonnets encouraging Grey to snap the trap shut. "The men heaped their plates high and left their womenfolk to forage through scraps of that fine meal—"

"The women won't begrudge the bachelors a chance to enjoy a little home cooking!" Huber burst out, spotting the danger and trying to forestall it.

Too late.

"The ladies served," Grey reminded their audience. "What did the men provide in return? A guarantee that their womenfolk would go hungry."

Finally understanding, the men began to shift restlessly. Some looked at their boots and mumbled. Others glared at Grey, foremost among them hotheaded Huber.

"They know full well there's no greater compliment than clean plates and empty tables."

"I, for one, would feel more flattered on a full stomach." The shopkeeper's sour-faced wife stepped forward and led a feminine chorus of agreement. "Gatherings aren't excuses for gluttony!"

Shocked by the uprising and shoved toward his wife by other men anxious to defray the ladies' ire, the shopkeeper cleared his throat. "If you all felt that way, why didn't you speak up before?"

"Your eyes work as well as your stomachs." Another older woman Grey didn't recognize joined the protest. "No matter how much food we made, you met the challenge."

"If we remarked, it would come too close to taking you men to task." The shopkeeper's wife held no such compunctions today. "So we held our silence until a stranger showed the manners to speak up on our behalf!"

Most of the menfolk certainly seemed shamefaced—or at least as shamefaced as a fellow with a bellyful of fantastic food could feel after the fact.

"Yet you side with that stranger over your own townsmen!" Huber bellowed the reprimand, spreading his arms wide. "Bring concerns to your men at home. In town, we stand together, and no stranger has the standing to judge how we treat our women!"

"Last I checked, Huber," Seamus growled, "you don't have a woman, and you're the one who started judging my guest."

"That's right." A young man standing beside the second matron, who looked to be his mother, crossed his arms and took up the cause. "Mr. Wilder held his peace until you tried to shame him for having better manners than most of the town."

Grey returned the fellow's nod, surprised to find a source of support and solidarity. If others showed the same amount of backbone, there might be hope for the town yet.

Uncowed, Huber circled back to solid ground. "Who's he to try and show us up?"

"Someone who dislikes injustice." Grey shrugged, pleased with the day's work. "The women deserve to be waited on when the men are so self-serving."

A tiny, rapidly swallowed sound told him Bea smothered a laugh at his turn of phrase. *I do like a woman who appreciates my wit.*

"You think your sense of 'justice' carries more weight than mine?" Huber stubbed a finger toward Grey but lacked the bravery to make contact.

"Ought to, considering Mr. Wilder here has a long history as a police guard back in Chicago." Seamus slowly rose to his feet, making sure to plant the tip of his cane atop the tip of Huber's boot as he levered upward. "In fact, we ought to be asking him to help us draw up some town regulations and nail down the requirements and duties for a sheriff."

"A man who causes so much disturbance isn't fit to take on the duties of peacekeeper." He eyed Grey with an animosity reserved for fending off threats.

Good. Grey didn't intend to take up permanent residence in TallGrass but vehemently opposed Huber's aspirations toward law enforcement. He clapped Huber's meaty shoulder. "Good of you to realize you're not qualified."

"What?" He jerked away, although Grey had already removed his hand. "I meant you! You're the source of this disturbance. I just tried to fetch Bea to ready the competition—a contest which will show how qualified I am to take care of troublemakers!"

No one present doubted who Huber would have targeted today, had he the authority to shoot more than his mouth.

"Today's match is about marksmanship and good, old-fashioned fun." Grey offered his hand to Bea and pulled her to her feet so they could both make a show of gathering their guns. "A sharp eye and a steady hand go a long way in a lawman, but an even temper and a dedication to fair play go farther."

"Competition couldn't be any more fair, so let's see if your eye and your aim can match your claims." Huber stalked off toward a scraggly stand of trees. When he realized the entire town moved en masse to follow, he snarled. "While we get things ready, only those who plan to do the shooting should take the field. The rest of you can wait for my call."

"Don't keep them away on my account." Though she'd wisely opted not to comment on the town's treatment of either her gender or her family, Bea found her voice as soon as the conversation turned to shooting. "No sense showing the way the machines work and explaining the rules more than once. Who needs privacy for a few practice rounds, when everyone will bear witness to the real shooting anyway?"

"I second that." Grey found it anything but a hardship to side with Bea against Huber but particularly approved any means of speeding them through the competition. The sooner Bea beat Huber, the sooner they could all get back to the farm.

After the shots he'd seen her make, first in tandem with her sisters' against the Spinster's Doom moving target, then against airborne clay discs, and finally *marbles* tossed by her sisters, he harbored no doubts about her ability to best him. Hands down. And he'd been one of the higher-ranked shots at Bogardus's Shooting Gallery, even going up against the legendary sportsman and holding his own from time to time.

Grey more than looked forward to the expression on Huber's face when Bea beat the stuffing out of him. If Grey's own skills also happened to top Huber's, even better. They'd have that much more to celebrate after they left the rest of the TallGrass rabble in the dust of their wagon.

Huber made quite the fuss over his trap mechanisms, obviously expecting to astound and intimidate his opponents with unfamiliar machinery. Disbelief soured his expression as Bea's eyes lit up and she insisted on touching everything firsthand. He impatiently passed over a pair of Ira Paine's Feather-Filled Glass Balls.

Bea removed her gloves, ignoring a few scattered gasps from the crowd, and rolled the targets across her palms to feel the thin-blown, smooth surface of the glass and test their heft. Frowning in concentration, she tossed them into the air, lightly at first, then with increasing force to check the speed of their descent.

"Load them into the machine and pull the lever if you want a real idea of what you'll be aiming at." For what Grey suspected was the first and last time, Huber issued an order Bea willingly followed. The trap loaded fifteen of the target balls at a time, though the lever required pulling for each individual launch.

Grey hung back, shaking his head when Bea raised a brow at him in silent invitation to join her inspection. His old gallery used the same trap machine, though Bogardus manufactured his own balls—thicker glass than these Ira Paine versions, which would be much easier to break. Weak but flashy, with their flutter of feathers, the targets matched the man who'd selected them.

Encouraged by Bea's enthusiasm, the other competitors swarmed forward to get a feel for things. Grey smiled to see the crowd push Huber off to the side, then took the opportunity to get a closer look at the various firearms he'd face off against.

He frowned to see the assortment also included shotguns, which provided a vast advantage when shooting at any kind of distance—and particularly when wielded against the weak-walled smoothness of the Paine targets. A shotgun's spray of bullets made targets much easier to hit versus the single bullet path of a rifle. It didn't make much difference to him—if anything, he felt as though it evened up whatever advantage his familiarity with the traps had given him. For Bea. . .

Well, those glass targets were at least ten times larger than the marbles he'd seen her strike last week, so he stifled his outrage. With the exception of Huber's fancy new model, everyone else toted guns that looked like they'd been passed down for at least a generation or two. Grey's own Sharps carbine looked positively modern and sleek in comparison. But at least he'd brought a rifle. Huber's shiny new shotgun was a just-released model Grey knew held at least twenty rounds.

Don't know why I'm surprised. He disliked the implications but decided to reserve judgment until after Huber announced the rules of his competition. So long as they didn't include too much of a weight toward a timing factor, Huber hadn't stacked the deck enough for him to point it out. A premature protest would sound like sour grapes, since they'd already brangled once today.

"Rules are as follows." Huber stuck his chest out, and his neck all but disappeared, calling to mind an overfed bullfrog. "A round's worth of practice for each contestant before we begin. For the competition, we won't be doing elimination cycles. A single event is all anyone gets to prove their mettle. One chance to win."

It'd be over sooner than any of them expected, but Grey wasn't grateful to hear it. By making the contest a single all-or-nothing round, Huber deprived everyone else the chance to find their footing with the unfamiliar targeting system—distinct advantage the bullfrog didn't deserve. Not only that, but none of Huber's posturing divulged the scoring system for this lone event, and that omission struck Grey as particularly ominous.

Ominous and intentional—Huber withheld the information to impress participants and observers alike with his status. It wasn't enough that he arranged the contest and held everyone's attention. He needed to shore up his already overinflated sense of importance by forcing the rest of them to ask for basic information.

"I didn't hear the rules." Bea's statement leveled the field. She asked nothing and gave nothing. No demands, no accusations, and no reason for Huber to vent his frustration.

Reasonable, Huber wasn't. "Have to listen to hear important information. If you paid attention, you'd have learned that in church today. Martha and Mary, serving men and listening to them. Two virtues you fail to display."

"You don't even listen to yourself, Huber." Grey rebuffed the attack before Bea wasted energy defending herself. "If you did, you'd know that you failed to outline any judging criteria. As before, when you embarrassed yourself about the serving issue, the fault doesn't lie with the lady."

"I've never embarrassed myself!"

"Only two kinds of men stand beyond embarrassment." Grey thumbed back the brim of his hat. "Those who've sunk so far beyond common decency that they no longer care, and those who've made fools of themselves so often they're inured to it. Whichever group you fall in line with, we're still waiting for those rules."

The man actually gnashed his teeth before coming up with a reply. "We'll see who looks foolish after the contest. Fifty targets. Five minutes. High score wins."

"Five minutes?" One of the townsmen looked from his own rifle to Huber's showy shotgun. "My gun holds half the rounds as yours, so I'll take twice as much time to load ammunition."

The fellow didn't bring up the shotgun versus rifle issue, but since his voice fell to a mutter and he'd taken a visible step back from Huber, he wasn't willing to make a stand. Nor did any of the other competitors speak up or step forward.

"Want to borrow my gun, Earl?" Soft and steely, Huber's invitation paid lip service to equality without any risk of putting it into practice. No man used an unfamiliar firearm in a competition if given a choice.

"Generous, but I'll keep mine." Earl looked like a man about to bolt.

"No other questions?" Huber glowered at Grey before bringing the force of his challenge to Bea.

She coolly met his challenge. "Shooting order?"

Huber rattled off a list of names that meant nothing to Grey, aside from the final three. He would shoot before Huber, with Bea taking the final slot.

In many competitions, last draw was an honor afforded to the best. Here, Huber attempted to put Bea in her place—following the men. What he intended to intimidate offered an extra advantage, and Bea's smile said she knew it. No other competitor would know the highest numbers, but she would know precisely how many balls to break for a winning score.

After they got through the practice rounds. For now, Huber insisted they watch his demonstration of. . .well, it certainly wouldn't be much of a show of skill, since his shotgun accomplished most of the work for him.

Each pull of his trigger sped an ever-widening spray of shrapnel toward the fragile spheres. The wider the margin of shot, the less need for accuracy. So long as Huber aimed in the general direction and timed it reasonably, the man couldn't fail to hit something. Grey watched dispassionately as Huber gave the order to release a few targets.

Five glass balls arced through the air, sparkling in the spring sunlight to shatter in a burst of feathers.

Five balls. . .seven shots.

Disgusted, Grey struggled not to scoff at such a mediocre performance. When he caught sight of Bea fighting for the same control, he lost a measure of his own. Not everyone would notice, but that slight twist of her lips rebuked Huber's ham-handed shooting. No wonder the clunch kept "number of shots fired" out of consideration for scoring.

In spite of that sorry display, Huber waved to the watching town as though he were royalty, generously ceding his place so his competitors could squeeze in a five-target practice round apiece. For those unfamiliar with their size, shape, launch, speed, and descent patterns, five targets offered precious little opportunity to become proficient. Particularly since the competition consisted of a single round. Even so, no one complained.

If anything, the other men seemed delighted to try their hand— and their eyes—at taking down their practice rounds. Their enthusiasm made the minutes fly faster than the targets, and Grey started to get into the spirit of the match.

None of the other contestants looked like they'd provide much in the way of competition, but Grey wouldn't sink into complacency. For all he knew the men of TallGrass might be a cagey bunch, holding back their best efforts for the match. He didn't make his sharpest showing either. Let Huber wallow in a false sense of security.

Even Bea made an uncharacteristic fuss over taking down her targets, firing the same seven shots as Huber. She refused to look at Grey or her family when she did this, and he wondered whether her reticence came from shame at her ploy or fear that she'd be unable to keep a straight face.

Huber, alternately sneering and leering at her from the sidelines, bought her performance. Grey could only hope the others felt as confident as the strutting banker, making the win that much easier for her. With the practice turns finished, the competition started with the expected bang.

But despite the cracking and booming reports from the variety of guns, the contest weakened to a whimpering mess within half an hour. The five contestants before Grey retired from the field, their scores so abysmal they ought to have retired their firearms for good.

If these strapping settlers relied on their shooting skills to put food on the table, the mercantile must make a small fortune selling ammunition. Any man who stood before his peers to fire a weapon owed to himself and his audience to prove his competency. While their practice shots didn't inspire awe or fear, they'd done passably well. No reason why none of those five men managed to bring down more than thirty targets.

Grey wished Bea an easy win, but winning implied a challenge. Thus far, the only challenge in sight was the struggle not to denounce their fellow contestants as cowards and the entire affair as fixed!

Chapter 30

Disgraceful. Mortification blazed in the tight knots of Bea's cheeks, the heat of humiliation making her smile that much more strained. If Huber held debts over everyone's head, he might as well have kept the competition one-on-one. Better a direct confrontation than this mockery of marksmanship.

Today wasn't the first time her townsmen humored Huber by throwing a competition, but it ranked as the most egregious. The men didn't only dishonor themselves. Their lack of backbone dragged all of TallGrass down into their disgrace.

Any hope Grey might consider staying scattered wider than a batch of buckshot. Bea ached to share a smile or give him a nod as he took his place, to offer the same support he so steadfastly gave her. Instead, she avoided his gaze. If those golden eyes reflected her fears, the disappointment might affect her shooting.

Bea's loyalty belonged to her family. They couldn't afford failure, so she couldn't risk any distractions. Every ounce of focus from here on out must remain fixed on the shooting.

No hardship, now that the intentionally inept surrendered the field. Grey possessed both the talent and integrity to restore the credibility of this competition. Although the contract stipulated that only Bea needed to beat Huber to reap the benefits, she set her sights higher. No one who'd seen Grey practice this past week would imagine Huber could match his score, much less best it. Bea set her goal as one better than

Grey's total, certain he'd stand unmatched.

And not only in TallGrass. Even the largest city would be hard pressed to produce a man who matched Grey's abilities. Whether shooting at targets or shooting the breeze, he offered an easy camaraderie she'd never expected to share with anyone but her sisters. Their interests and work habits matched so closely they became a team to rival Marco and Polo.

Perhaps because we make no other demands on each other, or our time together. Troublesome hopes aside, Bea nourished no illusions that Grey would actually decide to stay. For now, they worked in tandem and stayed in step together. The weight of expectation would tangle their traces and tie their tongues, making their time unproductive. And awkward.

Why ruin their remaining time together by counting the hours? Better to count the ways he'd turned a dreaded afternoon into a day worth remembering. Or the targets he prepared to bring down.

From the tilt of his head to the set of his shoulders and the way he gripped his gun, every aspect of his stance proclaimed his proficiency. Even the least knowledgeable onlooker could appreciate the contrast between Grey's confidence and Huber's arrogance—a contrast sure to sharpen with every shot fired.

Or at least every volley of shots. The rapid rounds of Grey's Sharp's carbine made it impossible to distinguish single shots. Little wonder Pa spoke so highly of the weapon. Its longer sights made for easier, more accurate aiming. But when Grey let her test his rifle, the booming report and punching recoil from the weapon's heavy weight slowed Bea's shooting.

It underscored the importance of finding a firearm to fit the user. Her trusty Winchester, with its less jarring burst of sound and steady, more controllable kick suited her far better. In Grey's hands, the carbine came to life. He snapped out rounds at a dizzying pace.

He stopped to reload before Bea registered the sixteen separate shots she knew were his, as the booming report of the gun itself became a constant background for the shattering of glass targets. Had she or the other spectators observed from the side, rather than from behind, Bea knew they would have been able to hear the swift, low hiss the bullets made when they passed by.

But then she'd lack the vantage point to appreciate the solid strength of his upraised arms, the taut vigilance of his shoulders, his pinpoint timing as he aimed through his sights. Patient but efficient, he completed his run in just over three minutes. Bea couldn't be certain of the precise final tally, but by her reckoning he'd shattered at least forty of the targets. Awed whispers broke out behind her as he lowered his smoking barrel. Applause burst from the crowd, their enthusiasm and volume almost as explosive as the shooting.

Not even his competitors withheld their approbation, though they fell silent when Huber turned and caught them clapping. Bea shrugged off her irritation and returned her attention to Grey—just as he returned to her. Boots planted wide enough to match the width of his shoulders, his rifle propped against his hip and lightly cradled in the crook of one arm, Grey looked every inch the conqueror.

"Forty-two!"

Not even Huber's bad humor could hold back the applause now. Grey maintained a stoic expression, but Bea saw the tightened lines at the corners of his mouth—the ones that tattled he was trying not to smile. A slight rising of his brows asked her a question, but Bea couldn't decipher what it might be. Did he ask whether his shooting earned her approval, or did he want to know whether she thought she could best his score? Either way, the answer would be yes.

Yes, Grey, you impress me. Bea tilted her head in a sign of agreement, indulging in a brief flashing smile their spectators couldn't catch. *And yes, Grey, I can still beat you.*

"You're not upset."

"Why would I be upset?" Every onlooker would see them engaged in close, animated conversation, but Bea ignored it. This afternoon the only rules related to targets and timed events. "I counted on you to give me something to shoot for."

"You're already shooting for something. And unless you count Huber's pride, you're the only one with anything on the line." He thumbed back his hat brim, casting a glance toward the left, where the other Darlyns cheered loudest of all.

"A person's honor is always on the line. If you'd held back, it would have been a blow against both of ours."

The gold of his eyes gleamed. Some people might assume she meant the brown of his gaze had warmed, but that wasn't the case. The color didn't deepen—it lightened. To others, it might even seem cold. They'd be wrong. His focus brightened the golden color, refining it as though to match the value he placed on her words.

"You are an incredible woman, Beatrix Darlyn."

He said my name. Bea couldn't speak, even if she'd found words to say. The compliment paled in comparison to the simple fact that he'd finally called her Beatrix. *He made it sound nice. It's never sounded nice before.*

The boom of a shotgun tore through the air, halting the excited conversation all around and putting an end to Bea's reverie. For once, Huber timed his interruption to good effect. Amazing, how a woman could appreciate even an idiot's utter disregard for everyone else, so long as it saved her from making a fool of herself in front of a far better man.

Let the townspeople and the already-beaten cheaters think what they liked—she refused to limit her enjoyment while watching Huber finalize his own defeat. Whatever advantages he vouchsafed when selecting his gun and drafting the rules of the competition to suit his own shooting, they couldn't compensate for his inferior ability.

And he knew it, too. Understanding that he'd been beaten at his own game contorted his smile into the snarl of a jealous dog. Aggression couldn't mask the panic any better than this contest could prove him capable.

It could, however, aggravate him into making more mistakes. Too tense, he missed the first shot. At this added humiliation, Huber lost his head, abandoning any attempt at accuracy in favor of haste. Unable to win on the merit of his marksmanship, Huber exploited his swift-loading gun, spraying wide, wild arcs of shot to inflate his score.

No one moved, much less cheered, as the judge moved forward to confirm the tally. Huber didn't deign to join them, standing with legs splayed wide and hands clasped behind his back as though the proceedings were beneath his dignity. His fine shotgun lay forgotten at his feet, where he'd thrown it in an appalling lack of consideration for basic safety measures.

"Thirty-seven?" Far from the ringing tones of certainty used to trumpet everyone else's scores, this number came out as a question. *How would Huber react?*

Quickly. He spun on his heel and marched toward Bea, sneering. "Ladies all seem to favor the stranger today. Even lady luck."

"Luck holds no sway here, Huber." Bea held tight to her temper. Pathetic, that he tried to disguise another man's accomplishment as luck rather than face his own failure. "Skill won Mr. Wilder every point of his high score. He's proven *his* ability."

She couldn't resist emphasizing that, so even Huber caught the real message.

"Your turn." Rage didn't do more for his looks than defeat. "Show us how well you can manage."

"Better than you." Grey wasn't about to let Bea walk onto the field with Huber having the last word. She'd leaped to defend his ability but wouldn't waste words on her own.

Huber made a point of looking Bea over before scoffing, "Never."

"Always."

Grey missed the man's reaction, too busy drinking in Bea's.

Her eyes widened, her lips parting in an exclamation so soft he might have imagined it. A delicate glow washed Bea's cheeks, her generous mouth curling into a smile he'd never seen before. Secretive, as though she'd sampled something forbidden. . .and found it to her liking.

Intoxicating, the notion that his words struck her so intensely.

"Her?" Huber's bellow broke through the moment. "Better than me?"

"In every way."

Had they been alone instead of standing in front of the entire town, Grey would have reached forward and cupped her cheek, testing to see if all that color warmed her skin the way it warmed him.

A narrow miss, but Grey kept his head long enough to end the exchange. "She'll show everyone."

"We'll see about that." His muttering broke into disjointed German as he swaggered toward the sidelines.

"Thank you." Before her whisper faded, Bea took the field with the same capable grace he'd noticed when they first met—the swift, sure stride of a champion.

Silence reigned until the first trap sprang its targets in a glittering spray across the field. Shots firing, glass shattering. . .fifteen times each. Grey watched with unabashed admiration as she loaded her rifle for another set. The first volley posed the greatest hurdle for any marksman, mistakes more common until they caught a feel for the target trajectory. Not only did Bea hit each one, but she hadn't needed a single extra bullet.

Fifteen shots more. Unless Grey's keen eyesight failed him, she'd repeated the feat. He waited with bated breath, hoping and even praying she could accomplish it one more time. A score of forty-five would silence her detractors once and for all.

Grey wasn't the only one transfixed. No one dared so much as cheer, for fear of distracting her and breaking her streak. The second before she began shooting for the third time stretched so silent, Grey could have tracked the rustle of a cricket in the grass.

Gunfire. Victory coming closer with every shattered target. . .until a cry cracked through the air, loud as the report of Bea's rifle. And every bit as fatal.

"Pa!"

Grey didn't identify the sister but instinctively knew the cry came from a Darlyn. So did Bea. She whipped her hand away from the trigger, curling her other palm around the Winchester's still-smoking barrel as she swung around. Without pausing, she raced toward the place her family had stood moments before, cheering.

No one cheered now.

Grey matched her motions, a heartbeat ahead of her since he stood closer to the crowd. Feet flying, his heart sunk when he couldn't see Seamus. Bea's height came from her father. If he didn't stand out among her much-shorter sisters, he'd fallen to the ground or been lowered there. A thicket of skirts blocked his view and their path. Grey paused, hampered by a lifetime's unwillingness to manhandle women—especially when they might be able to offer more help than he.

Bea shoved forward, so fiercely determined that the other women gave way long enough for Grey to shoulder through, too.

"Back away!" Flailing her arms as though beating back Satan himself, Judith narrowly missed Grey—and everyone within her surprisingly long reach. "Stop crowding!"

Spectators retreated enough for them to find Seamus stretched flat on the ground. Ariel knelt at his side, pressing her fingers against the pulse point of his throat. A small sob escaped her as she repositioned her fingertips, pressing harder in a desperate search. Blotches of a ruddy flush drained away to leave his skin an ominous, ashy shade. Despite Cassia's attempts at fanning him with his own hat, sweat shone from his upper lip and temples.

Grey immediately added his efforts to Judith's, establishing a wider boundary. Bea hit the ground knees first, reaching for her father's hands to tug off his gloves and push up his sleeves. She felt his wrist as Ariel laid her head against Seamus's chest.

"There." Her voice sharp with fear and relief, Bea groped for Ariel's hand. She positioned it atop the pulse point. "Faint. So slow. . . Can anything help?"

"Foxglove would speed his heart, but I don't have any."

"What does it look like?" Judith demanded. "I'll find it."

A choked sob escaped her older sister. "It has to steep to a certain darkness."

"I have it!" The shopkeeper's wife jabbed her husband. "The tea I give your ma when she falls faint—fetch the bottle from the icebox!"

"Thank you." Bea's voice shook, but her hands stayed steady as she unbuttoned her father's collar. "Ariel, what about his breathing tea? Can they be taken together?"

"Foxglove first, but yes. Judith?" Their youngest sister needed no further instruction to go hying off after the concoction. Anyone could see Seamus's breaths came in shallow, thin gasps forced through too-tight lungs.

"We need to prop him up." Grey crouched beside Bea and carefully slid his hands beneath Seamus's shoulders. Time might have rushed past or ambled by as they worked and worried. It felt like it took far too long before rough hands pushed a corked bottle into Ariel's keeping. Grey took up hat-fanning after they leaned Seamus against Cassia's lap. She cradled his head, holding it upright and steady while Bea and Ariel poured small sips of tea into his mouth, then rubbed his throat to make him swallow.

Slowly, they gained ground. Sweat no longer beaded his brow. Some of the ashenness left his skin, then color came to take its place. His breathing whistled fewer alarms. . .though not enough to satisfy Ariel. She decreed another mug of tea, though this time Seamus resisted her efforts. He tried to turn his head, choking and spluttering, but his daughters prevailed. They pulled him back when he tried to get up. They pulled him back when he tried to lie flat.

They pulled him back from the brink of death itself.

When Ariel deemed him stable enough to move, the girls lined the buckboard with their cloaks. His eyelids twitched, and he stirred as Grey and a few other men lifted Seamus atop the makeshift cushion, but Ariel's smile told Grey this was a good thing. The girls climbed carefully into the wagon, giving another round of thanks to the people who'd helped—especially the shopkeeper and his wife for their foxglove tea.

Glad beyond measure that he'd insisted on riding Daredevil instead of crowding the Darlyns in the wagon, Grey swung into the saddle. It gave them just enough room for Seamus to lie flat.

And it gave Huber just enough room to dart forward and snatch the reins from Bea's grasp. "You think you can drive away without so much as a word about the contest?"

Her empty hands closed into fists as Grey jumped to the ground. He plucked the reins from the banker's grasp and held them out to Bea, but her glare remained fixed on Huber with an unbreakable intensity. When Grey nudged the reins into her grasp, he realized her hands shook from the force of her rage.

"Words?" she choked out. "Like the ones you hissed into Pa's ear to make him collapse? What words did you use then, Huber?" She threw down the reins and rose to her feet, towering over everyone from her precarious perch. "Tell me."

"N–nothing," Huber stammered, eyes darting around wildly. Surrounded by stony-faced townsmen, he gave a hard swallow and composed himself. "I'm not to blame for your father's weakness, just as his weakness doesn't excuse yours."

"Weak? They possess strength you'll never know." Grey positioned himself between Huber and the wagon, keeping his back toward Bea. Instead of helping her down, he blocked her ability to do it herself.

"Not enough strength to finish the competition," he crowed. "Making me the winner!"

"Not even close." Grey's own fists throbbed from the strain of holding steady. "Thirty-two targets in thirty-three shots, and the last one only went wide because she heard the yells about her pa. Unquestionably better odds than thirty-seven out of fifty—even without asking how many rounds of ammunition you unloaded during your run!"

"Best out of fifty, and thirty-seven beats thirty-two with no question."

"And forty-two beats thirty-seven," Judith challenged. "Mr. Wilder beat you, and when my sister finishes her round, she will, too!"

"No she won't."

"Not today. I'm taking my father home," Bea gritted out, sinking back onto the wagon seat. "I'm certain I can hit at least eight of my remaining eighteen targets in however much time I have left."

"None." Huber shook his head so hard his jowls jiggled. "The match took place today."

An odd note of glee crept into that last statement, making Grey's gut twist as he remembered how much the Darlyns depended on Bea's triumph.

"If you insist, I'll repeat the entire round." She picked up the reins. "Once my father's well."

"No exceptions or addendums to the contract. Those five minutes are finished." Huber backed away from the wagon, his grin widening with each step. "Now the clock is running on your month to make good."

Chapter 31

Looks like you won't be the only one hauling some old bones out to Devil's Lake." Whatever strength Seamus lost physically, he funneled into his opinions. The old man was bound and determined to overrule physical infirmity through sheer obstinacy—with a dash of ornery, to keep things interesting.

Days after the shooting contest, Seamus could no longer explain away his obvious weariness. For the first time since his weak spell and Miles's return, he'd made it out of bed. All the way to the breakfast table, in honor of Miles's second departure that morning to haul off the rest of the bones. Instead of hauling, Grey held the opinion Seamus's bones needed all the rest they could get.

Watching how carefully he held his mug, Grey understood why Ariel insisted on a strict regimen of rest and sickroom fare. He'd never before seen the benefit of limiting an invalid to soft, bland foods. That sort of diet ate away a man's spirit, robbing the sick of one of the last joys left for them to savor.

But once again, the Darlyns proved to be the exception. In spite of the restrictions, the daughters who enforced them gave Seamus more joy than a lifetime of fine meals.

"Don't know where you got that idea, Seamus. Grey's going to leave me on my lonesome again." Miles made light of correcting his host.

"He is?" Bea's fork clattered to her plate, forgotten as her gaze sought his. "I mean, you are?"

For the life of him, Grey couldn't say why she sounded so surprised. Her hogs had all but attacked him and ravaged his clothes; Grey stayed. Her family hid bones in haystacks and asked for help; Grey stayed. Huber harassed her over a silly shooting match; Grey stayed. Her pa made him shovel more manure than any small farm could believably produce; Grey stayed.

With a track record like that, what made the woman imagine he'd leave now, when the Darlyns needed him the most? He should be insulted. He would have been insulted. . .but surprise wasn't Bea's most important reaction.

She'd gone a long time without blinking, lips pressed tightly together as though biting back more questions. Sitting so stiffly, with her arms clamped at her sides and fingers gripping the seat of her chair, she put him in mind of an old, slatted lantern. Everything might be locked down tight, but enough light seeped around the edges to see the brightness waiting to burst forth.

"Of course." Grey didn't have to wait for his reward. Immediately, a beaming grin broke across Bea's face like a rising sun. Out of her impressive arsenal of smiles, this unfettered expression of joy was Grey's favorite.

In stark contrast, Seamus glared around the table. "I didn't mean Grey, who is of course welcome to stay. I meant me. I'm the old bones being shipped out of town, and my own daughters are the ones doing the deed!"

"Pa, nothing is certain yet." Ariel tried to soothe him. "But if you want to stay home and avoid the doctor, you can't overexcite yourself!"

"Don't you want to enjoy the morning, before Miles leaves?" Cassia cajoled.

Miles added his charm to Cassia's. "You all set a high bar with that send-off last time. I'd hate to leave anyone on a sour note. Good memories all around, that's the way a man should take his leave."

"Just like Philippians, Pa!" Jodie blurted out. "Think on the good things."

Seamus wavered for a moment before giving in with better grace than he'd shown all week. "Aye, and I'm too blessed to keep on grumping about like an ungrateful wretch. Good thing I've got my favorite daughters to remind me."

"Jodie?" Bea's smile softened, but lost none of its radiance. "Why don't you fetch Pa's Bible and we'll finish reading the rest of that chapter. I can't think of a better way to see Miles off this morning."

As everyone else echoed their agreement, Grey tried to hide his own discomfort. Sitting around the table, so close and personal, made this sort of Bible reading worse than church. Church at least allowed him to sit silent in the pews. Perhaps not unnoticed, but nevertheless not expected to offer up any of his personal thoughts for public consumption. Here, Grey knew the Darlyns wouldn't let him wriggle out of these conversations forever. *I'll find something to say that won't offend anyone.*

Scripture might not apply to Grey lately, but he figured he'd already lost more than enough without letting his memory go soft. Verses like the ones he'd forgotten from Philippians once stood as the cornerstone of his conscience.

He'd worked alongside Pa and Miles too many times not to be alarmed by crumbling cornerstones. Too much rested on a solid foundation. Now that Grey acknowledged his faith no longer provided that foundation, what would he rest on? What had he rested on for the past two years?

Myself. Beyond his belief in the message of salvation and the moral guidance given in the Word, Grey didn't find daily strength in faith. Nor did he lean on friends or family. How could he lean on them when he shouldered responsibility for them as soon as he was able?

Grey grew up too quickly, eyes too busy looking out for others to look up to anyone or anything else. If his time with the police taught him nothing else, Grey understood that every man looked after himself. Relying on anyone—or anything, no matter how great and good—left too much room for mistakes.

When a man made his own errors, he could look back and see where he'd gone wrong—even if it was too late to set things right. *Some things just aren't possible.*

"I can do all things through Christ which strengtheneth me. . . ." Ariel's reading penetrated the gloom of his thoughts and brought him crashing back to attention.

Stunned, Grey missed some of what followed. The words shocked him, not only for the power of their promise but for the fact that he'd forgotten them. One of the most forceful verses in scripture and an old favorite of his, back in the days when belief seemed strong enough to carry him past the petty crimes he fought against, and he hadn't been able to call it to mind!

In the midst of that revelation, he managed to catch another, deeply familiar phrase as Ariel finished the reading. "But my God shall supply all your need according to his riches in glory by Christ Jesus. . . ."

Like a wolf caught in a trap, Grey wanted to howl. How could this family speak of God's provision when they stood to lose everything?

"I love the message that you don't need everything you might think you do to be content." Bea's voice snagged him as soon as she said "love," but the other words didn't match up.

Finding contentment ranked far below being able to do "all" things and having "all your needs" supplied. Grey realized he'd missed too much of the chapter to be able to follow the discussion—worse, even with the prompting of the last parts he'd listened to, his memory wouldn't recall the rest.

"Can I take a look at that?" It humbled him to have to ask, but no one looked at him askance. Bea simply lifted the Bible and passed it along. Her fingertips brushed against the back of his, warming his hands and melting a bit more of his resistance.

Grey couldn't help but savor another one of those all-too-rare times when he felt the softness of her skin with no barriers between them.

At least, nothing tangible. Differing opinions drove people apart, particularly when it came down to interpretation and application of the tome she'd handed him. When her hands withdrew, its weight seemed greater than ever. Grey lowered it to the table, gathered his thoughts, and read through the chapter. Then he skimmed over it a second time, amazed by the scope of what came before the oft-quoted assertion about doing all things through the strength of the Lord.

That line caught Grey when Ariel read it, and caught a good deal of his frustration as well. Now, reading the context of the promise, the two verses directly before it changed the way he responded to the passage.

Not that I speak in respect of want: for I have learned, in whatsoever state I am, therewith to be content.

I know both how to be abased, and I know how to abound: every where and in all things I am instructed both to be full and to be hungry, both to abound and to suffer need.

I can do all things through Christ which strengtheneth me.

He traced them with his forefinger, trying to imprint them upon his memory. Unbelievable, to realize he'd read the message incorrectly so long ago. . .and carried it around that way since. Such a difference between what he'd heard before and what he saw with his own eyes now.

God wasn't promising to fulfill all desires or offering His children the strength to do anything they wished. That simplistic accounting only looked at a few lines amid the whole. It didn't end with contentment and abundance—God acknowledged that these were gifts given alongside the more painful parts of life's path.

To be content, no matter one's state. To understand abasement as the counterpoint to abundance, to grow and to suffer. . .to need.

To need strength, and know your own would not suffice to carry you through the ordeal ahead. To call on the Lord for the strength to carry on. . .and believe He would do the carrying.

These weren't empty words painting pictures of perfect happiness. These were warnings that the road ahead would be harder than man could imagine. And the strength so powerful it allowed a man to accomplish anything? That came after a man humbled himself to ask for help. It ran contrary to how he'd been raised. Here was something a suffering believer could cling to through his darkest moments. Not mere platitudes or rosy promises. Real troubles...real life...

Grey let loose a breath he hadn't realized he'd held back.

Real truth.

✳

Bea tiptoed to the door and lifted her cloak from its peg. She should have gotten to town yesterday but hadn't managed to get a horse saddled before being called back to the house.

Her sisters wanted her to take at least one of them when she went to TallGrass. Pa didn't want any of them going to check for telegrams at all, fighting tooth and nail against having his sister come take him to the medical professionals in Lincoln. Already, he'd made such a fuss and gotten himself in such a bad state that they'd delayed sending the first telegram. Now a week since the incident, and time moved much too fast to leave them with so little to show for it. Especially when they needed every drop of daylight.

They'd scraped together every dime they could to give Aunt Mary for medical care. Once Miles came back, they'd stave Huber off with the bone money. But the windfall wouldn't stretch much further than that, which meant the farm's future hung on this year's harvest.

Which, of course, depended on their preparing and planting the fields in proper time. Without Pa. And until Aunt Mary came to fetch him, at least one of the sisters would keep to the house. Ariel desperately wanted to watch over him during the trip to Lincoln, but they couldn't spare the time or the expense of her traveling along.

If Pa tired easily before his attack at the shooting contest, collapse marked a dangerous development. Now, if he became overexcited or upset, it stressed more than his breathing. What he called the "flutters" left his pulse thready, his color slipping to an alarming clammy gray that sent Ariel running for more foxglove tea.

They refused to discuss the possibility that the doctors might not be able to do more for him than Ariel. But not talking about something didn't make it disappear, and sending Pa to Lincoln couldn't rid them of deeper fears. It was a mark of how drastically things changed that the prospect of protecting all three of her sisters during the Devil's Lake visit to drop off Pa at the train station wasn't one of Bea's bigger worries.

Compared to the ceaseless vigil over Pa's failing health and long hours frantically working in the fields to stave off foreclosure, a night in the rough-and-tumble town sounded downright tranquil. More than anything else, being together as a family to see Pa off would lend the Darlyn sisters a much-needed measure of peace.

But only after they knew when to expect Aunt Mary! Bea needed to get to the telegraph office and find out when they could expect her. Slipping into her cloak, she paused before pulling up the hood. *Is that a cough?*

Of course it was. Bea left her hood down and snatched up the teakettle. Of course she should have brewed up a batch of Pa's breathing tea before she left!

Silent as a shadow, Ariel emerged from the bedroom. She took the teakettle and waved toward the door. "I'll do it. Go, while you still can."

Bea grabbed Ariel and hugged her close, teakettle and all, before she left. The sound of her sister's chuckle followed her through the door, lifting her spirits as she snuck into the barn. Impossible not to light a lamp and make some noise when saddling a horse. Bea darted a guilty glance toward the hayloft, all too aware of the way Grey sided with her sisters yesterday. If she didn't get Marco out of the barn without waking Grey, he'd insist she wait for him to ready another mount.

"Morning."

Glancing up at the hayloft, Bea didn't see Grey standing beside Marco and Polo's stall. She might well have run into the man if he hadn't spoken up, but the shock of it made her jump. Putting a hand against her chest in a vain attempt to calm her speeding pulse, Bea realized she held the only lit lamp—one of the reasons he'd been able to catch her by surprise.

"What are you doing?" Compared to his greeting, she sounded downright waspish.

"Waiting for you." He opened the stall and led Marco out, already saddled. "Figured you'd get a jump on going to town this morning, since you didn't make it yesterday."

She took hold of Marco's reins, touched by his thoughtfulness. Strange, to have a coconspirator who wasn't related to her. With Ariel, the hug came easily. With Grey. . .the very thought of hugging him made her blush and sent tingles down to her fingertips. So she settled for something safer. "Thank you."

"Let's go." He led Polo from the stall. Also saddled and ready to go. His tone brooked no further argument, and since he'd saved her the time and trouble of saddling her mount and stood ready to go, Bea wouldn't waste time arguing with the man.

Chapter 32

It's slow going until we leave the coulee, but we'll make up time after the pass." Steep, uneven, and not overly wide, the curving pass in and out of the small valley also offered a challenging assortment of ruts. Speed could easily mean the injury of a good mount.

"You treat your horses well."

"Any animal should be treated well, but Marco and Polo deserve every consideration I can afford them." Bea leaned forward slightly to give Marco's neck an affectionate pat. "Strong backs and steady temperaments, they work hard without any fuss."

"Is that the way to a woman's heart?" He sounded curious enough that Bea didn't mind his amusement. As they reached the opening of the pass, he drew alongside her, taking the outside of the narrow pass and pressing her against the safer side, against the earthen wall. "To work hard without fussing? Because men appreciate those qualities, too, and you might have been describing yourself."

"Might more easily describe you." Somewhat less than thrilled at being compared to a draft horse, Bea deflected the compliment. "I don't know that I've seen anyone work so hard for so little and without complaint."

"You do it every day, from what I can see. Strong and steady."

Well, between that and my strong back, I should have men lining up and asking to see my teeth. Knowing Grey meant to compliment her didn't make the comparison more flattering. *What woman wants to be placed in*

261

the "strong back" category?

"My temper is not so steady, I'm afraid."

"A steady soul doesn't preclude a passionate heart."

A soft "Oh!" escaped her at the impact of his words. A passionate heart. . . He made it sound desirable. Bea glanced at him, struck again by the clear-cut strength of his profile and how it matched the straightforward charm of the words he chose.

"Is that how you see yourself?" She wanted to ask if that's how he saw her, but couldn't. "It's how I see you." He turned his head to meet her gaze, and the intensity of it made Bea glad she rode so close to a wall. It gave a sense of security against the exhilarating free fall of their conversation. "A woman who's both devoted and adventurous."

Flustered and pleased, Bea blushed and wondered what a woman should say to a comment like that. Not for the first time, she wished she could swap her strong back for a few of her sisters' strengths. Cassia instinctively understood how to draw men out without seeming forward. Ariel would have found something clever to say to keep the conversation going. But Bea? *I'll have to muddle through as best I can.*

"Most people seem made of contradictions. Some blend better than others." She took a breath and plunged ahead. "Like yours. You can't help but try to take charge, but it's not because you're controlling. You see a need to interfere, whether you intended to or not. Because you care about people. It's what made you stay and help us instead of going off to Canada on your own adventure."

"Don't stick me on that pedestal." All traces of good humor vanished. "Save Miles, I spent the past two years not caring about anyone. Stop giving me so much credit."

"Stop giving yourself so little." The chide came quicker than the compliment, but before Bea could despair over her own awkward ways, Grey chuckled.

"That may be the first time anyone's ever scolded somebody and made it sound like a compliment."

She laughed right along with him, their pace slowing to

accommodate their inattention to the road. All the reasons she'd rushed out for this ride remained the same, but suddenly Bea wished the coulee walls stretched a bit higher. Soon they'd reach level ground and kick into a gallop—killing a conversation she wasn't ready to end.

"I can lay claim to plenty of skills, but small talk eludes me."

"Small minds, small talk. There's nothing small about what you say or who you are—it's one of the things I like best about you." He thumbed up the brim of his hat and seared her with another one of those looks that hitched her breath. "Don't let anyone cut you down to their size."

Bea marveled that she hadn't melted clean out of the saddle while he said such beautiful things. Her bones abandoned her all at once, leaving her soft enough to let his words shape her into something more than she'd built before. Dangerous, but exhilarating. Bea's nose stung, caught in the middle of the storm gathering behind her eyes. Unleashed, its power would drench them both, and she didn't trust herself to try and speak.

So she gave him a nod. He noticed and shifted his hat back down to shade his eyes as they ambled on, neither one attempting to pick up the pace. When she wrested control back from her emotions and her bones began functioning properly, Bea discovered she wasn't willing to let the interlude end in such a mundane way.

"That may be the first time," she echoed his earlier jab, "that a man basically called a woman—and everything about her—'big' and managed to make it sound like a compliment."

It worked. By the time their laughter faded, they'd regained their easy footing. If they now balanced over a greater depth than what stretched between them before, now wasn't the moment to examine it.

"Once we reach flat land, we'll gallop." She didn't want to spur Marco without warning Grey that she might leave him behind. Then again, she might not. "Polo might speed up before you spur him, since they're so used to working together."

Amusement deepened his voice, lending it an extra richness Bea couldn't help but enjoy. "Must be nice for them, having a partner they can rely on to match their pace."

"You set an impressive pace even when learning new tasks," Bea praised, finding it got easier with a little practice. "I'd imagine it's harder for you to find someone to keep up."

"Me? I've been trying to keep up with you!"

"You would surpass me next season, if you had any interest in farming. I ought to be grateful we had your help when you were learning because you more than matched my efforts from the first day—and I'm an old hand at farmwork!"

"Hardly old."

She couldn't be sure he intended for her to hear him, so Bea kept her response to herself. *I wish you did have an interest. In farming. . .or in a "hardly old" spinster.*

"If you'd asked a year ago, I would have said I'd never have an interest in farming." His matter-of-fact tone made her heart heavy.

She had no right to hope for more. When she and Cassia invited him for dinner, none of them expected him to stay for three weeks, much less opt to stay behind and help in the fields. What Greyson Wilder had given her and her family went far beyond a week of work. But when he left for Canada, he'd leave behind a keen sense of loss.

"But that was before I came to TallGrass and you taught me a thing or two."

"Oh?" She tried to keep most of her hope hidden, but enough of it escaped into that syllable that he shot her an assessing glance.

"Yes." They were coming to the end of the pass, where the land leveled off enough to gallop—and to cut their conversation short. "I might have an interest now. If you wouldn't mind teaching me more, maybe I could stop by and stay for a few lessons the next time I pass through."

"Any time!" Bea felt lighter than she had in months. Grey coming back gave her something to look forward to beyond her hopes for the harvest and all the hard work in between. She looked over to see him wearing a smile to match hers just as they crested the pass and couldn't resist throwing down a challenge. "So long as you can keep up!"

✳

Grey chased her all the way to town, racing into a breeze that brought a chill to his cheeks and her laughter to warm the rest of him. He liked the way Bea laughed. She didn't try to swallow it back like some ladies he'd known. Why did any of them do that? Squeeze a laugh so hard it came out shrill and high and chittering—like an angry squirrel.

Any man would prefer Bea's bolder, more vibrant mirth. Especially considering the way she kept hold of her good humor no matter what circumstances she found herself in. The drought didn't keep a smile from her face when they'd first met. Huber's horrible revelation about the mortgage couldn't steal her joy. Nor could the man's manipulation of the shooting contest. Even her father's failing health didn't plunge her into long stretches of gloom.

She leaned forward as they galloped, cheeks rosy with the sting of the wind and her own exhilaration. If he could see her eyes, they'd be sparkling. The hood of her cloak fell back, revealing a bonnet too stubborn to oblige him by doing the same. What a sight she'd be, galloping across the prairie, her mahogany locks waving free. Grey let himself imagine it for a moment before deciding it didn't really matter. No matter what she wore, Bea would always be a wonderful sight.

A sight I'll be seeing more of. It pleased him, the way Bea challenged him to keep up with her—and keep close enough to come visit. Other things she'd said pleased him, too. She'd all but come out and told him she liked having him around and hoped he'd stay.

Stays could always be extended. Grey knew he wouldn't leave the Darlyn family until they'd gotten their father's condition stabilized and he'd returned home, at the very earliest. The edges of a plan to stay on until they'd resolved the matter with Huber kept tickling his mind, though if he understood correctly, they had another year before the end of the loan.

Alarming, that the thought of staying in TallGrass for an entire year failed to alarm him. Grey gave some consideration to the vacant—or, more accurately, not-yet-established—position of town sheriff but wasn't ready to commit himself indefinitely. Maybe a year wouldn't be so bad. As a trial run for everyone in town to get used to the idea. That way, even if he didn't stay on, he would have implemented the proper policies and protocols before the next officer took over. An officer he'd handpick and personally train to keep an extra eye out for the Darlyns.

Not that it would be difficult to convince any man to keep a close eye on the Darlyns. If they didn't attract so much attention, they wouldn't need to be watched over as much. Grey grinned at the irony of the idea as they closed in on the tiny town.

He followed Bea's lead, or perhaps Polo followed Marco's, slowing down to a more decorous pace as they approached the main street. Too early for town folk to open their businesses, but that didn't bother Bea. They hitched their horses and walked along, companionably preserving the early morning silence. Grey waited while she darted up to the mercantile, pulling something from one of her deep cloak pockets and carefully looping it around the door handle before returning to him.

"Ariel sent along some foxglove," Bea explained without making him ask, "to replace what the Muensche's gave Pa."

"More than what they gave, if I know you Darlyns."

She surprised him by shaking her head. Bea bit her lower lip, her long lashes fluttering shut for a bewildering moment. When she opened them, her eyes shone a little too bright. "Nothing we send will ever be more than what they gave."

He'd seen the herbs. She'd seen her pa's life. Grey swallowed against a growing tightness in his throat and fought his need to take her into his arms. Sleepy town or not, someone might see and get the wrong—or worse, the right—idea about why he held her. He voiced some sort of agreement, then walked with her to the telegraph and mail office.

It looked closed, but she skirted to the side of the structure and produced a small key. Small metal boxes, no bigger than bricks, marched across the building in two neat rows. She unlocked one of the steel doors, opening it to reveal a folded missive. Bea plucked it out, looked it over, and her eyes widened.

"Aunt Mary arrives the day after tomorrow!" Hastily, she clicked the door closed, turned the key, and shoved both it and the telegram into her pocket.

"So long as it wasn't today, it'll be fine." Hating to see her troubled, Grey searched for another topic. "Fancy post box setup you folks have for such a small town."

"Ah, yes." Her lips curved upward once again. "They used to be unsecured, but Huber stirred up quite a fuss making claims that some Nosey Nellies were riffling through his correspondence. He tried to install only one, for himself, but the town governance held firm and insisted on standardized mailing slots. Since he'd jawed about it so much, he bought one for every family rather than lose face and let the matter slide."

Grey grinned at the idea that someone made Huber pay for something, but lost his mirth when they rounded the building to see the very toad they'd been talking about, waiting near their horses. A low groan and the fleeting pressure of her hand against his arm told Grey that Bea hadn't missed the problem.

Even if they'd had time to squander, it was too late to turn back. Huber lifted his chin and positioned his hands so they rested along the collar of his vest, making it look a little like he was fighting a renegade piece of fabric for trying to choke him.

His gaze flicked toward Grey before dismissing him entirely to focus on Bea. "Wondered when you'd be coming to see me and settle our business."

"Not this morning, Mr. Huber." Edging around the man brought her close enough to brush against Grey, soft and citrus sweet.

"Yes, this morning," Huber thundered. "Time's running out."

"That's why we're leaving." Grey figured that since Bea pointed out his tendency to take charge of things, Bea wouldn't mind too much if he hastened Huber out of their way.

"What you do is no business of mine." He waved his hand as though swatting a fly. "The girl, on the other hand, owes me a reckoning."

Chapter 33

The Darlyns will go to your office when we're prepared to make a payment." As she spoke, Bea unwound her reins in obvious preparation to mount, but Huber stayed planted in her way.

"You expect me to believe you're going to pay in full?"

"Believe what you like, so long as you record the transaction properly when it takes place."

"I believe you won't come up with the cash, but I also believe I'll enjoy making frequent trips to the farm to see everything settled." The oily quality of his voice, the way he leaned too close to Bea, and his leer made insinuations Grey could not ignore.

He yanked his wallet out of his pocket, pulled out enough bills to cover the overdue amount—he recalled Seamus mentioning it equaled a little less than half of their expected income from the sale of the bones—and slapped it against Huber's chest. He made sure to pull the puffed-up frog out of Bea's way while he was at it. "There. All settled."

Gratified by both the astounded expression on Huber's florid face and Bea's alacrity in swinging into her saddle, Grey waited while the banker peered down at the money plastered against his waistcoat.

He made no motion to accept the cash. "Where's the rest?"

Bea squinted at the bills fanned against Huber's chest. "That's more than enough to cover the amount in arrears and bring us current for this month."

"Fine. Best bring it to my office so we can record the transaction properly." He took a step back, still not taking the money and looking far too pleased for Grey's peace of mind.

Caught by her own challenge, Bea reluctantly slid from her saddle. Without another word, she marched away, leading Huber to his own office. Though she needed to wait for him to dig a key from his coat pocket and let them in, nothing about Bea's movements spoke of defeat.

When Huber shoved his way in ahead of her, failing to hold the door open for a lady, Grey wasn't surprised. He stepped close to Bea and caught the door, using their proximity to press the bundle of bills into her palm. She favored him with a tight smile before following Huber into a small, dark room.

For a moment, Grey hesitated. No matter that he'd given her the money, that was only an advance payment against what he and Miles would owe her family for the bones. It didn't give him the right to insert himself in Darlyn business dealings. But the idea of standing on the other side of a closed door, leaving Bea to fend off Humphrey Huber in a small, dark room. . . His hand clenched, refusing to release the slab of wood.

"Grey?" She reached out and caught the edge of the door, even though he hadn't released it. Bea pressed, opening it wider in a silent invitation.

One step carried him ahead of Bea. His body blocked Huber's view of her just enough to make the banker scoot his chair over and crane his neck.

"Can't expect anyone to read something in here, much less sign off on it." Grey leaned over the desk, letting his size press Huber into a retreat. He held the position longer than necessary before reaching up and snapping open the blinds.

"Not so much!" Huber scrambled up to adjust the blinds, for once his greasy gaze not sliding all over Bea. A potted plant sprouted bright flowers, the smooth blossoms waving cheerfully from stalks that seemed sort of scrawny in comparison.

Grey glanced at Bea to catch her looking from the blooms, then to

Huber, before looking at him with the same puzzled disbelief he felt. Still, she managed to make her curiosity polite.

"I didn't know you held an interest in horticulture, Mr. Huber."

"Horti—naw. They're tulips." He cupped one stubby hand over the nearest blossom before skimming to the next, not touching any of them. "M' mother brought them to America. They do best outside, but not now. Got to keep the dirt moist."

He poked his forefinger at the bottom of the plants, rubbing a smudge of the soil between his fingers before nodding. "Can't let them dry out, you know."

In spite of himself—or maybe in spite of Huber's self—Grey nodded. No matter what a man made of himself in this world, he ought to honor the woman who'd brought him into it.

"Drought takes a toll on us all." Bea's sympathetic murmur brought Huber's attention back to the business at hand.

"Farms can't be potted." He wiped his finger on the knee of his pants, grabbed a pen, and fixed his beady gaze on Grey. "Let's get down to figures."

Bea laid the bills atop his desk, earning a quizzical look. Neither she nor Grey offered an explanation as to why Bea now offered the payment, and eventually Huber stopped trying to stare them into submission. For a few minutes, the only sounds in the office were a raspy slide of riffled papers and the sharp scratch of a riled writer. He shoved the papers, glistening with wet ink, toward Bea.

"There. Payment recorded. Still don't know why you'd do it this way, but it's that much more profit for me when you fail to bring the rest."

"You'll receive another payment next month, and so on." Bea checked the amount paid and slid the papers back to Huber.

"No I won't."

Grey was more than ready to end this interview. "She said you will, so you won't question her integrity."

"I'm not questioning her integrity so much as her timekeeping. Next month is too late." Huber's grin spread like an oil slick. "Her pa signed the contract. She failed to win the contest, so the Darlyns have one month to pay the amount outstanding on the loan."

Exasperated, Bea jabbed at the still-glistening figure in the "payment" column. "That is more than the overdue amount."

"Not overdue. *The full amount outstanding.*" Huber gave a great snort of laughter. "I worded that addendum specifically to make sure you got what you deserved for trying to make me look foolish."

"The full amount?" Bea paled before Grey fully understood what Huber meant.

"Fourteen hundred dollars remaining on the loan, less the payment you just made." Huber raised a sparse brow. "Still going to tell me you'll make that payment in time, little Darlyn?"

"It can't be legal!" Bea rallied. "We'll have you brought up on charges of usury!"

"Go ahead, but I filed the foreclosure documents the day your pa missed his third payment. You and your family will be out on your ears if you don't mind your manners."

"No." Grey said it loudly, so Bea looked at him. "The month's not up, but it's past time we left."

"You go ahead." Huber rose to his unimpressive height and waved Grey toward the door. "Bea and I need to discuss more. . .private. . . matters."

"There are no private matters between us, Mr. Huber." Bea stood. "You made sure of that the day you trumpeted the particulars of my father's loan to all and sundry."

She deserved applause but got the sound of Huber's fist hitting his own desk.

"Sit down and listen." He flattened his palms on the scarred wooden surface, leaning forward. "I'm willing to make other arrangements to settle your pa's account. I'm a good businessman but a bad bachelor. I want a bride, and lucky for the Darlyns, I've decided I want you."

Never. Grey bit his tongue to keep from telling Huber he could stick his "other arrangements" in his tulip pot and ship the lot back overseas. It wasn't his place to speak for Bea or the Darlyn family. . .but Grey couldn't help wishing, right now, that it was.

"I want to be permitted to finish my round from the shooting match, or even take another turn entirely. You've ensured that we can't have what we want."

"No. You'll give me what I want or you'll pay the price." He breathed in heavy gusts, angry and excited and everything Grey wanted to keep far, far away from Bea.

He stepped forward but stopped when Bea spoke.

"Give me my shooting round. If I don't best your score, I'll agree to the. . ."—she faltered—"other option."

"No." Grey couldn't keep silent. Not that he doubted her ability, but after last time, they all knew Bea's shooting skills weren't the only factor at play. Another crisis—he had no doubts Huber would manufacture one somehow—and Bea would slip straight into his clutches.

"No." Huber's denial matched Grey's vehemence. "We already played out that little game, Bea. You lost. I won then. I win again now. There's nothing left but to agree to my terms."

"I won't." Bea skirted around the short wooden chair.

Huber spluttered. "You can't just walk away from me!"

"You may be within days of owning the title to my home, but you hold no claim upon my time, Mr. Huber. It's my only commodity now, and I can't afford to waste it on a man who taxes my patience." She pulled open the door. "I'll invest my energies elsewhere."

With that, she sailed out of the office, head held high as a queen's. Huber rounded his desk, stretching one meaty arm after her.

Grey grabbed it and pulled it behind the banker's back, twisting the arm. Not enough to break or dislocate anything, but it didn't take much to make a worm writhe.

"You. Don't. Touch. Her." He gritted out the warning, digging his free hand into the side of Huber's neck in a pinch that promised far worse should this rule be broken. "Ever."

When he whimpered something that sounded more like a spineless plea than an agreement, Grey released his hold and let him drop to his own dusty floor. He strongly considered breaking the flowerpot over his head but manfully refrained.

When it came to innocent, lovely things, Huber already destroyed enough.

✳

Why, Lord? Bea's tears blinded her to everything but her despair at Huber's manipulations. She trusted Marco to lead her back to the coulee but couldn't help being surprised when the horse came to a stop so soon. Swiping her eyes with the back of her gloves, Bea realized Marco hadn't halted at the edge of the coulee on his own.

Gold eyes, bright as she'd ever seen them, clouded at the sight of her tears. Grey tugged off one of his gloves and lifted a warm, strong hand to cup her cheek and smudge away the traces of her sorrow. "When we talked about how men want to escape a woman's tears, you never mentioned that the woman might try to outrun them, too."

"Don't tell Pa." She heard the tremble in her voice and despised her display of weakness, even as she tilted her head to feel more of his touch. "If he heard what Huber said, there won't be enough foxglove in the world to keep him with us."

"Understood." He withdrew his hand, and Bea immediately missed the warmth of the connection. Then he dismounted and came around, raising his hands to clasp around her waist and steady her as she came down.

She didn't mind when his hands lingered. Today she needed someone to steady her, and Bea didn't want anyone but Greyson Wilder. It took the final dregs of her self-control not to pitch forward and cling tight to the one bright spot left on her horizon. "What am I going to do?"

"Take a few breaths and pray for wisdom. Then tell your sisters so you can all get your pa to Lincoln." Short, simple instructions. Steps she could follow.

"Yes." She managed her first deep breath since leaving TallGrass. *God, grant me strength.* "I can do all those things. And I will."

"Remember, you won't have to deal with this alone." His hands tightened around her waist, reminding her that he hadn't let her go yet. "Ask Ariel how much your father's heart can withstand and if he should be told anything. I'll distract him until you've formed a plan."

"I don't keep things from Pa." *And if he hadn't hidden this loan from me, we wouldn't be in this situation!*

"He took out the loan. He signed the shooting match agreement." Grey stated the facts without any hint of judgment, but those very facts were too damning.

"I agreed to the match, too. That makes it every bit as much my fault as Pa's!" Bea pulled away from Grey, immediately missing the warmth of his hands at her waist. "Put the blame where it belongs—on Huber's greedy, conniving, manipulating shoulders."

"I wasn't blaming anybody." He held his hands up as though pushing away the accusation. "Someone smarter than I once told me I couldn't be blamed when I lost what was precious to me."

"Oh, bother!" Bea grumbled. "My sisters do this same thing, Greyson Wilder. I vow, the only time anyone recalls my advice is when they can spoon-feed it back to me!"

She couldn't be sure, but it seemed as though he swallowed a snicker before replying.

"Good advice bears repeating," he intoned with a suspiciously straight face. "You pointed out that blaming someone for misfortune means you're acknowledging they're in control. You called me out for blaming myself over Alice's death."

No hint of snickering now. His long face tugged at Bea's overworked heartstrings.

"It's not often someone looks so sad when they're hearing they were right." His gentle admonishment cleared away some of the tension. "I couldn't prevent the fire, and I was wrong to think and act as if I alone controlled every aspect of my life."

"Only God possesses that kind of power," she agreed, more by rote than by conviction at the moment.

"Do you still believe that He's in control? That even when horrible challenges befall us, we need to trust that He'll give us strength enough to work through it?"

Yes. But it wouldn't budge from her lips. Bea pursed them against sudden misgivings. *Lord, I know Your strength is sufficient. But right now, I'm having a hard time feeling with my heart what I know in my head. I feel sad and small and so alone I ache with it even before the worst comes.*

We have to send Pa away. Our home is all but lost. Even Grey will leave for Canada soon. If I relied on him less, would You let him stay longer?

As soon as she prayed it, the truth knocked back. *If you relied on Me more, you wouldn't need him to stay.*

"I'm sorry," Bea whispered. To God, to Grey, and even to herself. "I've been blaming Huber's greed and leaning on your help with him and the farm, but most of all I've been trying to fix things my own way. And all of that is wrong."

"One day, Huber will answer for his greed. And it's no sin to take help when it's offered. But it's not up to you to save your family any more than it was in my control to save mine." A muscle ticked in his jaw, his throat working in a way Bea recognized all too well.

Strange, to see a man trying to swallow old sorrow. Strange and understandable, when the sadness became strong enough to choke away better things.

"Thank you, Grey." She wanted to reach out to him but couldn't. Not when it was already too hard to let him go. "I should have known you weren't blaming Pa."

"No, not blaming. Bea, your pa's health may be failing, but his mind isn't." Grey rubbed the back of his neck, speaking slow like a man trying to find the right words. "On some level, even if he doesn't want to admit it to himself, much less any of his daughters, Seamus Darlyn understands that you might not be able to save the farm."

"Hope is a handhold when health fails." She drew the back of her forefinger beneath her eyes, clearing away some of the salt still clouding her vision. "Pa's barely holding on as it is. Maybe he understands that we're losing, but as long as his daughters keep fighting, he'll fight to stay with us. If we tell Pa the battle's over, the farm won't be the most important thing we lose."

"I understand. I'm just trying to make sure you know that your father understands, too. Feeling guilty for keeping the news from him won't do either of you any good."

"I know."

He searched her eyes a moment, then nodded once, turning back toward his horse.

"Grey?" She waited for him to look back at her. "What you said about being surprised a woman might try to outrun her tears. . .that was wrong."

"So was what you said about me always trying to escape a crying woman." His flicker of a smile restored some normalcy to the afternoon. "You'll notice I came after you."

I noticed. Warmth sparked, beating back the chill that had settled in her chest since they'd seen Huber. But now wasn't the time to examine her reaction—or his reasons. Her head and her heart already held too many conflicting emotions for one day.

"Then, if you were paying attention, you already know I'm not running away from problems." She remounted her horse, held her head high, and nudged Marco into motion. "I'm trying to keep one step ahead of them!"

Chapter 34

They've fallen too far behind. . .over twelve hundred dollars. The Darlyns couldn't possibly come up with that sort of cash in a month. *No. Over a week's gone by since the shooting match, and Huber mentioned drawing up the documents before that. The date will be even earlier.*

If Grey didn't miss his guess, the girls had just over a week left before they forfeited the farm. Mere days to raise more than he used to earn in two years as a police officer. Impossible.

Impossible—but Bea would try anyway. Everything Grey knew about the woman warned that she'd shoulder this burden as her own, same as she did everything else. Memories jumbled together, pieces of the whole but parts he cherished for their own sake.

The scent of lemon as they leaned over the back of a buckboard, negotiating. How she gripped her gun, holding it as a barrier between her family and Huber. The hope she'd tried to hide as her family led him and Miles to their haystacks. An old gospel song brought back to life as she sang her way up and down the fields. Generous lips twisted in a wistful smile as she admitted that her travels with Marco Polo wouldn't extend beyond the edges of pages and plows.

Reddened palms stretched out atop a table as Ariel dabbed them with unguent—burns from where she'd grasped the still-smoking barrel of her rifle, refusing to endanger others by dropping her gun or holding it by the lever as she raced to help her father. The stubborn jut of her jaw as she ordered Grey to stop giving himself so little credit. The soft wonder in her eyes when he told her she was worth more than the small-scale surviving most people settle for.

"Don't let them cut you down," he'd told her, but why should a woman have to stand alone, much less stand between her family and catastrophe? God granted her strength, but maybe He'd gotten Grey to the Darlyn farm to stand with her as an ally others could see. Someone who could help.

"Stop giving yourself so little credit." She'd scolded him into smiling, but Bea inspired more than amusement. Resolve straightened Grey's spine, and he spurred Polo for an extra burst of speed. Then he prayed for an extra dose of strength.

Lord, it's been a long time since I came to You, but You brought me around by bringing me here. To her. I've made too many mistakes to count, and that makes me even more grateful for Your mercy and forgiveness. I confess to sinful pride, selfishness, and a slew of other vices I can't call to mind at the moment. And most of all, I ask for Your guidance as I set myself to complete the work You laid before me. Make me a man strong enough to serve Your will and be the man Bea deserves.

And I wouldn't quibble if You greased the wheels for my conversation with Seamus.

Incredible to think that a few short weeks separated him from the isolated bone picker who'd never heard of his Darlyn. Even more incredible considering how hard he'd tried to resist her. He'd drawn a line about how long they'd stay, only to have it slip as fast and as far as his own resolve. Every time he pushed back his departure, it pushed him closer to Bea. To think, he'd fought it every step of the way, never changing his plan to head in the opposite direction as soon as he caught the chance.

Thank God I'm not the one in control. Bea had been right all along. No matter how blind he'd been before, or how hard he'd fought to forge his own path, when Grey looked back he could see God's hand guiding even the most painful steps. Nothing else could have led him to TallGrass. Nothing else could have stretched a stop in TallGrass into an experience that stretched Grey back.

"Just supper" filled a man's stomach, but now Grey knew to look harder. An empty belly ached, but an empty heart left a man broken.

Even if he didn't know it.

Grey hadn't, until he'd seen the truth through the keen eyes of a sharpshooting farm girl. And it had taken every concession from chocolate cake through competing with Huber to give him enough time to change his mind. All those hours he'd once begrudged, Grey would give up without a second thought if it helped him become the man he should've been from the start. A man ready to stop taking small steps and make a leap of faith.

Bea believed there were two ways to begin difficult conversations. The first involved biding one's time, then pouncing on the guilty party. The element of surprise was a valuable tool to crack open confrontation. But when the conversation didn't revolve around a misbehaving sibling, Bea preferred a gentler approach.

Bad news needed no added dramatics. Tough times and topics like these required a gentle hand. . .but Bea's were shaking, and she didn't have time to find the right words.

"The springhouse?" Cassia's question made Bea look around.

"The springhouse. . .yes. " Bea hadn't planned to bring them here, but she didn't regret the location. Here, they'd begun their farm. Here, they'd learn their best efforts couldn't be enough to save it.

God, grant me the words to speak and the courage to lead my family through this—especially if it means leading them away from our home. Bea ducked inside and snugged into the far corner so they could all squeeze in around the supplies. She stared at the weathered wooden planks and their motley assortment of jars and cans, listening to her sisters spill into the room. Bea pressed the back of her hand against her mouth, pushing down a fresh swell of grief. Only when she'd gathered enough composure did she turn around.

"Is something wrong with Aunt Mary?" Cassia rubbed nervous

fingertips across her cuticles but didn't start picking at them.

"No." Bea welcomed the chance to offer any sort of assurance. "Aunt Mary is fine."

"Did she say she can't take Pa?" Ariel looked over her shoulder, as though she could see through both the springhouse and kitchen walls to catch sight of their father.

"She arrives in Devil's Lake two days from now to fetch him. It's something I'm especially grateful for." It might not be the best way to ease into the heart of things, but Bea ran empty on ideas. "I don't think his health would hold firm in the days ahead if Pa stayed on the farm with us."

"I hate to send him away." Jodie smoothed a yellowing catalog page against the wall. "After we lost Ma, he promised we would all stay together."

Nothing could be truer—or more painful to hear. Bea swallowed.

"This isn't like it was with Ma." Ariel shuffled around a sack of potatoes to rest a hand on Jodie's shoulders, offering comfort without the added burden of long-overdue explanations.

Let Jodie think Ariel meant that Pa would pull through and come home—Bea and Cassia understood how completely the situation had changed since eleven years ago. Ma's heart had been in the wrong place, and her feet followed. Pa's heart held true to his family, but his health pulled him away.

"I know, but he belongs here." Jodie leaned toward Ariel. "With us."

"He belongs where he can get better, so he can come home to stay." Cassia smoothed a hand over her hair, darting wary glances toward the aging paper above her head. Under any other circumstances, her sister's bug watch would make Bea smile.

Not today.

"Once Pa is well, we'll stay together." She started with a statement sure to get everyone in agreement, then plunged forward. "Even if we don't stay here."

Silence, broken by a series of thumps and thuds and crashes as

Ariel—the most graceful of them all—stumbled and brought down sacks of onions and carrots and crocks of stewed beef tumbling to the ground to keep her company.

"I'm all right." She waved them away but didn't jump up to put things to rights. "What happened in town?"

"Huber." She knew she needed to say more, but a round of outbursts proved her wrong.

"The toad!" Jodie shouted.

"Did he try anything?" Cassia started worrying her fingernails again.

"He. . .suggested. . .that he'd be willing to erase the debt if I agreed to marry him." Her stomach lurched, making the last words taste like bile.

"You can't be serious?" Cassia's jaw dropped. Then snapped shut with sudden ferocity. "*Never.* Do you hear me, Bea? Never Huber. I'll marry one of the Brauns if I have to, but—"

"No!" All three of them shouted at once.

"Cassia, hush. This is not one of your Gothic dreadfuls. You won't sacrifice yourself in marriage to save the family fortunes." Jodie rolled her eyes but betrayed her anxiety by raking her fingers through her hair and unraveling her braid. "Bea has more sense than to shackle herself to a worm. He'd wriggle out of any promises he makes!"

"The farm is a patch of land—we can find another and start over if we need to. I only have three sisters, and each of us only gets one life. It's too precious to waste. None of us will marry the wrong man to line Huber's pockets, and that's that." Ariel pulled herself up to a lumpy perch atop the sacks of vegetables. "Now tell us what else he said. Specifically."

Bea left out some of the more loathsome details, keeping her account sparse to spare her sisters any extra upset.

"I'll look at the documents and see if there isn't a way around it." Mind already slipping around possible loopholes, Ariel absentmindedly rose to her feet and promptly tripped again.

"He's already foreclosed, Ariel. Pa missed the payments—the

competition contract gave us a little extra time, but we have no recourse but to pay in full or. . ." Her throat stopped working when it came time to say the worst.

"Lose the farm?" Cassia questioned the entire situation, not just Bea's unfinished sentence.

"We can't! We won't!" Jodie aimed a vicious kick at the side of one of the metal tubs filled with larded pork, then hopped around with both hands wrapped around the injured foot.

Hopping mad. . .and Bea couldn't dredge up any amusement. She looked back at Ariel. "Grey heard everything."

Ariel's light complexion, already pale from their predicament, whitened until every freckle stood out in sharp relief, as if they were all preparing to dive from the tip of her nose. "And we left him with Pa!"

Bea caught her sister by the arm before she could rush for the door—and maybe bring the entire place down around their ears. "I asked him not to say anything. In fact, he encouraged me to ask you how much of this, if any, Pa's heart can withstand. Grey understands." *More than anyone I've ever known.* She remembered his solid strength as he'd helped her form a plan. One step at a time. . .

"None." Ariel's flat assessment chilled them all. "His heart is already weak—hearing that he's lost the farm will break it beyond any hope of repair."

"We." Jodie gingerly put her injured foot back on the floor and wiggled her toes, wincing.

Cassia looked at her. " 'We,' what?"

"If Huber wins, Pa won't lose the farm." Jodie lifted her chin, and Bea caught the gleam of tears in her younger sister's defiant stare. "We will. All of us. No matter whose name holds the deed, every Darlyn had a hand in building this place."

"Both hands." Bea slid one of hers down and threaded her fingers through Ariel's, reaching with her free hand to catch one of Cassia's. Jodie shuffled forward to finish the circle. "Not one of my sisters gives less than her all."

KELLY EILEEN HAKE

"And we're not done fighting yet." Ariel's freckles faded back into proper rank. "We may not have much time, but we owe it to ourselves to make every effort to raise that money."

"We owe it to Pa," Cassia agreed, squeezing Bea's hand. "We're already in the springhouse—let's set aside everything we can sell in Devil's Lake after we see Pa off. And before we dig in, why don't you say a prayer, Bea?"

"Yeah," Jodie muttered. "We need every prayer we can get!"

✳

Grey prayed Seamus's bad mood wouldn't spoil things. It seemed providential that Bea's need for a private conversation dovetailed so well with his need to speak with her father, but this was no run-of-the-mill favor he planned to ask.

Of course, if he didn't ask now, there might not be a time to seek a private audience with the king of the Darlyn castle. Not with Seamus scheduled for a train to Lincoln. Grey might not get another chance, so he'd have to cajole the thwarted monarch into a more beneficent mood.

"Going off to plot against me!" For a man with a weak chest, Seamus Darlyn produced an impressive harrumph. "Trying to decide when they can bundle their old man out of town, but I'll be having none of it, you hear?"

"I hear." Grey hoped Seamus wouldn't ask for his assistance in standing against the girls. Even if he didn't harbor a deep personal bias toward Bea, he would think twice before defying the women. And that went double for the times he happened to agree with them!

In spite of the rage coloring Seamus's cheeks and giving breath to his ire, his condition hadn't improved much since his collapse. Whatever troubles stole his strength, they used every ounce of it to resist the regimen of rest, nourishing food, and lots of love. Grey figured the affliction must be dire, if Ariel's buckets of herbal teas couldn't drown it.

"Good. Now tell me what the telegram said, so we can find a way to work around the arrangement."

"I don't think so." Not the most promising of beginnings, to disagree with a man before asking for his daughter's hand, but necessary. Grey's heart sank as Seamus's eyes brightened with the light of battle, in true Irish fashion.

"Reckoned you'd understand, of all people."

"Why?"

"You know what happens when a man leaves his womenfolk alone and unprotected—even for a short while! You've gone through it." Sorrow stole some of his anger, making his shoulders slump. His voice lowered, his words scratching from Grey's ears right down to his heart. "The loss. The guilt. The knowing. . .that if you'd been there when she needed you most, she might still be here when you need her. And you'll always need her. The ones we love don't take away our need for them when they go."

Grey hardened himself against a surge of self-pity. Now that he knew it for what it was, he couldn't pretend that the rage and regret he'd lived with for so long was the kind of grief that honored his late wife. Nor could he believe Seamus's ongoing despair paid homage to Bea's mother.

"Your daughters need you to get well, here and now." *And thanks to your dealings with Huber, now might be all you have here on the farm if no one steps in.* Grey tensed at the thought but calmed at the knowledge he'd be the one stepping in.

"And I plan to be here now and to keep on being here, no matter what the telegram said." The paper-thin lines on his face deepened to chasms. "Who else will look after my girls?"

"I will." Grey drew a long breath. He'd avoided taking responsibility for anything and anyone else for so long, it felt foreign.

Seamus didn't answer for a good long while, staring at the fire while he considered the offer. "You'll stay with them until I get back?"

"Gladly."

He gnawed on his lip and passed a hand over his eyes, before pinning Grey with a direct, assessing look. "And if I don't make it back?"

It was the first time Grey heard the old man admit the severity of his condition. It was a mark of honor and trust, for another man to acknowledge such weakness. Now that they'd bridged that divide, Grey needed to bring Seamus back up and bridge the distance.

Easiest thing in the world, to put a father back in the position of power when a man came asking for a wife. "Remember when you asked if I had any intentions toward one of your daughters, and I told you I never planned to marry again?"

A gleam of interest and relief eased those lines. "Aye."

"I've learned that when it comes to the Darlyns, plans have a way of flying out the window."

"Made a few new ones, then?"

"No, sir. I'm not holding plans. Just hope—that you'll give me permission to ask Bea to marry me." *And that she'll say yes.*

"Why should I give you my blessing?" Seamus demanded. "What makes you worthy of my favorite daughter?"

"Oh, I'm not. I'm hoping both of you can overlook it, but I definitely don't deserve her."

Seamus started to cackle. "When you ask her, be sure to lead with that."

Almost the moment Bea returned to the house, Grey led her back outside. First he headed toward the barn, then turned at the last moment to bring them behind the house. Here, they were sheltered from prying eyes and upwind of any unpleasant barnyard scents.

In spite of herself, she tightened her grip on his arm when they came to a stop. "Did Pa upset you?"

"He didn't upset me so much as I surprised him." His conspiratorial grin beckoned. "I even managed to make him laugh."

"Really?" That was more than an improvement in mood. . .it was a miracle! "We've all been trying to wrangle a smile from him for days, with no success. How did you do it?"

He shifted closer. "Simple."

"H–how?" Bea heard the start of a stutter and resolutely squashed it.

She'd already accepted blushing. No matter how attractive or intriguing the man, she refused to slide any further toward ninnydom.

Then he rested one of those large, capable hands on her hip, and Bea stopped worrying about it altogether. Stuttering stopped being a problem when a girl couldn't speak!

His eyes darkened to the color of the aged whiskey Pa reserved for special occasions. Bea never tried it, but she doubted the spirits held half the heat or intensity of Grey's gaze as he whispered to her:

"I wanted his blessing before I asked you to be my bride."

Chapter 35

Wind rushed in Bea's ears, and her pulse fluttered in the back of her throat, making it hard to hear him or to say anything in return. Probably not a bad thing, since she would've let out a croaky "yes!" and fallen into his arms, too overcome to think straight.

But she didn't. For one thing, telling her he'd asked for permission to propose didn't count as an actual proposal. No greater ninny ever lived than the woman who agreed to marry a man who hadn't asked her yet!

That very morning, Grey talked about leaving the farm. Oh, he'd mentioned the possibility of coming back for a visit, but that was a far cry from a proposal! The only thing that changed between then and now was the deepening mire of her family's debt to Huber. . .which wasn't an encouraging thought. *He didn't propose to Alice until he knew she needed a hero. Is he only proposing to me now because he wants to save my family?*

Perhaps he'd said something to her father that would banish these pesky doubts. After all, he hadn't given Ben his blessing so easily. He'd taken days to think it over, then discussed it with her directly.

So how had Grey bypassed Pa's thinking time? Pa wasn't given to drastic changes in the way he handled things—especially something as important as this. He must've had good reason.

"Why did Pa give you his blessing?"

Grey's grip tightened then loosened, but he still didn't let go. "You don't think your father should approve of me?"

"No, no, no. That's not what I meant at all." She wondered where her wits went but didn't have time to start a search. "You know you've earned my family's respect and gratitude, but Pa's approval is something else."

"Good. I don't want your gratitude." The lines along the corners of his mouth deepened, tattling of a held-back scowl. "When your father told me to start our conversation by telling you what he'd asked, I thought he was joking."

"What did he ask?"

"He asked what made me worthy of you."

Interesting. Bea wondered whether Ben had needed to draw up some sort of list. "What did you say?"

"That I wasn't worthy, but I hoped you'd both be willing to overlook the fact that I don't deserve you."

Bea's knees went wobbly as a newborn colt's. "That's the most romantic thing I've ever heard." She allowed herself a single sigh before she let common sense resume control. "Utter nonsense, you know, but very romantic."

"It's not nonsense, and it's not romantic. Just the truth."

"Lucky for you, I disagree."

"That's supposed to be lucky?"

"A woman has no business accepting a proposal from a man if she can't come up with a few reasons why he's worth marrying. You think there aren't any. . . . I think you're wrong."

"And my being wrong means I'm the right man for you?" He shook his head, bemused.

"Darlyn logic is unusual, but at least it's consistent. Your father said that if I knew I didn't deserve you, he knew I'd treat you right. Then he told me to go ahead and ask you."

"But why are you asking? Why now?"

"Why does any man propose? I asked because I want you to say yes." A little tendril of warmth wrapped around her heart at his response, but it was too thin to overcome her concerns.

"Would you have asked if you didn't know we were about to lose the farm?"

"No."

One syllable, utter devastation. Bea looked down at her boots, choking back disappointment as he slipped one hand from her waist. Then he crooked a finger beneath her chin and tilted it back so she couldn't avoid his gaze.

"Not yet." Grey spread his fingers and slid his hand to the side to cup her cheek again.

"Then don't. Not now. I don't want a man to marry me because he thinks I need to be rescued. Pity or charity can't carry a lifetime commitment."

"If I had asked before Huber's threat, would you have said yes?"

The smallest of smiles stretched its way from her heart to her lips as she acknowledged his point. "Not yet."

"Are you going to say yes now?"

"Not yet..."

Before she said another word, the window crashed open, bringing Jodie right into the middle of the moment. Jodie levered herself over the ledge until she stuck halfway out of the house, and from the amount of wriggling and kicking going on, Bea knew Cassia and Ariel were trying to pull their youngest sister back.

"Eavesdroppers!" Bea denounced all three of them.

"You never would have known if Jodie hadn't opened the window!" Ariel yelled.

"I wouldn't have needed to open the window if you and Cassia had the sense to keep quiet until it was over!" Jodie hollered back.

Cassia gasped. "A crack would've been enough. What made you think you needed to crawl through it?"

"The sash broke!"

"So why don't you go back inside?" Bea gritted out. She slanted a horrified look at Grey, only to see him smiling at her sisters' antics.

He grabbed Jodie's hands and tried to nudge her back through the window, only to have her cling like a limpet.

"Pull me loose," she pled. "Do you have any idea what those two will do to me if you push me back inside?"

"I can come up with a few ideas," Bea muttered, but sure enough Grey was already tugging Jodie free. *I was right. The man can't resist the impulse to save someone!*

"Listen, I know I botched things here." Jodie looked up at Grey with a mixture of adoration and urgency. "But just in case Bea turns you down—"

"Judith Rachel Darlyn, that is enough." Bea leveled the Finger of Doom at her youngest charge. "You get back inside the house this second."

"Yes, Bea." Jodie backed up...but didn't back down. "But if you don't have the good sense to say yes, and if Grey wouldn't mind waiting a couple more years, I'd take him!"

With her face burning brighter than a new copper kettle, she rounded the corner and ran off, leaving Bea and Grey to gape after her.

Cassia and Ariel stuck their heads out the window, craning their necks and trying to see which way Jodie went.

Cassia recovered first. "Did my little sister just propose? To a man who..."

"Who's trying to propose to your older sister?" Grey finished. "Yes. She did. And yes, I am. And yes, I'm going to ignore all of it and finish what I started."

With that, he wrapped one arm around Bea's shoulders, slid the other beneath her knees—no longer wobbling, at least—and scooped her off her feet. She let loose a small squeal before circling her arms around his neck and holding tight while they stalked away from her sisters.

"At some point, I think I promised your pa that I wouldn't sweep you away...but I'm banking that he'll forgive me."

"Sweeping me off my feet...sparing Jodie from the wrath of my sisters...proposing marriage when you know we're going to lose the farm. . ." Bea refused to allow him to distract her from the important points, no matter how strong he might be, or how warm and tingly it made her feel to be tucked up close against him, or how secretly delighted she was by his decisive action. None of it was enough to change her mind.

"I can't marry a man who only offered out of pity."

"Pity?" He rounded the barn and slid her back to her feet, leaving the arm around her shoulders to hold her close. Somehow his snort reassured her. "Even if you refuse to be my bride, I'll pay off the loan."

Bea's mouth gaped. "How?"

"I have some savings." He gave a wry grin. "Bone picking has proven to be quite beneficial."

"We'd never be able to pay it back."

"Can you come up with a reason why you might want to marry me anyway?" His tone remained light, but his fingertips stopped brushing against her skin, too tense while he awaited her answer.

"One or two." She shifted, releasing his hand from her hip so she could thread her fingers through his. "What about you? Are there any reasons, beyond saving the farm, why you want to marry me?"

"Hundreds." He didn't even hesitate, turning her teasing into the sort of avowal every woman longed for. Grey lifted their joined hands and slid them apart until only the tips of their fingers touched. "Your faith. Your strength. Your steady soul and passionate heart."

With each reason, he tapped one of her fingers, curling it against the warmth of his palm. With each reason, the warm tendril he'd wrapped around her heart grew stronger.

"Your beauty." His hand closed over hers, and he reached for her other hand to repeat the process.

"Wait. My turn." She wiggled loose before he could begin again. "Your protective nature. Your willingness to listen. Your generosity. Your ability to laugh at the little things. And most of all,"—she paused before the final one, just as he had, though her hand could hardly claim to cover his as she finished—"how much you care for others, even though you don't like to admit it."

"If I admit it,"—his voice deepened with the rumbling intensity of a growl—"will you say yes?"

She tilted her head back, considering both the man and the question and knowing she wanted both. "Yes."

"Then I admit it." With one swift motion, he released their hands and swept her into his arms. Grey lowered his mouth to hers, and neither of them said anything for what might have been a moment or a month.

Thanks to Grey, Bea didn't need to worry anymore about time passing them by.

Time ran out when a man least expected the ending. Miles winced at the sharp shrill of the steam engine whistle and braced himself as best he could against the seats. The smallest of movements—every breath, in fact—sent fresh shards of pain spiking through his chest and shoulders. Every time the train applied the brakes, the jolt multiplied his agony.

Not that he didn't deserve the punishment. . .but he opted to minimize it as much as possible. A broken rib took a good stretch to heal, so Miles figured he had plenty of punishment ahead. As best he could figure, he had three of the plaguey things.

Along with two broken fingers, a dislocated shoulder he'd popped back in for himself, and a mottled, swollen mess of a face where his winning smile belonged. A smile now missing one of his back teeth, but Miles wouldn't concern himself with that just now. He wouldn't be doing any smiling for a good while anyway. And besides, he figured it was far enough back that no one else would notice. In the grand scheme of things, losing a molar didn't mean much.

Especially to a man who'd lost every cent he had to his name, and a solid ninety percent of his partner's savings to boot. And at the worst possible time, too. If things between Grey and Bea went well while he'd been gone, as Miles hoped and planned for it to, his partner needed those savings to send Huber scuttling back to whatever dank hole he'd climbed out of.

Maybe the broker wanted some company. After he confessed everything to Grey, Miles figured he'd need to find a dank hole of his very own to crawl into.

So long as it stayed still, it had to be better than a train!

✳

Jodie wished she was the Darlyn with a train waiting to take her away, but wishes weren't going to carry her past the consequences of her outrageous behavior.

After she shook loose of Ariel and Cassia, she'd headed for the old river line. There, the skeletal old trees and resolutely thriving shrubs offered her mournful company—and, more importantly, cover. Childish, to keep silent when she heard her sister's shouts change from angry to worried. Absolutely infantile to wait while the day faded away, through the supper bell, until darkness deepened enough for her to expect that Grey had returned to his hayloft.

But she couldn't face him. Hard enough to have to face Bea. . .Jodie buried her face in her hands, trying to rub away the reality of what she'd done. Had she truly proposed to Grey in the middle of his proposal to her sister?

Outrageous.

Unbelievable.

Inexcusable.

Jodie thumped her fists against her temples with every description, hammering home the enormity of her transgression. *What was I thinking?*

Nothing. To lose one's head so completely, thinking couldn't be part of the equation. She'd been too busy *feeling*. Rage against Huber nicely eclipsed a niggling disappointment in Pa. Desperation to find a way to save their home. . .and their family. No matter what the others said, the two were intertwined. The farm without the Darlyns? No good. The Darlyns without the farm? Even worse—because that was what they'd all have to live through.

Grey gave them a chance. A way to put Huber in his place, keep the family together, and put everything back the way it should always be. . .with a nice addition to the family, to boot. Was it so bad that she wanted to keep him, one way or another? Deep down, Jodie didn't really mind that Grey wanted Bea. She certainly couldn't fault her sister for wanting Grey!

But both of them could—and should—fault her. What sort of self-absorbed nitwit had she turned into, to try such a stupid stunt?

Jodie buried her hands in her hair and pressed her fingernails against her scalp, wishing she could claw out the memory. Of all people to thoughtlessly trample over, why, oh why, did she unleash her idiocy against Bea? Not many people in this world were loved by someone so much that they'd stand as mother, sister, and friend for a lifetime.

She took a gulping breath, rose to her feet, and pushed through the pricker bushes toward home for the third time, finally finding all the windows dark. Bea was probably the one who figured out that she was waiting for everyone to go to bed before she slunk through the door—and instead of putting a candle in every window, Bea had drawn the shades.

Maybe she'll forgive me. Jodie hesitated, cold from the inside out and longing for the warm bed she shared with the sister she'd betrayed. Knowing she didn't deserve to be there. Knowing how badly she'd messed up. . .but knowing that nothing could budge the deeper truth. No matter what Jodie had done, Bea still worried about her. Still waited for her to come home so she could keep her safe and sound.

What a shabby way to repay that, lurking outside and letting her sister worry all night when she never got enough sleep to begin with.

Mind made up, Jodie hurried to the door and tested it. It gave. Had she ever really wondered whether they'd lock her out? Relief tempered her shame as she slid inside and made her way to the bedroom. She waited for her eyes to adjust to the total blackness of the indoors, where curtains blocked the moonlight, then crossed the final threshold.

She saw Ariel and Cassia, fast asleep, then tiptoed toward her own bed, where a lump under the covers told her she'd find Bea. As soon as she reached the edge, the blankets flapped up. Bea grabbed her and hauled her into the warm cocoon and held her tight.

"Don't you ever do that again, Judith Rachel Darlyn," she hissed.

"I'm sorry, Bea." The tears she'd thought all cried out came back in hot streams as she turned and buried her face in Bea's shoulder and shook them both with her sobs. "So sorry."

"Hush, now. You're back where you belong." And, just as she had for as long as Jodie could remember, Bea ran her hand through her hair until she finished crying. All the while, humming a tune that had no name and never followed the same melody twice. It was the song of belonging, and Jodie let it wash over her like a warm bath.

It was the sound of coming home.

Chapter 36

He'll be back," Ariel repeated for the hundredth time that morning, as the train puffed out of sight.

Jodie, who hadn't met his gaze since she'd stammered through an agonizingly heartfelt apology two days before, snagged her sister's hand and patted it. "We know."

Bea told him to give it time and Jodie would bounce back to the mischievous imp he already missed, so Grey didn't push for her to talk to him. At least those painful blushes didn't sweep over her face every time he glanced in her direction, and she stopped dashing out of the room the second she came up with an excuse.

Aside from making everyone else uncomfortable, the awkwardness never failed to catch Seamus's curiosity. And since Jodie had already left the room, that left everyone else with the increasingly impossible task of fielding her father's questions. Though, on the balance, Grey found himself grateful for those interrogations. Seamus's attempts to solve the mystery were one of the few times he'd left off moping about his upcoming journey.

Grey took advantage of his fiancé status to snag Bea's hand, wishing she weren't wearing gloves. "I liked your aunt Mary."

"She liked you, too." Bea bumped her shoulder against his arm in a friendly sort of way. "Even more so when you slipped her that money to make sure Pa gets the best possible care."

"I thought I'd snuck that past you." He'd actually been proud of how smoothly he'd pulled off the maneuver, palming the cash to Mary when they'd exchanged farewells.

"Oh, you handled it so smoothly I would never have guessed if Aunt Mary's eyes hadn't bugged out." Bea's laugh was worth getting found out for.

Grey'd been afraid his girls wouldn't laugh as much once their father set off.

"Your attempt at discretion, while admirable, couldn't overcome Aunt Mary's surprise." Even Ariel looked cheered by the memory.

"What could?" Cassia asked. "When she turned her hand over, opened it, and gawked at the bills?"

"Speaking of bills, I'll need to pay a visit to Wells Fargo. It's down the row and to the left. I can take you to the hotel first, if you like, but that shop I mentioned is on the way." Grey figured Honest Al's would wring another set of smiles from the sisters. Even more so, since Al wouldn't hesitate to buy up every blessed jar, sack, crate, and barrel they'd brought to Devil's Lake—filling the entire farm wagon with goods and leaving the ladies to squeeze any luggage for their father's trip and their own overnight stay into the buckboard with the rest of the family.

"Oh, can we please go to the shop?" Cassia begged, eyes round with anticipation as he helped everyone back into the wagons.

Remorse jabbed at Grey when he realized the ladies probably hoped to find exactly the sort of "silly-frillies" Al banned from his establishment. Belatedly, he tried to temper their expectations. "It's not a fancy place. More hardscrabble than most around here, but he'll give you a fair price when it comes to buying your goods. All the same, I plan to go in first and make sure there aren't the sort of excitable characters who'll play keep-away with your pickle jars."

This prompted giggles from Bea and Cassia, at least, who knew exactly what he meant.

Grey pulled his wagon along the side of the building and got everyone's agreement to stay put until he came back. Even Jodie grudgingly chorused along with the others when he made it clear he wouldn't budge until she joined in.

The front of the store remained unchanged by the past weeks. Dust lovingly coated the boarded-up window and faded the misspelled sign Grey was so glad to see. The bell on the door gave a single sullen clank. "Al? Bill?"

A string of thunks sounded overhead, followed by the clatter of boots on stairs.

"Hello there and welcome to Honest Al's, where—" Bill had launched into his sales greeting before he got close enough to squint at Grey.

"Nothing has changed," Grey interrupted, sticking out his hand. "And I'm glad to see it."

"Al!" Bill squawked with enough volume to leave his ears ringing. "Gotta repeat cust'mer. Looks sorta fermiliar!"

A few more thuds, a murmur of male voices, and another set of boots hit the steps. His impressively large stream of tobacco missing the spittoon by an even more impressive margin, Honest Al made his grand entrance. He didn't bother to look at Grey before growling at Bill.

"What I tell ya 'bout interrupting me when our guest is learnin' me how to beat Barney at the next citywide poker competition?"

"Don't do it." Bill scratched the side of his nose before flinging a forefinger toward Grey. "But if'n my eyes ain't playing tricks, I do believe this here gent'man is—"

"Course your eyes is playing tricks! Keep telling you to git some specs. You can't recognize your own horse, much less a stranger. Who hopped on old man Mickey's old mule last night, instead of Sadie?"

"That were the likker's fault and none o' mine."

"You drank it, it's your fault." Grey wasn't going to waste any more time waiting for these two to finish bickering. "But Bill's right. My business partner and I did come through here a couple weeks back."

When Al finally bothered to look him full in the face, he just about jumped back in surprise. "Bill! This here's Miles's pal."

"What I been tryin' to say?" Bill demanded, looking mighty proud of himself. "These eyes can spot a razor blade on a grate. That keen."

"Yes, but Miles isn't with me." Grey tried to steer them back to the conversation at hand. He'd left the ladies alone for too long already.

"We know." Al tilted his head back and stared at his ceiling. "Hauled him here yesterday, an' all."

"Miles is here?" Grey considered the time frame and figured that if Miles had made good time and not stopped to enjoy a little extra luxury in Chicago, he could've made it back by now. He'd crossed the store and reached the bottom of the steps before either of the other men moved. Grey cupped his hands around his mouth and bellowed. "Miles? You up there?"

A couple faint creaks and a low groan preceded a sheepish, "Grey?"

"Get down here!"

"Easier for you to go up." Al sent another tobacco stream into the corner. "Had a heckuva time gettin' him up them stairs, with the state he's in."

"What—" Grey looked at the pair before him and decided to save himself some frustration. He shouted at Miles instead. "What's wrong with you?"

"Ribs," Al proclaimed, with Bill bobbing his head in agreement.

"All right. Al, come outside. I brought some ladies with me, and I need to introduce them and get them safe inside before I can go up and see Miles."

"Ain't a ladies' shop."

"They're not the sort to be bothered by a little grit. Trust me. They've got plenty of their own."

Al scowled. "Don't do business with hussies."

"I'll forget you said that. The Darlyns are ladies, through and through, but you're risking a lot if any one of them hears you speak against one of their sisters." *Especially Bea.*

"Darlyns?" Al's eyes lit up, and Bill shouldered in. "Didya say Darlyn sisters?"

Miles. Grey glowered at the stairwell. What kind of fool ran on about four beautiful farm girls within a day's ride, without stopping to think he'd be sending trouble their way?

"My partner needs to hobble his mouth. The Darlyns don't need either one of you chin-wagging, either. The last thing they should have to deal with is a group of good-for-nothings who got curious."

"Right." Al nodded a few too many times. "Wouldn't want nobody hurting those gals. Miles says they're sweet as can be."

Trust Miles not to trumpet that the men would be the ones who got hurt. Grey shot another glare upward and stomped to the door. "Don't mention Miles to the ladies until after I've seen him. Maybe we can avoid upsetting them."

"Sure!" Bill scuttled ahead, beating Al to the door but stopping to tussle over the handle.

Grey couldn't be sure, because Bill whistled like a man with a mouth full of gumballs, but he thought he caught the strains of "Oh My Darlin'" as the men rushed outside.

Just as Bea began to wonder whether they should go check on Grey, since he'd been gone so long something had to have gone wrong, the shop door burst open and burped out an odd, raggle-tag set of men. The pair raced forward, looked around forlornly, then brightened when they spotted the wagons nudged up to the side of the store.

Bea freed her pistol from its holster and held it hidden among the folds of her skirts. Smart men didn't run at a wagon of strange women. Best be prepared, even if she had a hard time seeing these two as a serious threat.

The first stood tall and round, with a mustache so luxurious it might explain where all the hair went when it left his shiny pate. The second skittered behind him, short and wiry but nondescript until he drew closer. Then she saw that this one's hair seemed determined to expand its borders, bristling forward in odd patches along his upper cheeks and sending scouts spiraling from his eyebrows in absurd lengths.

"Miss Darlyn?" They called in unison, reaching the buckboard and bowing several times. "Miss Darlyn. Miss Darlyn."

Ariel ended the recitation with her best schoolmarm tone. "That will do."

The pair subsided into silent stares as Grey joined them. "As you've guessed, these are the Darlyns. And these..." He looked at the haphazard set of men hovering beside him with ill-disguised impatience. "Come to think of it, I don't know their last names."

"No need." The wiry one waved a thin hand from himself to his friend. "I'm Bill, and he's Al."

"Of Honest Al's." The bigger one gestured as though pointing to a sign before realizing they weren't standing beneath one, clustered as they were at the side of the building.

"He owns the store." Grey reached up and swung Bea down so fast, she barely had time to reset the safety on her gun and stick it in her pocket.

Bill and Al assisted Cassia and Ariel, while Jodie took one look at them and jumped for it on her own. When everyone trouped around to the front of the store, Ariel started snickering.

Bea followed her sister's line of vision until she caught sight of a woebegone sign whose faded letters still spelled out HONEST AL'S SUPPLES. She bit back her own giggle and shifted so she could swat Ariel's elbow and hiss. "Don't be rude."

Too late. By now Cassia and Judith were both chuckling.

"We're just appreciating the sign!" Jodie protested.

"Ain't nice to laugh at a man's sign," Bill grumbled in a show of loyalty for his poor speller of a friend.

"But it's so clever!" Ariel let loose another peal of laughter. "*Supples!*"

"Clever? Oh!" Judith caught it at the same time as Bea. "You left off the *i* on purpose!"

"Because Honest Al doesn't deal in 'lies.' " Grey's solemnity got them chuckling all over again as they entered the store.

Bea decided the warm welcome and good humor made up for the boarded-over window and air of neglect. That, along with Grey's recommendation, kept her from herding her sisters right back to the wagons.

"I'll be right back. Going to check on that shipment upstairs." With that, Grey left them to browse.

The shelves mapped an erratic perimeter around a potbellied stove and cracker barrel. Merchandise cluttered the dingy shelves with no discernable system. Socks straggled alongside holsters. Vermin catcher nestled atop pillows. Cough drops cozied up to spittoons. . .though on second thought, Bea saw a glimmer of logic in that one.

In no time at all Cassia progressed from praising the store to working the shopkeepers into a lather over what waited in the back of the wagon. Ariel haggled with a hapless Bill, who looked more and more moonstruck with every moment. It took almost no time before they'd struck a deal for more money than Bea could possibly have hoped for back home.

Nothing compared to what Grey would contribute toward Huber's mortgage, but at least they'd be able to contribute something. Bea plucked a dusty shotgun from its ironic place beneath a large clock and started buffing it clean. When it came to dust and debts, every little bit counted.

"All of it?" Grey sank down onto a spindly chair and ignored its creak of protest. He had plenty of protests of his own.

"All but the two hundred bucks I keep tucked in my sock." Miles lifted his left leg a little and set it back down in a hurry, biting his lip the whole time. "Had to use a little of that to buy a ticket back."

"Gambling, Miles?" Grey wanted to rage at the man who'd been part friend, part father to him over the years, but Miles looked so completely miserable and pathetic he couldn't. "All these years?"

"Never was a drunk." He shaped every word carefully, keeping his breaths so shallow it was a wonder he didn't pass out.

"And you welshed on a loan from the McDonald outfit?" Grey's temples thudded in protest against such unimaginable idiocy.

Miles nodded then hissed in pain.

"It's a miracle they didn't come after you ages ago to set an example!"

"About that." Miles closed his eyes as though unable to bear what he had to say. "I think they might've tried. What with the company still in your da's name, I wondered. . ."

He faltered, eyes shining with unshed tears amid a repulsive display of blue bruises fading to sickly greens and bilious yellows.

"What?"

"If they moved against the company but didn't know you weren't your da. Same name and all." The tears left glistening snail trails across his patchwork bruises.

"The fire?" Grey shot to his feet, ignoring the way the chair teetered behind him and crashed to the floor. "All this time, you've thought the fire was your fault, and you didn't tell me?"

"How could I? After what I'd done. . .to try and keep you safe." Miles pulled at loose threads along the edge of his finger bandage. "When I fed you enough drinks during the nights after the fire to keep you from showing your face where anyone would know you. If they were looking for a Greyson Wilder, the only way to protect you was to let them think you died in the fire, too."

"The funeral." Grey's head swam, and he backed into the chair—or onto it. The sound of splintering wood sliced the air as Grey crashed down. He sat amid a pile of kindling, staring at the man he'd trusted so completely for so many years, catching sight of the betrayer beneath the friend, painted in the sickly shades of a beaten man.

"Aye." Miles let his head drop back against the pillow and mopped his face with a soggy bandanna. "I kept you from it. Easy enough to help a man drink himself senseless when he's never danced with the devil in the shotglass before."

Grey surged to his knees and emptied his stomach into the chamber pot. He shoved it back under the bed, not speaking until he'd convinced himself that letting Miles go on feeling guilty about the fire was almost as despicable as Miles watching him blame himself for missing Alice's memorial for the past two years.

Chapter 37

It was the neighbor." Grey poured himself a splash of water from the pitcher at the side of the bed, swallowed, and ran the back of his hand over his mouth. "Turns out his boy stole a knapsack from school and someone fingered him for it. . .so the kid tried to burn the evidence. Too bad the pack was oiled against rain."

"You're trying to make me feel better, when I don't deserve it." Miles lifted a hand and swatted it through the air like he was trying to kill a fly. He dropped his arm with an anguished cry, quickly stifled but no less difficult to hear. "Don't make up stories for me."

"I didn't. I put a call in to my station house a couple weeks after we started collecting bones." Grey leaned against the nearest wall. "Kid caught fire, lost his head, and ran around spreading the flames. His mother covered him with a blanket and dragged him down the stairs. Both of them made it to the hospital, badly burned. She lived. The kid didn't."

He thumped the back of his head against the wall, anchoring himself in the physical discomfort to keep from being dragged under by the deeper current. "Not the sort of story to cheer anyone up."

"No. It isn't." A rattling, moist honk told Grey Miles blew his nose. "So I kept you from the funeral for nothing. And I've been keeping you from the truth ever since. . .all for nothing."

"You should've told me." Another knock against the wall. "But you can't take all the blame. No one forced me to swallow those drinks. I wanted a way out, you offered oblivion, and I took it with both hands."

"Grief kept you from thinking straight. I knew better."

"Like you knew better than to gamble?"

"Yeah."

"Or to take out a shady loan."

"Or to run out on it," Miles added with so much humility it left no room to browbeat him.

"Or to keep going back to Chicago, knowing the risks?" Grey reached down, picked up part of the smashed chair, and started snapping it into smaller pieces. "You're lucky they didn't kill you."

"I know."

"*I'm* lucky they didn't kill you." Grey tossed away the remains of the stick and got to his feet again.

Miles gave a morose sigh. "Dunno about that. Don't want you to be stuck with me like this."

"What do you think I would've done if you disappeared?" Grey demanded. "You think I wouldn't have gone looking for you? You think I wasn't a good enough officer to uncover what happened, and go after the men guilty of murdering my friend?"

Surprisingly, a man swollen and swathed in bruises could still go pale. "The second they heard you asking questions, you'd have been dead."

"Yep."

Miles let out a shuddering breath that sounded suspiciously like a sob. "I'm not worth that. I'm not worth any of it."

"You won't hear me arguing with you about it right now." Grey finished splintering a chunk of seating. "Don't you dare start crying, Miles."

"I'm"—a blubbering sniff—"not."

"Our money saved your skin, and while I'm glad there was enough to keep you breathing, you don't have the right to cry about it." He threw the next chunk of seating against the far wall. "Not when your old debt just cost the Darlyns their farm, and maybe lost me my fiancée."

Ignoring Miles's spluttering questions, Grey stalked down the stairs to find Bea. Not hard to do, when the woman he wanted to marry stood in the center of the store, aiming her pistol at Honest Al.

✳

Stretch out your arm as far as you can, keeping the card between the very tips of your finger," Bea directed the shopkeeper, knowing full well the man would keep as much of himself as far away from the target as he possibly could without any extra prompting.

She eyed the shivering spade at the center of the ace and pulled the trigger.

"Well, I'll be." Bill snatched the card from Al and held it up to let light stream through the neat hole her bullet had punched through the center.

"You're every bit as good as your sisters said!"

"That's nothing," Jodie snorted. "You want to see something special, turn the card around."

Bill gave her an odd look before balancing on his tiptoes and stretching out the card with its blue backing facing forward. "Okay, then."

"Not like that." Cassia plucked it from his grip, turned it sideways, and wedged it back between his thumb and forefinger. "This way."

Al looked from the razor-thin edge of the card to Bea, then back again, and shook his head. "You split that card with one shot, I'll come out to see you gals practice with that target thingamajig you talked about."

Bea laughed, squeezed the trigger, then laughed harder as Al fell to his knees and groped around for the fallen top half of the card, then matched it to the piece Bill still held.

"I'll be." He shook his head. "If that don't beat all."

"Sorry for telling you 'bout that cigar trick," Bill hastened to apologize. "Never meant to imply you used a cheap advantage like that."

"What trick?" Grey's voice had Bea turning toward the stairs. She'd heard him come down but didn't want to compromise her concentration.

Now she wished she hadn't waited. A glance was all she needed to see that something was terribly wrong. Bea holstered her pistol and made her way to him, leaving the explanations to Ariel.

"Bill and Al say there are trick cigars with loops that go around a man's tongue, so when someone fires a shot he pulls the loop and it makes the ash burst loose." Ariel sounded more fascinated than aggrieved. "Can you imagine how much time went into designing something so silly?"

"I can think of worse things." Grey stepped off the bottom stair, picked up Bea's hand, and put it on his arm. "Bea and I will be back in a moment."

With that, he tugged her out a side door, onto a small stoop, and stepped away from her as soon as the door shut. "Miles is upstairs."

"What? Why?" She clasped her hands together to keep from batting Grey's hands from his hair. He raked his fingers through those black locks with so much force it should've made a ripping sound.

"History caught up with him in Chicago and took a heavy toll."

Bea rubbed her hand along the base of her own throat, which suddenly felt too tight to pipe out any words. "What kind of toll?"

"Just about every dollar Miles and I made over the past two years went toward the bill. They took the rest out of his hide until he gave up the cash."

"Is he all right?" Stupid question. She immediately corrected herself. "Is he going to be all right?"

"Far as I know, there's no cure to fix a gambling, cowardly, low-down liar." Grey pulled off his hat and smacked it against his thigh. "But he'll heal up, given enough time."

"So will we." Bea moved toward him, but he transferred his hat to the hand nearest her and kept smacking it against his leg—a barrier she couldn't ignore. "Even though you're angry right now, you'd mourn him terribly if he didn't pull through. We can't replace Miles, but we can make more money." *Just not in time.*

"Not quick enough to settle up with Huber." Grey slammed the hat back on his head. "I put my trust in a man who didn't deserve it.

That makes his mistakes my mistakes. Miles lost the money. . . ." He swallowed. Hard. "But I lost the farm after I promised to save it."

"It wasn't yours to lose." Bea knew better than to try and coddle anyone through this sort of mood. "It wasn't even mine or my sisters'. It was Pa's. And none of us asked to be rescued."

Even though it would've been nice.

"That doesn't absolve me for breaking my promise." His fists clenched. "So I can't in good conscience hold you to yours. I don't expect you to tie yourself to a man who can't provide what you need most."

"Pa taught us to take care of ourselves." Stung, Bea lashed back in hopes of surprising him to his senses. "And any man who asks me to marry him should know better than to think the thing I need from him is money."

He shook his head but wouldn't look at her.

In that moment, something inside her broke. Bea felt herself deflate, felt something vital give way, and realized it was the shiny, buoyant bubble of hope and happiness that started growing when Grey decided to stay.

He'd changed his mind. He planned to walk away. Just because Miles told him he couldn't afford to buy her hand in marriage.

As if her hand made the decisions. *Why doesn't he care about my heart, Lord? That's what I promised to him. That's what I wanted from him. . .not the farm. Not money. . .just him.*

"I didn't agree to join our lives for money." She whispered it, not willing to say it any louder than that. "I wanted more from you than that, Greyson Wilder. Maybe I wanted too much, but never money."

She groped for the door handle, pushing it open and backing inside. "I'm not a whore."

His hand shot out, closed over hers, and yanked the door closed again. The move pushed her closer to him, but he gave no quarter. The gold of his eyes she loved so well gleamed sharp and cold as the metal he thought made him a man worth wanting.

"Never say that." He planted his hands on either side of her head.

"You're anything but a whore. You're everything I stopped letting myself want, because I told your father the truth."

Some small pocket of hope stretched again. "That you want to marry me?"

"No." He pulled his arms back. "That I don't deserve you. But at least I won't stand in the way of you finding someone who does."

✳

Grey watched her shove her way back into the store, obviously trying not to cry, and somehow let her go.

Why, God? I admitted I can't control everything. That I wasn't good enough for her. But I did earn enough to give her family their home. Why did You take that away from me? From them?

No small voice answered back. No sign crashed down from the heavens. Sometimes the answer was just no. And there was nothing he could do about it, except try to keep from dragging anyone else down with him.

He went back into the store to find Bea bracketed by her sisters, all of them talking over each other and trying to describe the Spinster's Doom to an obviously interested—and just as obviously confused—Honest Al.

"All right! I'm convinced!" He held up his hands to stop all the talking. "Bill and I will make the trip out to your place to see this contraption firsthand. If the rest of you have half your sister's talent, I'll arrange for the four of you to take top billing in Grand Forks next week."

"Top billing?" Grey didn't like the sound of that.

"That's right." Al sent him a smug grin. "Thanks to your partner's tips, last night I won half ownership in a Vaudeville theater. These little Darlyns could be just the ticket to fill the seats and line our wallets. I'm thinking they'll bring in every man for miles around!"

Chapter 38

They're here!" Jodie cantered Daredevil in a wide ring around the targets before sliding to the ground.

"Wonderful." Grey tried not to sound too sarcastic. The Darlyns needed to make a living; Al needed to fill his playbill. Grey had no right to try and keep the two separate. The best he could do was keep himself as separate from the girls in general—and Bea in particular—as he possibly could. That meant bolting meals and heading directly to the barn after dinner. It meant keeping clear while the women mapped out a show designed to win Honest Al's patronage.

Gone were late afternoons spent trading questions with the woman he'd hoped to marry. Gone were the long meals filled with easy conversation. In spite of Bea's insistence that she hadn't wanted his money, her sisters withdrew their approval in a mighty hurry as soon as his bank account shrank.

Every day, he rode to the telegraph office hoping for word that Seamus experienced a miraculous recovery and would be coming back to take charge of his daughters. Every day he rode back the way he'd left—empty-handed. Something Grey didn't think he'd ever get used to. A full wallet might not be what made a man, but no one could deny that in times like these, it was what made him useful.

✸

"What do you use this for?" Bill poked at the sandbag. He'd been poking at everything they showed him, except for Daredevil. Bea couldn't say whether it was Jodie's glare or the horse's that made him keep his fingers to himself on that score, but nothing else matched the feat. Not even nicks from Ariel's arrows or gouges from Cassia's knives deterred him.

"I shoot the rope to make it drop down and send Bea's targets flying through the air." Ariel alone maintained an amused patience after so much prodding—probably thanks to her experience managing a schoolroom.

"Let's see it in action!" Al stuffed a fresh wad of tobacco into his bulging cheek and sprayed the ground nearby with his enthusiasm.

Jodie's trick riding and a few rope stunts had set the tone early on. Then Cassia had provided a quick demonstration of simple throws with good, solid sticks. They'd decided not to show off too much. Better to hit every mark, every time, with less complicated tricks, than to miss even one of the hard ones.

Besides, like Ariel pointed out, the Dangerous Darlyns shouldn't bring out their greatest feats during the first show—if this became lucrative enough for them to save up for a new home, they needed to leave room to make the show bigger and better.

"All right." Bea tried to call everyone's attention but finally had to resort to her whistle. It never failed. "Gentlemen, I'm going to ask you to come back behind this line while Ariel demonstrates a few shots with her arrows. We'll run through Spinster's Doom afterward."

In seconds, everyone had taken their places. Bea watched with burgeoning pride as Ariel sent arrow after arrow winging toward the target, until they ringed the heart-shaped bull's-eye. The next shot went right into the center. All they needed was for her to make the final trick—splitting that center arrow straight down the middle—and they'd be golden.

But her sister hesitated, tilting her head as though trying to locate the source of some sound. Bea heard it, too. The shape of the coulee walls carried sound better than anyone imagined. It sounded like horses.

"Did you ladies invite anyone else?" Bill shaded his eyes even though he wasn't squinting into the sun.

"No." Bea watched as the dark shape in the distance divided into small specks around a darker blob, and knew exactly who it was. "These guests aren't people we'd ever choose to invite."

Al ambled around and wandered toward the approaching visitors, taking slurping sips from his canteen as if still enjoying a show.

Bea grimaced. If Huber didn't watch himself, Al and Bill might get more of a show than they bargained for.

Father, we've worked hard to get this far. We've come together and given the fate of the farm into Your hands and followed this new opportunity as far as You've brought us. Please don't let Huber take away this chance. Even if it's not Your will, please show it another way. Make me miss my targets. . .but please don't make Huber the one who ends this.

The back of her neck prickled, and when Bea looked up, she found Grey standing beside her. Closer than he'd come since the day he'd learned of Miles's misfortune and made it into their own. He'd kept his distance since then—and Bea hadn't been the only one kept at arm's length. Even her sisters felt the sting of his withdrawal because they all saw it for what it was. Rejection.

Grey snapped open his rifle chamber, checked to see it was full, and snapped it back into readiness. "Huber."

It wasn't a question, but Bea answered anyway: "Huber."

In spite of the approaching ordeal, Bea couldn't suppress a spurt of happiness to have Grey beside her again. Even if the only thing she read on his face was grim determination and the only thing that brought them together was Huber, Bea relished the return of her ally. If only he'd realize this was enough for her—that dependability mattered more than financial stability ever could. . .maybe he'd choose her over his pride.

By the time Huber reined in that ridiculous buggy and the rest of his posse pulled in alongside him, cold determination replaced any warm feeling from seeing Grey step up. Bea spotted someone clinging to the seat in the back of the buggy and counted three men riding with them. Two Braun brothers—including the one who'd felt the bite of that jar of pain extractor—bracketed the buggy on either side, with the youngest

Kalb brother bringing up the rear.

"You're not welcome here, Huber." Bea motioned with her rifle. "Take your men and leave."

"Since I hold the deed, I decide who is and isn't welcome." He jumped down from the buggy and swaggered up to Al and Bill. "Who are you two, and what are you doing on my land?"

They mumbled something about the Darlyns' invitation before Bill beat a hasty path back to the barn, with Al abandoning his canteen to follow in close pursuit.

Not exactly a show of strength to send Huber packing with his tail between his legs.

Bea tightened her grip on Chester.

"You can't claim ownership until after you've served notice to vacate." Ariel let the tip of her bow touch the ground but kept her arrow notched.

Grey rested the butt of his own rifle against the inside of his elbow, raising the gun to a more prominent position. One that made it easier to swing into place and start shooting.

Huber pulled out his own pistol and tapped it against a sheaf of papers he retrieved from the seat and held in front of his horsewhip. The thickheaded Braun brother hopped from his horse and gained a few steps toward Cassia, while his brother followed Huber's example and raised his shotgun.

The Kalb kid looked like he wanted to be anywhere else, and the shadow in the buggy either couldn't keep still or was shaking so hard he made the whole thing quiver with him. Bea dismissed them both and kept her attention fixed on the three main threats—dividing half her focus between the two Brauns and devoting the remaining half to Huber.

Who sneered at their weapons and had enough nerve to come close enough to throw the papers toward Bea's boots. "There's your notice. You've got one month to move out." He took another step forward, and Bea decided he'd gone one step too far.

Apparently, Grey thought the same thing, since the two of them raised their rifles to their shoulders in unison, as though they'd rehearsed the motion.

Huber faltered but didn't fall back. "Or you can make nice, so you and your sisters don't have to leave TallGrass. I've arranged everything."

"The only thing I want you to arrange is your departure," Bea warned. "Leave now, and if you come back before the end of our month, you won't claim more privileges or protections than any other trespasser."

"You don't want to provoke my temper, Bea."

"Miss Darlyn," Grey corrected, showing that even if he no longer claimed her, he wouldn't let Huber take his place.

It would've been Mrs. Wilder, if you hadn't thrown me over. Fresh pain stiffened her spine and sharpened the snarl she aimed at Huber. "I don't want attention from you at all."

"Don't you want to stay?" Huber's eyes raked over her, practically leaving streaks of oil down her new dress.

"Don't you need to leave?" Cassia called back, wiping one palm against her skirts, then the other, before sliding her blades back into place.

"No." Huber uncurled his fingers, letting the lash from his horsewhip spiral to the ground. Behind him, his horse shied away, prompting a frightened yelp from the figure still shadowed by the buggy. "I told you, I made all the arrangements."

"They don't seem interested," came a placating voice from inside the buggy.

"Come on out, Pastor Rickets." Huber grinned.

"Pastor Rickets?" Cassia sounded more horrified than curious—a sure sign that Bea wasn't the only one who suddenly understood the nature of Huber's so-called arrangements.

"The circuit rider!" Jodie craned her neck. "Join us, Pastor. Let your good influence soften those who harbor ill will toward my family!"

From what Bea gathered, Rickets's good influence barely had the strength to keep the buggy from shaking.

"But we offer the best of intentions," Huber oozed. "The stuff of every girl's dreams and every father's fondest hopes."

"So you *are* leaving." Ariel's wry comment twitched the grin away from their unwanted visitor.

"I'm sending you into the arms of your new husbands. I considered offers from most of the unmarried men in town and settled on fine matches for each of you." Huber waved toward the buggy, where Pastor Rickets still perched. "Even brought the pastor to do it up proper."

The oldest Braun stole another step toward Cassia. "Huber said I can have you, and my brother can take that scrawny sister of yours."

"And he's giving Judith to me!" Kalb's voice cracked on the last syllable in a way that might have been funny if he were saying anything else.

"You have no right to speak for us." Bea's incredulity steadied her rage and kept her finger from twitching against the trigger.

"Your father's weak and waning. Once we marry, I'm head of the household—and that gives me the right to select suitors for your sisters." Huber's voice lowered. "You might be grateful that I demanded they marry the minxes before I'd allow them to be carted off."

"Grateful?" Bea lowered her head, eyes finding the sight line atop the barrel of her rifle. She followed that line, then adjusted until it led straight to Huber's black heart. "I'll give you one minute, Mr. Huber, before I and my sisters unleash the full force of our *gratitude* on you and your so-called suitors."

"Get your gals!" At Huber's roar, he and his men started to move.

Slowly, it had to be said, but with a foolhardy determination that left the sisters no option but to fight back. Kalb hopped from his horse and raced toward Jodie, who sent her rope sailing and jerked the boy from his feet in less than a second. He hit the ground with a bone-jarring thud.

At first, Bea kept her eyes on Huber and his pistol, but he was too busy enjoying the show to budge. For now, the Braun brothers presented the greatest threat.

"Stop." Cassia's warning bounced right off Braun's thick head— until he felt a breeze and looked up to see his hat pinned to the side of the barn.

Ariel's arrow held drawn and tense, directed at the idiot's brother. An idiot in his own right, he brandished his shotgun with unsettling eagerness, shifting from Grey to Bea to Cassia and completely ignoring the arrow his "intended" was prepared to sink into his chest.

Cassia sent another blade so close to the eldest Braun that if he'd moved any faster she would've pinned his nose to the barn. Instead of heeding the warning, he wiggled the knife free and kept coming.

A second later, Cassia's beau crashed to the ground, knives bristling from both of his boots and one of his shins. He curled into the fetal position, fingers finding and feeling the edges of the blades and coming away bloodied.

Instinct snapped Bea's attention back to Huber in time to see him raise his pistol. She pulled her trigger without an ounce of remorse, shooting the gun from his hand and bringing him to his knees. She looked at the Braun still sitting atop his horse, chilled to see him take aim at Cassia.

Chapter 39

Grey's yell distracted Braun long enough for Grey to grab Al's abandoned canteen and hurl it toward the horse. Braun smirked at such a weak weapon, but Bea immediately understood Grey's gambit. Their shots fired almost simultaneously, still ringing when the canteen exploded. The burst of leather and liquid sprayed Braun and spooked his mount into rearing back and bucking his rider.

The fourth fool joined his cohorts and found his place on the ground.

Thank You, Lord, that no lives were lost. Forgive me if part of my relief comes from knowing my sisters won't bear that burden.

A snarl grabbed Bea's notice in time to see that Huber had gotten to his feet and raised his horsewhip—but not in time to evade it. She tried anyway, squeezing her eyes shut and hitting the ground in an attempt to duck the lash, all the while waiting for it to fall. She heard the smacking strike of leather against flesh, astonished to realize she didn't feel it.

Bea skimmed her fingertips across her face, expecting the sickening warmth of blood. When she found none, she opened her eyes to see Jodie's rope arc around Huber, pinning his arms to his sides but failing to bring him down. He shrugged out of it and ducked away from Grey's tackle to scoop up one of the knives protruding from Braun's boot.

Grey followed, holding his rifle and steadily closing in.

But he didn't shoot. He didn't even try to close the distance between them, just steadily tracked Huber like a cat toying with a mouse. Bea grabbed Chester and rushed to join him, reaching Grey's side at the same time Huber backed into Spinster's Doom.

The loud thunk of the sandbag hitting Huber's head drowned out the soft twang of Ariel's arrow. The sandbag tumbled to the dirt first. Huber swayed for a moment before collapsing atop the weight that felled him.

Bea snatched Cassia's knife from his clammy palm, grimacing at damage done to the other. When she'd shot the pistol from Huber's hand, the bullet left torn and gory stumps where his middle and ring fingers belonged. Ariel nudged her out of the way, bending to loop a length of twine around what remained of the digits before tightening it with several strong tugs, then knotting it.

"Can't save the fingers, but this will keep him from bleeding to death." Sure enough, the gush of blood slowed to a sluggish stream, then a thin trickle.

"Better than he deserves." Grey turned away in disgust before Bea could look him in the eye and thank him for his quick thinking. Together, they hog-tied all four of the trespassers, using the Braun brothers' own grubby handkerchiefs to staunch their unceasing whines. Bea filched a spare and used the handle of Huber's own whip to shove it into his mouth. No sense waiting for him to wake up—she wouldn't put it past the man to start biting.

With the danger past, Bill and Honest Al emerged from the barn. Hesitant at first, both were swaggering by the time they reached the side of the buggy, where Grey and the Darlyns propped up all four captives.

"Ladies," Al intoned, sweeping the hat from his head and giving a flourishing bow, "I've never seen a better show. You're hired."

"These weren't part of the show." Jodie jostled the bigger Braun brother with the toe of her boot.

"Ya don't say." Bill's eyes went wide beneath his untamed brows, making him look more than a little wild.

"In that case," Al gaped at the four trussed troublemakers before setting his hat back on his head, "you're still hired!"

"He'd be afraid to turn you down, and that's a fact. You Darlyns really are dangerous!" Bill hunkered down to poke at the captives, then went green around the gills when he caught sight of Huber's hand.

"Here." Al shoved some papers toward Grey. "Stage passes, so they can't try to run you out of my theater. I never met my co-owner, but the guy I won the theater from swore that these will grant you access to everything from the dressing rooms to the stage."

"Al?" Grey kept their benefactor's attention. "You got room in that wagon of yours to take this bunch of lawbreakers to lock up in Devil's Lake? There's no jail or even sheriff here in TallGrass."

"Sheriff won't keep 'em long on account of assault, but he'd probably stretch it out if we made sure to tell him they attacked ladies." Bill bent down and started poking at the ropes, checking to see that the knots were tied tight enough.

"Try to keep them tied up for a couple days," Grey encouraged. "Long enough for the ladies to pack their bags without wasting time looking over their shoulders."

"Done." With that settled, the men turned their attention to shoving the prisoners into Al's weather-baked wagon.

"You think Miles will be in any shape to join us in Grand Forks?" Grey's question answered one of Bea's.

So he's managed to forgive his friend. Good for Miles. . .bad for Bea. Not only did it rob her of one of the few things she disliked about Grey, but his concern for his fellow bone picker might rob her of his company once they returned to Devil's Lake.

After all, Grey had no obligation to go to Grand Forks with them.

The sound of hooves broke through her thoughts and pounded new worries in their place. Bea grabbed Chester and started walking, determined to meet this newly arrived challenge before it got the chance to scare her sisters. With the men occupied putting the prisoners in Al's wagon and her sisters following Bea's wave to stand down, she stood alone to meet the newest rider.

✳

"Who's that?" Grey shrugged Ariel away, impatient with her fussing. He tried to place the man walking beside Bea, leading his horse behind him. The fellow looked familiar. Grey recognized him as the townsman who'd taken his side during Huber's lunchtime attack.

"Lionel." Ariel stepped forward but stopped and waited for the newcomer to join them. "Lionel Fuller."

Jodie gave him the answer Grey needed. "Ben's younger brother."

"Back when Ben spent a lot of time here, Lionel joined him quite a bit. Didn't he, Ariel?" Cassia gave her sister the sort of meaningful look Grey knew meant trouble.

Lionel probably nursed a longing for his older brother's fiancée. Grey grimaced at the thought but consoled himself with the knowledge that the upstart had chosen the worst possible time to come calling. It wouldn't take Bea long to send him packing.

"Ariel?" Bea started to say something to her sister, but it faded into nothing when she caught sight of Grey's face.

He'd been careful to keep his head turned away—to keep the burning, swelling gash across his cheek hidden from her.

"Grey! What—" She reached toward his cheek, fingers hovering above the long gash laid open across his left cheek. He met her gaze for half a heartbeat before he pushed her hand away.

Don't let her close. Grey fought the urge. *You know you'll want to keep her.*

She flattened her palm against the center of his chest, blocking him from walking away. Even looking at what he knew would be an ugly wound, the blue behind her hazel eyes glowed soft and full of wonder. "You stepped in front of Huber. You took the lash for me."

In that moment, they connected as strongly as before he'd found Miles.

"Bea?" Ariel intervened. "Lionel would like a word. In private."

Grey's cheek stopped hurting when Bea turned, answering Lionel's summons. Useless rage shredded his chest, blocking any other, lesser pain. *She's going to him.*

But first, she reached over to give his hand a motherly pat. "This won't take long."

"Take as long as you need." His voice sounded gruff, but Grey couldn't help that. "Take private conversations with whomever you want. I told you I wouldn't hold you to our engagement. You don't owe me any explanations."

With every word, her jaw hardened a little more. When he finished, she gave a brittle nod and marched toward the house without a backward glance. Why look back at him, when she had Lionel to look forward to?

✳

Jodie peered around the barnyard, spotting Grey by the chicken coop. She squared her shoulders and fixed her courage.

Now wasn't the time to remember her own foolishness from before. Not when she'd gotten a chance to make up for it! So she marched right up to him and slapped a wad of cotton-wrapped ice into his hand.

"Stick that on your cheek." When he didn't immediately comply, she drummed her fingers on one of the fence posts circling the chicken yard. "Believe me. Ariel's no slouch when it comes to stitching skin, but it'll go a lot smoother if you can numb it first."

"Don't want stitches."

"Fine. Leave it unwashed and open to every breeze, bug, and bit of dust to blow your way. Scar your face to spite whatever's sent you on your stubborn spree." Jodie stuck out her hand. "I'll take the ice though. No sense letting it go to waste."

Grey laid the clumsily wrapped bundle across his cheek. He spread his palm over the ice and pressed it more firmly against the angry red wound it pained Jodie to see.

But it would have pained her more to see it on Bea.

"You rolled into town and walked onto our farm like something out of a fairy story. All black hair and golden eyes and the ability to get Pa to sell the bones and save the farm. A hero."

"No I'm not."

"No, you're not." His quick, disgruntled look made her grin. "But you kept acting like one anyway. Choosing to stay and help us put in the crops—always standing up against Huber. Showing that you can shoot almost as well as Bea. Offering to save the farm. Everything you did made you seem larger than life. But the bigger the character, the bigger the mistake when they mess up."

"That's true for everyone."

"Maybe. But I'm trying to give you credit, here." She stuck the toe of her boot into the chicken wire and wrapped her arms around a fence post to hoist herself up to eye level. "You've done a doozy of a job with my sister."

"Because I proposed."

"No. The proposal goes down as one of my mistakes. But you did one better." For the first time, she glared at him. "What kind of man *unproposes?*"

"Unpropose? What's that supposed to mean?"

"You undid your proposal. You took it back." If he hadn't also shielded Bea from Huber's whip, Jodie might've wanted to smack him. "Where's the honor in that?"

✳

Never had Grey seen a conversation go downhill so fast. "I didn't undo anything. But I was honorable. I won't hold Bea to our agreement when I can't keep my end of it."

"So Miles lost the money, and you ended the engagement." Jodie's jaw jutted forward. "Admit it."

Grey wished he had more ice to lay against his cheek. It stung almost as bad as Jodie's accusations. "A man has no business marrying a woman when he can't provide what she needs."

"There've been at least three men who've tried to marry my sister. She turned down two of them." Jodie tapped the bottle of witch hazel against the fence post. "Do you know why?"

"Ben chose Oregon. And Huber. . .is Huber." More than reason enough.

"Huber's a chicken. Struts around and rules the roost, making a big show about whatever he runs across and always claiming the best bits for himself. Bea won't humor him. No Darlyn will answer a birdbrain's every peck and call."

Grey started to grin before the searing pain in his cheek stopped him. *Peck and call.*

"Ben wasn't much better. He chose Bea then thought he could change the deal and choose Oregon, too."

"I knew better than to change the deal," Grey pointed out.

"Did my sister ever tell you that she would only marry you if you paid our mortgage? Or did she just agree to marry you?"

"We had an understanding."

"You have no understanding!" Jodie hopped down from the fence and planted her index finger in the middle of his chest. "Bea didn't demand a farm. Ben offered her a fine one in Oregon. Huber would've let her stay here. Either one of them would've given her that much, but she turned them both down." She jabbed him again. "What does that tell you?"

Lord, did I make a mistake? Doubts rattled his brain like marbles.

"The farm isn't the most important thing." He'd known that, but. . . "It still matters."

"Not as important as having a husband she can count on the way everyone else counts on her. You had the chance to prove you'd be that kind of husband, but you unproposed instead."

Hope rose but quickly deflated. "She obviously agrees, or she wouldn't go off for a private chat with Lionel Fuller!"

"Lionel?" Jodie blinked then groaned.

"I can read between the lines."

"You've got the story backward, Grey." Jodie rolled her eyes. "Lionel's sweet on *Ariel.* With Pa gone, Bea's head of the family. He doesn't want Bea—just her blessing."

Chapter 40

Bea!"

Her heart thumped at Grey's shout, then picked up the pace even more when he grabbed her hand and started tugging her around the house.

"What is it?" Reluctantly, she tugged her hand from his when they stopped behind the house—just beside her bedroom window. The same place where he'd once proposed.

"I made a mistake."

"Several," she agreed. "Which one do you want to talk about?"

"I know I've got more than my share of flaws, and the longer I look, the more I see."

"Opportunities," she reminded him. To Bea's mortification, she felt the sting of tears behind the bridge of her nose.

"Yes. I've decided to stop letting opportunity pass me by." His hand found hers and enveloped it. "Especially a beautiful one who smells like lemon."

"You can't keep changing your mind, Grey." *I can't take it if you do. I've already lost too much.*

"I never stopped wanting to marry you, Bea. I wanted to be a man you could rely on to keep his promises. . .but it felt like losing the farm meant I'd already failed to be that man. And instead of trusting God the way I thought I'd grown into, and trusting you to tell me if you changed your mind, I blamed myself and figured you would, too."

"You weren't to blame for the farm. I told you that." Tears snuck down her face in spite of Bea's best efforts to hold them back.

"I forget things." He rubbed his thumb across her knuckles. "Important things, like the part of Philippians that talks about finding contentment in times of want. To know God is with us in times of abundance and in suffering. Right now, the Darlyns are going through some of both, and I regret that I've added to your suffering."

Bea swallowed, not knowing what to say. When he reached up to wipe away her tears, they burst free with new vigor.

"This is the second time I've seen you cry." He pulled a fresh handkerchief from his pocket and brushed it against her cheeks. "Remember what I said about why men want to escape when a woman cries?"

"Because he can't fix it, and he hates admitting there are things he can't fix." Bea wiggled her nose, trying not to sneeze when he passed the hanky over her face in another feather-light caress.

"This is the second time I haven't wanted to walk away from your tears. The first time, I thought I could fix it by buying the farm."

"And this time?" *Tell me you can fix it.* Bea's heart squeezed.

"This time, I know I can't."

Pain shot through her heart.

"I know that I can't give you everything you deserve or fix everything that goes wrong. Not now, not in the years to come. I can't promise you perfection, Bea." He gave a rueful smile. "I can't even promise I'll always patch things up well enough. I can only promise that I'll always be there to try."

"For years to come?" *Lord, if You don't want Grey to be my husband, stop him now. Stop my willful heart from falsely hoping—when the hope is false, the pain is still real.*

"Do you know what I told Miles, the first time we rode into TallGrass?"

Bea blinked at the shift. "No."

"We'd stop—but just for bacon and butter." His smile widened. "That's how I met you. The second I saw you, I knew I'd found something special. But I knew it meant change, so I kept trying to fight it."

I know the feeling.

"Do you know what I told Miles, after you and Cassia offered to make those ducks? That we'd go—but just for supper. Just supper, then we'd leave."

"But I invited you to stay the night in our hayloft." She was starting to enjoy this.

"And I swore it would be just for that night."

"Until Pa asked you about the bones."

He nodded. "Just one haystack."

"So when Huber challenged you after church, and you changed your mind about staying. . ."

"Just one week." He chuckled. "I swore that every step would be the last, but you kept making offers I just couldn't pass up."

"And now?"

"I know it wasn't the offers I couldn't resist; it was the woman who made them." He reached into his back pocket and pulled out a slip of yellow paper.

Bea stared at it before she recognized it. "This is one of the theater stage passes! Why are you giving it to me now? And why is it yellow?"

"Not yellow." He rubbed his fingertips together, sending a fine spray of yellow trickling toward the ground.

"Pollen?"

"Gold, Bea." A note of exasperation crept into his voice. "It's supposed to be a golden ticket."

She rubbed her fingertips along the edge, unable to stop smiling. "Like Marco Polo's? To grant me passage through exotic adventures?"

"Exactly. So I made that for you."

Suddenly, fear doused her joy. Surely he wasn't telling her that he wouldn't be coming to Grand Forks? "Where's yours?"

"Holding the one I made."

Bea looked from the "gilded" ticket in her hand to the man who'd made it, and back again.

"It's you, Bea." He folded his hand around her wrist again. "You're my golden ticket. You give me all the wonder and adventure a man could ever need."

"Oh, Grey."

"Now, there's one more thing I'm hoping you'll be willing to share with me." His hand tightened around hers as he sank down on one knee.

"Just one thing?" she teased, trying to calm her speeding pulse.

"Just one, but it's a big one." He waggled his brows.

"What do you want with me, Greyson?"

"Just forever." There was a catch in his voice that told Bea how much he meant it. "See, I've come so far, I can't settle for anything less."

"Well, I can't think of anything bigger or better than that." Bea sank into his embrace and smiled. "So 'forever' will just have to do!"

Coming soon from Kelly Eileen Hake—
the Dangerous Darlyns series continues with

Slings & Arrows
Fire & Knives

Here is an exclusive scene from
the Darlyns' next adventure in

Slings & Arrows

Chapter 1

June 1889, on the Darlyn Family Farm
in TallGrass, North Dakota

W*hoosh.* Ariel Darlyn nocked her seventh arrow, feeling the telltale 'click' as wood clasped sinew in a snug embrace. *Thunk.* Her last shot hit its mark, drowning out the softer sound and completing her six-arrow outline of the bulls-eye one hundred yards away. Shaped like a heart upon her sister's request, that distinctive target would serve as the calling card of the Dangerous Darlyns—if Ariel shot true today.

Bea's sharpshooting, Cassia's throwing knives, and Jodie's trick roping and riding all went off without a hitch. Ariel's archery was the last hurdle, the final piece to prove that Honest Al should book the Dangerous Darlyns act for his vaudeville theatre in Grand Forks. The proceeds of the opportunity would be both too small and too slow to salvage the farm, but might be enough to see all four sisters safely to their father's sickbed in Lincoln.

Ariel loosed the seventh arrow. This time, the twang of the bowstring underscored the more dramatic *whoosh-thunk* as her missile found its mark: dead center of the target. She didn't ready her final arrow as swiftly as the times before, intentionally allowing her bowstring its victory dance. Uninterrupted, the resonant vibration literally added a note of drama before her final, most difficult shot.

The slight scrape of wood against stiffened leather grated as she withdrew her final arrow, unnaturally loud against the absolute stillness of her expectant audience. This time, the slight *snick* as she slid it against the nocking point seemed as loud as the report of Bea's rifle-though not nearly as distracting as the muffled squeak from her far right.

I forgot. Ariel's heart pounded out an alarm at her sister's dismay. How could she have forgotten to employ the theatrical flourish Cassia quizzed her on so many times? Ariel disliked dramatics but even she understood the vital necessity of such things when selling showmanship.

Eyes wide with worry and apology, Cassia raised her hand, then jerked it downward. She'd caught herself before succumbing to her own nervous habit. When anxious, Cassia tended to pick and nibble at her cuticles.

When anxious, Ariel tended to make errors.

No more mistakes. Lord, don't let my nerves be the downfall of my family. Ariel repeated the silent, fervent prayer she'd been offering in some form for days. *I cannot fail them.*

I *will not* fail them.

She began to raise her bow, highly conscious of the slight shift in weight and balance for this shot. Those others, tapered reed with blunted target tips, served well for the speed of snap shooting. This final arrow, entirely solid and footed with a hardwood splice for durability and balance, she'd tipped with a four-sided bodkin. Under any other circumstance, she'd never notice the difference. A half-ounce was nothing...

But in archery? Two-hundred and forty grains of additional heft—particularly when concentrated toward the head—made a critical difference to an arrow's flight path. Switching seamlessly between the two types demanded complete concentration.

Ariel drew a deep breath, knowing she'd release it with the shot. The world narrowed to the two hearts, one a cheery challenge awaiting her arrow. The other beat out a quick, steady rhythm, her very pulse an insistent cheer: DAR-lyn, DAR-lyn, Dar-lynNNNnnNN...

Something altered the rhythm, a low rumble that seemed to travel up her spine. Ariel halted, bow far too low and still pointed to the ground. She let out the breath she'd barely begun to hold, letting the world rush back. Nestled between two of the sloped, earthen walls of a dried riverbed, Darlyn land carried sound much farther than level ground. Ariel tilted her head, searching for the source of the disturbance...hooves.

More than a single horse—oxen never moved at such a swift pace—thundering an inexorable descent down the sloping path to the Darlyn farm. With Honest Al and his buddy Bill already accounted for, no one else belonged anywhere near their land. No one else was wanted; but the most unwanted man in TallGrass took no notice of such things. Only he would dare race into their small valley with the frenzy of an invading force. *Huber.*

"Huber." The grim assessment came from Greyson Wilder, Bea's former fiancé.

Somewhat former...possibly somewhat future. Ariel suspected that Grey would soon recover from the news that his business partner lost all of their profits for the past two years, and launch a campaign to win Bea back. Since he'd remained on the farm, still expending every effort to help their family, he might even manage it. It all depended on whether he acted in time to persuade Bea that his idiocy was a temporary affliction and rendering him resistant to further outbreaks.

With the mortgage due and Huber infesting the farm, it looked like time had run out.

Ariel considered raising her bow but decided against it. With no way of knowing how long she might need to hold the shooting position, prudence dictated that she wait. She could draw back in an instant, but maintaining tension for an extended period would compromise the stability of her hold, and thus the power and accuracy of her release. A poor bargain, considering how little heed Huber would pay her. Even on occasions when none of them stood armed, his attention fixed on Bea with unsettling intensity.

Bea and Grey stood side-by-side, braced against the oncoming onslaught with rifles raised and ready They made a formidable match, even more intimidating thanks to their recent and well-deserved reputations as crack shots. If any threat could impact a man like Huber, he'd respect a sharpshooter's bullet before any archer's arrow.

Kelly Eileen Hake received her first writing contract at the tender age of seventeen and arranged to wait three months until she was able to legally sign it. Since then, she's fulfilled two dozen contracts ranging from short stories to novels. In her spare time, she's attained her BA in English literature and composition, earned her credential to teach English in secondary schools, and went on to complete her MA in writing popular fiction. She lives with her chef husband and two mischievous mutts in Southern California.

Also available from Shiloh Run Press

Unabridged Audiobook